SARATOGA TRUNK

ALSO BY EDNA FERBER

Great Son

American Beauty

Cimarron

Show Boat

So Big

Giant

Ice Palace

edna ferber

SARATOGA TRUNK

HARPER ● PERENNIAL

NEW YORK ● LONDON ● TORONTO ● SYDNEY

HarperCollins books may be purchased for educational, business, or sales promo-
tional use. For information please write: Special Markets Department, HarperCollins Publishers Inc., 10 East 53rd Street, New York, NY 10022.

First Perennial Classics edition published 2000.
Perennial Classics are published by Perennial, an imprint of HarperCollins Publishers.

Library of Congress Cataloging-in-Publication Data has been applied for.
ISBN 0-06-095671-2

12 ❖/RRD 10 9 8

SARATOGA TRUNK

I

✦

They were interviewing Clint Maroon. They were always interviewing old Colonel Maroon. Though he shunned publicity, never had held public office and wasn't really a Colonel at all, he possessed that magnetic flamboyant quality which makes readable news. It wasn't his wealth. America had fifty men as rich as he. Certainly it wasn't social position. He and the spectacularly beautiful Clio Maroon never had figured in formal New York society. It could not have been his great age merely which had brought the reporters into his hotel suite at Saratoga on this, his eighty-ninth birthday, for the newspapers had seized upon him with yelps of joy when first he had dawned dramatically upon their horizon at thirty. They had swarmed on him throughout the three-score years that had elapsed since then; when he turned forty; at his dashing half-century mark; at sixty, when there was scarcely a glint of gray in the reddish-brown hair that was exactly the color of a ripe pecan shell; at seventy, eighty, eighty-five. If Clint Maroon bought an old master or a new yacht, sold short or emerged from a chat with the President of the United States, streamlined one of his railroads or donated a million to charity or science, won the Grand National or took up ice-skating (ever so slightly bow-legged, proof of his Texas past) there the reporters were, clamoring for him.

"I'm from the *Times*, Mr. Maroon . . . *Herald Tribune*, Colonel

. . . *News* . . . *American* . . . *Sun* . . . *Post* . . . *World-Telegram* . . . My paper would like to know if it's true that you . . ."

They liked him. He never said, "Hiyah, boys!" with that false jocularity they so quickly detected. He never whipped a brown oily cylinder out of his vest pocket with a patronizing, "Have a good cigar." His manner was courteous without being hearty. Quietly he answered their questions when he was able, always taking his time about it. Just as deliberately he had said, on occasion, "Sorry, young man, but I can't answer that question at this time." Curiously soft-voiced and rather drawling for so big and full-blooded a man, he sometimes gave the effect of being actually shy. Easterners for the most part, the New York newspapermen did not realize that in the Far West of the bad old days the man who was slowest in his speech was likely to be quickest on the draw. They had, in fact, forgotten that Texas was Clint Maroon's early background. He never had reminded them.

Certain wise ones among the fraternity said it was Mrs. Maroon who really ran the show. "She's always there," these wily craftsmen observed, "if you'll notice, standing beside him with her hand on his arm, like royalty, looking so damned beautiful and queenly you think, Boy! She must have wowed them when she was young. She doesn't talk much, but watch those eyes of hers. Big and black and soft, and what they miss you could put in your own eye. But when she does speak up, very soft and sort of Southern, she says something. Nice, too, both of them, but I don't know, cagey, in a way. I've seen her pinch him when he was headed for a boner, with that lovely kind of heartbreaking smile on her face all the time he took to cover up and start fresh. Some day I'd like to dig way back on those two. I'll bet there's gold in them thar hills."

Mr. and Mrs. Clinton Maroon, Fifth Avenue and Seventy-third Street. Clint and Clio back in the old Texas, New Orleans and Saratoga days. But curiously enough, for all their interviewing, none of the newspapermen or women really knew about that. These two had been rich, respectable and powerful for sixty years. Newspaper reporters die young, or quit their jobs.

Possessed of a dramatic quality, together with vitality and bounce, a zest for life and an exquisite sense of timing, the Maroons had brightened many a dull Monday morning news page. They were almost incredibly handsome, this pair, with a splendor of face and figure that had crumbled little under the onslaught of the years. Hospitable, friendly, interested in life—particularly in your life, your plans, your conversation—hundreds liked and respected them, but amazingly few really knew them. Seeming frank and accessible, the truth was that they went their way in a kind of splendid isolation. They consistently shied away from the photographers. It was the one point on which they met the news fraternity reluctantly.

"Oh, come on now, Colonel! Please, Mrs. Maroon! Just one shot. You haven't murdered anybody."

"That's what you think," Clint Maroon retorted.

Much as they liked him, the general opinion among the newsmen lately had been that the old boy was cracking up. When they came to interview him on business or political or philanthropic or international affairs he now tried to tell them outrageous yarns palpably culled from Western thrillers and lurid detective stories. It was difficult to lead him back to the hard modern facts about which they had come to see him. Among themselves they confided, "Old Maroon's getting a little balmy, if you ask me. At that, he's good for his age. Crowding ninety. Gosh, ninety! You should live so long, not me."

And now on this, his eighty-ninth birthday, old Clint Maroon, in spite of wars, panics, and world chaos, still was triumphantly news. Cameras, candid and flashlight; reporters, male and female, special and news, all had traveled up to Saratoga on this broiling August day. They were there not only because the ancient's natal day found him at the quaint little spa at the beginning of the racing season when the thermometer kissed the ninety-degree mark, but because he had just made a gesture so lavish, so dramatic that it promised to land him on the front page of every newspaper in the country along with other world phenomena.

Reporters had swarmed by plane, motorcar and train. It was four o'clock on a brilliant summer afternoon. "What the hell's the good of living to be eighty-nine and piling up eighty-nine millions and more if you can't take yourself a nap or go to the races at four in the afternoon on a day like this!" demanded Matt Quinlan.

"You're above all that at eighty-nine, with eighty-nine millions," said the astringent Trixie Nye of the *Post*.

Short, squat little Balmer of the *Sun*, oldest of the lot and most canny, shook his head while he lighted his pipe, in itself no mean feat. "Not that old bird. Clint's up to something, or Gaffer Balmer has missed his calling all these years."

They roamed the room or sat mopping their flushed faces or stared down at the street below which, for one brief month in the year, wakened from its Victorian serenity to receive the sporting blood, the moneyed, the horse-lovers, the gay, the social, the gambling fraternity of the whole country. The great ancient elms in front of the United States Hotel cast an ineffectual shade upon the burning asphalt and cement.

In the high-ceilinged dim old sitting room of the Maroon suite at the United States Hotel there was something incongruous about those modern hard young faces, that slick mechanical equipment. The carved walnut tables with their liver-colored marble tops, the prancing rockers, the Victorian drapes and steel engravings, the faded ingrain carpets and lumpy upholstery were anachronistic as a background for this dynamic group. The women writers stared with amused eyes at the gas globes of the ponderous chandelier, the men took a sporting shot at the vast cuspidor. Quinlan's lean, worldly face broke into a grin as he noticed the coil of stout rope dangling from a hook near the window. "It's a rope fire escape, by God! I heard they still had 'em but I never believed it."

Ellen Ford of the *Tribune* said, wistfully, "I wish they'd let me see the bathroom. They say the tub and the loo and the washstand are all boxed in black walnut, like coffins."

Tubby Krause wagged a fat and chiding forefinger. "Papa told you to go when you were downstairs."

There was a discreet tap at the outer door, they turned swiftly to face it, but it was a waiter, it was a little flock of waiters in the best Saratoga manner, white-clad, black-skinned, gold-toothed, aware of the dignity of their calling and the tradition of the house. Trays and trays and trays. Scotch, rye, bourbon. Ice coffee, iced tea. Mint and gin pleasantly mingled. Lemon, cream, sandwiches. Tinkle of ice, clink of silver.

"Hepp you ladies and geppmen or you prefer to hepp youseff?"

"Hepp ourself," said Larry Conover, and lost no time. "One you boys got a tip on a horse?"

"Honey Chile, straight," the procession answered as one man; bowed and withdrew with a rustle of starched white uniforms.

"Is it always like this?" inquired one of the newer men. Before anyone could answer, the door to the adjoining room opened, the newspaper reporters turned their alert faces like a battery of searchlights on the pair who entered.

"Good afternoon, ladies! Glad to see you, gentlemen! Keep your seats. Go on with your drinks."

"Hiyah, Mr. Maroon!"

They looked like royalty—rowdy royalty, and handsome. Almost a century of life rested as rakishly on his head as the sombrero he so often wore. A columnist once said that Clint Maroon, even in top hat and tails, gave the effect of wearing opuro, chapo and sombrero.

"Clio, these are the ladies and gentlemen of the press. Some of them you have met before. . . . Mrs. Maroon." He pronounced her name with such effect that you felt you had almost heard a brass horn Ta-TA-ah-ah-ah!

Both wore white; there was almost an other-world look about them. The reporters reproached themselves inwardly for being so hot, so sweaty and unkempt. As though sensing this, Mrs. Maroon now said in her lovely leisurely voice, "How young you all are! It refreshes me just to look at you. Don't you feel that, Clint?"

"Swap you ten years for ten millions, Mr. Maroon," said the brash Quinlan.

"Wish I could do it, Matt. Or there was a time when I'd have wished it. Not so sure, now. Take your coats off, take your coats off! Be comfortable."

Clio Maroon at seventy-nine stood straight and slim as a girl. Her unwithered lips were soft and full, her skin was gently wrinkled like old silk crepe, its lines almost unnoticeable at a distance. Even the least perceptive among those present must have felt something exotic and quickening about her. Ten years younger than he, she still was beautiful with a timeless beauty like that of ivory or marble or a painting that takes on added magnificence with age. Her white hair was still so strongly mixed with black that the effect was steel-gray. In certain lights it had a bluish tinge. Springing strongly away from brow and temples, it was amazingly thick and vigorous for a woman of her age. But all this you remarked at a second or third glance. It was the eyes you first saw, liquid, clear, softly bright; merry, too, as though she enjoyed outer life with the added fillip of an inner secret. She stood beside her towering handsome husband, but a little behind him, too, as women of Victorian days had walked in deference to the male. Certain seasoned newspapermen knew there was more than mere symbolism in her standing thus. They had watched the workings of her quiet generalship; they knew she sustained and directed him. Her delicate brown hand resting so trustingly on his arm was not above giving him a furtive little pinch in warning or reproof. They had even seen him wince on occasion, and once or twice he had been known to emit an ouch of surprised remonstrance at a particularly sharp and sudden tweak.

"Oh, Clint, *chéri!*" Mrs. Maroon would say, her tone one of fond sympathy. "Is it your arthritis again?"

Though she appeared fragile there yet was about her a hair-wire resilience that bespoke more vitality than he possessed in spite of his bulk, his high color and the auburn still glowing in his hair that even now was only sprinkled with white. Though marked for the woodsman's ax, the juices still coursed through the old tree.

Now the photographers sprang into action. Almost automatically he and she raised protesting hands; then she smiled as though remembering something. Clint Maroon waved one great arm. "All right. Shoot! I'm through with skulking. My grandpappy fought in the Alamo. I reckon I can face a battery of cameras without flinching." Suddenly he winced. Then he reached across his own girth and patted his wife's hand that lay so innocently in the crook of his other arm. "No more pinching to shut me up, Clio. Time's past for that, too. From now on I'm making a clean breast of it. This is going to be a different America. We won't live to see it, but we said we were going to try to make up for what we'd done to it."

She smiled again, wistfully, and shook her head a little, and the reporters thought, she must have a time of it managing the old boy now that his mind is slipping a bit. The candid camera men stood on chairs and surveyed their victims from strange angles; the little boxes clicked. The two white-clad figures posed smiling and serene.

Len Brisk of the *Telegram* dismissed the camera men with a gesture of clearing the decks for action. "All right, boys! You've got yours. Beat it."

You heard the well-bred authoritative voice of Keppel of the New York *Times*. "Mr. Maroon, there are certain questions my paper would like me to ask you. Is it true . . ."

The barrage was on. Is it true you are giving your Fifth Avenue house to the city, outright, to be used for a Service Clubhouse? Is it true you've turned your collection of paintings over to the Metropolitan Museum? Is it true your yacht is to be a government training ship? Is it true your Adirondacks estate is to be a free summer camp for boys? Is it true you're giving away every penny of your fortune to the government after you've pensioned your old employes? And that you're keeping just enough for you and Mrs. Maroon to live on in comfort? Is it true . . . is it true . . . is it true . . .

He replied in the soft-spoken Texas drawl that had taken on the clipped overtones of authority. "All true. But unimportant. That stuff's not what I want to tell you about. This time I can give you a real story. It isn't only something to write about. It's something for Americans to read and realize, and remember. They'll hate me for it. But anyway, they'll know."

"Yeah, that'll be fine. Uh—look, Colonel, we want——"

"All right, Colonel, but first——"

"First hell! This is first I tell you. In another year, if I live, I'll be ninety. The way the world is headed I don't know's I want to. Ninety, nearly, and I'm sick of being a railroad magnate and a collector of art and a Metropolitan Opera stockholder and director of a lot of fool corporations. It's damned dull, and always has been. If I was thirty I'd learn to run an airplane. Might anyway. Next to breaking a bucking bronco that must be more fun than anything."

"May we say that, Mr. Maroon?"

"God, yes. Say anything you like. I've got nothing to lose now. I'm coming clean. Listen. Millions, and I had to be respectable. Me, a terror from Texas. Here you are, smart as they make 'em, you and your kind have been interviewing me for sixty years, ever since I found that fool railroad hanging around my neck—and you don't know a thing about the real Clint Maroon. Not a damned thing. Or if you have got it filed away in the morgue somewhere you're scared to print it while I'm alive. Well, go on. Use it! I'm a Texas gambler and a killer. I've killed as many men as Jesse James, or almost. I've robbed my country for sixty years. My father, he ran the town of San Antonio back in 1840 before the damn Yankees came along and stole his land for a railroad. That's one reason why I didn't hesitate to steal it back from them. My grandpappy, old Dacey Maroon, fought the Santa Anna Mexicans along with Jim Bowie and Bill Travis and Sam Houston. That's the stock I come from. And what did I do for my country! Stole millions from millionaires who were stealing each other blind. Another year and I'll be ninety—the meanest old coot that ever lived to be nearly a hundred——"

"Oh, come on now, Colonel. You know you're a wonderful guy and everybody's crazy about you and Mrs. Maroon. So stop kidding us and give us our story in time for the first edition."

"God A'mighty, I'm giving it to you, I tell you! They called us financiers. Financiers hell! We were a gang of racketeers that would make these apes today look like kids stealing turnips out of the garden patch. We stole a whole country—land, woods, rivers, metal. They've got our pictures in the museums. We ought to be in the rogues' gallery. My day you could get away with wholesale robbery, bribery in high places and murder—and brag about it. I was brought up on the stories my father told about 'em—Huntington and Stanford and Crocker. Two hundred thousand dollars is all they had amongst them in 1861. And they wanted to build a railroad across a continent. So they paid a visit to Washington, and they left that two hundred thousand there. Made no secret of it. They came away with a charter and land grants and the government's promise to pay in bonds for work in progress. What did the Central Pacific crowd do! I heard my pa tell how in '63 Phil Stanford—he was brother of the Governor—drove up to the polls in a buggy when they were holding elections in San Francisco over a bond issue. Reached into a bag and began throwing gold pieces to the crowd at the polls, yelling to 'em to vote the bond issue. They voted it, all right. Do that today and where'd you land? In jail! Lives and principles, they didn't matter. Same thing in 1880 when I got started. Say, I was as bad as the worst of 'em——"

"Sure, Colonel, we know, we know. You were a bad *hombre* all right."

"You tell us all about that some time. Some other time. And about the day you rode your horse right up to the bar of the Perfessor Saloon in San Antone."

They were being good-natured about it, but they did wish Mrs. Maroon would stop the old coot's nonsense. Pretty soon it would be too late, the races would be over and they'd have to hop back to New York without a chance to use that tip on Honey Chile.

"Sixty years ago, young fella, I'd have wiped that grin off your face with a six-shooter. Fights and feuds and fiestas and fandangoes, that was the program back in Texas where I came from in 1880. People call it romantic now. Well, maybe it was. Anyway we had the use of our legs and arms instead of being just limbless trunks riding around in automobiles the way you softies are today. It's got so you have to jump into a car to go down to the corner to get a pack of cigarettes. Two years ago I went down to Texas, went in an airplane from New York in less time than it used to take us to gallop into town on a Saturday night in the old days. Houston's a stinking oil town now, Dallas sets up to be a style center, San Antonio's full of art and they're starting a movement to run gondolas on the San Antonio River for tourists. My God, I almost had a stroke."

"That's very interesting, Mr. Maroon, but look——"

"I can tell you things if you think that's interesting. Ninety, or nearly. Let 'em put me in jail. If I was to eat two pieces of chocolate cake this minute and drink a quart of champagne I'd be dead in an hour. What can death do to you at ninety that life hasn't done to you already!"

"You're right, Colonel. Uh, look, we've got our edition to make, see. And if you'll just give us what we came for, first, and then——"

"You're deaf and dumb and blind, the lot of you!" His face was dangerously red considering his age and the weather. He snatched his arm free of his wife's restraining hand, his voice rang out with a resonance incredible in an organ that had known almost a century of use. "I tell you I'm giving you the real story if you'd have the sense to see it. I'm giving up my money now because I robbed widows and orphans to get it. That was considered smart in those days. But I'll say this for myself—I didn't want money or position or power for myself. I wanted Clio Dulaine and I had to have those to get her. So I outwitted them and I've outlived them, too, the whole sniveling lot of them—Gould and Vanderbilt and Rockefeller and Morgan and Fisk and Drew. We skimmed a whole nation—took the cream right off the top."

Tubby Krause spoke up soothingly, but even his unctuous voice had the gritty sound of patience nearing exhaustion. "Yep, that's right, Mr. Maroon. You ought to write a book about it. I bet it'd make 'em sit up. Ever read *The Robber Barons?* Great book. Yeh, those were the bad old boys all right. Now, Mr. Maroon, if you'll just answer a couple of questions."

Mrs. Maroon took his great freckled hand in her own two delicate ones; she looked up into his face, earnestly. "You see, Clint, they don't want to hear it. I told you they wouldn't. They don't believe it. Let it go. What does it matter now?"

"Thanks, Mrs. Maroon." It was Quinlan with an edge to his voice. "You understand how it is. We're here to get our story. We've always been on the square with you and the Colonel. And you've been more than square with us. This is our job, see."

"Yah, your jobs!" snarled Maroon to their astonishment, for he had always been as charming as he was considerate. "You young fools! You deserve to lose 'em. I suppose if I told you that Mrs. Maroon is the daughter of a Creole aristocrat and the most famous *placée* in New Orleans back in the '60s, you wouldn't be interested!"

"What's a *placée?*"

"I suppose you never heard of José Llulla, either? Pepe Llulla, they called him, isn't that right, Clio? Long before your day. He fought and won so many duels that he had to start his own cemetery to take care of them. Cemetery of St. Vincent de Paul on Louisa Street. Anybody'll show it to you. Well, now, Mrs. Maroon's grandmother was killed by Pepe Llulla. Jealousy."

The newspaper people were smiling rather uncertainly now. After all, a joke's a joke, they thought, but the old boy was going too far. Mrs. Maroon's musical indolent laugh reassured them. Mischievously she shook her husband's arm as one would remind a dear forgetful child.

"Don't leave out the important things, Clint, *chéri.*" She shut one handsome eye in an amazing and confidential wink. "Surely you won't forget to tell them that Mama was accused of murder. And the scandal was hushed up," Clio Maroon went on, equably. "They said he had died of a heart attack. So then Mama was smuggled out of New Orleans, they sent her to France, and of course that's how I——"

"——came to be educated in a convent," chimed in two or three rather weary voices.

Someone said, "Oh, listen, Mrs. Maroon! You going to start kidding us too? After we've given you the best years of our lives!"

Clio Maroon smiled up at her husband. "You see, dear? Next time. Next time."

"That's right," Len Brisk assured her. "Next time we'll run all that movie stuff, Mr. Maroon, just to show you our hearts are in the right place, even if our heads aren't. Then what'll you do to us?"

"Sue you for a million dollars," Mrs. Maroon put in, swiftly.

"But it's all true!" Clint Maroon shouted. "Damn it, it's all true I tell you! I just want you boys and girls to write it—to write it so that Americans will know that this country today is finer and more honest and more free and democratic than it has been since way back in Revolutionary days. For a century we big fellows could grab and run. They can't do it today. It's going to be the day of the little man. Tell them to have faith and believe that they're the best Americans in the decentest government the world has ever seen. It's true, I tell you. We're just coming out of the darkness. Don't let anyone tell you that America today isn't the——"

"Sure. Sure. We know."

She turned to go then, with a glance at them over her shoulder—a whimsical and appealing glance from those fine eyes that seemed to convey a little secret understanding between her and them. I am leaving an old and sick man in your care, the glance said. Be lenient. Be kind. Aloud, "Don't keep Mr. Maroon too long, will you? And please help yourselves to drinks and sandwiches there on the table. If I come back at the end of—oh—fifteen minutes don't be too cross with me. Mr. Maroon finds this heat rather trying."

"Thanks, Mrs. Maroon. You've been swell. . . . Think it's safe to leave a bunch of newspapermen with all this scotch and rye?"

She went then, carrying herself with such grace and dignity that if it had not been for her steel-gray hair you might have thought her a woman of thirty, her soft draperies flowing after her, her head held high. As she closed the door and vanished she heard Keppel's voice, not quite so suave now, for time was pressing. "Now then, Mr. Maroon, is it true that you . . ." And then the hard incisive tone of Larry Conover's voice keyed to the tempo of the tabloid he represented. "Hi, wait a minute, fellas. Something tells me Mr. Maroon isn't kidding. Are you, Mr. Maroon? Say, listen, maybe we're missing the real story. What was that again about——"

She made as though to turn back and re-enter the room. But she only hesitated a moment there before the door, and shrugged her shoulders with a little Gallic gesture and smiled and did not listen for more.

She and Clint Maroon had met and fallen instantly in love at breakfast in Madame Begué's restaurant that April Sunday morning in New Orleans, almost sixty years ago. Though perhaps their encounter in the French Market earlier in the day should be called their first meeting. Certainly there he had persisted in staring at her and following her, and he had even attempted to speak to her. She had had to administer punishment, brisk though secondhand—for his boldness.

Clio Dulaine was back in New Orleans after an absence of fifteen years. Though she had left it as a child and had not seen it again until now, when she had just turned twenty, she was as much at home in it, as deeply in love with it as if she were a Creole aristocrat with a century's background of dwelling in the *Vieux Carré*. Throughout the years of her life in France she had heard of New Orleans and learned of it through the memories and longings of two exiled and homesick women—her mother, the lovely Rita Dulaine, and her aunt Belle Piquery. These two, filled with nostalgia for their native and beloved Louisiana city, had lived unwillingly and died resentfully in the Paris to which they had been banished—the Paris of the 1870's. In those years the mind of the girl Clio had become a brimming reservoir for their dreams, their bizarre recollections, their heartsick yearnings. Though they dwelt perforce in France, they really lived in their New Orleans past. The Franco-Prussian War, the occupation of Paris had been to them a minor and faintly annoying incident. Their chief concern with it was that in those confused years their copy of the New Orleans French newspaper *L'Abeille* sometimes failed to arrive on time. Its arrival was an event. They fell upon its meager pages with the eager little cries of women famished for news from home. They devoured every crumb of information—births, deaths, marriages, society, advertisements. Though these two women belonged to that strange and exotic stratum which was the New Orleans underworld, Rita's life had been for many years entwined with that of one of the city's oldest and most aristocratic of families. In that fantastic society she had been the mistress of Nicolas Dulaine, only son of that proud and wealthy family; not only that, she had been known by his name, she was Rita Dulaine, she had lived in the charming little house he had purchased for her in Rampart Street, she had borne him a daughter, she was queen of that half-world peopled by women of doubtful blood. She was a *placée*, she had taken the name of Dulaine, she was the acknowledged beauty in an almost macabre society of strangely lovely women. Her gowns came from Paris, her jewels from the Rue de la Paix, she had traveled abroad with Nicolas Dulaine as his wife. Love, luxury, adulation, even position of a sort, Rita Dulaine had had everything that a beautiful and beloved woman can have except the security of a legal name and a legal right as the consort of Nicolas Dulaine.

The tragedy of Dulaine's death had changed her from a high-spirited and imperious woman to a dazed and broken creature, suddenly sallow and almost plain at times. Even Aunt Belle Piquery, her older sister, Belle the practical, the realistic, had been unable to urge her out of her valley of *douleur*. Usually after a ship's mail had brought them a little bundle made up of back numbers of *L'Abeille*, Rita was plunged deeper than ever in gloom. Whenever the words appeared in the newspaper's columns—Madame Nicolas Dulaine—they seemed to leap out at her as though printed in red letters a foot high. This was his widow. This woman lived and he was dead. It was she who had really killed him with her possessiveness and her arrogance and her spite. Rita was long past weeping, but she would begin to weep again, dry tears. Her face, lovely still, would become distorted, her eyes would stare out hot and bright, her hand would clutch her throat as if she were choking, the sobs would come, hard and dry, racking her.

Then Angélique Pluton, whom they called Kakaracou—Kaka, her maid and Clio's nurse—would hold her in her arms like a baby, and soothe her and murmur to her. She spoke in a curious jargon, a mixture of French, Spanish, New Orleans colloquialisms, African Negro. "Hush, my baby, my baby. Spare your pretty eyes. There are dukes over here and kings and princes waiting to marry you. You will go back to New Orleans in your own golden carriage and they'll crawl at your feet, those stony-faced ones."

"I'll never go back, Kaka. I'll die here. They won't let me come back. They said they'll put me in prison. They said I killed him. I was only trying to kill myself because I couldn't live without him."

Brisk Belle Piquery would say, "You're only making yourself sick, Rita. I think you enjoy it. After all, they threw me out, too, and said they'd put me in prison if I ever showed my face in New Orleans. And I was only your sister."

"There you go reproaching me. I wish I were dead too. Why didn't I kill myself! I wanted to."

"You didn't really," the practical Belle would say. "People hardly ever do. You wanted to keep him, of course, and you thought if he saw you pressing a pistol against your heart—well, there, there, let's not talk about it. He should have known better than to snatch it away, poor boy. Anyway, he's dead. Nothing can bring him back now. We'll be dead, too, first thing you know. So let's enjoy life while we can."

"You've never really loved, Bella. You don't know."

"I've loved lots of them," Aunt Belle retorted blithely. "I spent my life at it, didn't I! Only with me it was a career and with you it was your whole existence."

This elicited a little scream of pained remonstrance from the New Orleans Camille. "Belle! How can you speak like that of my love for Nicolas!"

"Now don't flare up, Rita. I just meant I know he was your life, but you expected too much. You even thought he would marry you after Clio was born. Imagine! Such a *bêtise!*"

"He would have, if it hadn't been for Them and Her."

"If it makes you feel better to believe that, then go on believing it. All I ever expected in life was a little fun and a chance to die respectable and to be buried in the cemetery of St. Louis with my name in gold letters—Belle Piquery—and chrysanthemums on All Saints' Day—though who'd bring them I don't know. But when I die, that's where I want to be. They'll let me come back to New Orleans then. You'll do that for your Aunt Belle, won't you, Clio?"

It was a strange life the two women lived in the charming little Paris flat overlooking the Bois—the flat paid for by Them with threat money and hush money. But it was stranger still for the child Clio when, at sixteen, she emerged from the convent school. And strangest of all was the sight they presented as they drove in the Bois or walked in the Champs Elysées. Rita Dulaine, tragic in black, her great dark eyes demanding sympathy, her sable garments chic as only the Paris couturiers could make them. By her side the bouncing Belle in such a welter of flounce and furbelow that it was almost impossible to tell where bosom began and bouffant draperies left off. Their carriage was a landaulet with a little cushioned seat opposite the large tufted one, and on this, her back to the driver's box, perched Clio, her legs, far too long for this cramped little bench, doubled under her voluminous skirts, primly. Beside her, bolt upright, her spare, straight back disdaining the upholstery, sat Kakaracou with dignity enough for all. Her skin was neither black nor coffee-colored but the shade of a ripe fig, purplish dusted with gray. Above this, and accentuating the tone, reared the tignon with which her head always was bound, a gaudy turbanlike arrangement of flaming orange or purple or pink or scarlet, characteristic of the New Orleans Negro.

Certainly the occupants of the landaulet were bizarre enough to attract attention even in the worldly Paris. But the figure perched on the driver's seat held the added fillip of surprise. Seated there, his legs braced against the high footboard, his knees covered with a driver's rug, his powerful arms and hands managed the two neat chestnuts with a true horseman's deftness of touch, there seemed nothing remarkable about the coachman, Cupidon. It was only when he threw aside the rug, clambered down over the wheel as agilely as a monkey and stood at the curb that you saw with staring unbelief the man's real dimensions. The large head, the powerful arms and chest belonged to a dwarf, a little man not more than three feet high. His bandy legs were like tiny stumps to which the wee feet were attached. This gave him a curiously rolling gait like that of a diminutive drunken sailor on shore leave. The eyes in the young-old face were tender, almost wistful; the mouth sardonic, the expression pugnacious or mischievous by turn. This was Cupidon, whom they fondly called Cupide; bodyguard, coachman, major-domo. When he spoke, which was rarely, it was in a surprisingly sweet clear tenor like that of a choirboy whose voice has just changed. He might have been any age—fifteen, twenty, thirty, forty. There were those who said that, though white, he was Kakaracou's son. Certainly she bullied and pampered him by turns. Sometimes you saw her withered hand resting tenderly on the tiny man's head; sometimes she cuffed him smartly as though he were a naughty child. She managed to save the choicest tidbits for his plate after the others had finished, she filled his glass with good red wine of the country as they sat at the servants' table, he in his specially built high chair on which he clambered so nimbly up and down.

"Drink your red wine, Little One. It will make you strong."

Instead of thumping his chest or flexing his arm he would rap his great head briskly. "I don't need red wine to make me strong. I'm strong enough. Here's my weapon." But he would toss down the glassful, nevertheless, giving the effect as he did so of a wickedly precocious little boy in his cups. Everyone in the household knew that his boast was no idle one. That head, hard and thick as a cannonball, was almost as effective when directed against an enemy. Thigh-high to a normally built man, he would run off a few steps, then charge like a missile, his head thrust forward and down, goat fashion. On a frontal attack, men twice his size had been known to go down with one grunt, like felled oxen.

Except for her years at the convent in Tours this, then, was the weird household in which Clio Dulaine had spent her girlhood exile. But then, it did not seem strange to her. Kakaracou and Cupidon both had been part of the Dulaine ménage in Clio's infancy when they had lived so luxuriously, so gaily in the house on Rampart Street in New Orleans. They were as much a part of her life as her mother or Aunt Belle Piquery. And all four of them dinned New Orleans into her ears, all four spoke of it with the nostalgia of the exiled, each in his or her own wistful way.

Rita Dulaine from her couch before the fire would stare into the flames like one hypnotized. It was as though she saw the past there, flickering and dying. "There's no society here in Paris to compare with the salon that your papa and I had in Rampart Street. The élite came to us. Oh, not those Creole sticks with their dowdy black clothes and their cold, hard faces."

"But Papa was a Creole. The Dulaines, you always told me, were the oldest and most——"

"Yes, yes. But he was my—he was your papa. His family, though, they were cruel and hard, they made me leave New Orleans after the—the—accident—after your papa was hurt—after he had a heart attack——" She would fall to weeping again, after all these years, if the dry gasping sounds she made could be called weeping.

Clio would rush to her, she would put her strong young arms about the woman's racked body, she would press her fresh young cheek against the other's ravaged one. "Don't, chérie, don't. Let's not talk about that any more. Let's talk about Great-Grand'mère Clio Bonnevie, how she came to New Orleans with the troupe of Monsieur

Louis Tabary, and how they had to play in tents or vacant shops, and how the audiences behaved—go on, tell me again, from the beginning."

The girl herself had the face of an actress, inherited from that other Clio who had come to New Orleans in 1791, one of a homeless refugee band of players who had fled the murderous Negro uprising in the French West Indies. The features hadn't quite crystallized yet, but the face was one of potential beauty—mobile, alight with intelligence, the eyes large and lustrous like her mother's, the mouth wide and sensual like that of her father, the dead Nicolas Dulaine.

"Well," Rita would begin, suddenly gay again. "I heard it only from Grand'mère Vaudreuil who was, of course, as you know, the daughter of Great-Grand'mère Bonnevie." Hearing her reminiscing thus, one would have thought her a descendant of a long line of Louisiana aristocrats rather than the woman she really was. The formality of marriage had not been part of her lineage. Grand'mère Vaudreuil and Great-Grand'mère Bonnevie had lived much as she lived. Men had loved them, they had begotten children, Rita Dulaine had emerged from this murky background as a water lily lifts its creamy petals out of the depths of a muddy pond. "Of course you know Grand'mère Vaudreuil was the talk of New Orleans in her day because she was so beautiful and because José Llulla—Pepe Llulla, they called him—fought a duel with her protector. The duel was fought in St. Anthony's Garden just behind the Cathedral of St. Louis. They say he had his own cemetery, José Llulla, he was such a hothead and so formidable a duellist. . . . Oh, yes, Great-Grand'mère Bonnevie, they say she was a superb actress, you know she came over from the French West Indies with Monsieur Tabary's troupe, they played in the very first theater in New Orleans. You should have heard Mama tell of how Great-Grand'mère told her about the way the audiences used to fight to get in, the roughs and the élite all mixed up together. We've always loved the theater, our family, it dates from then, no doubt. . . . Your papa and I used to go to the French opera, and sometimes after the play we entertained friends at home. . . . The house in Rampart Street had a lovely garden at the back paved with red brick, cool and fresh, and a fountain in the center. There were camellias and azaleas and mimosa and crepe myrtle. In the evening, the perfume was so heavy it made you swoon . . ."

She would forget all about Grand'mère Vaudreuil and Great-Grand'mère Bonnevie, she would live again her own past, drinking deep though she knew it would not slake her thirst, as a wanderer in the desert drinks of the alkaline water because there is no other.

"Before you were born your papa had built a little *garçonnière* at the far end of the garden facing the house. You were to live there with Kaka as nurse; all the little New Orleans boys of good family lived in their own houses—*garçonnières,* they are called—near the big house. He was so sure you were going to be a boy. He was disappointed at first, but then he said the next would be a boy. I said we should call him Nicolas Dulaine, I am sure he would have consented if he . . . Your little dresses were the finest embroidery and handmade lace, they were brought from France; he always said there was nothing in New Orleans fine enough. My dresses, too, came from . . ."

Clio began to find this a trifle dull. Aunt Belle Piquery's memories were of lustier stuff.

"You needn't talk to me about the food of Paris. I never tasted here such bouillabaisse and such shrimps and crab as we have in New Orleans. Marseilles bouillabaisse isn't to be compared with it. And the pompano, the lovely pompano, where else in the world is there a fish so delicate and at the same time so rich . . . ? *Bisque écrevisse Louisiane* . . . the *bouilli* . . . the hard-shell crab stew . . . soft-shell turtle ragout . . . the six-course Sunday morning breakfasts at Begué's . . . I used to love to go the French Market myself in the morning, it made you hungry just to see the vegetables and fruits and fish spread out so crisp and appetizing almost with the dew still on them. On Sunday morning the French Market is like a court levee"—unconsciously Aunt Belle lapsed into the present tense, so vivid were her longings and memories—"it's the meeting place for society on Sunday mornings after early Mass at St. Louis Cathedral. Or we sometimes go to late

Mass and then to Begué's for breakfast. But first usually we like to spoil our appetite by eating hot *jambalaya* in the French Market, and delicious hot coffee——"

"Jambalaya! What's that, Aunt Belle? It sounds heavenly."

"It's a Creole dish, hot and savory. Garlic and *chorices* and ham and rice and tomatoes and onion and shrimp or oysters all stewed up together——"

By this time Clio's mouth would be watering. Aunt Belle Piquery was off on another excursion into the past. "During Mardi Gras we'd have a tallyho or a great victoria and there we'd sit, viewing the parades, or we'd see them from a balcony in North Rampart or Royal Street. We never went near Canal, it wasn't chic. Your mama never went with us. She and Nicolas were very grand and stayed by themselves; you'd have thought Rita was *chacalata*. But then, I never held it against her. If Rita did go out people stared at her more than at any Carnival Queen, she was so much more beautiful."

The girl, listening avidly, would press a quick clutching hand on her aunt's plump knee. "Am I beautiful, Aunt Belle? Like Mama?"

"You, *minette!* A little scrawny thing like you!"

"I will be, though."

"Maybe, when you fill out. Your eyes, they're not bad, but your mouth's too big."

"You wait. You wait and see. I'll be beautiful, but I shan't be the way you and Mama were. I shall marry and be very rich and most respectable. But quite, quite respectable. Not like you."

A smart little slap from Aunt Belle's open palm. "You nasty little *griffe,* you! How dare you talk to me like that!"

The girl did not even deign to put her hand to her smarting cheek. Her eyes blazed. It was the epithet she resented, not the slap. "Don't you dare call me that! I'm a Dulaine. The royal blood of France flows in my veins."

"*Quelle blague!* Your Grandmama Vaudreuil was a free woman of color. Your mother's a——"

"I'm a Dulaine! My father was Nicolas Dulaine. "You wait. You'll see! My life will be different."

Aunt Belle Piquery laughed comfortably and took another chocolate from the little silver bonbon dish that always somehow managed to be on a tabouret beside her chair. "You'll be a fool about men just the way we all were—your mama and me and your Grandmother Vaudreuil and Great-Grandmama Bonnevie."

"I won't I tell you!"

"Though I honestly can't say I regret a thing I've done. I've had a fine time and would have yet if Rita hadn't gone waving pistols around. Don't take 'em seriously, I always told Rita."

The girl Clio looked at the overplump aging woman; her eyes were pitying but not contemptuous. "You and Mama aren't Dulaines. I am. My life's going to be different. I shan't be a fool about men. They'll be fools about me."

At this Aunt Belle laughed until she choked on a bit of chocolate, gasped, coughed, and waddled off to regale Rita and Kakaracon with this chit's presumption.

"Wiser than her elders," Kakaracou commented sagely when she heard it.

And now Rita Dulaine lay in the little cemetery outside St. Cloud; and Aunt Belle Piquery too knew at last the belated respectability of a solitary—though earthy—resting place in the cemetery of St. Louis in New Orleans, with her name in gold letters on the tomb and Clio and Kakaracou and Cupidon to place upon it the chrysanthemums that marked All Saints' Day. Years before she had slyly bought the space under another name, for the cemetery of St. Louis was not for the Belle Piquerys. The stately whitewashed tombs bore the names of the socially elect of New Orleans. There was sardonic humor in the fact that even in death respectability was not to be granted Aunt Belle. For by the time Clio, an orphan of twenty, had brought Belle Piquery's earthly remains back to the New Orleans she loved and had seen her safely entombed among the city's élite, certain changes had taken place in these hallowed precincts. The railroad had edged its way along the outskirts of the cemetery, and at night the red light of the semaphore glowed down upon the tomb as though the sign of Belle Piquery's earthly profession haunted her even in this, her last resting place.

II

⭐

From France they had sailed back together in the early spring—this strange trio, distributed as befitted their state of being and their station in life. A quartette they might really have been called, for Aunt Belle, the erstwhile voluble and bouncing, now went as a silent passenger in the freight hold; Kakaracou and Cupidon, in the servants' quarters, baffled the ship's officers, what with the color of Kakaracou and the impish proportions of the little man; while the girl Clio, silent, lovely, black-clad, was a piquant source of mystery to the other passengers. New Orleans was their destination, and they seemed to melt into the teeming picturesque city as though they never had left it. Daily, for fifteen years, they had talked of it, had heard its praises sung, had longed for it through the nostalgia of the languishing Rita and the lusty Belle.

But even Kakaracou, who treated her like a child, was a little awed by the imperious and strategic generalship with which Clio Dulaine took possession of her New Orleans patrimony. Shabby and neglected though it was, Clio went immediately to the old house on Rampart Street. Mice scuttled and squeaked in it, windows were cracked or broken, the jalousies rattled eerily, rank weeds choked the garden once heavy with the fragrance of camellias and mimosa. The little brick *garçonnière* that faced the house at the rear was overgrown with a tangle of wistaria and bougainvillaea so that the iron lacework of the lovely gallery was completely hidden. The very street itself had taken on a look of decay.

Clio Dulaine stood surveying this scene of ruin, the half-smile on her face curiously cynical for one so young. Then to the shocked dismay of Kakaracou and Cupidon she began to laugh. She looked at the dust and the torn brocades and the broken glass and the weather-stained draperies and she laughed and laughed until she held her sides and then she held her head, and the tears of laughter streamed down her cheeks.

At first Kakaracou had laughed with her, companionably, though not knowing why. But then she looked sober, then serious, finally alarmed.

"Hysterical," said Cupidon, in French. "Slap her. Hard, on the cheek. I'll go into the next room."

Kakaracou had gone to her, had taken her gently in her arms as she stood there, but Clio had shaken her off and gone on laughing. "Don't *bébé*, don't *chérie*," Kaka had murmured. Then, seeing that this was unavailing, she took Cupide's advice. She slapped the girl's cheek a stinging blow. Clio's laughter ceased as though turned off by a piece of mechanism, her eyes blazed at the Negress, she raised her hand to strike her, the woman cowered, and Clio's hand came down on her thin shoulder, gently, gently.

"Thank you, Kaka. I'm all right now. It was that sofa with one leg off. It looked so crazy and frowsy and dirty, like that old woman who used to limp along the quay in Paris, selling fish."

Kakaracou stared at it. Then she began to laugh with something of Clio's hysterical note in her voice. "So it does! Oh, that's very funny! So it——"

"Stop it! Don't you begin. That wasn't why I was laughing, really. Anyway, it's better than crying. That sofa was the one Mama always talked about. It was made and carved by Prudent Mallard, she said, and the crimson brocade came from France. Solid mahogany. Not so solid now, is it?"

Kaka leaped to the defense of her dead darling. "You should have seen her as she sat on it in her silks and jewels——"

"I know, I know. She told me a thousand times. This house—I remembered it as the most exquisite and luxurious——" She began to laugh again, then pulled herself together with an actual physical effort. She stood there, surveying the mildewed walls, the decrepit furniture. Her young face was stern, her eyes resolute and almost hard. "I suppose nothing in life is what we dreamed it would be. She spoke of this house as if it had been a palace. It's a shanty, tumble-down and filthy."

"Is it?" Kaka asked, dully, staring about her as though seeing the room for the first time. "Is it? Why, so it is!"

"It is not!" Clio then retorted with fine inconsistence. "It's beautiful! You wait. You'll see. We're *cagou* because we are sad and tired and everything's so neglected. But we'll make *ménage,* you and I and Cupide. We'll sweep and scrub and polish. The jalousies will be mended and the *garde-de-frise* out there, and the walls and the windows."

Kaka, the imitative, looked a shade less doleful, but she hugged her thin shoulders and edged closer to the doorway. "In the street they say this house is haunted. That's why it looks as it does. No one has come near it since he died here."

"It's very chic to be haunted by a Dulaine. Buy yourself a *gris-gris* from the *mamaloi*. That will keep off the spirits, you've always said. You used to complain because there was no voodoo woman in Paris to furnish you with one."

"You may laugh, but I know——"

"Yes, I can laugh. I'm going to be happy. Not like Mama. She had no pleasure in living those years in France. She talked of nothing but this house and its wonders. Look at it! She might much better have been enjoying a gay time—she and poor funny Aunt Belle. Well, I'm going to have a gay time! Glorious! This house will be lovely again."

"How? We've nothing."

"Mama's jewelry."

"You wouldn't part with that!"

"How else? Not the best of it, of course."

"The best! You haven't got the best of it. That went long ago. The magnificent pieces. She was extravagant, my poor *bébé* Rita, no doubt of that."

"*Stupide!* I'll keep the best for myself, of course, until someone gives me better. The unimportant pieces will pay for what I shall do to make this place right again. It won't be much. We shan't be here long."

Kakaracou was accustomed to dolorous middle-aged mistresses who wept on her bosom, required to be dressed and undressed like children, asked her advice as though she were a sibyl and berated her by turn. She now rolled her eyes at this strange new note of authority so that they seemed all whites. "Where we go!"

"Oh, wherever there's money and fun."

"Not here! Not New Orleans!"

"Pooh! It's dead here—finished. I saw that the moment I set foot in this town. I only came here to show them they can't frighten me and bully me the way they did Mama. Clio Dulaine! That's me. If they threaten me I'll tell the whole business. They can't do anything to me. I would, anyway, if it weren't for Mama. . . . Come on, I want to see the bedroom. She always said the dressing table—she called it a *duchesse*—was carved of palissandre, and the four-poster bed that Papa gave her was made long ago by Francois Seignouret, of rosewood, too, and signed by him, like a painting, it's so valuable. Will they be like that sofa, I wonder . . . well . . ."

At that moment Cupide waddled in from the dim bedroom across the wide central hall that divided the drawing room and dining room from the two bedrooms. His gait was a rollicking thing to see, quick, light, rolling, like the gay little Basque fishing boats that used to come bouncing into port from the Bay of Biscay with the sardine and herring catch. They had watched them on many a holiday along the Côte d'Argént. As he trotted, Cupide was whistling through his teeth, a talent in the perfection of which he was aided by nature, his two large square yellow incisors being separated by a generous eighth of an inch. He jerked a thumb over his shoulder.

"Blood in there on the carpet by the bed," he announced blithely.

Kakaracou shrieked, but Clio Dulaine stared at him a moment, silent. "Let me see," she said, then. She crossed the hall swiftly, her silken skirts flirting the dust. "Open the jalousies."

It had been the bedroom of a lovely and beloved woman. This was apparent in its furnishings, in its delicate coloring, in its arrangement. The exquisitely carved armoire of rosewood was meant to hold only the most fragile of silks and laces; the great arms of the vast palissandre bed were built to cradle love. The light that shone dimly through the broken blinds gave to the room a pale green translucence as it filtered through the rank growth of vines and trees that had spread a verdant coverlet protectingly about the house. The pastel grays and rose and fluid greens of the charming Aubusson carpet formed a pattern of wreaths and roses, faded and dusty now, but still lovely except for that great blotch there by the side of the bed. It must have been a pool, once, a pool that had grown viscid before it had been scoured in vain by hands that had striven to erase its marks. A great rusty brown irregular circle defacing the wistful flowers that strewed the floor.

Cupidon pointed with one tiny blunt forefinger. Kakaracou shrieked again and covered her staring eyes with her two hands, but she peeped through her latticed fingers, too, at once fascinated and terrified. The girl only stared in silence.

"I saw him as plain as if he was there now, the blood spurting out of his shirt like the fountains at Versailles," began the dwarf with gusto, "and she kneeling there screaming, her hair was dipping in it——"

Kakaracou leaped to him; she cuffed him a thwack across his hard head. He did not even blink. He merely brushed her hand away lightly as though it had been a mosquito.

"Let him be," the girl commanded. "I want to hear it." She dropped to her knees beside the sinister stain, she peeled off her fine French glove and, stooping, she passed her hand slowly, caressingly, over the rusty brown spot on the carpet. "His blood. My blood. They are the same. I love it, this spot. I will sleep here tonight, in this bed."

"No, no, no!" screamed Kakaracou. For a moment it looked as though she would run from the room, from the house, from the street itself.

"Yes, I say. Why not?"

"You can't. It isn't—it isn't decent." Then, as the girl's eyes blazed again, "It needs airing—the whole house—it's like a tomb."

"Cupide, open up here. Run down to Canal Street and fetch a pail, a mop, a broom. Tomorrow we'll find women to scrub and clean but we'll make it do for tonight. Kaka, open the bags and find me an old *blouse-volante*. This afternoon I'll engage workmen. A little paint, a few nails. A glazier. The garden made neat. Today is Monday. By the end of the week everything will be shining and in order."

Cupide rubbed his tiny hands together, he kicked up his heels like a colt. "This is fine!" he cried. "I like this. Are we going to eat here? Shall I bring things from the market?"

"Get on there!" shouted Kaka, entering into the spirit of the thing. "The marketing is my affair, you whelp. The stove probably doesn't march, and the chimney's sure to be stopped up. Well, we'll see."

"Shrimps!" ordered Clio. "And a *poulet chanteclair* and *omelette soufflée*. How Aunt Belle would love it, poor darling."

"You're crazy," Kaka muttered. "What do you think I am? A magician! If I can give you the plainest of omelettes and a cup of black coffee it will be a miracle. . . . Here is the *blouse-volante*. What do you want it for?"

"To put on, of course. I'm going to scrub too."

"Your hands!"

"Oh, the creams will put them right. I can't wait to see everything neat and gay, the chandelier glittering in the drawing room, and pots in the kitchen and flowers everywhere and the fountain singing in the garden. And Sunday!"

"Sunday?" Kaka was plainly afraid to hear what Sunday might bring out of this new strange mad mind, but she listened nevertheless.

"Sunday we'll go down to the French Market, just as Aunt Belle used to tell it. We'll buy everything. Everything delicious. I'll wear my gray half-mourning. We'll go to Mass at St. Louis Cathedral. We'll go to Madame Begué's for breakfast. Perhaps They will come in for breakfast. Mama said They sometimes did. Then—well, I don't know. I may stare at Them—like this. Or I may go up to Them and say, 'How are you, Grandmama, how do you do, Grandpapa.'"

"You wouldn't do that!"

"Ha, wouldn't I! What are they? Rich. Rich and dull and clannish, drooping around in black like those Paris snobs who think they're so grand that they have to dress down to keep from dazzling the *canaille*. I'll be richer than they. I'll be grander than they. I'll dress in the most exquisite——"

"Yes, well, that's very fine. Meantime, that dress you're wearing was your poor mama's but it was made by Worth. I can copy it, but where would I find such material? So take it off and put on the *blouse-volante* or stop pulling furniture about, one or the other. You won't get another dress like it in a hurry."

Clio Dulaine had never done a day's manual labor. It was a lesson in the adaptability of youth to see her now as she scrubbed, polished, scoured with Kakaracou and Cupidon. She produced carpenters, plumbers, glaziers, cabinet-makers and charmed them into doing their work at once, and swiftly. All that week there was a cacophony of sound throughout the house and garden, a domestic orchestra made up of the swish of the broom, the rub-a-dub of the washboard, the clink-clank of the plumber's tools, the sharp report of the carpenter's hammer, the slap-slap of the paint brush, the snip of the gardener's shears, the scrape of trowel on brick. Above this homely symphony soared the solo of Clio's song. As she worked she sang in a rich, true contralto a strange mixture of music—music she had heard at the Paris

Opera; songs that Rita Dulaine had hummed in a sweet and melancholy tremolo; plantation songs, Negro spirituals, folk songs with which Kaka had sung her to sleep in her childhood; songs that Aunt Belle Piquery had sung in a shrill off-key soprano, risqué songs whose origins had been the brothels and gambling houses of the New Orleans of her heyday. *Po' Pitie Mamze Zizi,* she caroled. Then, *Robert, toi que j'aime.* Three minutes later her fresh young voice would fling gaily upward the broken beat of a Negro melody:

> *Tell yuh 'bout a man wot live befo Chris'—*
> *He name was Adam, Eve was his wife,*
> *Tell yuh how dat man he lead a rugged life,*
> *All be-cause he tak-en de woman's ad-vice. . . .*
>
> *She made his trouble so hard—*
> *she made his trou-ble so hard——*
> *Lawd, Lawd, she made his trou-ble so hard. . . .*

It had been Kakaracou who had taught her *Grenadie, ça-ça-yie,* a Creole song with its light and fatalistic treatment of death and love. Kaka, too, had taught her those mixtures of French and Negro dialects such as rose so naturally now to her lips in the Creole lullaby:

> *Pov piti Lolotte a mouin*
> *Pov piti Lolotte a mouin*
> *Li gagnin bobo, bobo,*
> *Li gagnin doule, doule,*
> *Li gagnin doule dans ker a li.*

The dialect was Gombo, soft and slurred; she hardly knew the meaning of the words, but her slim white throat pulsed and her voice swelled in song. She was happy who had been bred in such *douleur,* she was definite and sure who had been so bewildered by her life, shuttled as she was from convent to Paris flat, hearing of her real background always in terms of nostalgia and resentment, never hoping to see it. She worked singing or she worked silent, the tip of her little pink tongue just showing between her teeth as she rubbed and polished, an unusual glow tinting the creamy pallor of her cheeks. She had the happy energy of one who at last belongs; of the vital female who has been dominated all her life and who now, at last, is free. As she sang and polished and flitted from room to room, from garden to kitchen, from *garçonnière* to street, the house magically took on life, color, charm. She was like a butterfly emerging from a grub; the house was a *bijou* once dingy with long neglect, now glowing rich and lustrous. The fine chandelier, always too magnificent for the little drawing room, was now a huge jewel whose every handcut crystal gave back its own flashing ruby and topaz and sapphire and emerald.

Every few minutes she ran to the door or window at the call of a street vendor. Here was another opera, high, low, melodious, raucous. The chimney sweep came by. "R-r-ra-monay! R-a-ramonez la cheminée du haut en bas!" The French words fell sweetly on her ear, but the voice came from a black giant in a rusty frock coat, a battered and enormous top hat, over his shoulder a stout rope, a sheaf of broom straw, bunches of palmetto. She beckoned him in, he shook his kinky head over the state of the fireplaces and chimneys. Like a magician he pulled all sorts of creatures out of their nests of brick and plaster—bats, mice, birds. Clio would not have been surprised to learn that the cow that jumped over the moon had come to rest in one of the chimneys of the Rampart Street house.

The coal peddler, a perfect match for his wares, had his song, too.

> *Mah mule is white*
> *Mah face is black;*
> *Ah sells mah coal*
> *Two bits a sack.*

The brush man called, "*Latanier! Latanier!* Palmetto root!" Clothes poles and palmetto roots dangled from his cart. Fruit women, calling. Berry women. Clio bought every sort of thing, her lovely laughing face popping out at this door or that window. Vast black women stepped down the street carrying great bundles of wash on their heads; they walked superbly, their arms swinging free at their sides. Generations had carried their burdens thus; their neck, waist and shoulder muscles were made of steel. Clio Dulaine threw pennies to every passing beggar or minstrel. Street bands, ragged and rolling-eyed, made weird music done in a curious broken rhythm that later was to be called ragtime or jazz.

Now the doorstep, scoured with powdered brick, shone white. Kaka, down on her knees with pail and brush, gave short shrift to inquisitive neighborhood servants who loitered by in assumed innocence, but who obviously had been sent out on reconnaissance by their mistresses.

"Where you come from? France, like they say?"

"I come from New Orleans. Not like you, Congo."

"You make *ménage?*"

Kaka had easily dropped into her native New Orleans patois. "What you think! We carpetbaggers like you!"

"Your lady and you, you going stay here?"

The time had come to close the conversation. *"Zaffaire Cabritt ça pas zaffaire Mouton."* The goat's business is none of the sheep's concern. The inquirer moved on, little wiser for her pains. Cupide gave them even less information, but a better show. Among his talents was that of being able to twist his face into the most appalling shapes and expressions. His popeyes, his wide lips, his outstanding ears, his buttonlike nose were natural contributors to this grisly gift. Perched on a ladder, busy with his window-washing or occupied with brush and pail on the doorstep, or even shopping in one of the neighborhood stores he would ponder a question a moment as though giving it grave consideration. Then in a lightning and dreadful transformation he would peer up at his questioner, his face screwed into such a mask of distortion and horror as to send his questioner gibbering in fright. At first the neighborhood children and the loiterers in the nearby barrooms and groceries had mistaken him for fair game. But his cannon-ball head, his prehensile arms and his monkeylike agility had soon taught them caution and even respect. *Bébé Babouin*, they called him. Baby baboon.

At the end of the first week the house seemed to be in a state of chaos from which order never could emerge. Dust, plaster, paint, soapsuds, shavings, glue mingled in dreadful confusion. But by Friday of the second week order had miraculously been wrought. Kaka's waspishness waned, she began to talk of toothsome Creole dishes; Cupide, who had seemed to swing like a monkey from chandelier to mantel, from mantel to window, came down to earth, donned his Paris uniform of broadcloth and buttons and announced that the time had come to search New Orleans for a suitable carriage and pair.

Clio, disheveled and somewhat wan, looked down at him with affectionate amusement. "Our carriage and pair will be ourselves and our own two legs, Cupide. At any rate, until someone buys us others. So you may as well lay away your maroon coat and gold buttons."

"My livery goes where I go. And I go where Mad'moiselle goes," he announced dramatically. This was not so much loyalty as fury at the thought of being parted from the uniform he loved, the trappings which, in his own eyes, made him a figure of importance in spite of his deformity. Young as she was, Clio Dulaine sensed this. She laid her hand gently on his head, she tipped the froglike face up and smiled down at him her lovely poignant smile. "You are my body-guard, Cupide. My escort. And we'll have carriages and the finest of horses. You wait. You'll see."

He brightened at that, he capered like a frolicsome goat, he rushed off to the kitchen to tell Kaka that he was once more Cupidon of the maroon livery, the gold buttons, the shiny boots. Kaka, the realist, did not share his happiness. "On the street! You'll look like a monkey without a string."

"*Carencro!*" Cupide spat out at her, for by now he had renewed acquaintance with old half-forgotten New Orleans epithets. This Acadian corruption of carrion crow or black vulture he found particularly suitable in his verbal battles with the sharp-tongued Kakaracou.

Now it was Saturday, and the house was not only habitable, it was charming and even luxurious. From the street one saw only a neat one-story dwelling of the simple plantation type, built well off the ground to avoid dampness. Its low-hanging roof came down like a hat shading its upper windows. It gave the house a misleading compressed look, for inside the rooms were high-ceilinged and spacious, with a wide central hall running straight through the house from front to back. Drawing room, dining room, bedroom, boudoir; beautifully proportioned rooms in this cottagelike structure. But the real life of the house was at the back. There was the courtyard with its paving of faded old orange brick; kitchen and servants' rooms were separated from the main house, forming an ell at one side of the courtyard. At right angles to this, and facing the house, was the *garçonnière*. Its two rooms, with a lacework balcony thrown across the front, were protected from dampness by the little basement that formed the ground floor. Here and there, where the plaster had fallen off, the old brick of the foundation showed through yellow-pink like the courtyard pavement.

Inside the house the white woodwork had been freshly painted, the carpets scoured, the windows mended. The rosewood and mahogany of the fine furniture had been rubbed until it shone like satin. The gilt mirrors gave back the jewel colors of the chandeliers. Clio had brought to America bits and pieces from the Paris flat—plump little French chairs, Sèvres vases, inlaid tables of rosewood and tulipwood. These had stood the journey bravely and now fitted into the Rampart Street house as though they dated from the lavish New Orleans day of Rita Dulaine.

And now the three stood surveying their handiwork: the big-eyed girl with that look in her face of one whose life will hold surprising things, but who, even now, is planning not to be taken by surprise; the Negress, wiry, protective, indomitable; the dwarf, rollicking, pugnacious, always slightly improbable, like a creature out of a drawing. Each wore the expression of one who, having done his work, finds that work well done. An ill-assorted trio, held together by a background of common experience and real affection and a kind of rowdy camaraderie.

"It looks well," said Kakaracou even as she breathed on a bit of crystal and rubbed it with her apron, needlessly.

The little man cocked an impish eye up at her. "It's well enough—until we can manage something better."

Clio's grin was as impish as his. "Now I know what Mama meant. Do you remember she used to say there was an old Louisiana proverb: 'Give a Creole a crystal chandelier and two mirrors to reflect it and he is satisfied.' Well, I've got the chandelier and the two mirrors. But I'm not satisfied."

"Who's Creole here?" demanded Kaka, sourly. Always, when speaking to outsiders, she boasted that the Creole blood flowing in Clio Dulaine's veins actually was tinged with the cerulean hue of royalty. In private she never missed an opportunity to remind the girl that her origin was one-half aristocratic Creole and one-half New Orleans underworld. Perhaps this was her instinctive desire to protect the girl from bruising herself against her own ambitions as her mother before her had done.

Yet, "I am!" Clio shouted now. "I'm Creole!"

"Take shame on yourself, denying your own mama."

"That's a lie! Don't you dare!" She stopped in the midst of her protest as though suddenly remembering something. She stood looking at these two human oddments as though seeing them clearly for the first time. It was a deliberate and measuring look. In that moment she seemed to shed her girlhood before their very eyes and become a woman. The daughter of a *placée*, the niece of the hearty shrewd strumpet Belle Piquery, most of her life had been spent in the company of two women whose every thought was devoted to pleasing men. Convent-schooled though the girl was, she had absorbed the very atmosphere of courtesanship. Because she had loved them, her voice, her glance, her movements were an unconscious imitation of theirs. Yet there was a difference even now. Where they had been fluid and easy-going she was firm; where they had wavered she was direct.

The square little chin balanced the sensual mouth; the melting eyes were likely to cause you to overlook the free plane of the brow. Wan and disheveled with her two weeks of concentrated work, she now seemed to gather herself together in all her mental and physical and emotional being.

"Now then, listen to me, you two. You, Angélique Pluton. You, Cupidon." They stared at her with uncomprehending gaze as though she had spoken in a strange language. Never in her life had she called the woman anything but Kaka, or—crowing mischievously—Kakaracou. The dwarf had always been Cupide. "Do you want to stay with me?"

The little man's mouth fell open. It was the wrinkled woman who said, with an edge of fear in her voice, "Where else!"

"Then remember that no matter what I say I am—that I am. I shall be what it suits me to be. Life is something you must take by the tail or it runs away from you. . . . Now where did I hear that! That's clever. I must have made it up. Well, anyway, I don't want to hear any more of this telling me who I am and what I am to do. Do as I say, and we'll be rich. Which do you choose—stay or go?"

"Stay!" shouted Cupide, cutting a caper with those absurd bandy legs. The Negress voiced no choice. The fear was gone from her eyes. She stood with her lean arms crossed on her breast, assured and even a trifle arrogant.

"Play-acting," she sniffed, "Like your great-grandmother. That's the Bonnevie in you. You and your cleverness! What will Your Highness choose to be tomorrow? Queen of England, I suppose!"

Clio dropped her role of adventuress. She pouted a moment as she had in her childhood when her nurse Kaka would not bend to her will. Then she threw her arms around the woman and hugged her. "Tomorrow, Kaka, we'll dress in our best and we'll have a wonderful time, you and Cupide and I. We'll go first to the Cathedral and then to the French Market and then to Begué's for breakfast—or we may go to the French Market first and then to Mass—well, anyway, now I'll have my hair washed, Kaka, and such a brushing, and my hands in oil, and then you'll rub me all over with that lovely sweet stuff that you used when Mama had one of her sad times and couldn't sleep. And tomorrow morning I'll wake up all fresh and gay in my own home in New Orleans. Oh, Kaka!" Here she gave an unadult squeal and clapped her hands. There was something touching, something moving about this, probably because it made plain that her stern and implacable role of the past fortnight had been only an acting part. At sight of this the faces of the two changed as a summer sky grows brilliant again when the sun drives off the clouds. For two weeks she had been a stranger to them, a managing mistress, hard, almost harsh, driving them and herself in a fury of energy. Now she was young again and gay; the house was fresh, cool, orderly; in the kitchen just off the courtyard Kaka's copper pans shone golden as the sauces they soon would contain, and on the kitchen table was a Basque cloth of coarse linen striped with bright green and red and yellow. The window panes glittered. The steps were scoured white. The courtyard bricks were newly swept and the fountain actually tinkled its lazy little tune; inside the high-ceilinged rooms you were met by the clean odor of fresh paint; silver, crystal, satin and glass reflected each other, surface for surface; the scent of perfume in Clio's bedroom, her peignoir softly slithering over a chair back.

"*En avant, mes enfants!*" cried Clio, satisfied.

"*A la bonne heure!*" shouted Cupide.

But, "*Tout doux,*" the acidulous old woman cautioned them. "Not so fast, you two."

III

✦

But next morning even Kakaracou's grim mask was brightened by a gleam of anticipation. Sunday morning, April, and steaming hot. New Orleans citizens did not remark the heat, or if they did they relished it. They were habituated to that moist and breathless atmosphere, they thrived on it, they paced their lives in accordance with it. Clio and Kaka and Cupide slipped easily into the new-old environment as one allows an accustomed garment, temporarily discarded, once more to rest gratefully upon one's shoulders.

Kaka's broad nostrils dilated with her noisy inhalations as the three emerged into the brilliant April morning sunshine of Rampart Street. Over all New Orleans there hung the pungent redolence that was the very flavor of the bewitching city.

First, as always, the heavy air bore the scent of coffee pervading everything like an incense wafted from the great wharves and roasting ovens. Over and under and around this dominant odor were other smells, salty, astringent or exotic. There were the smells of the Mississippi, of river shrimps and crayfish and silt and rotting wood and all manner of floating and sunken things that go to feed the monster stream; of sugar, spices, bananas, rum, sawdust; of flower-choked gardens; of black men sweating on the levees; of rich food bubbling in butter and cream and wine and condiments; the sweet, dank, moldy smell of old churches whose doors, closed throughout the week, were opened now for the stream of Sabbath worshipers. The smell of an old and carnal city, of a worldly and fascinating city.

"M-m-m!" said Clio. And "M-m-m!" chorused Kaka and Cupide.

Any one of the three, as they set out this Sunday morning, would have been enough to attract attention on the streets of New Orleans, sophisticated though the city was. Certainly Clio Dulaine alone was a figure to catch the eye and hold it, to say nothing of the bizarre attendants who walked in her wake.

She was wearing a dress of stiff rich gray silk faille, and it was amazing that so prim a color could take on, from its wearer, so dashing and even brilliant a look. Perhaps it was that the gray of the gown was the shade of a fine pearl with a hint of pink behind it. It made her black hair seem blacker, her skin whiter. It had, in fact, an effect almost of gaiety. For contrast, and doubtless because this gown was supposed to represent mourning in its second stage, the overskirt and basque were trimmed with little black velvet bows as was the pancake hat with its black curled ostrich tips, tilted well down over her eyes. Beneath this protection her eyes swam shaded and mysterious like twin pools beneath an overhanging ledge. In her ears were pearl screws, very foreign and French, and a pearl and black onyx brooch made effective contrast just beneath the creamy hollow of her throat. If one could have seen her brows below the down-tipped pancake hat it might have been remarked how thick and dark and winged they were—the brows of a forceful and vigorous woman. She was a figure of French elegance as depicted in the fashion papers. No well-bred French woman would have ventured out of doors in a costume so rich, so picturesque.

Beside her and perhaps just a half step behind her paced Kakaracou, looking at once vaguely Egyptian, New Orleans Negro duenna, and a figure out of the Arabian Nights. Her handsome black grosgrain silk gown was as rich and heavy as that of any grand lady, though severe in style. Over it her ample white apron and fichu were cobweb fine and exquisitely hemstitched. In the withered ears dangled heavy gold earrings of Byzantine pattern, and where the fichu folded at her breast was a gold brooch of Arabesque design. Surmounting all this was a brilliantly gay tignon wound about her head. The gray-brown face, like an old dried fig, had the look of a rather sardonic Egyptian mummy, yet it had a vaguely simian quality due partly to the broad upper lip but more definitely to the eyes, which had the sad yet compassionate quality found in an old race whose heritage is tragedies remembered. As she walked she had a way of turning her head quickly, almost dartingly like a bird, and this set her earrings to swinging and glinting in the sun. The eyes beneath their heavy wrinkled lids noted everything.

Behind these two, a figure out of Elizabethan court days, except that he wore no brilliant turban, no puffed satin pantaloons, walked the dwarf Cupidon. He walked without self-consciousness other than that of pride; the tiny bandy legs, the powerful trunk and shoulders, the large head, the young old face were made all the more bizarre by his coachman's plum broadcloth uniform ornamented with gilt buttons and topped by a glazed hat with a gay cockade on one side. The wistful yet merry eyes watched the slim, graceful figure that walked ahead of him as a dog watches his mistress even while he seems busy with his own affairs. A mischievous and pugnacious little figure yet touching and, somehow, formidable. Hooked over one tiny arm was a large woven basket, for they were on their way to the French Market, these three on a fine hot, humid New Orleans Sunday morning, just as Clio Dulaine had planned.

Now and then the girl would turn her head to toss a word over her shoulders to the stern, stalking figure just behind her.

"It smells exactly the way Aunt Belle said it did." A long deep inhalation. "But precisely!"

"How else!"

The little procession moved on up the street. Passers-by and loungers stared. In their faces you saw reflected a succession of emotions like the expressions of rather clumsy pantomimists. First there was the shock of beholding the three in all their splendor; then the eye was lit with admiration for the lovely girl; startled by the mingled magnificence and gaudiness of the Negress; shocked or amused by the little liveried escort strutting so pompously behind them. The three figures made a gay colorful frieze against the smooth plaster walls of the *Vieux Carré*. Past the old houses whose exquisitely wrought iron-work decoration was like a black lace shawl thrown across the white bosom of a Spanish *señora;* past the Cabildo with its massive arches and its delicate cornices, pilasters and pediment. The sound of music came to them as they passed the Cathedral, but Clio did not enter.

"America is lovely," said Clio graciously, gazing across the Place d'Armes to the stately double row of the Pontalba buildings facing the square. The remark was addressed to the world, over her shoulder, and was caught deftly by Kakaracou who in turn tossed it back to Cupide, like an echo.

"America is lovely."

Cupide looked about him, spaciously. "It's well enough."

With one little gray-gloved hand Clio pointed across the Place d'Armes to the stately brick front of the Pontalba buildings with their lacy festoons of ironwork. "As you probably know, Kaka, my Aunt Micaela, the Baroness Pontalba, built those apartments." She turned her head slightly to catch Kaka's eye. For a moment it seemed that Kaka must reject this statement, but Clio Dulaine's look did not waver, her eye held the other in command. The turbaned head turned again to enlighten the little man.

"Mad'moiselle's Aunt Micaela, the Baroness Pontalba, built those fine apartments, Little One."

Pattering along behind them the dwarf rolled his goggle eyes in mock admiration of this palpable fantasy. "*Ma foi!* My uncle, the Emperor Napoleon, built the Arc de Triomphe."

Clio laughed her slow, rich laugh that was so paced and deep-throated. This morning she was gay, eager, this morning nothing could offend her. She was finding it to her liking, this colorful, uncon-ventional city. She sniffed the smells of river water and good cooking and tropical gardens; her young eyes did not flinch from the glare of the sun on the white buildings; as they approached the busy French Market she felt at home with these people walking and chatting and laughing. Some of them had come there solely for sociability, some had market baskets on their arms or servants walking behind them carrying the laden hamper. She liked the look of these people, they were dark and juicy like the lusty people of Marseilles; indeed she thought the city itself had the look of Marseilles down here by the French Market so near the water front. These people thronging the streets on a spring Sunday morning had French and Spanish and American blood running strong in their veins, a heady mixture. And the Negroes were here, there, everywhere accenting the scene, enriching it with their expressive tragi-comic faces, their fluid movements. You heard French spoken, Spanish too, English; the Negro dialect called Gombo; the patois called Cajun, which had been brought to the Bayou country by the Acadian settlers from Nova Scotia.

And now they were in the midst of the Market's clamor, the crackling of geese, the squawk of chickens, vendors' cries, the clatter of horses' hoofs. Footsteps rang on the flagstoned floor, the arcaded brick and plaster structure was a sounding board, the arched columns formed a setting for the leisurely promenading figures or the scurrying busy ones. Creole ladies severe in their plain street dress of black were buying food for the day fresh from the river or lake or nearby plantations, while the basket on the arm of the servant grew heavier by the minute.

Greeks, Italians, French, Negroes, Indians. Oysters, fish, vegetables, oranges, figs, nuts. Delicate lake shrimp like tiny pink petals; pompano, trout, soft-shell crabs, crayfish. Quail, partridge, snipe, rabbits.

"Oh, Kaka, look, some of that! And that! Look, Cupide, herbs and green for *gombo-zhebes* that Aunt Belle longed for in Paris and couldn't get. I can't wait to taste it. Kaka! Kakaracou! Where are you! Look! Crayfish for bisque. Or shall we have redfish with *court-bouillon*? Cupide, come here with that basket."

Fat Negro women, their heads bound in snowy white turbans,

baskets of sandwiches on their arms, lifted the corner of a napkin to tempt the passer-by with the wares beneath. A hundred appetizing odors came from charcoal braziers glowing here, there, behind stalls or at the pavement's edge. The fragrant coffee stands with their cups of *café noir* or *café au lait* were situated at opposite ends of the market, but in the very heart of the food stalls they were selling hot Creole dishes to be served up on the spot and eaten standing. There was the favorite hot jambalaya steaming and enriching the already heavy air; the mouth watered as one passed it.

The trailing skirts of Clio's exquisite French dress had swished from stall to stall, the basket on Cupide's arm had grown heavier and heavier. The market men and stall vendors, their Latin temperament quick to respond to her beauty and her strong electric attraction, gave her overweight measure. Cupide was almost hidden behind the foliage of greens in his basket; now and then a crayfish claw reached feebly out to nip the maroon sleeve of his uniform only to be slapped smartly back in place by the little man. They were followed now by quite a little procession of the curious and the admiring and the amused. They paid no heed. Even in Paris they had become accustomed to this.

Clio stopped now and pointed to the pot of bubbling jambalaya. "Some of that!" she said. "A plateful of that. Mm, what a heavenly smell!"

"No. It will ruin your breakfast at Begué's."

"Nothing will ruin my breakfast. I have the appetite of a dock laborer. You know that. Here, Cupide. Set down that basket and fetch me a plateful of that lovely stuff. What's that it's called, Kaka?"

"Jambalaya. Heavy stuff. You'll be——"

"Quick, Cupide. Tell the man a heaping plateful for me—for Madame la Comtesse."

Cupide, in the act of setting down his basket, straightened again with a jerk "For who!"

"You heard!" barked Kakaracou. "A plateful of jambalaya for Madame la Comtesse. Who else, *stupide!*"

The dwarf shook his bullet head as though to rid it of cobwebs, grinned impishly and trotted off. "Heh, you! A dish of that stuff for Madame la Comtesse."

"Who?"

"Madame la Comtesse there. And be quick about it."

The man looked up from stirring the pot, his eyes fell on the girl's eager face, he became all smiles, his eyes, his teeth flashed, he spooned up a great bowlful and placed it on a tray and himself would have carried it to her but Cupide reached up and took it from him and brought it to her miraculously without spilling a drop, brimming though it was. Then, because he was just table-high with arms strong as steel rods, he stood before her holding up the tray with its savory dish and she stood and ate it thus, daintily and eagerly, with quite a little circle of admiring but anxious New Orleans faces, black, olive, cream, *café au lait,* white, awaiting her verdict.

"Oh," Clio cried between hot heaping spoonfuls, "it's delicious, it's better than anything I've ever eaten in France."

Cupide, the living table, could just be seen from the eyes up, staring over the rim of the tray. He now turned his head to right to left while his stocky little body remained immovable. "Madame la Comtesse," he announced in his shrill boyish voice, "says that the dish is delicious, it is more delicious than anything she has eaten in France." He then lowered the tray an inch or two to peer into the half-empty dish. "*Relevé,*" he said under his breath. "Hash! Pfui!"

Clio took a final spoonful, her strong white teeth crunching the spicy mess; she broke a crust of fresh French bread, neatly mopped up the sauce in the bowl and popped this last rich morsel into her mouth. The onlookers breathed a satisfied sigh, and at that moment Clio encountered the bold and enveloping stare of one onlooker whose admiration quite evidently was not for her gustatory feats but for her face and figure. It was more than that. The look in the eyes of this man who stood regarding her was amused, was tender, was possessive. He was leaning indolently against one of the pillars forming the arcade, his hands thrust into the front pockets of his tight fawn trousers, one booted foot crossed the other. Under the broad, rolling brim of his white felt hat his stare of open and flashing admiration was as personal as an embrace. Clio Dulaine was accustomed to stares, she even liked them. In France, especially at the races, the Parisians had followed the fantastic little group made up of the lovely Rita Dulaine, the full-blown Belle, the great-eyed girl, the attendant dwarf and Negress. They had stared and commented with the Gallic love of the bizarre. But this man's gaze was an actual intrusion. He was speaking to her, wordlessly. In another moment she thought he actually would approach her, address her. She felt the blood tingling in her cheeks that normally were so pale. Abruptly she set down her plate and spoon, she shoved the tray a little away from her.

"Bravo Madame la Comtesse!" cried the jambalaya man behind his brazier of charcoal. "Eaten like a true Creole!" The onlookers laughed a little, but it was an indulgent laugh; they liked to see a pretty woman who could polish off her plate with gusto. It flattered them. They, too, knew good food when they saw it. They knew a good-looking woman, as well, though she did have a fast look about her—or maybe it was merely foreign.

Kakaracou nudged her with one sharp elbow. "Come, I don't like the look of this. It's common. You, Cupide, take that miserable stuff away." Her sharp eyes had not missed the tall stranger lolling there against the pillar with his bold intent gaze. She was still muttering as they moved on, and the words were not pretty, made up as they were of various epithets and obscenities culled from the French, from the Congo, from the Cajun, from the Negro French.

"Stop nudging me, you wicked old woman! I'm not a child. I'll go when I please." But Clio moved on, nevertheless, with a flick of her eye to see if the tall figure lounging against the pillar took note of their going. Here and there they stopped at this stall or that, though the basket by now squeaked its protest and Cupide was almost ambushed behind its foliage. Clio was like a greedy child, she wanted everything that went to make up the dishes of which she had heard in her Paris exile. Kaka, too, was throwing caution to the winds. All through the Paris years she had complained because she could not obtain this or that ingredient for a proper Creole dish. And now here it all was, spread lavishly before her. Native dainties, local tidbits. Her eyes glittered, the artist in her was aroused.

"Quail!" she could cry like a desert wanderer who stumbles upon water. "Pompano! Red beans! Soft-shell crabs! Creole lettuce! Oh, the wonderful things that I could never find in that place over there."

A turbaned Negress came by calling the wares from her napkin-covered basket. *"Calas tout chaud! Calas tout chaud!"* Undone, Kaka bought a hot rice cake and gulped it down greedily, poked another into Cupide's great mouth. Down it went with a single snap of his jaws.

So it happened that when they reached the end of the arcade there leaning against a pillar exactly as before was the sombreroed stranger of the burning gaze. He was refreshing himself with a cup of coffee bought at the near-by stall, and as he stirred this lazily and sipped its creamy contents he did not once take his eyes off Clio over the cup's rim.

New Orleans knew a Texan when it saw one. New Orleans regarded its Texas neighbors as little better than savages. Certainly this great handsome product of the plains made the New Orleans male, by contrast, seem a rather anemic not to say effeminate fellow. He was, perhaps, an inch or so over six feet but so well proportioned that he did not seem noticeably tall. His eyes were not so blue as his bronzed face made them appear. His ears stood out a little too far, he walked with the gait of the horseman whose feet are more at home in the stirrup than on the ground. Any of these points would have marked him for an outlander in the eyes of New Orleans. But even if these had failed, his clothes were unmistakable. The great white sombrero was ornamented with a beautifully marked snakeskin band, his belt was heavy with silver nailheads, his fawn trousers were tucked into high-heeled boots that came halfway up his shin. But as final contrast to the quietly dandified or somber garments of the sophisticated Louisiana gentry he wore a blue broadcloth coat of brightish hue strained across his broad shoulders and reaching almost to the knees; and his necktie was a great stiff four-in-hand of white satin on which blue forget-me-nots had been lavishly embroidered by some fair though misguided hand. He was magnificent, he was vast, he was beautiful, he was crude, he was rough, he was untamed, he was Texas.

"There he is!" hissed Kaka, rearing her lean black head like a snake ready to strike. "There he is, that great *badaud,* leaning there."

Clio was intently examining a head of cauliflower. She hated cauliflower and never ate it. "Who, Kaka dear?" she now asked absentmindedly. "H'm?" with an air of dreamy preoccupation which would have deceived no one, least of all the astute Kakaracou. "What a lovely *choufleur!*"

"Who, Kaka dear, who, Kaka dear!" Wickedly the Negress mimicked her in a kind of poisonous baby-talk. "You and your cauliflower head there, you're two of a kind."

Clio decided that the time had now come for dignity. In her role of Madame la Comtesse she now drew herself up and looked down her nose at Kaka. The effect of this was somewhat spoiled by the fact that Kaka glared balefully back, completely uncowed. "We will now go to the Cathedral. Kaka, you will accompany me. Cupide, you will go home with your basket, quickly, then return and wait outside the church. *Vite!*"

At the Market curb stood an open victoria for hire, its shabby cushions a faded green, its two sorry nags hanging listless heads. The black charioteer was as decrepit as his equipage. "We'll ride," Clio announced, grandly. "I'm tired. It's hot. I'm hungry."

The black man bowed, his smile a brilliant gash that made sunshine in the sable face. His gesture of invitation toward the sagging carriage made of it a state coach, of its occupants royalty. "Yas'm, yas'm. Jes' the evening for ride out to the lake, yas'm."

"Evening! Why, it's hardly noon!"

"Yas'm, yas'm. Puffic evening for ride out to the lake."

She set one foot in its gray kid shoe on the carriage step.

"Ma'am," said a soft, rather drawling voice behind her, "Ma'am,

I hate to see anybody as plumb beautiful as you ride in a moth-eaten old basket like this, let alone those two nags to pull it. If you'll honor me, Ma'am, by using my carriage, I'm driving a pair of long-tailed bays to a clarence, I brought them all the way from Texas, and they're beauties and thoroughbreds, just like—well, that sounds terrible, I didn't mean to compare you, Ma'am, with—I meant if you'd just allow me——"

Standing there on the carriage step she had turned in amazement to find her face almost on a level with his as he stood at the curb. The blue eyes were blazing down upon her. He had taken off the great white sombrero. The Texas wind and sun that had bronzed the cheeks to startlingly near her own had burned the chestnut hair to a lively red-gold. For one terrible moment the two swayed together as though drawn by some magnetic force; then she drew back, and as she did so she realized with great definiteness that she wanted to feel his ruddy sun-warmed cheek against hers. She said, "Sir!" like any milk-and-water miss, turned away from him in majestic disapproval and seated herself in the carriage, whose cushion springs, playing her false, let her down in a rather undignified heap. His left hand still held the coffee cup. Unrebuffed, he strode toward the stall to set this down, and at that moment the outraged Kakaracou gave the signal to Cupide. That imp set down his laden basket. The Texan's back was toward him, a broad target. With the force and precision of a goat Cupide ran straight at him, head lowered, and butted him from behind. The coffee cup went flying, spattering the *café au lait* trousers with a deeper tone. Another man would have fallen, but the Texan's muscles were steel, his balance perfect. He pitched forward, stumbled, bent almost double, but he did not fall, he miraculously recovered himself. The white hat had fallen from his hand, it rolled like a hoop into a little pile of decayed vegetables at the curb. Across the open square, skipping along toward the *Vieux Carré*, you saw the figure of the dwarf almost obscured by the heavy basket.

A gasp had gone up from the market, and a snicker—but a small and smothered snicker. The flying blue coattails had revealed the silver-studded belt as being not purely ornamental. A businesslike holster hung suspended on either hip.

Kaka had whisked into the carriage, the coachman had whipped up the listless nags, they were off to the accompaniment of squeaking springs and clattering hoofs and the high shrill cackle of Kaka's rare laughter.

Clio Dulaine's eyes were blazing; her fists were clenched; she craned to stare back at the tall blue-coated figure that had recovered the hat and now, standing at the Market curb, was brushing its sullied whiteness with one coat sleeve even while he gazed at the swaying vehicle bouncing over the cobblestones toward the Cathedral.

"I'll whip him! I'll take his uniform away from him. I'll send him up North among the savages in New York State. I'll never allow him to walk out with me again. I'll lock him in the *garçonnière* on bread and water. I'll——"

"Oh, so Madame la Comtesse enjoys to have loutish cowboys from Texas speak to her on the street. What next! Even your aunt Belle——"

"Shut up! Do you want to be slapped here in front of the Cathedral!"

Kaka took another tack. She began to whimper, her monkeyish face screwed into a wrinkled knot of woe. "I wish I had died when my Rita *bébé* died. I wish I could die now. I promised her I'd take care of you. It's no use. Common. Common as dirt." The carriage came to a halt before the church, Clio stepped out, her head held much too high for a Sunday penitent. "Wait here," Kaka instructed the driver, her air of injured innocence exchanged for a brisk and businesslike manner, "and if that lout in the market asks you if we are inside say no, we left on foot. There'll be *pourboire* for you if you do as I say."

Within the cool dim cathedral Clio's head was meekly bowed, her lips moved silently, she wiped away a tear as she prayed for the souls of the dead, for her lovely unfortunate mother, for her father, for her lusty aunt, but her eyes swam this way and that to see if, in the twilight gray of the aisles and pillars, she could discern a tall waiting figure. Out again into the blinding white sunshine of the Place d'Armes, the carriage was there, awaiting her; Cupide was there perched on the coachman's box, the reins in his own tiny hands; the Sunday throngs were there, but no graceful lounging Texan, no clarence drawn by long-tailed bays.

"Oh!" The girl's exclamation of disappointment was as involuntary as the sound of protest under pain. Kaka was jubilant. They had thrown him off. He had overheard the driver speaking of the lake. Plainly Clio was pouting.

"It's too late for Begué's, don't you think, Kaka? And too hot. Let's drive out to the lake, h'm? I'm not hungry. All that jambalaya."

Cupide had wrought a startling change in the broken-down chariot. Evidently he had brought back with him from the house sundry oddments and elegancies with which to refurbish his lady's carriage. A whisk broom had been vigorously plied, for the ancient cushions were dustless now and the floor cloth as well. Over the carriage seat he had thrown a wine-red silk shawl so that the gray faille should not be sullied further. He had rubbed the metal buckles of the rusty harness, he had foraged in the basement of the *garçonnière* for his cherished equipment of Paris days and had brought out the check reins, which now held the nags' heads high in a position of astonished protest. He himself, in his maroon livery, was perched on the driver's seat, his little feet barely reaching the dashboard against which he braced himself. It was the Negro, dispossessed but admiring, who clambered down to assist the two into the transformed coach.

"Never see such a funny little *maringouin!* He climb up there he make them nags look like steppers. Look him now! Hi-yah!"

Sulkily Clio took her place on the wine-silk shawl against which her gray gown glowed the pinker. Kaka triumphantly took the little seat facing her, her back to the coachman's seat. "Begué's!" she commanded over her shoulder to Cupide.

"Fold your arms!" Cupide commanded of the chuckling Negro beside him on the box. "Sit up straight, you Congo! Eyes ahead!"

The man wagged his head in delighted wonder. "Just like you say, *Quärtee*. Look them horses step! My, my!"

Kaka, victorious, decided to follow up her advantage. "Madame la Comtesse looked very chic talking to that dock laborer. Is it for that we crossed the ocean and returned to New Orleans to live!"

"I didn't talk to him. He talked to me. He isn't a dockhand. He's a Texan, probably. Can I help it if——"

"Texan! Savages!"

"A clarence, he said. Thoroughbred bays. And serve you right if he has Cupide brought into court."

"That one! Not for him, courtrooms. I know the look of them. He's probably wanted in Texas himself, and skipped out with somebody's carriage and pair."

"Oh, Kaka, let's not quarrel. I was going to have such a lovely day. I looked forward to it." The morning was sunny; she was young; a clarence drawn by long-tailed bays and driven by a huge Texan in a white sombrero could not long remain hidden on the streets of New Orleans; instinct warned her that danger lay ahead, common sense told her that Kakaracou was right.

They turned into Decatur Street and drew up at Madame Begué's with quite a flourish.

"Let him wait," Clio commanded, loftily.

"No such thing. Sitting here, doing nothing, while we pay him for it. I'll pay him off now. If he wants to wait until we come out that's his business. You, Cupide!"

Cupide had heard. He tossed the shabby reins into the hands of their owner, and, agile as a monkey, scrambled out on the heaving back of one of the astonished horses, retrieved his check reins (at which the horses' heads, released, immediately slumped forward as though weighted with lead), leaped down and handed Clio out in his best Paris manner. The check reins he tucked away under his coat; he sprang to open the restaurant door, and the strange little procession of three climbed the narrow stair and entered as Rita Dulaine had entered so often twenty years before, with the woman to attend her like a duenna, the dwarf to stand behind her chair as though she were Elizabethan royalty.

IV

✦

New Orleans of the late '50's had itself been sufficiently bizarre to have found nothing fantastic in the sight of the beautiful *placée* followed by her strange retinue. But the New Orleans of Clio's day, breakfasting solidly in its favorite restaurant, looked up from its plate to remain staring, its fork halfway to its mouth.

The three stood a moment in the doorway, their eyes blinking a little in the sudden change from the white glare of the midday streets to the cool half-light of the restaurant. In that instant Monsieur Begué himself stood before them in his towering stiffly starched chef's cap, his solid round belly burgeoning ahead of him. He bowed, he clasped his plump hands.

"Madame! But no. For a moment I thought you were—but of course it isn't possible——"

"I have heard my mother speak of you so often, Monsieur Begué. They say I resemble her. I am Comtesse de—uh—Trenaunay de Chanfret. But this is America, and my home now. Just Madame de Chanfret, please."

She was having a splendid time. She relished the little stir that her entrance had made; it was pleasant to be ushered by Hippolyte Begué himself to a choice table and to have him hovering over her chair as he presented for her inspection the menu handwritten in lively blue ink. Having entered with enormously dramatic effect, she now pretended to be a mixture of royalty incognito and modest young miss wide-eyed with wonder. She had seated herself with eyes cast down, she had handed her parasol to Cupide, her gloves to Kaka, she had pressed her hands to her hot cheeks in pretty confusion, she had thrown an appealing glance up at the attendant Begué.

"I want everything that you are famous for, Monsieur. You and Madame Begué." She cast an admiring glance at the plump black-garbed figure reigning behind the vast cashier's desk at the rear. "All the delicious things Mama used to describe to me in Paris."

"She spoke of my food! In Paris!" He was immensely flattered. He snapped his fingers for Léon, the headwaiter, he himself flicked open her napkin and presented it to her with a flourish. Then the three heads came close—the restaurateur, the waiter, the audacious girl—intent on the serious business of selecting a Sunday morning breakfast from among the famous list of viands at Begué's. Madame Begué's renowned crayfish bisque? Not a dish for even Sunday New Orleans breakfast. Pompano? Begué's celebrated calf's liver *à la bourgeoise*? *Filet de truite, Poulet chanteclair?* With an *omelette soufflée* to follow? *Grillades? Pain perdu?*

Clio, speaking her flawless Parisian French to the two attendant men, ordered delicately and fastidiously. Hippolyte Begué himself waddled off to the kitchen to prepare the dishes with his own magic hands.

Clio Dulaine now leaned back in her chair and breathed a gusty sigh of relief and satisfaction. She looked about her with the lively curiosity of a small girl and the air of leisurely contemplation befitting her recently assumed title and station. She was attempting to produce the effect of being a woman of the world, a connoisseur of food, a *femme fatale* of mystery and experience. Curiously enough, with her lovely face made up as Aunt Belle had taught her, her rich attire, her bizarre attendants, her high, clear voice speaking the colloquial French of the Paris she had just left, she actually achieved the Protean role.

That choice section of New Orleans which was engaged in the

rite of Sunday breakfast at Madame Begué's stared, whispered, engaged in facial gymnastics that ranged all the way from looking down their noses to raising their eyebrows.

Well they might. Behind the newcomer's chair stood Cupide, a figure cut from a pantomime. He brushed away a fly. He summoned a waiter with the Gallic "P-s-s-s-s-t!" He handed his mistress a little black silk fan. He glared pugnaciously about him. He stood with his tiny arms folded across his chest, a bodyguard out of a nightmare. His face was on a level with the table top as he stood. Each new dish, on presentation, he viewed with a look of critical contempt, standing slightly on tiptoe the better to see it as he did so.

From time to time Clio handed him a bit of crisp buttered crust with a tidbit on it—a bit of rich meat or a corner of French toast crowned with a ruby of jelly, as one would toss a bite to a pampered dog.

Breakfasting New Orleans snorted or snickered, outraged.

"Not bad," Clio commented graciously from time to time, addressing Kaka or the world at large. "The food here is really good— but really good."

Kakaracou sat at table an attendant, aloof from food and being offered none. Certainly Begué's clients would have departed in a body had she eaten one bite. Her lean straight back was erect, disdaining to relax against Begué's comfortable chair. The eyes beneath the heavy hoodlike lids noted everything about the table, about the room; she marked each person who entered at the doorway that led up the stair from the hot noonday glare of Decatur Street. For the most part her hands remained folded quietly in her neat lap, the while her eyes slid this way and that and the darting movement of her head set her earrings to swinging and glinting. Occasionally the purple-black hand, skinny and agile, darted forth like a benevolent spider to place nearer for her mistress's convenience a sugar bowl, a spoon, a dish. She viewed the food with the hard clear gaze of the expert.

"Red wine enough in that sauce, you think? . . . The *pain perdu* could be a shade browner."

The delicate and lovely girl slowly demolished her substantial breakfast with proper appreciation. She might have been a lifelong *habituée* dawdling thus over her Sunday morning meal. The room watched her boldly or covertly. Monsieur Begué hovered paternally. The waiters approved her and her entourage. Here was someone dramatic and to their fancy; someone who, young though she was, knew food. Titled, too. From France. There was about these serving men nothing of the appearance of the gaunt and flat-footed of their tribe. They were fruity old boys with mustaches and side whiskers. In moments of leisure they sat in a corner near Madame Begué's high desk reading *L'Abeille* and engaging in the argumentative talk of their fraternity. Nothing meager about these servitors. They, like Madame and Monsieur Begué, were solid with red wine and gumbo soup and the rich food for which the city was famous. Their customers were clients; each meal was a problem to be weighed, discussed. They advised, gravely. They were quick to see that the lovely stranger knew the importance of good eating.

From time to time Léon reported in a sibilant whisper, "A Comtesse, that little one . . . The little monkey is old, his face is marked with wrinkles when you see him close . . . She orders like a true Creole. Grits, she said, one must always have with breakfast at Begué's."

The talk between mistress and maid was not at all the sort of conversation ordinarily found in this relation. It resembled the confidences exchanged between friends of long standing or even conspirators who have nothing to conceal from one another. And conspirators they were. As guest after guest entered the dim coolness of the restaurant Kaka commented on them succinctly and wittily. The girl munched and nodded. Now and then she laid down her knife and fork to laugh her indolent deep-throated laugh.

The women who entered now, decorously escorted by the men of their family, were, for the most part, dressed in quiet, rich black, like Parisian women; the men wore Sunday attire of Prince Albert coat or sack suits with dark ties. Sallow, reserved, rather forbidding, they conducted themselves like royalty incognito, aware of their own exalted state but pretending unconsciousness of it.

"*Chacalata,*" Kakaracou said, witheringly. It was a local New Orleans term, culled from heaven knows where, to describe the inner circle of New Orleans aristocracy, clannish, self-satisfied, resenting change or innovation.

"The same dresses they wore when we left for France fifteen or more years ago. They're so puffed with their own pride they think they don't have to dress fashionably. They'd come out in their *gabrielles*, those *chacalata* women, if they thought it decent."

Clio giggled at the thought of beholding these stately New Orleans Creole women in the informality of the loose wrapper locally known as a *gabrielle*. She preened herself in the consciousness of her own rich finery. "Dowdy old things, in their snuffy black. I could show them black. I wish I'd worn my black ottoman silk with the Spanish lace flounces."

"Too grand for the street," Kaka observed. "Ladies don't dress up on the street. But then, you're not a lady." She said this, not spitefully or insolently, but as one stating a fair fact to another.

"Not I!" Clio agreed, happily. "I'm going to enjoy myself, and laugh, and wear pretty clothes and do as I like."

"Like your mama."

"No, not like poor dear Mama. She didn't have any fun—at least not since I can remember. Always moping and reading old letters and trailing around in her *gabrielle*, ill and sad."

"She wasn't always like that, my poor *bébé* Rita."

"Look!" Clio interrupted, in French. "There! Coming in. Is it They?"

The head in its brilliant tignon jerked sharply in the direction of the doorway. The spare figure stiffened, then relaxed. "No. No, silly"

"Are you sure? You're sure you'd know them, after all these years?"

"I would know them, those faces of stone, after a hundred years. . . . Stop staring at the door. Drink your good red wine and eat another slice of that delicious liver. It will bring you strength and make your eyes bright and your cheeks pink."

Clio pushed her plate away like a willful child. "I don't want to be pink. Pink women bore me, just to look at them, like dolls."

Indeed the naturally creamy skin was dead white with the French liquid powder she used, so that her eyes seemed darker and more enormous; sadder too, and the wide mouth wider. Almost a clown's mask, except for its beauty. It was a makeup that Aunt Belle Piquery had taught her—Aunt Belle of the round blue eyes and the plump pink cheeks and the pert little nose. "I'm the type men take a fancy to, but you're the type they stay with and die for," the hearty old baggage used to say to Clio. "Like your ma."

"All right, pink or not, eat it anyway," Kaka now persisted.

"I won't. I'm not hungry. I just ordered everything because I wanted to taste everything."

Like an angry monkey Kakaracou chattered her disapproval. "I told you! It's that jambalaya you stuffed yourself with in the French Market."

"Oh, what's it matter! I eat what I like when I like. . . . It's getting late, isn't it? They're not coming. You said yourself They stopped coming after Mama and Papa—after They—when Mama moved into the Rampart Street house. It isn't likely They started coming after Papa died. Anyway They're millions of years old by now."

The eyes of the Negress narrowed, they were knifelike slits in her gray-black face. "They stopped. But They came again, after. Creoles are like that. Customs. Habits. Everything de rigueur."

The girl leaned forward, eagerly. "Do I look enough like her? When They come in will it be a shock to Them to see me sitting here? Do I look like the picture Mama and Papa had taken together? Will They think I am Mama—just for that first moment?"

The woman's eyes regarded her sadly across the table; she shook her turbaned head. "You are like her, yes, perhaps even enough to startle anyone who knew her when she was your age. But she was beautiful. She was the most beautiful woman in New Orleans."

"I'm beautiful too."

"You're well enough. But she! At the balls they used to stand on chairs just to see her come in. Pale pink satin—shell pink—with black lace, sent from Paris, and all her jewels."

"I'll have jewels too. You wait. You'll see."

"But you have hers."

"Second best."

"Her second best were finer than the best of other women."

The girl's eyes were always on the door, though she pretended to be busy with her food. Each time it opened she glanced swiftly to see who it was that stood outlined against the bar of blinding white sunshine that leaped into the carefully shaded room. She smiled now a little secret smile. "Mama was more beautiful perhaps, but I have more chic and more spirit. You've said so yourself, when you weren't cross with me. I'll find a rich man—but colossally rich—and I'll marry him. Not like mama. No Rampart Street for me."

Her eyes always sliding around to the door. Kakaracou saw this. Kakaracou saw everything. "Yes, that will be fine. That's why you are watching the door like a spaniel. Don't think you're fooling me. It isn't that you expect to see Them come in. You are watching to see if he has followed you here, that tramp, that roustabout, that *cagnard* in the French Market. That's why you wanted the carriage to wait outside. He might see it there, and know."

"That's a lie!" Clio snapped, too hotly. "I'd forgotten all about him until you mentioned him, that *picaioun.*" To prove this she busied herself with the dish before her, her eyes on her plate, so that though the door swung open she did not glance up to see who entered.

Cupide behind her chair leaned forward suddenly and stood on tiptoe so that the great head was close to her ear. "There he is! That *Gros-Jean!* Shall I butt him again?"

The girl's face and throat flushed pink—the pink she despised—beneath the sallow white of her skin and the white powder overlaying it.

"It is he!" breathed Clio, drawing herself up very fine and straight and looking tremendously happy.

Kaka knew an emergency. "Come. We will go. Cupide, run, ask Madame Begué the bill. *Vite! Vite!*"

"No!" Clio commanded sharply as the dwarf started off with his waddling bandy-legged gait. "Back, Cupide! I'm not leaving."

The man had not blinked or peered as he entered the room. Those eyes were accustomed to the white-hot sun of the Texas plains. He loomed immense in the doorway, then he smiled, he took off the great white sombrero and gave it a little twirl of satisfaction on one forefinger before he crossed the room with his long, loping stride, the high heels of his boots tap-tapping smartly on the flagstoned floor. He ignored Léon, who was about to approach him, he deftly side-stepped waiters with laden trays, he made straight for the table just next to the one on which his gaze was concentrated. Pulling out a chair he sank into it with a sigh of relief that almost drowned out the protesting creak of the chair as it received his great frame. His long legs sprawled under the table and into the aisle, he flung the sombrero to the floor beside his chair, he smiled broadly and triumphantly even as he summoned Hippolyte Bergué with one beckoning finger and a "Hch, cookee!" Monsieur Begué did not pause; he did not even look in the direction of the man; he walked on with the leisurely pushing strut of the potbellied and vanished into the kitchen.

Kakaracou leaned forward. Her undertone was a hiss. "You see! He's sitting at the next table. Come. We are leaving."

"And I say we're staying. I'm not nearly finished. I'm going to have an *omelette soufflée* and after that some strawberries with thick cream."

Kaka glared, her wrinkled face working. "Yes! Burst your corsets! Stuff yourself! With a figure like a cow you'll get a fine husband, oh, yes! Or maybe you've already picked that Texas *vacher* for a bridegroom. He's used to bulging sides."

"Texas, Texas! How do you know he's from Texas? Besides, what does it matter! I'm not even looking at him. What do I care where he's from!"

Kaka smothered a little cackle of contempt. "Well, look at him then. He's mumbling over the menu. He can't read a word of it; he never saw a French menu before. Beef and beans, that's what he's used to, that *imbécile!* Look. Léon is laughing at him; he doesn't even care to put his hand before his mouth to hide his laugh. Now he points—the *stupide*—with his great thick sausage finger."

"I think he's beautiful," Clio said, deliberately. She put one hand to her throat. "I think he's beautiful."

As Kaka said, the man was pointing with one forefinger; he looked up at the contemptuous waiter and smiled boyishly; there was something engaging, something infinitely appealing about this great creature's perplexed smile.

"What's that, sonny? I'm no Frenchy. In Texas where I came from we print our bill of fare in American."

"I make no doubt," sneered Léon.

The Texan mopped his forehead with a vast red handkerchief. "It sure is steamy in New Or-leens," he said.

You would have said that Clio had not even looked at him. Industriously she had cleared her plate in the good French manner, pursuing the last evasive drop of sauce with a relentless crust. Her gaze was on her empty dish; she had not seemed to flick an eyelid. Yet now she said to Kaka's horror, "If he were mine I would have for him four dozen of the finest white handkerchiefs of handwoven linen and you would embroider the initials in the most delicate scrolls."

"I!" Kaka's remonstrance was pure outrage. "Embroider for that cowboy! He's never seen a white linen handkerchief."

"Linen, too, for his shirts," Clio went on equably. "Fine pleated linen and his initials on that too."

"Initials, initials!" barked the infuriated Kaka. "What initials!"

"What does it matter?" Clio murmured with maddening dreaminess.

The man at the next table had made his reluctant decision. "I don't know what the hell runions are, but I'll take a chance on it. They say anything here is licking good."

Clio tapped smartly three times with her knife against her water glass. At the sound Léon, smirking at the adjoining table, turned sharply toward her. "Léon!" She beckoned him, he sped toward her, he leaned deferentially over her table, forsaking his later client without so much as a word of apology.

"Léon, please tell Monsieur Begué I will have one of his marvelous *omelettes soufflées*."

Léon was all admiration. "It is *prodigieux*, the fine appetite that Madame la Comtesse has! Monsieur Begué will be enchanted, he——"

"P-s-s-s-s-st!" The sibilant sound came so venomously from Kaka that even the chunky Cupidon gave a jerk of alarm, stationed though he was so stolidly behind Clio's chair. "They're here! They're entering. I told you so! See, Madame Begué herself comes down from her desk to greet them. Now will you try to act the lady!"

"Good," said Clio calmly, not even deigning to turn her head. "And Léon, tell Monsieur seated there at the next table—that one with the big hat and the boots—tell him that if he is having difficulty in choosing his breakfast I shall be happy to assist him."

Léon stared, his mouth agape. "What! That one, you mean!"

"Oh, yes, we're old friends. Only this morning we happened to meet him in the French Market. That's why he is breakfasting here. Ask him if he wouldn't, perhaps, prefer to be served here at my table. Then we can chat." Stunned, he turned away. "A moment! Léon! That old couple there—Madame Begué is speaking to them—now Monsieur Begué is showing them to a table. Is that—are they the old Monsieur and Madame Dulaine?"

The man stared, startled, then burst into discreet laughter. "Madame will have her little joke. For a moment you fooled me. Of course Madame knows that old Monsieur and Madame Dulaine are"—he coughed apologetically—"are, in a word, dead."

Léon approached the near-by table with a new deference. Clio turned a dazzling smile upon Kakaracou. The natural prune color of Kaka's skin had turned a sort of dirty gray. Her lips were drawn away from the strong yellow teeth.

"Wait out in the hallway, Kaka. Or go home if you like. Cupide will stay."

"You're crazy. You're as crazy as your mother was. Worse! I've a mind to slap you right here."

"Oh, have you! You're not my nurse any more, you know. You're my maid. You'll do as I say, or I'll send you away to starve. You'll never see me again. Look! He's coming. Now I'll have a man at my table to protect me, like those other women. The handsomest man in the room. The handsomest man I ever——"

He was standing by her chair looking down at her. He flushed, he stammered. In his haste and astonishment he had left his great white sombrero on the floor by his chair. "Did you—that fellow said you said—pardon me, Ma'am, do you want me to sit here—did you mean——"

"Please sit down. Kaka, a menu. Cupide, fetch the gentleman's hat at the other table beside the chair."

"Well, say, thanks. Back where I come from we carry our hats with us on account of not knowing just when we might want to pull out of a place quick." He jerked out a chair and bumped the table so that the water and the red wine slopped over the glasses' rims. His face would have grown redder if that had been possible; he sat down in embarrassed bewilderment yet with the kind of grace that comes of superb muscular coordination.

Kaka had risen; she stood at the side of the table as though rooted to the spot; she clung to the chair back with one skinny hand so that the knuckles showed almost white. But the two were not looking at her, they were looking at each other. He sat forward in his chair, one great arm thrown across the white cloth; she sat back in her chair, cool, silent, her eyes enormous in the white face, the pearl and onyx brooch at her throat rising and falling quickly, giving the lie to her cool silence. So they faced one another, measuring quietly as combatants eye each other with wary curiosity before the beginning of a struggle. Then in a kind of exultant hysteria she began to laugh her deep-throated deliberate laugh. After a moment he joined in, ruefully at first, like a giant boy, then delightedly, like a man who senses victory. The restaurant rang with their laughter. Begué breakfasters looked up from their plates, frowning at first. Monsieur Begué in his towering white cap stood in the doorway that led to the kitchen; Madame Begué of the shrewd black eyes held her busy pen suspended in momentary disapproval; the waiters glanced over their shoulders at the unwonted sound. Then the infection of hysterical laughter made itself felt. As the fresh high sounds of young laughter pealed through the sedate room you saw Monsieur Hippolyte Begué's great white-aproned belly begin to shake with sympathetic mirth; Madame Begué's vast black silk bosom heaved; the waiters giggled behind their napkins; the guests smiled, chuckled, laughed foolishly and helplessly. A plague of laughter fell upon the place. Only Kakaracou showed no taint of senseless mirth. And Cupidon behind his mistress's chair, though he smiled broadly, was too bewildered by the sudden favors accorded the lately despised Texan to relax into the mood of the room.

"Forgive me," Clio gasped, rather wildly. "You looked, sitting there, so—so big!"

"Far's that goes, you look kind of funny yourself, Ma'am, with all that white stuff on your face."

As suddenly as it had begun, the laughter of the two stopped. The Texan wiped his eyes. Clio Dulaine pressed one hand to her heart and leaned back in her chair, spent. The breakfasters, looking a little foolish and resentful, applied themselves again to their food.

He said, companionably, as though they had known each other for years, "I don't know what we're laughing at, but I haven't had so much fun in a coon's age. And down in Texas they told me people were stand-offish in New Or-leens."

"New Orleans," she said, gently correcting him.

"You fixing to learn me the English language? They told me you were French."

"I'm not French. I'm American. And it's teach, not learn."

"All right. Play schoolma'am if you want to. I'll learn anything you say. When I first saw you there in the Market I thought you were a town woman parading around with those two, all dressed up——"

"How dare you!"

"Well, I'm just coming out and telling you like that because I want to explain how come I spoke to you there. I had you wrong. I want to start fair with you because something tells me you and me——"

"Pardon." The waiter placed before him the dish at which he had pointed just as Clio had summoned him to her table. It turned out to be Begué's famous kidney stew with red wine, at which the Texan looked rather doubtfully. Hours had gone into the preparation of the dish before it had reached the stage of being ready to serve at a Begué breakfast. Hippolyte Begué allowed no one but himself to take part in the rite of its cooking.

"*Rognon. Ragoût de rognon.*"

The Texan stirred it doubtfully with his fork. He looked up. "Got any ketchup."

The waiter recoiled. "Ketchup! But this *ragoût* is cooked with Monsieur Begué's own sauce, it is prepared by the hands of Monsieur Begué him——"

"Ketchup!" commanded Clio, crisply. Then, in French, "In Paris now everything is eaten with ketchup. It is the chic thing for dinner in Paris. Ketchup for Monsieur."

Stunned, the man went in search of the condiment. "What's that you're talking—French? I thought you said you were American."

"I am! I am American. But I was brought up in France. I am Comtesse De Chanfret."

"Shucks! You don't say! Well, honey, I don't believe it. But just to prove to you I'm playing square with you I'll tell you my real name though I'd just as soon they didn't know where I am, back in Texas. My name's Maroon. Clint Maroon. Now come on—tell me yours."

"Clint Maroon," she repeated after him, softly. She looked up at the grim-visaged Kaka still stationed behind the chair in which she lately had been seated. "Do you hear that, Kaka? The initials to be embroidered are C. M. You may go now and wait in the hall."

V

He had driven her home behind the high-stepping bays that Sunday afternoon—home to the Rampart Street house. Cool and straight and fragrant she sat beside him in the clarence. Now and then he turned his head to look at her almost shyly. His was not a swift-working mind. His growing bewilderment aroused an inner amusement in her mingled with a kind of tenderness; a mixture of emotions whose consequences she did not yet recognize. She looked at the muscles of his wrists and at his strong bronzed hands as, gloveless, he held the reins. The two had been voluble enough in the restaurant. Now they were silent. Once, as though obeying an overmastering impulse, he shifted the reins to one hand and reached over as though to touch her knee. She drew away. He flushed, boyishly; flicked the bays smartly with the whip.

"I can't figure out about you."

"Is that why you whip your horses?"

In the back seat sat Kakaracou, an unwilling chaperon whose glare of disapproval would have seared their necks if their own emotional warmth had not served as counteraction. Cupidon had walked home—rather, after one wistful look at the fiery horses and the dashing equipage he had whisked off at an incredible pace on his own stumpy legs. Taking short cuts, dodging through alleys, there he stood, purple-faced and puffing what with haste and the heat, waiting at the carriage block when the turnout drew up before the house. He took the horses' heads, one tiny hand stroking their necks and withers with the practiced touch of the horselover.

Clint Maroon handed Clio out. Agilely Kaka stepped down, but she stood waiting like a demon duenna. Maroon stared at the neat secret house, he looked around him at this neighborhood that had about it something flavorous, something faintly sinister, something shoddy, something of past dignity. He looked the girl full in the face.

She hesitated, she glanced at the waiting Kaka; like a young girl still a pupil at the school in France she said, primly, "Won't you come in?"

He said, crudely, "Say, what kind of a game is this, anyway?"

Without a word she turned and walked swiftly toward the house. Cupide dropped the bridle-hold, Kakaracou seemed to flow like a lithe snake into the house, the front door closed with a thud, leaving him staring after them. As if by magic the three had vanished. The house-front was blank as a vault. From the sidewalk there was no hint of the garden at the back with its vines and shrubs, its magnolia tree, its courtyard green with moss, the tiny fountain's tinkle giving the illusion of coolness.

For a week he haunted Rampart Street. At first he came with his horses and carriage and the neighborhood marked him and watched and waited, but the house door did not open to his knocking, and small boys, white and black, gathered to stare and the horses fidgeted. Clint Maroon felt a baleful eye upon him from somewhere within the house—an eye with yellowish whites in a prune colored face. But there was no sound. He took to loitering in the neighborhood, he sauntered into the near-by provision shops and asked questions meant to be discreet. But the shopkeepers were sneeringly polite and completely noncommunicative; they looked at him, at his white sombrero, at his high-heeled boots with the lone star stitching in the top, at his wide-skirted coat and the diamond in his shirt front and at his skin that had been ruddied by sun and whipped by wind and stung by desert sand. They said, "Ah, a visitor from Texas, I see." The inflection was not flattering. He had a room at the St. Charles Hotel, that favorite rendezvous of Louisiana planters and Texas cattle men. Its columned façade, its magnificent shining dome, its famous Sazaracs made from the potent Sazarac brandy, all contributed to its fame and flavor. From here he laboriously composed a letter to her, written in his round, schoolboyish hand and delivered in style by a dapper Negro in hotel uniform. He had spent an entire morning over it.

> DEAR LADY,
>
> You might be a countess like you said but you are a queen to me. I did not go for to hurt your feelings when I said that about how I did not understand about you. I guess back in Texas we are kind of raw. Anyway I sure never met anybody like you before and you had me locoed. I think about you all day and all night and am fit to be tied. You were mighty kind to me there in Begué's eating house and I acted like a fool and impolite as though I never had any bringing up and a disgrace to my Mother. If you will let me talk to you I can explain. I have got to see you or I will bust the house in. Please. You are the most beautiful little lady I ever met.
>
> Ever your friend and servant,
>
> CLINT MAROON.

This moving epistle was wasted effort. Clio never saw it. Delivered into the hands of the ubiquitous Kakaracou, it was thrust into her capacious skirt pocket and brought out that evening under the kitchen lamplight. But reading was not one of Kaka's talents. Discretion told her to throw the letter into the fire. Curiosity as to its contents proved too strong. Over the kitchen supper table with Cupide she drew out the sheet of paper and turned it over in her skinny fingers. She had deciphered the signature, and this she had torn off in the touching belief that without it the letter's source would be a mystery to its reader.

It was characteristic of Kaka's adaptability that, after an absence of more than fifteen years, the old New Orleans Negro patois and accent were creeping back into her speech. Gombo French, Negro English, Cajun, indefinably mixed; the dropped consonants, the softly slurred vowels, the fine disregard for tenses. Naturally imitative and a born mimic, she was likely to fit her speech to the occasion. Weary, she unconsciously slipped back into the patois of her childhood. To impress shopkeepers and people whom she considered riffraff, such as Clint Maroon, she chattered a voluble and colloquial French of the Paris boulevards and the Paris gutters. Her accent when speaking pure English was more British than American, having been copied from Clio's own. Clio's English had been learned primarily from the careful speech of Sister Félice at the convent. And Sister Félice had come by her English in London itself, during her novitiate. Not alone Kaka, but Clio and Cupide were adept in these lingual gymnastics. They were given to talking among themselves in a spicy *ragoût* of French, English and Gombo that was almost unintelligible to an outsider.

Kaka now fished the crumpled letter out of her capacious pocket, smoothed it, and turned upon Cupide an eye meant to be guileless and which would not for a moment have deceived a beholder much less astute than the cynical Cupidon.

"I find letter today in big *armoire* in hall I guess must be there many years hiding heself."

"What's it say?"

Kaka rather reluctantly pushed it across the table to him. St. Charles Hotel. New paper, palpably fresh ink. Cupide, his fork poised, read it aloud in a brisk murmur. Intently the old woman leaned forward to hear. Finished, Cupide said. *"Tu mentis comme un arrachour de dents."* You lie like a dentist. And went on with his supper.

"What does it say, you monkey, you!"

He shrugged. "Wants to see her. He'll break into the house if she doesn't see him. Crazy about her. *A la folie.*"

A flame of fear and hate flared in Kaka's eyes. She pushed back her plate. She remembered the days when strange people had come into Rita Dulaine's house, forcing their way into the room where she lay weeping after Nicolas was dead.

"We must leave here. It is no good for us here in New Orleans. It was good in Paris—*triste* but good."

Cupide wiped his plate clean with a crust of crisp French bread and popped the morsel into his mouth. "Old *prune sèche!* What do you know! It's fine here in America. Don't you bother your addled head about little Clio. She knows her way about. Anyway, I like that big *vacher* from Texas. He knows about horses. Yesterday I heard he won a thousand dollars at the races. At night he gambles down on Royal Street and wins. At Number 18 they say he never loses."

"Number 18, Number 18! What are you talking about!"

"That big marble building on the Rue Royal—the one that used to be the Merchants' Exchange. Everybody knows it's a gambling house now. You ought to see it! Mirrors and velvet, and supper spread out on tables——"

"So that's where you've been at night! Leaving us here two women unprotected alone in the house." A sudden thought struck her. "Has he seen you there? Have you been talking——"

"No, but I might if you don't feed me better. You with your everlasting pineapple and strawberries with kirsch, you're too lazy to prepare a real sweet—*baba au rhum* or a lovely *crème brûlé.*"

"Little One, I make you sweets—*omelette soufflée—crêpe suzette*—baba cake—pie Saint-Honoré—effen you not speak to her about letter."

He strutted superior in his knowledge as a male. His answer fell into Gombo French. "Make no difference about letter, Old One. This going to be something. You see. You better go to voodoo woman get black devil's powder. But if you do I tell. Anyway, I am sick of nothing but women in the house, here and in Paris. A man around suit me fine."

Now Clio was definitely bored with her week of dignified seclusion. It was not for this that she had come to New Orleans—to sit alone in the dusk in a garden swooning sweet with jessamine and roses and magnolia. She dressed herself all in white and, with Kaka and Cupide keeping pace behind her, she walked to the Cathedral of St.

Louis in the cool of the evening, prayer book in hand, eyes cast down, but not so far down that she failed to see him when he entered. For at last he was rewarded for his daily vigil at the corner of Rampart Street. He did not remain in the shadow of the dim cathedral columns but came swiftly to her and knelt beside her, wordlessly, his shoulder touching hers, and suddenly the candlelights swam before her eyes and there came a pounding in her ears. She did not glance up at him. She closed her eyes, she bowed her head, she thought, irreligiously, I must tell him not to use that sweetish hair pomade, it isn't chic. When, finally, she rose, he rose. Together they moved up the aisle and, dreamlike, walked out into the tropical dusk. Kakaracou and Cupide fell in behind them.

"Send them away," he said. It was the first word that had been uttered between them.

She turned and spoke to them in French. "Go home, you two, quickly. There will be two of us for supper. The cold *daube glacé*, soft-shell crabs—Cupide, fetch a block of ice from the *épicier* and get out a bottle of the Grand Montrachet."

They ate by candlelight with the French doors wide open into the garden. They ate the delicate food, they drank the cool dry wine, they talked a great deal at first and laughed and did not look at one another for longer than a flick of the eyelash; but then they talked less and less, their gaze dwelt the one on the other longer and more intently until finally, wordlessly, they rose and moved in a pulsating silence toward the French doors, down the cool stone steps into the velvet dark of the garden, and the white of her gown merged with the dark cloth of his coat and there was only the soft tinkle of the little fountain. In the bedroom the gaunt figure of Kaka was silhouetted against the light as she made her mistress's room ready for the night.

VI

*

Just as she had inherited all that remained of her mother's magnificent Rue de la Paix jewelry, just as her mother's exquisite Paris gowns fitted her as well as her own frocks, so Clio Dulaine had been bequeathed other valuables of courtesanship less tangible but equally important. Now, in the Rampart Street house, she slipped fluidly into the way of life that had been Rita Dulaine's many years before. But with a difference. There was an iron quality in this girl that the other woman never had possessed.

From her lovely languorous mother and from her hearty jovial aunt Clio had early learned the art of being charming to everyone. A trick of the socially insecure, yet there was nothing servile about it. Clio had seen Rita Dulaine's poignant smile and wistful charm turned upon the musty old concierge as he opened the courtyard door of the Paris flat. The same smile and equal charm had been bestowed upon any man numbered among her few Paris acquaintances whom she might encounter on her rare visits to the opera or while driving in the Bois. Her graciousness was partly due, doubtless, to the inherent good nature of a woman who has been beautiful and beloved for years; partly to the fact that gracious charm was a necessary equipment of the born courtesan.

So, then, the manner of the girl Clio Dulaine stemmed from a combination of causes: unconscious imitation of the two women she most loved and admired; observation, training, habit, innate shrewdness. She had, too, something of her buxon aunt's lusty good humor; much of her mother's sultry enchantment.

Without effort, without a conscious thought to motivate it, Clio had turned the same warm, personal smile on the waiter Léon and on Monsieur Hippolyte Begué; on the painters and glaziers who had smartened the Rampart Street house; on Clint Maroon.

The relation between these two, begun as a flirtation, had, in two weeks, taken on a serious depth and complexity. Though so strongly drawn together there was, too, a definite sex antagonism between them. Each had a plan of life selfishly devised, though vague. Each felt the fear of the other's power to change that plan. Each, curiously enough, nourished a deep resentment against the world that had hurt someone dear to them. Hers was a sophisticated viewpoint, for all her youth and inexperience; his a naïve one, for all his masculinity and dare-devil past. Cautiously at first, then in a flood that burst the dam of caution and reticence, the two had confided to each other the details of their lives. Through long lazy afternoons, through hot sultry nights each knew the relief that comes of confidences exchanged, of sympathies expressed, of festering grievances long hidden brought now to light and cleansed by exposure. Adventurers, both, bent on cracking the shell of the world that was to be their oyster.

Though they did not know it, they were like two people who, searching for buried treasure, are caught in a quicksand. Every struggle to extricate themselves only made them sink deeper.

She had never met anyone like this dashing and slightly improbable figure who seemed to have stepped out of the pages of fiction.

"Tell me, the men in Texas, are they all like you?"

"Only the bad ones."

"You're not bad. You're only mad at the world. You are like someone in a story book. When we lived in Paris I read the stories of Bret Harte. Do you know him? He is wonderful."

"No. Who's he?"

"Oh, what a great stupid boy! He is a famous American writer.

His story-book men carry a pistol, too, like you, at the hip. I don't like pistols. They make me nervous. You know why."

By now he knew the story of Rita Dulaine. The Comtesse de Trenaunay de Chanfret had vanished early in their acquaintance. "This is different, honey. You don't have to worry about a gun on me."

"But why! Why do you wear it? It is fantastic, a gun on the hip, like the Wild West."

"The West is wild, and don't you forget it. Anyway, I wouldn't feel I was dressed respectable without it, I'm so used to it. I'd as soon go out without my shirt or my hat."

"Tell me, *chéri*, have you killed men?" He was silent. She persisted. "Tell me. Have you?"

"Oh, two, three, maybe. It was them or me."

"They," she said automatically and absurdly.

"Aim to make a gentleman out of me, don't you, honey?"

"I don't want to change you. You are perfect. But perfect!"

"Ye-e-es, you do. You're like all the rest of 'em. They all try to make their men over."

"Their men! You are not my man. You belong to that little lady who you say is the finest little lady in the world—she who made you the amazing white satin tie embroidered with the blue forget-me-nots. Oh, that tie!" She laughed her slow, indolent laugh.

"What's the matter with it! You're jealous, that's all."

"It is terrible. But terrible! Tell me about her—the finest little lady in the world who made you that work of art. Blue eyes, you said, and golden hair, and so little she only comes up to here. How nize! How nize!" When she mocked him she became increasingly French, but rather in the music-hall manner, very maddening. "Tell me, when are you going to marry, you two?"

She could not be sure whether the finest little woman in the world really existed back there in his Texas past or whether he had devised her as protection. Grown cautious, he would say, "I don't aim to marry anybody. Me, I'm a lone ranger out for big game."

She in turn had no intention of allowing this man to shape her life. She, too, had her armor against infatuation. "I shall marry. I shall marry a husband very, very rich and very respectable."

"Yes, and I'll be best man at the wedding."

"Why not? But no, you would be too handsome. All the guests would wonder why I had not married you. Very, very rich and very respectable men are so rarely handsome. But then one can't have everything."

"Say, what kind of a woman are you, anyway!" he would shout, baffled. Back home in Texas the codes were simpler. There were two kinds of women; good women, bad women. But here was a paradoxical woman, gay, gentle, fiery, prim; brazenly unconventional, absurdly correct; tender, hard, generous, ruthless. Sometimes she seemed an innocent girl; sometimes an accomplished courtesan.

Even after their first week together they were watching one another warily, distrustful of the world and of each other, stepping carefully to avoid a possible trap.

The very morning after their reunion in the church of St. Louis she had sat brushing her hair that hung a curtain of black against the sheer white dotted swiss of her *gabrielle* with its ruffled lace edging of Valenciennes. She wielded the silver-backed brush and sniffed the air delicately and half closed her eyes. "A house isn't really a house," she murmured, "unless it has about it the scent of a good cigar after breakfast."

He stared at her, he strode over to her seated there before the rosewood *duchesse*. With one great hand he grasped her shoulder so that she winced. "Where did you learn that?"

"Mama used to say that, poor darling. Or maybe it was Aunt Belle."

"Did, heh? Look here, all that stuff you were telling me last night in the garden—it's the truth, isn't it? I don't mean that first stuff about being a countess, and all that. Sometimes you talk like a schoolgirl—and sometimes I think you've been——"

She looked up at him from the low bench before the dressing

table. He put his hand on her long throat, tipping her head still farther back so that his eyes plumbed hers.

"Ask Kaka. Ask Cupide."

"Those two! They'd lie for you no matter what."

"Well," she said gently, with his hand still on her throat so that he could feel the muscles moving under his palm as she spoke. "Well, if you think that I am lying and Kaka is lying and Cupide is lying why don't you finish your business here in New Orleans and go back to the finest little lady in Texas?" His great fist doubled against her jaw, he pushed her delicate head back gently, ruefully, in tender imitation of a blow.

He was a bewildered, love-smitten Texan who had met a woman the like of whom he never had seen or dreamed of.

For a week—two—three—they spent lazy hours talking, listening. The girl always until now had taken third place. Her mother had come first, then Aunt Belle; Kakaracou had waited on them, cooked New Orleans dishes for them, sewed for them. Cupide had run about for them tirelessly; he had been coachman, footman, butler, boots, page. Clio had worn second-best, had fetched and carried for the two women, had played bezique with Belle Piquery, bathed her mother's forehead with eau-de-cologne when she was suffering from headache, pressed her fresh young cheek against Rita's tear-furrowed one when she was sad, fed the two with her youth and high spirits. Now she found it wonderful to be the center of interest. Now she and Clint Maroon, suspicious of the world and resentful of it, could pour out to each other their hopes, their schemes, their longings, their emotions. It was almost as fascinating to listen as to speak. Not quite, but almost. He had told her his story disjointedly, in bits and pieces, for he was not an articulate man, and he had been taught to think that emotion was weakness.

"I haven't got any money, honey. I mean, money. I make my living gambling. I wouldn't fool you. I raise horses some—or did, back home in Texas. Sometimes I race 'em. That's how come I left. I shot the man we caught trying to lame my three-year-old, Alamo.

He's almost pure Spanish, that chestnut. He steps so he hardly touches the ground; it's like the way you see a dancer that never seems to have a foot on the floor he's so light. It was a plain case; no jury in the Southwest could convict me, but I reckoned I'd better leave for now, anyway. And besides, I was ready to go. I always told Pa I'd come up North and get the land and money back they'd stole off him. Why, say, they came in and they took his land away from him as slick as if he'd been a hick playing a shell game at a country circus. Everybody in Texas knew Dacey Maroon, the town we lived in was named after him, Daceyville. Grampaw Maroon fought the siege of the Alamo; I was brought up on the story; it was sacred history like the stories in the Bible, only more real. He had fought over the very land he owned. Pa used to say that Daceyville and San Antonio were watered with the blood of their defenders. In Texas schools they teach the young ones about Bunker Hill and Valley Forge and battles of the Civil War like it was history, but mighty few up North know the story of the Alamo and San Jacinto. They're as much a part of American history as the Revolution or Gettysburg, and more. Pa had come in and settled his land and married Ma and brought her to Texas from Virginia. Brought up gentle as she was you'd think she never could have stood what she had to. She was little——"

"Like the one who embroidered the forget-me-not tie?"

"Why—maybe."

"Men often marry their mothers," Clio observed, dreamily. Then, hastily, she added, "I heard Aunt Belle say that, too."

But his was too literal a mind for Belle Piquery's unconsciously sound psychology.

"There'll never be anybody like her. Everything around the house just so, and yet she'd never chase the menfolks out of the house to smoke, the way some women would. I reckon that was the way she was brought up in Virginia. She could gentle the orneriest horse in Texas, and her two little hands weren't any bigger than magnolia petals. Time she was married they drove into Texas from Virginia, through hell and high water. Pa worked that land there in Texas, staked it and claimed it and laid out the town of Daceyville, but Grampaw, he came in with Austin when Texas belonged to Mexico. That was real pioneering. They cleared, and they built cabins and planted grain. Funny thing about Texas. Do you know about Texas, honey?"

"No. I have read that it is big. Enormous. And wild."

"It's big, all right. Bigger than France, bigger than Germany, bigger than most of Europe rolled into one. Lots has been written about Texas, but it's unknown territory. Maybe it's because it's so allfired big. Grampaw Dacey Maroon, and Sam Houston and Martin and Jones and Pettus—the Old Three Hundred—and Bowie and Travis and Davy Crockett, why, they were my heroes the way other youngsters think of Washington or Napoleon or Daniel Boone. Bowie, sick and dying of pneumonia there in the Alamo, and hacking away at the Mexicans from his cot because he was too weak to stand up or even sit up, and twenty dead Mexicans heaped up on the floor around him when finally they got him—that's what I mean when I say Texas. And then along through the West came a fellow named Huntington that used to be a watch peddler, and Mark Hopkins, and a storekeeper named Leland Stanford and a peddler named Charley Crocker. Smart as all get-out. Well, say, they pulled deals in Washington that no cattle or horse thief would have stooped to. They began to survey in Daceyville and they sent a low-down sneaking polecat to Pa and said, 'You'll give us your land and right of way through here and so many thousand dollars that you'll raise among the folks here in Daceyville and we'll run our railroad line through here and make a real town of it. If you don't we'll go ten miles the other side and you might as well be living in a graveyard.'

" 'I'm damned if I will,' " Pa said, and he got his gun and he chased them off the place. They turned Daceyville into Poverty Flat; they built the depot ten miles away and we found we were living in a deserted village, everything closed up; you had to drive ten miles to get a sack of salt. Daceyville was nothing but a wide place in the road. Everybody moved out except us. Pa said we'd stay, and we did. The railroad they built yonder wasn't even a decent road, but they'd been granted all that land by a rotten Congress that they'd bought up—land on both sides of the tracks for miles and miles, east and west. That's what they were after, you see. They got all that land along the right of way—hundreds of thousands of acres—and it never cost them a cent of their own money. A handful of men owned the West. They were like kings. Pa said it wasn't like America, it wasn't taking a piece of land from the government and settling it and making it fit for civilized folks to live on. It was taking the land by force and by tricks—land that others had worked on and settled. Ma said it was like the days of the feudal lords in Europe, only this was supposed to be free America. It was free for them, all right. All the silver and iron and copper in the land they'd stolen, and the forests that stood on it and the rivers than ran through."

"But couldn't your father fight them? Couldn't he go to Washington and couldn't he see those Congressmen? If it was his own land!"

"He tried. That's all he did for years till he was old and broke. I saw my mother and my father die in poverty on the land they'd cleared and built up. Pa couldn't even take her back to Virginia to be buried with her kin the way she'd always asked to be. Texas was Grampaw Maroon's lifeblood, and Pa's—and mine, for a while. Not now. Reckon it's turned to gall, my blood."

"It is bad to be bitter, Clint."

"Cleent," he grinned, mocking her. "Can't you talk American! Short, like this—Clint." He clipped it smartly so that the sound fell on the ear like the clink of a coin. "Clint."

"Clint," in brisk imitation.

"That's it, *muchachita!*"

"What? What is that word?"

"Oh, that. I learned that off the Mexicans down home. Spanish, I reckon. *Muchachita*. Means—uh—pretty little girl, kind of. Sweetheart."

"Very nice—that *muchachita*. But rather long for a dear name. And to be called *muchachita* one must be little."

He passed his hand slowly over his eyes as though to wipe away an inner vision. "That's so. It doesn't suit you, somehow. It just slipped out. It belongs to Texas."

"But I like you to be Texas. It is right for you. You must never be different. I want to know more about Texas and these men. Tell me more."

"Nothing more to tell, honey. They're the men I hate—them and their kind. Ever since I grew up I made up my mind they'd never get me like they'd got Pa. I was going to live off the rich and the suckers—and I have. Let 'em look out for themselves. I live by gambling and racing once in a while and turning a trick when I can—decent most of the time. Not always. When I can get it honestly, I do it. When I can't, I get it the best way I can. I've lived a rough life. The way I talk, I know better. But I want to talk the way the cowhands talk, and the folks back in Texas. I've come a far piece and I aim to go further, but Texas is where I belong. I'm going to make my pile off of them. I hate 'em all. I'd as soon shoot them as I would a gray mule-deer or a cottonmouth out on the Black Prairie. I might as well tell you I've killed men, but never for money. I've known a lot of women; I've never married one of them and don't aim to. I could be crazy about you but I ain't going to be."

She looked at him as though seeing him clearly for the first time. "In a way, chéri, we're two of a kind. You heard your mother and father talking of the wrong that had been done to them and it cut deeply into you. I heard my mother and Aunt Belle talking the same way when I was very young and they thought I didn't hear or didn't understand. I wonder why grown-up people think that children are idiots. I made up my mind early that some day I would pay them back, those people. I'm going to be rich and I'll make them pay for what they did to Mama and Aunt Belle. Mama never hurt any-body——"

"Well, excuse me, honey, but even back in Texas if shooting a man and killing him ain't hurting him none, why——"

"She didn't kill him, I tell you. She——"

"I know, I know. Anyway, she had the gun, no matter which way she was pointing it, and he grabbed it and the bullet went into him and he died. And they got an awful ugly name for that in the courts of law."

"If they thought she had killed him then why did they send her money all those years in France, to the day of her death?"

"Not aiming to hurt your feelings, honey, but that's called hush money where I come from."

"Then New Orleans is going to learn that a Dulaine has returned from France. I'm going to see New Orleans and New Orleans is going to see me."

"They'll come down on you."

"They'll wish they hadn't."

"I've seen a lot of women but I never saw any woman like you, Clio."

"There isn't anyone like me," she replied quite simply. Then, "They'll come to me. You'll see."

"Better not rile 'em. They'll find a way to make it hot for you. Anyway, you don't want to stay down here steaming like a clam. We can clear out, go up to Saratoga for the races. That's where I'm heading for. I wouldn't be here this long if it wasn't for you. You got me roped and tied, seems like."

"Saratoga? Is that a nice place?"

"July and August there's nothing like it in the whole country. Races every day, gambling, millionaires and pickpockets and sporting people and respectable family folks and politicians and famous theater actors and actresses, you'll find them all at Saratoga."

"I'd like that. But I haven't enough money, unless I sell something."

"Shucks, you'll be with me. I can make enough for two."

She shook her head. "No, I am going to be free. You want to be free, too. Perhaps we can have a plan together though. Tell me, is it cool there in Saratoga—cool and fresh and gay?"

"Well, not to say real cool. I've never been there before, but I've heard it's up in the hills beyond Albany, and there's pine woods all around, real spicy. And lakes. July, I was fixing to go up North. Come on."

She sat a moment very still, her eyes fixed, unblinking, deep in thought. When finally she spoke it was in a curious monotone, as though she were thinking aloud. "Two more months here. That will be enough for me. I have a plan. There are things I must find out, first. These past few weeks—lovely—but no more drifting, drifting." She sighed, straightened, looked at him with a keen directness. "Clint, will you stay here in New Orleans for a month or perhaps a little more?"

He laughed rather shortly. "Wasn't for you I'd been on my way before now. It's too soft and pretty down here for me, and wet-hot. A week or two here and I was heading for St. Louis or maybe Kansas City and up north to Chicago. Clark Street, Chicago."

"Go then."

He looked down at his own big clasped hands, he glanced at the letter C so beautifully embroidered on the lower sleeve of his fine cambric shirt as he sat, coatless. In his hip pocket was a fine linen handkerchief hemstitched and marked in a design even more exquisite by the same hand—that of Kakaracou, expert though unwilling.

"You got me roped, tied—and branded. It's all over me, burned into my hide. C. Stands for Clio."

"It is for Clint, the letter C. You know that!"

"I'd have a tough time making 'em see that down in the cattle country back home in Texas. Me, Clint Maroon, embroidered and hemstitched. God! I'll be wearing ruffles on my pants, next thing."

"Is it kind to talk like that?"

"No, honey. Only I was just thinking how you can start something just fooling around and not meaning anything but a little fun, like that day I up and spoke to you at the Market."

Another woman would have said the obvious thing. But Clio Dulaine did not say, "Are you sorry?" She sat very still, waiting.

He stood up. "I'm staying," he said, and came over to her and put a hand on her head and then rocked it a little so that it lolled on her slender neck; a gesture of helpless resentment on his part. Then he strolled toward the garden doorway, where the hot sun lay like a metal sheet. She watched him go, high-heeled boots; tight pants, slim hips, vast shoulders, the head a little too small, perhaps, for the width and height of the structure of bone and muscle; the ears a little outstanding giving him a boyish look. She rose swiftly and came up behind him and put her two arms around him so that her hands just met across his chest. She pressed her cheek against the hard muscles of his shoulder blade. "I am so happy."

"Say that again."

"I am so happy, Clint."

"Say it again."

She gave him a little push toward the garden doorway. He had told her he loved to listen to her voice, sometimes he caught himself listening to it without actually hearing what she said. Hers was an alive voice, it had a vital note that buoyed you like fresh air or fresh water, it had a life-giving quality as though it came from the deep well of her inner being, as indeed it did. He had once said to her, "Back home in Texas the womenfolks are mighty fine, they don't come any finer, but they've got kind of screechy voices; I don't know, maybe it's the dust or the alky water or maybe having to yell at the ornery menfolks to make 'em listen. Your voice, it puts me in mind of the Texas sky at night, kind of soft and purple."

Clint Maroon stood a moment on the steps facing the courtyard and looked about him and listened and let the sun beat down upon his bare head and on his shoulders covered by the unaccustomed fineness of the cambric shirt. From the house, from the kitchen ell, from the *garçonnière* with the stable beneath came the homely soothing sounds and smells of life lived comfortably, easily, safely. In the kitchen Kaka was preparing the early midday meal that followed the morning black coffee. Clio, vigorous, healthy, was an early riser, a habit formed, doubtless, in her schooldays in France. She had, too, the habit of the light continental breakfast and the hearty lunch. Clint

Maroon sniffed the air. The scent of baking breads delicately rolled, richly shortened; coffee; butter sputtering. He thought of the chuck wagon. Beans. Pork. Leaden biscuits. Come and get it! Under Clio's tutelage he had learned about food in these past three weeks. He had learned to drink wine. Whisky, Clio said, was not a drink, it was a medicine. Wine, too, was something you cooked with, oddly enough. As for frying—that, it seemed, was for savages. Back in Texas everything went into the frying pan. You even fried bread. Clio was shocked or amused. Kaka was contemptuous. Things à la. Things au. He had learned about these, too.

From the stable came a swish and a clatter and the sound of Cupide's clear choirboy tenor. Cupide was in high spirits these past weeks. The little man worshiped the Texan. He scampered round him as a terrier frisks about a mastiff, he fetched and carried for him, he tried to imitate his gait, his drawling speech, his colloquialisms. Sprinkled through his own *pot-au-feu* of French, English, Gombo, this added a startling spice to his already piquant speech. *"Bon jour!"* he would say in morning greeting. "Howdy! *Certainement!* I sure aim to. It is a pleasure to see you as you drive the bays, Monsieur Maroon. Uh—you sure do handle a horse pretty. Yessiree!"

Triumph irradiated the froglike face; the great square teeth gleamed in a grin. "I speak like a true *vacher*, yes?" Maroon delighted in teaching him bits of cowboy idiom. The peak of Cupide's new knowledge was reached when one evening, standing in the drawing-room doorway to announce dinner, he had shouted, gleefully, "Come and get it or I'll throw it away!" Ever since the death of Nicolas Dulaine the little man had been ruled by women in a manless household—Rita Dulaine, Belle Piquery, Clio, Kaka. Now he and Clint Maroon were two males together; it was fine; he smoked Clint's cigars, he tended his horses; together they went to the horse sales, to the races. He loved to polish the Texan's high-heeled boots, to brush his clothes; he neglected the work in the house where, in his little green baize apron, he used to rub and polish floors, furniture, crystal.

Now, as he sluiced down the horses in the stable, he sang and whistled softly a song he had picked up with a strange rhythm. Queer music with a curious off-beat that you caught just before it dropped. He had heard it played by a tatterdemalion crowd of Negro boys who wandered the streets, minstrels who played and danced and sang and turned handsprings for pennies. The Razzy Dazzy Spasm Band they called themselves. Their instruments were a fiddle made of an old cigar box, a kettle, a cowbell, a gourd filled with pebbles, a bull fiddle whose body was half an old barrel; horns, whistles, a harmonica. Out of these *dégagé* instruments issued a weird music that set your body twitching and your feet shuffling and your head wagging. A quarter of a century later this broken rhythm was to be known as ragtime, still later as jazz. Cupidon, whose ear was true and quick, had caught the broken rhythm perfectly. He had learned, too, not to strike the high note fairly but to lead up to it—"crying" up to it they called it later. His whistle sounded jubilantly above the swish and thump as he worked.

The man standing on the steps in the sun's hot glare was thinking, Clint, you better be drifting. Say *adios*. You're fixing to get into a sight of trouble. You're locoed. Suddenly, from within the house, Clio began to sing. A natural mimic, she was imitating the song of the blackberry woman who passed the house on her rounds, having walked miles from the woods and bayous, her skirts tucked high above her dusty legs, her soft, melancholy voice calling her wares. Now Clio imitated her perfectly and with complete unconsciousness of what she was doing. Artless and lovely the song rose above the fountain's faint tinkle, above Cupide's whistle, above the clatter of pans in the kitchen.

> *Black-ber-ries—fresh an' fine,*
> *Got black-berries, lady, fresh f'om de vine,*
> *Got black-berries, lady, three glass fo' dime,*
> *I got black-berries, I got black-berries, black-BER-ees!*

The man looked back over his shoulder into the cool dim room he had just left. He looked about him. In the sight and the sounds of the mossy courtyard there was something blood-stirring, exhilarating. The pulse in his powerful throat throbbed. He knew he could not go.

He went down the steps, quick and light. The bedroom, the stable, the kitchen. The kitchen. Discord there, he knew. Kakaracou was a powerful ally or an implacable foe. She knew no middle course.

He had spoken to Clio about her. "That mammy of yours, she hates me like poison. Every time I look at her she turns away from me like a horse. I'm just naturally peaceable, but I'm fixing to have a little talk with Kaka."

"It isn't you. It's men. You see, she lived with Mama and Aunt Belle all those years. Men, to her, mean trouble and tears."

Now he strolled across the courtyard to the kitchen doorway and stood there a moment while the delicious aroma of Kakaracou's cookery was wafted to him from stove and table. Kaka did not glance up as his broad shoulders shadowed the room. At the French Market she had got hold of some tiny trout, cool and glittering in their bed of green leaves, and these she was broiling delicately. Her workday tignon of plain brilliant blue was wound around her head; she was concentrating on her work or perhaps away from him. Her wattled neck stretched forward, her lower lip protruded, she looked like a particularly haughty cobra.

"You ain't got one kind thought for me, have you now, Mammy?"

Her swift upward glance at him, jagged and ominous, was like a lightning stroke. He went on, evenly,

"Funny thing. When I meet up with somebody I don't like, or they don't like me, why, either I get out or they do, depending on which is doing the hating. I'm staying."

She eyed him balefully; she began to speak in French, knowing that he comprehended no word of it; taking great satisfaction in spitting out the venomous phrases. "Lout! Common cowboy! Scum of the gutters! Spawn of the devil! I hate you! Je t'déteste!"

"My, my!" drawled Maroon. "I don't parley Frongsay myself, but I sure do admire to hear other people go it. I kind of caught the drift of what you were saying, though, on account of that last word;

it's the same in American as it is in French. So I caught on you weren't exactly paying me compliments, Mammy."

Suddenly, swiftly, like a panther, he stood beside her; he caught her meager body up in his two hands. Her own hands he pinned behind her neck, one of his powerful hands held them there, the other grasped her skinny legs at the ankles and thus he held her as if she had been a sack of feathers. A little series of tooting screams issued from her throat like the whistle of a calliope coming down the river on a showboat. But they could not be heard outside, what with Clio's singing, Cupide's whistling and swishing and the cries of the hucksters in the street. Kaka's eyes protruded with hate and fear. Her face had turned a dirty gray.

Clint Maroon looked down at her. Suddenly his eyes were not blue at all, but steel color. When he spoke he was smiling a little and his voice was gentle and drawling, as always.

"Holding you the way I am, Mammy, I could give you a little twist, two ways, would crack your backbone like you split those fish. You'd never talk or walk again and nobody'd know I'd done it."

Like a snake she twisted her head and tried to sink her teeth into his arms. "Uh-uh. Shucks, I won't hurt you. I just thought you ought to know. We're going to be friends, you and me." The glare she now cast up at him made this statement seem doubtful. "Oh, yes, we are. Miss Clio, she never had any fun—not to say, fun. Two sick old women a-whining and a-bellyaching all the time. Now you and me and maybe Cupide there, all together, maybe we can fix it so's she'll be rich and happy. She wants fun and love and somebody to look after her. I don't aim to do her any harm. I want to help her."

Suddenly he set her on her feet and gave her a gentle spank on her bony posterior cushioned with layers of stiffly starched petticoats. She swayed and put out one hand, gropingly, as though about to fall. Then he curved his arm about her meager shoulders and pressed her to his side a moment and hugged her like a boy. "I love you because you love her," he said.

Kakaracou looked up at him. "You mean she will be rich? And everything *comme il faut*. Respectable."

"Sure respectable. But we got to play careful."

She looked up at him with the eyes of an old seeress, bright and wicked and wise and compassionate. She ignored his threatened brutality, his mad display of strength as though they never had been used against her.

"How you like pie Saint Honoré for dinner tonight, effen you and Miss Clio going to be home for one time?"

He replied in the wooing dovelike tones he reserved for all females of whatever age, color or class.

"What's in it, Mammy? Is it something lickin' good?"

"Uh, puff paste, first thing, and filling of striped vanilla and chocolate cream with liddy dabs of puff paste on top."

"Yes ma'am!"

She rolled a bawdy old eye at him. "It is good to have a man in the house to cook for. To cook only for women all these years, it make *un feu triste*."

"Whatever that is, Mammy."

"*Un feu triste*—oh, it mean a dull fire. To cook for women, *cela m'ennuia à la mort*. Though she eat well, my little Clio." She clutched his arm with one clawlike hand. "Only one thing I ask you. Do not call me that."

"What?"

"This—mammy." She drew herself up very tall. "It is a thing I hate. Out of the slave days."

"Why, sure. Name your own name. She calls you——"

"Me, I am Angélique Pluton. If you like you call me Kaka."

He eyed her with a measuring look that was a blend of amusement and resentment. "They sure ruined you in Paris, nigger."

Curiously enough, she laughed at this, her high cackling laugh. "Sure nuff, Mr. Clint. But don't you pay me no never mind. Half time I'm play-acting jess like Miss Clio."

VII

⬦

"*Faire du scandale*," said Clio, as though thinking aloud.

"How's that?"

"I shall make a scandal. Not a great scandal. Just a little one, enough to cause them some worry."

"Now just what are you figuring on doing? You fixing up some sorry mischief in that little head of yours?"

The jalousies were three-quarters drawn, they were sitting in the cool dimness of the dining room facing the garden. It was too hot now that May was well on its way to sit at midday in the courtyard. Not even a vagrant breeze stirred the listless leaves, the air was heavy with moist heat. They had finished their delicate breakfast-lunch of trout and asparagus and pale golden pineapple dashed with kirsch. Clio's face had a luminous pear-like quality in the gray-green shadow of the sheltered room. She wore one of her lace-frilled white *gabrielles;* her eyes, her hair seemed blacker, more vital in contrast.

"You put me in mind of a spring I used to come on out on the Great Plains near the Brazos. You'd come on it, unexpected, and there it was, cool-looking and fresh, you'd kneel to touch it and you'd find it was a hot spring, so hot it like to burn your fingers."

She laughed her slow indolent laugh that was so at variance with her real character. "Some day we will go to Texas, Cleent. Before I am settled for life with my rich and respectable husband."

"Trying to tease me?"

"No. Haven't I told you from the beginning?"

"Honey, sometimes you talk Frenchified and now and again you talk just as American as I do. Are you putting on, or what?"

She shrugged her shoulders, her smile was mischievous. "Great-Grand'mère Bonnevie was an actress, you know. And if I am the Comtesse de Trenaunay de Chanfret, why then——"

"Shucks! I keep forgetting you're nothing but a little girl dressed up in her ma's long skirts."

She sat up briskly. "I am not! I am very grown up. I have planned everything. I am an adventuress like my grandmother and my mother, only I shall be more shrewd. I am going to have a fine time and I am going to fool the world."

"You don't say!" he drawled as one would talk to an amusing child.

"*Ecoute!* There is nothing for us here in New Orleans, for you or for me. To stay, I mean. But I have a plan. Will you listen very carefully?"

"I sure would admire for to hear it. You look downright wicked."

"Not wicked, Clint. Worldly. They were worldly women—my dear Mama, and Aunt Belle. And Kaka is a witch. And Cupide is a dear little monster. And I have been with these all my life. And so——"

"I love you the way you are. I wouldn't change a hair of your head."

"Listen, then. I have sent Cupide out through the town, and Kaka, too, and they have listened and learned. They can find out anything, those two. All the gossip, all the scandal. Well, there is a daughter. Charlotte Thérèse."

"Daughter?" he repeated, bewildered. "Now, wait a minute. Who? What daughter?"

She explained with the virtuous patience of the unreasonable. "The daughter of my father, Nicolas Dulaine, and his wife. Charlotte Thérèse she is called. My half-sister she is. Isn't she?"

"We-e-ell——"

"But of course. Now then. She is fifteen, she is Creole—*chacalátu*—very stiff they are and clannish and everything *de rigueur*. She is to be introduced into society next winter, at sixteen. All very formal and proper, you see. But not so proper if there pops up an old scandal in the family."

He had been lolling in his chair, interested but relaxed. Now he sat up, tense. "Hold on! You're not fixing to try blackmail!"

"Clint! How can you think of such a thing!"

"There's a look in your eyes, I've seen the same look on a wild Spanish mare just before she rares up on her hind legs and throws you."

"How I should like to see that! The Wild West! Well, perhaps some day. But now we have work to do."

"What kind of work? What's going on in that head of yours? Sometimes I'm plumb scairt of you, especially when you look the way you do now, smooth as a pan of cream, but poison underneath if you was to skim it off."

"But it is nothing wicked! I am only arranging a gay little time for you and for me. Now will you listen—but carefully."

"Sure, honey. I like to hear your voice, it just goes over me like oil on a blister. I'm a-listening."

She held herself very quiet; her eyes were not looking straight ahead but were turned a bit toward their corners in the way of a plotter whose scheme is being made orderly.

"When I came back to New Orleans—before I met you, *chéri*—I was much much younger than I am now. Don't laugh! It is so. Only a few weeks ago, but it is so. I didn't know what I was going to do. Like a child I came back to my childhood home. I cleaned this house, repaired it, made it as you see, quite lovely again. I was going to live here and be happy like someone in a storybook. How childish! How silly!"

"What's silly about it?"

"Because I do not want to stay in this house. I do not even want the house to exist after I have finished with it. But now it is the house in which Nicolas Dulaine was k——died. I am now going to bring that sad accident to life again."

"Hi, wait a minute!" He sat up with a jerk.

"No. You wait. It is very simple. I shall make New Orleans notice me. I shall go everywhere—to the restaurants, to the races, to the theater if it is not too late now, to the French Market; I shall ride in the Park, I shall wear my most extravagant frocks—and you will go everywhere with me in your great white hat, and your diamond shirt stud and your beautiful boots——"

"But what——"

"No. Wait. All these weeks I have been living quietly, quietly here in this house—I here, you at the St. Charles Hotel, all very proper and prim and decorous."

A glint in his eye, an edge to his drawling voice. "Well, hold on, now. I wouldn't say it was all so proper, exactly."

"Proper on the surface. And in my eyes because I am so fond of you, Clint. But now we must be different."

"How d'you mean, different? What you fixing to do?"

"Only what I have said. We will go everywhere, and everywhere we must attract attention. Everything orderly, but bold—dashing— much *éclat*—everything conspicuous. People will say, 'Who is that beautiful creature who goes always everywhere with the handsome Texan? Look at her clothes! They must come from Paris. Look at her jewels! See how she rides, so superbly. Who is she?' Then another will answer, 'Oh, don't you know? . . . She is the daughter of Nicolas Dulaine who died. You remember? There was a great scandal——' "

"Why, say, Clio, you wouldn't be as coldblooded as that, now, would you? What do you want to go and do that for? What's the idea?"

"Because it will revive the old scandal. That would be very inconvenient for a family whose daughter will be of marriageable age next season—a family that is very conventional—in a word—*chacalata*. And the daughter—this Charlotte Thérèse—she is, I hear, quite plain.

And thin. *Maigre comme un clou.*" Clio smiled a dreamily sweet smile. "She was not made with love."

"They'll run you out of town."

"I'll go—for a price."

He stared at her while the meaning of this fully resolved itself in his mind. "You mean to say you came here to New Orleans knowing you could make these people pay——"

"No, Clint! I came because—well, where else could I go? All my life I had heard of nothing but New Orleans, New Orleans. It was home to them. That was because they were exiles. It isn't home to me. It is nothing to me but a dim blurred copy of the city Mama and Aunt Belle loved."

"That's a fine speech, honey. But I've got so I'm not more than one jump behind that steel-trap mind of yours. Sometimes I'm even ahead of it. Come on, come on, Clio. I'm not just a big dumb cowboy from Texas. What's in that head of yours, for all you're looking so droopy about the dear old days in New Orleans—you little hell-cat, you!'"

She looked at him with utter directness. She was no longer a woman and he a man; it was the cold, clear, purposeful look of the indomitable.

"One must be practical. Will you help me?"

"Likely they'll have us both corraled. I'll do it—just for the hell of it, and if it's going to make you happier feeling. But don't say I didn't warn you."

"The idea was mine. The risk is mine, really. We can share the expenses—restaurants, races, theaters—it will not be cheap. Perhaps you should have more than one-third——"

He stood up then, his eyes were steel slots in the blank face, he pushed her roughly away from him so that she staggered backward and would have tripped over the flounced train of her *gabrielle* if she had not grasped a table for support.

"Why, you no-'count French rat, you! You offering to pay me— like a fast man, like I was a pander."

"Clint! You a *paillard!* No! I did not mean—I only meant—we are partners, you and I——"

His slow venomous drawl cut under her passionate denial. "Yes, you're right. The idea is yours, the risk is yours, the whole rotten outfit is yours, your murdering mother and those two freaks out there——"

"Clint! Don't! Don't talk like this to me. I only meant—I was only trying to be fair—businesslike and practical—not like Mama and Aunt Belle! Don't you see?" She went to him, she clung to him, so that the thin white robe, the flowing sleeves, the perfumed lace ruffles hung from his shoulders, covered his face, swirled about his legs.

"Get away from me!"

"No! No! I will give it up. I only thought then we would be free. It was just a little plan—not bad, not wicked. Then we can go together to Saratoga, where it is gay and fresh with pine woods and the little lakes."

He was listening now, he was holding her against him instead of pushing her away, his anger was less than half-hearted. "I don't want any part of it."

"But when you said you would help me I thought we would be partners."

"Not in this. Maybe up North, if we hit on a scheme. But this here—this is different. This goes way back to—to something else. It ain't a clean grudge. Maybe they owe you something—you and your ma. I'll tote you around, like you said. You know I'm crazy about you. But I ain't that crazy. Any money you get from throwing dirt at them, why, it's yours to keep. I'll have no part of it."

"Clint, you are marvelous, *je t'adore!*"

"Listen, honey," he said, plaintively. "You take things too hard. Why'n't you just gentle down and quit snorting and rarin' and take it in your stride?"

"Now it is you who are trying to make me different."

"No, not different. Only let's be more ourselves if we're going to run together. All this play acting. You being so French and me playing Texas cowboy."

"But I am! I mean, I lived so long in France. And you—well, you are from Texas, you were a cowboy—at least you said——"

"I sure am. But we both been working too hard at it. Let's just take the world the way you would a ripe coconut down in the French Market. Crack the shell, drink the milk, eat what you want of the white meat and throw the rest away."

New Orleans had a small-town quality in spite of its cosmopolitanism. No couple so handsome, so vital and so flamboyant could long escape notice in any city. Her beauty, her Paris gowns, his white Texas sombrero, his diamond stud, the high-stepping bays and the glittering carriage—any of these would have served to attract attention. But added to these were the fantastic figures of Cupide and Kakaracou. The spectacular couple were seen everywhere, sometimes unattended, sometimes followed by the arrogant, richly dressed black woman and the dwarf in his uniform of maroon and gold.

It was late May, hot and humid, but the city had not yet taken on the indolent pace of summer. Summer or winter, New Orleans moved at a leisurely gait. It still closed its places of business at noon for a two-hour siesta, one of many old Spanish customs still obtaining here in this Spanish-French city. New Orleans deserted commerce for the races; it flocked to any one of a score of excellent restaurants there to lunch or dine lavishly; it gambled prodigally in Royal Street or in Southport or out at Jefferson Parish. New Orleans adored the theater, it was stagestruck en masse. As for the opera, that was almost a religion. Summer was close at hand. Now New Orleans, between the excesses of the Mardi Gras recently passed and the simmering inertia of the summer approaching, was having a final mid-season fling.

Into this revelry Clio Dulaine and Clint Maroon pranced gaily. The long, lazy mornings in the cool shaded house, the tropical dreamlike evenings in the scented garden were abandoned. The bays and the clarence were seen daily on Canal Street or in the Park. Purposely

Clio overdressed—lace parasols, silks, plumes, jewels. In France she had learned to ride, and frequently in Paris she had ridden in the Bois while Rita Dulaine and Belle Piquery had followed demurely in the carriage. Now she got out the dark blue riding habit with the very tight bodice, the long looped skirt, the high-heeled boots, the little hat with the flowing veil. Clint rode à la Texas; sombrero, boots, handkerchief knotted at the throat, tight pants, the high-horned Western saddle silver-trimmed. They tore along the bridle paths, her veil streaming behind her, he holding his reins with one hand while the other waved in the air, cowboy fashion. "Yip-eee! Eeeee-yow!" New Orleans, sedately taking the air in carriages or on horseback, stared, turned, gasped. Sometimes she rode without Maroon, Cupide as groom following, perched gnomelike on the big horse and handling his mount superbly. If possible, this bizarre escort attracted more attention than when she rode with the Texan.

She had inherited plenty of the acting instinct from her lively and gifted ancestor. When they went to the theater they entered just before the curtain's rise. Between the acts she stood up and surveyed the house through her jeweled opera glasses, leisurely, insolent.

"That looks like real bad manners to me," Clint observed when first she did this. "Who you looking for?"

"It is the continental custom."

Then one night on their way to the French Opera she said rather defiantly, "Cupide has found out that they are going to the play tonight. She and this Charlotte Thérèse and two others—an uncle and a young man. These Creoles marry very young, you know."

"Look, Clio, you're not figuring on anything wild, are you? Tonight?"

"Don't be absurd, darling. Cupide discovered that they are to sit in a box, the first stage box at the right. Very indiscreet of them. The mother must be a stupid woman."

She wore her pink faille with the black lace flounces and Rita's jewels, and when, after the first act, she stood up to survey the house through her glasses, the audience sat staring as though at a play within a play. Their seats were well front. She turned her head slowly toward the right box, she adjusted her opera glasses on their tiny jeweled stick, her back to the stage, so that there was unmistakable intention in her long, steady stare at the sallow middle-aged woman in black and the sallow young girl in prim white. She stared and stared and stared. All the audience, as though slowly moved by a giant magnet, turned its head to stare with her, hypnotized. Through her glasses Clio saw the dull red rise and spread over the woman's face and throat and bosom; she saw the girl twiddle her fan and look down and look up and then speak to her mother. And the woman made a gesture for silence and the two men bent forward to shield them and quickly made conversation. And finally Clio turned her head indolently away from them and toward Maroon, who by now was looking as uncomfortable as the four in the box.

"Very *chacalata*. Very plain. Very dowdy."

When the lights went up after the second act the four in the box were gone.

They went everywhere, Clio and Clint; she made sure that wherever they went all eyes should follow them. They went to the French Market on Sunday morning, they breakfasted at Hippolyte Begué's. The white sombrero, the Lone Star boots, the coat-tails; the Paris dresses, the plumed hats, the exotic attendants were restaurant talk now and coffee-table gossip. They say his collar button is a diamond . . . that woman down in Rampart Street, remember? Very beautiful . . . mistress . . . shot him . . . hushed up . . . Charlotte Thérèse . . . Rita, she called herself Dulaine . . . Clio . . . this is the daughter . . . demi-mondaine . . . Paris . . . must be twenty years ago . . .

She actually went with him to the gambling houses where respectable women did not go and in many of which women were not allowed. She accompanied him to the old marble building in Royal Street that once had been the Merchants' Exchange where traders, gamblers, auctioneers and merchants had met in the old days for the transaction of every sort of business. The second-floor rooms, topped by the beautifully proportioned domes, were used as a gambling house now. Number 18 Royal Street. She stood at the gaming table with Clint, she placed her money quietly and decisively.

"Why do they stare so! After all, I'm only playing quietly."

"They don't see many women here, I reckon. Not like you, least-ways."

"I always went with Mama and Aunt Belle when we were in Nice or Cannes or Monte Carlo."

"It's different here. Out West, the girls in the gambling saloons, why—if that's where they were, that's what they were. New Orleans is no cow-town, but I can't help seeing they kind of look at you funny. Let's go home, Clio."

"But that's what I'm here for, foolish boy!"

He rubbed his hand over his eyes in that bewildered way. "I should think sometimes you'd get mixed up yourself not knowing which kind of a woman you are."

"I do! Get mixed up, I mean. Sometimes I am all Mama's family and sometimes I am all Papa's family."

"But there's times when you're both at once."

"Then look out!"

New Orleans, in spite of its Creole aristocracy with their almost royal taboos, looked with a tolerant and sophisticated eye on manners and customs that would have shocked many larger American cities. Its ways had a tang of the old world; it liked its food, its fun, its women, its morals spiced with something racier than the bland and innocuous American cream sauce. So the Texan and the girl with their flamboyant ways and their *outré* clothes, their bizarre attendants and their lavish spending became a sort of feature of the town. One day you saw them at the races, the next they were shopping at the French Market, or driving the length of Canal Street down to the banana wharves where, to the mystification of the townspeople, they watched the giant black men unloading or loading the sugar, bananas, or coffee that made up the fragrant cargo.

"I love to watch it," Clio had said. "It is so beautiful and rhythmic and mysterious, too, like the jungle. See the muscles of their arms and backs. They move like panthers, these black men."

Clio Dulaine was enjoying herself, no doubt of that. Interspersed with her flauntings and posturings as a florid woman of the world she managed to see the best and the worst of New Orleans. She was saying hail and farewell to the city whose praises and whose shortcomings, whose fascination and whose sordidness had been dinned into her ears all her life. "Oh, I remember that!" she would say of a beautiful building or a shop or a restaurant. She never before had seen it except through the eyes and the memory of the two nostalgic women. "They've remodeled the front of that building. . . . They should have used a ham bone instead of bacon strips in this Gombo Zhebes, and I don't think they've browned the flour enough in the *roux*. . . . This used to be the shop of Prudent Mallard the cabinetmaker, he was a great artist. Oh, dear, it's a meat market now! He made the great palissandre bed in my bedroom."

Though her childhood and girlhood in France had been a fantastic mélange of conventional school life and haphazard household she had an eye for architecture, an ear for music, a taste in food, a flair for clothes, a love of horses, and even some knowledge of literature.

So she and Clint Maroon, walking or driving about the streets of the heady old city, were frequently drunk with its charm, its potent perfume, its mellow flavor.

"Funny thing," Clint Maroon said. "Going up and down the town like this, you and me together, it's like being with a man sometimes."

"I don't know that I like that, quite."

"Maybe that does sound funny. I didn't mean it that way. Only you make things come alive, the way you see them and talk about them."

"I love to see new sights and visit strange cities. I want to see all of America. And I shall, too."

"You and me."

"No, we mustn't get used to each other—too much. Here, yes. And perhaps Saratoga."

"If I didn't know different I'd say you were a coldblooded piece."

"That isn't coldblooded. It is just sensible. I want respectability and security and comfort. Most people don't give as much thought to planning their lives as Kaka does to a dinner menu. Then when it turns out wrong they think the world is to blame."

"But suppose you plan it and know just where you're heading and even then it turns out wrong?"

"This is fate. You can do nothing about that."

Now the newspapers were beginning to mention the two. The French newspaper *L'Abeille,* usually too conservative to make mention of so spectacular a pair, published a sneering reference to the beautiful and mysterious visitor who calls herself the Comtesse de Trenaunay de Chanfret and her devoted escort, the Texan, Monsieur Clint Maroon.

"La Comtesse," the story went on, "chooses to reside in a section of our beautiful city not ordinarily favored by members of the foreign nobility visiting our shores. It is said that the house at least is closely connected with a certain notorious New Orleans *femme fatale* now dead."

"It isn't enough," Clio said. "It must be something more. Something touched with *bizarrerie.*"

"I won three thousand dollars at Number 18 last night," Clint drawled, plaintively. "And there was a piece about it in the *Picayune.* Seems they got a woman there runs that paper, name of Mrs. Holbrook. I never heard of such a thing. Women'll be going into politics, next. This Mrs. Holbrook, she writes poetry, too, signs her name Pearl Rivers. Piece in the paper called me that romantic Texan. The boys back home ever get wind of that I'll never get shut of it. They'll ride me ragged."

Clio surveyed him thoughtfully, speculatively, the light of invention slowing dawning in her eyes. "A duel," she said, meditatively, as though thinking aloud. "Of course it really should be over me, but—

what of Mr. Holbrook? Why doesn't he—you're a marvelous shot—you could challenge——"

"No ma'am! You won't make any José Llulla out of me. Besides, she's a widow woman."

Regretfully she abandoned the idea. "If only your race-horse Alamo were here. Cupide could ride him. That would make *réclame*."

"It's getting too late for the races here. Besides, they're shipping him up to Saratoga. And I'm going to have my horse up there for you to ride, Blue Blazes, she's so black she's blue, the way your hair looks sometimes, and her little hoofs they never touch the ground. They'll sit up in Saratoga when they see you on her."

"It's going to be wonderful to feel the air clear and cool with pine trees. You know, Clint, I am a little tired of shrimp and pompano and magnolias and all things soft and sweet."

"Then come on!"

"No, first I must finish here. I must have money. I will not sell my jewels because I shall need them. Besides, I have a sentimental feeling about them. I have made up my mind that I shall not be sentimental about anything. But Mama's jewels—that's different."

"There you go! Taking things hard again. You put me in mind of the way I used to be; I never would just open a door and walk through, I had to bust it down for the hell of it. I just naturally liked doing things the hard way. Always shooting my way through a crowd instead of shouldering."

"But people make way for you now, don't they?"

"Oh, it's all right—long's somebody doesn't think of shooting me first."

"Now it's you who are taking things hard. After all, what can they do to me! I have done nothing but enjoy myself in New Orleans, and I've harmed no one. But I should think their pride would have sent them to me before this." She stared out at the hot little courtyard with its unavailing fountain, its brick paving oven-hot in the sun. "I suppose," musingly, "it's too late and too hot for a concert."

"Concert! Who?"

"I sing quite nicely. You've said so yourself. A concert—a public concert—that would be very annoying, I should think. But it's too hot, isn't it?"

"Hell, yes. Anyway, honey, that's the first really bad idea you've had. Stand on a platform, open to insult!"

"M-m, perhaps you're right. Let me see. I could say that this place is to be opened as a gambling house. Cupide and Kaka could spread the rumor in no time at all."

"Now you're talking wild, Clio."

"Am I, *chéri?* Well, perhaps you're right."

But she must have mentioned it. Or perhaps the implike Cupidon was eavesdropping as they talked. Within two days there arrived at the Rampart Street house a messenger with a letter in a long legal envelope and written in a dry legal hand. Though the envelope was addressed to the Comtesse de Trenaunay de Chanfret the letter itself dismissed her briefly, thus:

MADAM:

> Will you call at my office at the address given above so that I may communicate to you a matter of importance.

> I trust that you will find it convenient to come within the next two days, and that the hour of eleven will suit you.

> May I add that the matter which I wish to discuss will prove to be to your advantage.

> With the hope that I may be favored with your immediate reply I beg to remain,

> Your obedient servant,
> AUGUSTIN MATHIEU HAUSSY.

This curt epistle was greeted by Clio as though it had been lyric with love. "There! That's what I've been waiting for."

"How do you know it's because of them?"

"Who else!"

"Want me to go along with you?"

"I'm not going. This Monsieur Augustin Mathieu Haussy—he will come to me."

"Suppose he won't?"

"He will."

And two days later Kakaracou in her best black silk and her finest white fichu and most brilliant tignon opened the door of the Rampart Street house to a dapper little man carrying a portfolio. Clio received him alone in the dim drawing room, as she had arranged. "It is better that I see him alone, Clint. I am really a very good, shrewd woman of business. I learned to be because Mama and Aunt Belle were so bad."

She wore a childishly simple little dress of white china silk like a girl at her first Communion: puffed sleeves like a baby's, and a single strand of pearls. Curiously enough, this was the one piece of jewelry which always had been hers. Nicolas Dulaine had given it to this, his child, on her first birthday.

She had been seated on the crimson brocade and mahogany sofa. As the visitor entered rather hesitantly, for the dimness was intensified in his sun-dazzled eyes, she rose, slowly, a slight, almost childish figure.

Cupide, in livery, bawled from the doorway, "Monsieur Augustin Mathieu Haussy!"

She inclined her head, wordlessly. She put out her hand. He bowed over it. When he straightened to look at her he had to raise his eyes a little, for she was tall, and he was of less than medium height. They looked at one another—a long measuring look.

A little man, with a good brow, a quizzical eye: not more than thirty; a keen face, a long clever nose. "This is no dusty fool," Clio thought.

As his eyes grew accustomed to the dimness of the room he saw that the demure white figure resolved itself into a purposeful and lovely woman.

"You are younger than I thought—from your letter," said Clio.

"And you, Mademoiselle, are so young that I am certain you do not yet consider it a compliment to be told that you seem younger."

"Madame," she corrected him, smiling; motioned him to a chair.

He perched on the edge of his chair like a sharp little bird, his toes pointing precisely ahead. "I had hoped that we were going to be honest and straightforward."

She thought, this is not going to be so easy. He has a brain, this little man. Charm, too. Aloud she said, "But of course. I hope you noticed that I did not say to you, 'To what do I owe the honor of this visit?' "

"Good. I think I should tell you that I do not belong to the old-school New Orleans tradition. I belong to the post-war New Orleans. I have seen the Carpetbaggers come and go; I have seen New Orleans under Negro rule; I have lived through the yellow-fever scourge of two years ago; I am one of those who wish to rid New Orleans of its old-time unsavoriness. New Orleans of the Mississippi steamboat must pass. By the end of the year five railroad trunk lines will enter——"

"You did not come here to discuss railroads with me, Monsieur Haussy."

He laughed a little laugh, like a chirp, and sat back in his chair as though he had been given a cue to relax. "I was only going to add that in another two years Canal Street will be lighted by electricity. I was talking, Mademoiselle, in order to give myself a chance to study you."

"And now your lesson is learned, Monsieur."

"By heart," he replied, gallantly, with a little bob forward that gave an absurd effect of bowing while seated. "I am here——"

"I know," she interrupted, almost rudely. "One of my unpleasant habits is to be impatient of long discussions. I know why you are here."

He began to untie the portfolio that rested on his knees, "I have here——"

"Please, no papers. I am bored by papers. May I offer you some refreshment? A glass of sherry? A *coquetier?*" She raised her voice. "Cupide!"

"Nothing. You are brusque, Mademoiselle, for so young and so lovely a woman."

"It was you who asked for this interview, and you who proposed honesty and straightforwardness. . . . Cupide, go to the kitchen and stay there until I ring."

"You are right. Well, then I shall come straight to the point. You are causing a great deal of pain to my client, Madame Nicolas Dulaine, and her daughter, Charlotte Thérèse."

"I should be interested to meet my half-sister, Charlotte Thérèse Dulaine."

"I should scarcely call her that."

"I should. And do. Her father was Nicolas Dulaine. My father was Nicolas Dulaine."

"But there was a difference."

"Yes. My father loved my mother dearly. He did not love the mother of this little Charlotte Thérèse. It is curious, isn't it—the child of real love is usually beautiful, like me, and the child of a marriage *de convenance* is dull and sallow, like this Charlotte Thérèse. Poor child!"

Now he knew this was an adversary to be respected. He said again, "Your conduct is causing a great deal of pain to my client."

"Your client," Clio retorted, evenly, "for many years caused my mother and me much greater pain."

"The conditions are different."

"How?"

He waived this as being too obvious to require an answer. "We object to your calling yourself Dulaine."

"My mother and my father traveled everywhere, in this country and in Europe, as Mr. and Mrs. Nicolas Dulaine."

The little man smiled at her confidingly. "Mrs. Dulaine is very far from wealthy, you know."

"Not so far as I, Monsieur."

"Is this blackmail?"

Clio's dramatic instinct told her that this was the time to rise. She rose. Augustin Mathieu Haussy jumped to his feet, dropped the portfolio, picked it up. By this time her effect was somewhat spoiled. "I did not come to you. I was living here quietly, in New Orleans, in my mother's house——"

"Quietly!"

"Quietly. Disturbing no one. After all, I am young; I like to go about to the shops and the theaters and the races and the restaurants. I am not a nun. Still, if, as you suggest, your actions can be construed as blackmail——"

"Me!" squeaked Haussy. "It is you who are attempting something very like that ugly word."

She made a gesture toward the bell. "I shall live my life as I please. You cannot frighten me as you did my mother. Good day, Monsieur Haussy."

But he seated himself and opened his portfolio. "I have here five thousand dollars. It is that or nothing. It is all that my client can afford, I assure you. New Orleans is a pauper today. Well, Mademoiselle?"

"Five thousand dollars for—what?"

He extracted a paper from the portfolio, adjusted his glasses, looked at her over them as though to make sure that he had her attention, and read in his quiet, rather pleasing voice.

"I, who call myself Clio Dulaine, sometimes known as the Comtesse de Trenaunay de Chanfret, daughter of the woman Rita who called herself Dulaine, hereby agree and promise that I shall leave New Orleans within the period of the next thirty days, never to return . . .

"I shall cease to call myself Dulaine . . .

"While remaining in New Orleans I shall conduct myself quietly, taking care to attract no undue notice or attention . . .

"After leaving New Orleans never to return I shall do and say nothing that could in any way associate me with the family of Dulaine or the history or background of the family of Dulaine . . .

"I hereby promise . . ."

She listened quietly, her hands resting easily in her lap, her fine eyes thoughtful and untroubled, as though considering an impersonal legal problem.

When he had finished she sat silent a moment. The tinkle of the fountain in the courtyard came faintly to them, and the sound of Cupide's high boyish voice chattering in eager French to Kaka in the kitchen.

"And if I do not sign this very inhospitable paper?"

"I have political influence. I can make things very uncomfortable for you indeed."

"Not as uncomfortable as I can make them for you and your client. I have the hope of security and even respectability in my life. It is just as important to me as to the little Charlotte Thérèse. But if you try to make it impossible, I have little to lose, you know. I shall make the most frightful noise, I shall do something to make such a scandal that the old affair will seem nothing in comparison."

"Yes," the little man agreed, soothingly. "I am sure you could. But you won't. You are too intelligent."

"Ten thousand."

Now the bargaining began to earnest. Five! Ten! Six! Ten! Seven! Ten! She actually achieved the ten.

"Now then, I, too, have certain demands."

"Impossible!" said Augustin Haussy, exhausted.

"Oh, don't be alarmed. They are mostly sentimental. Nothing, really. The money is to be paid me as if for the sale of this house, and I should like the house to be torn down. Now, now, wait a moment. Don't you see that your client probably would like that too? I am sure of it. Then, in my absence, there is to be placed a bunch of chrysanthemums on the grave of my Aunt Belle Piquery once each year, on All Saints' Day. And her tomb is to be kept whitewashed. The furniture in this house will be destroyed——"

"But my dear child!"

"Burned. I myself shall see to it. Except for such bits and bibelots as I shall see fit to save. I want no dirty eyes gloating over these chairs and tables—the armoire—the dressing table—the bed——"

Augustin Haussy looked around the charming room. "But this— all this—is in the best tradition of the furniture of the period. That couch you are sitting on—it must be the work of Prudent Mallard."

"It is."

"This chandelier—the Aubusson carpet——"

Clio Dulaine rose as though to close the interview. "My mother and father both possessed great good taste, Monsieur Haussy. . . . I signed so many, many papers in France after Mama's death, and then Aunt Belle's. I know this one must be properly witnessed and notarized. Will you come again tomorrow, so that no time may be lost? And do you think you could bring Charlotte Thérèse to see me?"

He stared at her in horror. "But that is impossible!"

"I suppose it is. But I think she might have liked to learn something of her father's real life. She never knew him, you see. Oh, well, she must always live a very conventional and dull existence, the poor little one. Always *chacalata*. How I pity the child!"

"A strange thing for you to say."

"No. My father would have felt the same, I am sure."

She rang for Cupide. You heard his little feet pattering across the courtyard. The lawyer tucked his portfolio under his arm, he paused to regard the girl with an eye no less keen but now definitely unprofessional.

"I am interested to know what you are going to do. As a—a— man—an acquaintance, not a lawyer, I mean. Ten thousand dollars— that can't last long—at least, with you. Those pearls you are wearing are easily worth more than that."

Clio stared a moment, rigid. Then she melted into her slow, indulgent laugh. "You were right to say that you were not of old New Orleans, Monsieur Haussy. I was little more than a baby when we left here. But I am sure your manners are of a more recent and unfortunate day."

"I thought you were too worldly to take offense. I meant none."

"Dear Monsieur Haussy, I am not offended. I am amused. I

don't in the least mind telling you. I am going to marry a very rich and powerful man."

He stared, his face almost ludicrous in its astonishment. "You mean this fellow—this—pardon me—this Texan is——"

"Oh, no. Not a penny except what he wins, gambling. A charming boy. No, I am going to Saratoga, where I shall become the fashion. Mrs. De Chanfret. It may be that I shall have to call upon you for verification. I shall do nothing objectionable. Daring, perhaps, but not too indiscreet."

"But marry—who?" so mystified as to be ungrammatical.

"How should I know? What does it matter?"

He turned toward the door. Cupide of the big ears stood in the hallway. The man came back a step or two. "I shall see you tomorrow, then."

"Yes."

He stammered, "You are—very—beautiful—that is—beautiful."

"Yes," Clio Dulaine agreed, placidly. "Isn't it lucky!"

The legal mind must reach its conclusion. "Even so, you seem very sure of achieving this—this rich and—uh—powerful, wasn't it?—uh—husband."

She shrugged her shoulders; her tone was more wistful than blithe. "I have been in America such a short time. And I have seen nothing of it, really. But even here in New Orleans I can see that this country is a little ridiculous, it is so simple and so good. Its people. Clint—the one you call the Texan—he has told me such stories! Some day those Europeans they will find out how simple and how good and how rich this country is and they will come and try to take it, I'm afraid."

"You know a great deal—for one so young."

"Oh, I know things without learning them, like a witch. And I am adventurous, like my great-grandmother, who traveled here to New Orleans so long ago from the French West Indies. I am going to have a fine time. And I am going to fool the world."

He bowed in farewell. "I hope the ten thousand dollars will be of help."

"A little, Monsieur Haussy. A little."

VIII

⭐

She was giving the Texan last-minute counsel, for it was June, moist and sweltering, and he was off for the North.

"Go to the best hotel in Saratoga. As soon as you've had a good look around, write me—write me everything."

"I feel like a skunk leaving you here in this heat, and everything to do. Why'n't you get shut of it all and come on along with me? We'll light out tomorrow, a couple of days in St. Louis, then up to Saratoga."

"I've told you, Clint, we must not come to Saratoga together. We do not even know one another. Remember that. Don't seem eager to make friends. Swagger with the coat-tails. But do nothing until I come. Always be Texas. The white hat, the boots, the new blue satin tie, the diamond collar button and the diamond stud—everything is perfect. You have only to be yourself as you are. Only—*écoute, chéri*—you are very rich but you do not want this known—and you are a Western railroad and mining man—but you do not want this known, either. I should tell no one if I were you except, perhaps, the hotel manager and a *croupier* in the largest casino. There is a casino, you are sure? For gambling?"

"What's that? Croup—uh—what——?"

"A—a dealer, I suppose you'd call him."

"Oh. Faro dealer. He sure is a good one to tell your secrets to. Look, Clio, you'll be there in two weeks? Sure?"

"But sure. Where else! But write me—names—everything. It's going to be wonderful! I feel it. In my witch's bones. New places! New faces! A whole new life!"

"Don't talk that way." He was genuinely horrified.

"Why, what have I said?"

"You can't trifle like that with luck! Bragging about what's going to be wonderful. Luck's just naturally ornery and goes the other way if you try to drive her like that. You got to just ease her along."

"Luck—fate—you've got to make your own. Bad luck—bad judgment. Good luck—good judgment. Well, my judgment is good, so my luck will be the same. You wait. You'll see."

The bays and the clarence had been shipped to Saratoga. "Sure you'll be all right, honey?" Clint Maroon said over and over again. "What're you studying to do that keeps you here two weeks and more?" A sudden fear smote him. "Look here! You're not playing any tricks with me, are you? Fixing to light out somewheres?" Actually his hand crept to the gun that always hung beneath the flowing skirt of his coat. He carried it as other men wear a wallet, quite naturally.

Clio Dulaine watched this byplay with almost childlike delight. "You are perfect, Clint! But perfect! All my life in France I read about you, and here you are, melodrama come to life." She grew serious. "Not another shooting in this house, Clint. Think how uncomfortable you would be in prison in New Orleans during August."

He passed his hand over his eyes with that rueful and bewildered gesture made so touching because of his size and the swashbuckling clothes and the gun which was his symbol of defiance against the world.

"Play-acting again, the both of us. I thought we'd be shut of that when we got to Saratoga."

"No, foolish boy! We're really only beginning there."

"Shucks, all I aim to do is play me a little faro and clean up on those suckers they say are hanging around Saratoga with the money choking their wallets. Maybe enter Alamo in a race if she looks likely. And buy you something pretty in New York."

"New York! Oh, Clint! Really!"

"Why not? Maybe, by September, if we're lucky."

So they parted, and their panic at parting was real enough. They had come together so casually, the ruthless powerful girl, the swaggering resentful man. A month or two had served to bind them, the one to the other. Each had been alone against a hostile world; now each sustained the other.

"I've a good mind to stay and wait for you, no matter what you say."

"No. No! that would spoil everything."

"I sure would like to. I get to thinking somebody might do you harm here in New Orleans. That's what's eating on me."

"Kaka would scratch their eyes out, and enjoy it. Cupide is better than a gun—you ought to know that. I have a thousand things to do. I shall never see New Orleans again. We are Southerners, you and I. Those Northerners are sharp."

"Any sharper than you, they're walking razors."

"We'll see."

"Anything goes wrong you'll send me a telegram, won't you, honey? I'll mosey back here in two shakes."

"Remember to talk like that in Saratoga. . . . Send me a telegram just as soon as you are sure of your hotel."

Suddenly she began to cry with her eyes wide open—great pearly drops that made her eyes seem larger and more liquid, her face dew-drenched.

"How in tarnation can I go when you do that! Crying!"

"Pay no attention. I often do that when I'm excited. You know that. It doesn't mean anything. Just tears."

"Well, you sure cry pretty."

The tears were running down her cheeks and she was smiling as he left. It was he whose face was distorted with pain at parting. Cupide had begged to go with him. The big Texan had shown one of his rare flashes of anger. "Why, you little varmint, you! Go along with me and leave her alone with only Kaka! You'll stay. And remember, if I find you haven't done just like she wants, everything she says, when you get to Saratoga I'll kill you, sure. No regular killing. I'll tromp you to death like a crazy horse."

"Sure," Cupide agreed, blithely. "*Mais certainement.*"

In the little musty shops whose shelves were laden with the oddments and elegancies of a decayed French aristocracy of a past century Clio and Kaka had little trouble finding the things they sought. Leather goods, jewel cases, handkerchiefs, bonbon boxes, lacy pillows, purses, jeweled *bibelots,* all monogrammed with the letter C. On these forays she dressed in the plainest black and oftener than not did not take Kaka with her. Cupide, instead, trailed far behind and lolled innocently outside the shop door until she emerged.

Kaka's needle flew. But Clio's wardrobe needed little replenishing. Her silks, satins, muslins, jewels were of the finest. Some of them were of a fashion that had not yet even penetrated to America.

Having made a gesture of melodramatic magnificence in speaking to Augustin Haussy about the furnishings of the Rampart Street house, she now thriftily changed her mind and her tactics, in part at least. The fine Aubusson carpets, the massive crystal chandelier, the unmarked silver and glass and such other impersonal pieces had an intrinsic market value almost as permanent as that of precious stones. She sold deliberately and shrewdly, driving as hard a bargain as she could. Certain exquisite pieces of porcelain and glass she had packed in stout packing cases, and these she sent to be stored at a warehouse. Luxury-loving, and possessed of a sure dramatic sense, she set aside for her own use such odds and ends as would lend authority and richness to a hotel suite—heavy wrought-silver photograph frames, antique brocade pillows, vases; the bonbon boxes from which the plump Belle Piquery had nibbled until her plumpness grew to obesity; a Corot landscape, misty and cool, that Nicolas Dulaine had long ago purchased for his Rita because she had said that just to look at it revived her on the hottest day; a paper-knife with a jeweled handle; a cloisonné desk set from the Rue de la Paix; a fabulous little gold clock.

A kind of frenzy of exhilaration filled the three—Clio, Kakaracou and Cupidon. They had an unconscious sense of release, of impending adventure. None of them had felt really secure or at peace in the New Orleans to which they had been so eager to return.

"Now then, my children," Clio announced to Kaka and Cupide, "we are going to have a bonfire and to the tune of music. Not one thing will be left that people can finger and gloat over and point at and say, 'See! That belonged to Rita Dulaine. There is the mark.' Cupide, you will take the hammer and you will pull apart the big bed and the couch and the dressing table and the armoire, and you will roll up the carpet in the bedroom. You will burn all these, a little at a time, in the courtyard."

"No," screamed Kaka, in real pain. "No!"

"I say yes. The marked glass you will throw against the brick wall of the *garçonnière* so that it breaks into bits, and then you will gather it into the dust bin to be thrown away. The center of the courtyard, Cupide. Smash up the fountain first."

There was something dreadful in the sight of the glee with which the little man went about his task of destruction. Ghoulish, powerful, grinning, he rent and pounded, hammered and smashed. Now the massive hand-carved posts and headboard, the superb mirror frames, the delicate chair legs went to feed the fire that rose, a pillar of orange and scarlet destruction, at the rear of the Rampart Street house. The heat was dreadful, though the fire had to be fed slowly, for safety's sake. The mahogany burned reluctantly. Cupide's face became soot-streaked; he pranced between house and courtyard, between fire and wall. Crash, tinkle. Crash, tinkle, as the glass was hurled against the brick wall by his strong simian arm. Then another load of wood on the flames. Begrimed, sweating, filled with the lust for destruction, he was like an imp from hell as he worked, trotted, smashed, poked, hammered. The day was New Orleans at its worst—saturated with heat and moisture, windless, dead. Fortunate, this, or the Rampart

Street house itself might have taken part in the holocaust. Perhaps Clio had hoped it would.

"More," she urged Cupide. "More. Everything. I will sleep on the mattress on the floor these next few days. Nothing must be left."

The telegram came from the Texan, and then, as speedily as might be, his letter, written in his schoolboy hand, round and simple and somehow touching.

> DEAR CLIO (it began, formally enough)
>
> Honey I miss you something terrible. I thought I was used to being alone but it seems right queer now and lonesome as the range. This place beats anything I ever saw. Hotels pack jammed and you talk about style and some ways rough too all mixed up the old days in Texas couldn't hold a candle to it. The United States Hotel is the place to stay which is where I am as you see. The biggest gambling place is called the Club House it was built by Morrissey he is dead. You ought to see it, the carpet alone cost $25,000 they say, there is a colored woman housekeeper runs the kitchen and so on her name is Mrs. Lewis I found this out and thought that Kaka could get friendly there. Honey you ought to see who all is here. This is a bigger lay-out than we figured on. William Vanderbilt, Jay Gould, Whitney, Crocker, Keene, Bart Van Steed, why they are all millionaires fifty times over besides a thousand who are just plain rich with only a million or so in their pants pocket. Jay Gould sits on the front porch he is here at the United States and rocks a soft-spoken quiet-stepping fellow I wouldn't trust him with a plugged dime. I notice he's got a bodyguard since they tried to shoot him a while back. They call it the Millionaires' Piazza. The turnouts would take your breath away. A four-in-hand is nothing out of the ordinary. Vanderbilt drives a pair I would give anything just to get my hands on they are Maude S. and Adelina, the horses I mean, the prettiest team I ever saw and the fastest pair in the world. Bart Van Steed drives

a pair of big sorrels to a dogcart with a footman sitting up behind like a monkey. We got acquainted through my bays racing him on Broadway. They are as fine a pair as there is in town except of course Vanderbilt's if I do say so.

Well, honey they call me White Hat Maroon. I am playing up Texas like you said. Peabody of Philadelphia has a pretty team of dapple grays he drives to a landau. The races are just beginning. Better get you one of those new trunks they call Saratoga trunks big as a house and it will hold those fancy dresses of yours I haven't seen anybody can come within a mile of you for looks and style though they dress up day and night like a fancy dress ball. It beats anything I bet even Paris France. The girls are all out after Bart Van Steed and even yours truly they say their mamas bring them here to catch a husband. And a lot of the other kind here too, bold as brass. The race when it comes to looks and clothes and bows is between a Mrs Porcelain from the East somewhere and Miss Giulia Forosini her pa is the banker from California she drives three white mares down Broadway with snow-white reins, it's as good as a circus. Well honey sweetheart that gives you some idea. Van Steed is a mama boy they say afraid of his ma, she isn't here yet but coming and he is trying to make hay while the sun shines they say if he looks at a girl his ma snatches him away pronto. Bring all your pretty dresses. My room number is 239 at the front of the house there are rooms at the back on the balconies facing the garden very expensive they call them cottages which they are not but too quiet for my taste. Try to get 237 and 238 bedroom and sitting room they are vacant I paid for them for a week I said I wanted plenty of room and talked big. You make up a good reason for wanting them specially and I'll be a little gentleman and give them up when the manager asks me to. There is something big here if we play our cards right. Hurry up and come on but let me know everything about it as soon as you can. You drive to the lake for fish dinners and catch the fish yourself if you want to as good as New Orleans or better—black bass, canvasbacks, brook trout, woodcock, reed birds, soft shell crabs, red raspberries. You won't even remember Begue's with their kidney stew they make such a fuss about. They give you something called Saratoga chips it is potatoes as thin as tissue paper and crackly like popcorn. Everything free and easy, plenty of money, not too hot and big shady trees and you can smell the pines. This is bigger than I thought. I wish there was some way I could get at the big money boys I am studying how I can do it. I hate them worse than a cow man hates a sheep man. Well, if the cards run right and the horses run right and the little ball falls right we ought to clean up here. And if I do honey I'm going to buy you the biggest whitest diamond on Fifth Avenue New York. Only hurry away from that stew-kettle down there and come up here to,

Your friend,

WHITE HAT MAROON.

P.S. Crazier than ever about you I don't like you being down there alone old Kaka and Cupide don't count.

Clio Dulaine's reply to this rambling letter was characteristically direct and astute.

CLINT CHERI:—

It has been very queer here. All things. But I am well and I am safe and I shall arrive in Saratoga on July 14th at half-past two. Do not meet me. Be at the hotel desk when I enter. The hotel will expect me on the 15th. Find out immediately, as soon as you have read this letter, if Van Steed's mother is arriving in Saratoga before that time. Telegraph me at once. This is important. If she is not there he will receive a telegram sent by me en route at the last minute to say that she is on the train and that he is to meet her. It may not work but I shall try. Remember, you do not know me. I think this will not be a little holiday with perhaps some luck at cards and horses. This is the chance of a lifetime. I am bringing Kaka and Cupide of course and eight trunks besides boxes. *A bientôt chéri,* Big Texas. Remember we are business partners. I have written the hotel.

CLIO DE CHANFRET.

Her letter to the United States Hotel was as brief and more to the point.

MY DEAR SIR:—

My physician Dr. Fossat has advised me to go to Saratoga for the waters following my recent illness due to my bereavement of which you doubtless have heard. I shall require a bedroom and sitting room for myself and accommodations elsewhere in the hotel for my maid and my groom. Many years ago my dear husband occupied apartment 237 and 238 in the United States Hotel. It will make me very happy if you can arrange to give me this same apartment. If it is difficult I shall be happy to recompense the hotel for its trouble.

One thing more I must ask of you. Though I am the Comtesse de Trenaunay de Chanfret I wish to be known only as plain Mrs. De Chanfret. I want to remain quiet while at Saratoga. I wish no formal ceremonies. I must rely completely on you to comply with my request to remain incognito.

I shall arrive on July 15th at half-past two o'clock.

I remain,

Sincerely yours,
COMTESSE DE TRENAUNAY DE CHANFRET

(MRS. DE CHANFRET *please!*)

Twenty-four hours after the arrival of this letter everyone in Saratoga knew that nobility was coming incognito. Saratoga made much of its train arrivals in this, the height of the season. The natives themselves flocked down to see the notables and fashionables as they stepped off the train. The bell in the old station cupola added its clamor to the pandemonium of train bell, whistle, screech; the cries of greeting or farewell; the shouts of hotel porters and omnibus and hack drivers; the thud of heavy trunks; the stamp of nervous horses' hoofs. Landaus and dogcarts and phaetons and even a barouche or two were drawn up at the platform's edge. There was a swishing of silks and bouncing of bustles and trailing of draperies. Bewhiskered and mustached beaux in midsummer suits of striped seersucker or checked linen, horsey men in driving coats of fawn color or buckskin made a great show of gallantry as they bowed and postured and twirled their mustaches and took charge of the light hand-luggage and gave authoritative masculine orders regarding the disposal of trunks and boxes.

Clio Dulaine had lingered and dawdled in the train so that she was almost the last passenger to step onto the depot platform. The confusion was at its height. Bells clanged, whistles tooted, horses plunged and reared, the hotel runners shouted, "Grand Union bus here! Take your bus for the United States Hotel! Clarendon! Congress Hall this way!"

As she stepped off the train at Saratoga Spa it was characteristic of Clio Dulaine that she was not dressed in the utilitarian black or snuffy brown ordinarily worn for traveling by the more practical feminine world. She was wearing gray, sedate yet frivolous, the costume of a luxurious woman who need not concern herself with travel stains and dust. The little gray shoulder cape of ottoman silk was edged with narrow black French lace and its postilion back made her small waist look still tinier. Even her traveling hat (known as a Langtry turban) was relieved by its curl of gray and mauve ostrich tips nestling against the black of her hair. A traveling costume de luxe; a hint of half-mourning whose wearer has long since dried her tears.

As she stepped off the train she looked about her in pretty bewilderment, her expression touched with the half-smile of expectancy. The noise and confusion were at their height as passengers were swept off into waiting carriages or buses; then the whistle, the clangor and the slow acceleration of the engine's choo-choo-choo-choo-choo-choo-choo-choochoo as the train drew out. The noise reached a crescendo, died down, became a murmur. Sheriff O'Brien's sorrels whirled him off in his dogcart, the Bissells' long-tailed bays were twin streaks of red-brown against the landscape, the Forosini landau rolled richly off, the coats of the blooded blacks glinting like satin in the sunlight. Cupide had trotted off to wrestle with the pyramid of trunks and boxes. And still the slim gray-clad figure, drooping a little now, stood on the station platform. Behind her, a sable pillar of support, was Kakaracou. But Clio's speech, incisive though whispered, belied her attitude of forlorn uncertainty.

"Yes, I was right, Kaka. He's the one who has been running up and down like a chick without its hen-mother. That must be his carriage with the sorrels and the groom. Look! Now he's rushing into the waiting room. Quick, fetch Cupide, never mind about the trunks, when he comes out we must be standing near his cart, the three of us, put on your gloves, fool! Hold the jewel box well forward. Cupide! Quick! Here!"

She maneuvered the little group so that they stood between the waiting-room door and the team at the platform's edge. When he came out he must pass them. And now Bartholomew Van Steed emerged, a somewhat frantic figure. A final searching look up and down the station platform—a look that included and rejected the group of three as being no part of his problem—and he sped, dejected, toward the waiting groom and horses. As swiftly Clio intercepted him.

"Pardon, Monsieur!" He stopped, stared. "Can you tell me where I may find a carriage to take me to the United States Hotel? Please."

"Uh—why——" He waved a vague arm in the direction of the public hack stand, for he was full of his own troubles. He now saw that the space was deserted. Frowning, he looked back at her, into the lovely pleading face, seeing it now for the first time. His gaze traveled to the black woman behind her, to the strange little man in livery, then returned to her, and now her lip was quivering just a little, and she caught it between her teeth and clasped her gray-gloved hands.

"I was to have been met. Naturally. I cannot understand." She turned and spoke rapidly to Kakaracou in French, "This is terrible. I don't want to embarrass this gentlemen. Can we send Cupide somewhere, perhaps——" Her appealing look came back to Van Steed. And now for the first time he seemed to see the striking group as a whole—the richly dressed young woman, the dignified Negress, the dwarf attendant, all surrounded by a barricade of hat-boxes, monogrammed leather cases, fine leather bags, all the appurtenances of luxurious travel.

The brusqueness of perplexity now gave way to his natural shyness. He blushed, stammered, bowed. A tall man who appeared short perhaps because of his own inner uncertainty, perhaps because he stooped a little. Side whiskers and a rather ferocious mustache that did not hide the timidity of the lower face; a fine brow; amber eyes with a hurt look in them, a strong, arrogant hooked nose—the Van Steed nose. Clio Dulaine saw and weighed all this swiftly as she looked at him, her lips parted now like a child's. Something of a dandy, poor darling, she thought, with that fawn-colored coat and the *sans souci* hat like that of a little boy playing in the Luxembourg Garden.

"Madame," he began, "that is—Miss—uh——"

"I am the Comtesse—I mean I am Mrs. De Chanfret. I am sorry to have troubled you. It has been such a long and tiring trip. I had expected to be met. I am not fully recovered from——"

Two great pearly tears welled up, clung a moment to her lashes; she blinked bravely but they eluded her and sped down her cheeks. She dabbed at them with a tiny lace-bordered handkerchief.

"But Mrs. De Chanfret! Please! Uh—allow me to drive you to the United States Hotel. I am stopping there myself. I am Bart Van Steed, if I may——"

"Not—not Bartholomew Van Steed!" He admitted this with a bow and with that air of embarrassment which, oddly enough, seizes one when confronted with one's own name. "But how enchanting!

Like being met unexpectedly by a friend in a strange land. It is a strange land for me. But perhaps you are meeting someone else——"

At this his worried look returned, he glanced right and left as though the possibility still remained that he might have overlooked a passenger on the little depot platform. "I was expecting my mother. She telegraphed me that she would be on this train."

Clio was all concern. "And she didn't come?"

"I can't imagine what happened. Maybe she's on another train. But she never misses a train. And she never changes her mind."

"Perhaps someone was playing a joke."

"People do not play jokes on me," said Bart Van Steed. "I shall send a telegram as soon as we reach the hotel." He waved her toward the waiting carriage. "Lucky I drove the phaeton. Mother won't ride in the dogcart. But I'm afraid there isn't room for all——"

"You are so kind. This will do beautifully—for all of us." The groom had jumped down, had handed the reins to Van Steed, and now was barely in time to hand Clio up, for her foot was on the step and she was seated beside Van Steed before he had well adjusted the ribbons. "My woman can sit back there with your groom—she's very thin. And Cupidon can stand on the step, if necessary. . . . The bags just there . . . So . . . Kaka, have you my jewel-case? . . . That large bag here at my feet. I don't mind. . . . The hotel porter will see to the trunks. . . . Cupide! There, on the steps . . . You see he's so very little you will never notice he's . . . It's not far, I suppose . . . This is wonderful! So kind! So very kind! I don't know what I should have done if you hadn't appeared like a shining knight. . . ."

She leaned a little toward him, she smiled her lovely poignant smile. She sighed. She thought, well, lucky I know how to manage, we'd never have been able to pile in. Not with this weak-chinned one.

Away they whirled. White-painted houses. Greek revival columns. Gingerbread fretwork. Ancient wine-glass elms. Smooth green lawns. "Oh, I like this! This is very American!" Clio clapped her hands like a child, and for once she was not acting. "Charming!" She turned slightly to call over her shoulder to Kakaracou, speaking in French. "Look, Kaka, look! This is America—but the real America!"

"*Tiens!*" said Kaka, putting incredible sarcasm into the monosyllable.

"I gather that you have not visited Saratoga before," said Bart Van Steed, weightily. "I—uh—I speak some French." Then, as she turned to him, eager to express her delight in the language with which she was most at ease, he added, hastily, "But only a little. A very little. I—uh—read it better than I speak it. You haven't been here before, I gather."

"I haven't been anywhere. I am discovering America. It is amazing! So big! So new! All my life I have lived in France." She was having a fine time being very French; little Gallic gestures; her hands, her inflection, the cooing note in her voice. He had noted the crest on her luggage, the initials on the filmy handkerchief, the tiny jeweled monogram on her reticule. The letter C was entwined with vines and fragile leaves and spirals.

"Are you here for the racing season?"

"I am a lover of horses. But I am here in the hope that the waters and the air will help me. Not," she hastily added, "that I am ill. I never have been ill in my life. But I have heard that the waters are tonic and I hoped that the fresh bracing pine air and the tonic waters would restore my appetite."

His full blond mustache quivered, his pale gold eyes turned to her sympathetically. "I've got a delicate digestion too."

She thought, grimly, I'll be bound you have! Aloud she said, "All sensitive people—especially those whose lives are lived in the midst of great responsibilities—are likely to have delicate digestions. Because of his diplomatic duties my husband the Count de—I mean for years my late husband had to have everything *purée,* almost like an infant's food, really. Yet he was a man of the most brilliant mentality and marvelous achievement, like yourself."

"My mother," he announced, plaintively, "can digest anything. Anything. Sixty-seven."

"How marvelous! But then, she probably isn't your tempera-ment. Not so delicately organized."

"She's as strong," he announced with surprising and uncon-scious bitterness, "as an ox—that is—she's got great strength and—uh—strength."

"How—wond-er-ful!" she cooed in that paced leisurely voice. "And yet, do you know, sometimes these very, very strong wonderful people become sort of annoying to more highly sensitive ones like you and me—I don't mean your dear mother, of course."

He had barely time to say, "No, certainly not!" with guilty emphasis when they drew up before the fantastically columned entrance of the United States Hotel. The three passengers in Bartho-lomew Van Steed's equipage stared in stunned unbelief at a sight which could be duplicated nowhere else in America—or in the world, for that matter. Slim columns rose three stories high from a piazza whose width and length were of the dimensions of a vast assembly room. A gay frieze of petunias and scarlet geraniums in huge boxes blazed like footlights to illumine the bizarre company that now crowded the space on the other side of the porch rail.

"Grand Dieu!" was wrung from Clio Dulaine as she stared in shocked unbelief.

"Nom d'une pipe!" squeaked Cupide.

"Mais, bizarre! Fantastique!" muttered Kakaracou.

Up and down, up and down the length of the enormous piazza moved a mass of people, slowly, solemnly, almost treading on each other's heels. The guests of the United States Hotel were digesting their gargantuan midday meal. Carriages and buses had already dis-gorged the passengers who had arrived on the half-past-two train, and these had been duly viewed, criticized and docketed by the promenad-ers. It was part of the daily program.

And now here was an unexpected morsel—a delicious bit to roll under the tongue. The vast company goggled, slowed its pace, came almost to a standstill like a regiment under command. En masse they stared with unabashed American curiosity at Bart Van Steed's carriage and its occupants. Bartholomew Van Steed, the unattainable bachelor, the despair of matchmaking mamas, the quarry of all marriageable daughters, dashing up to the hotel entrance in broad daylight with a woman—with a young, beautiful and strange woman. One could discern that before she emerged.

Down jumped a midget in livery, gold buttons and all. Out stepped a majestic turbaned black woman looking for all the world like an exiled Nubian queen. Out jumped Bart Van Steed's groom, then Van Steed threw him the reins and himself handed out the modish figure in gray and mauve.

A simple day, a crude society. Like figures in a gigantic marionette show the piazza faces turned toward the little procession as Clio, her skirts lifted ever so slightly, swept up the broad steps of the piazza into the vast white lobby. Beside her strode Bart Van Steed, and behind her a stream of satellites. Out rushed a covey of black bellboys and joined the parade, each snatching a hatbox, a case, a bag. The women noted the cut of the stranger's ottoman silk gown, the fineness of the black French lace so wantonly edging a traveling cape; they saw the sly line of the Lily Langtry hat, the way the gray kid boots matched the richly rustling skirt. The men saw the slender ankle beneath the demurely lifted skirt, the curve of the figure in the postilion cape, the lovely cream-white coloring and the great dark eyes beneath the low-tipped hat.

"Why, the sly dog! I wouldn't have believed it of him! He said it was his mother he was going to meet."

Out pranced Roscoe Bean, the oily head usher, from his corner under the great winding stairway—Roscoe Bean, who winnowed the hotel wheat from the piazza chaff, who boasted he could tell the beau monde from the demimonde at first glance. A snob of colossal proportions, unctuous, flattering, malicious, he now skimmed toward the party so that the tails of his Prince Albert coat spread fanlike behind him. His arms were outspread, he swayed from the hips, it was a form of locomotion more like swimming than walking.

"Your ladyship!" he began, breathlessly, for his pervasive eye had glimpsed the omnipresent monograms and crests. "Your ladyship!" We didn't expect you until tomorrow."

"Please!" She raised a protesting hand. "I am Mrs. De Chanfret."

"Yes, of course. Beg your pardon. Your letter said——"

She approached the desk. She did not even glance at the tall figure lounging against a pillar just next the clerk's desk—a figure whose long legs were booted Western style, whose broad-brimmed white sombrero was pushed back slightly from his forehead, whose gaze lazily followed the spiraled smoke of the large fragrant cigar in his hand.

Even as she signed her name in the bold almost masculine hand—Mrs. De Chanfret—maid—groom—the room clerk, the subclerk, the hastily summoned manager and assistant manager wrung their hands and wailed in unison like a frock-coated Greek chorus.

"But Mrs. De Chanfret! Your letter said the fifteenth. Here it is. In your own hand. The fifteenth! Two thirty-seven and two thirty-eight were to be vacated early tomorrow morning. We were sending a staff of cleaners in to prepare them for you first thing in the morning. We wouldn't have had this happen for the world!"

"Perhaps I should have gone to one of the other hotels."

"Mrs. De Chanfret! No! We can give you a temporary suite in one of the cottages——"

"Cottages!"

"Magnificent suites at the rear——"

"I! At the rear!"

"But the cottages aren't cottages—that is—they're suites on the balconies overlooking the gardens. Our most élite guests refuse to occupy any other rooms . . . Mr. William Vanderbilt . . . Lispenards . . . Chisholms . . . Mr. Jay Gould himself . . . even President Arthur has . . ."

She shook her head gently; she turned away. To his own astonishment Van Steed heard himself saying, "This is preposterous! You must accommodate Mrs. De Chanfret. I myself will give up——"

The turmoil had now reached a dramatic height exactly to Clio Dulaine's liking. Behind her stood Kakaracou, an ebony statue, the jewel case clutched prominently in front of her. Cupide, his tiny legs crossed, was lolling negligently against a stack of luggage while his froglike eyes made lively survey of the immense lobby. A group of Negro bellboys, their clustered heads like black grapes on a stem, stared down at him, enthralled. Inured though the little man was to the cruel gaze of gaping strangers, he now was irked by the attention he was receiving. Suddenly he contorted his face into the most gruesome and inhuman aspect, accompanying this with an evil and obscene voodoo gesture unmistakable even to these Northern boys. They scattered, only to peer at him again, eyes popping, from behind a near-by pillar or desk.

And outside, the piazza-walkers were savoring this unexpected after-dinner delicacy, or dropping into the lobby on any pretext. . . . it's that countess or whatever she is . . . but I thought she wasn't coming until tomorrow . . . did you see the midget I thought it was a little boy until I saw his face he looks . . . this morning I happened to meet Bart he said he was expecting his mother on the two . . . well all I can say is that when old Madame Van Steed hears of this she'll have a . . . rules him with a rod of iron . . . Mrs. De Chanfret . . . they say she doesn't want to be called . . .

For this hotel was like a little self-contained town; the piazza like a daily meeting of a rural sewing society made up of gossips of both sexes. Every one of the promenaders longed to be in the lobby now. Yet even they realized that a concerted move in this direction would inevitably result in a stampede. Still, the hardier souls among them would not be denied. Singly or in pairs you heard them muttering a trumped-up excuse as they drifted out of the throng and made for the door that framed the enormous lobby.

"Well—uh—guess I'll get me forty winks after all that dinner . . . if I'm going to the races I'd better be starting . . . I'll go up to the room and see how Mama is. She had one of her headaches and wouldn't come down to dinner . . . Mr. Gillis said he'd have the information for me at the desk this afternoon so I'll just drop by and ask . . ."

Within the hotel the apologies and explanations behind the desk now rose to a babble through which could be heard a single word emerging like a leitmotif. Maroon. Maroon. Maroon. Colonel Maroon's occupying those rooms, but by tomorrow he——

Now the tall figure that had been so indolently viewing this scene from the vantage point of the near-by pillar uncrossed its legs, came forward with a slow easy grace and, removing the white sombrero with a sweeping gesture that invested it with imaginary plumes, bowed before the elegant and somewhat agitated figure of Mrs. De Chanfret.

"Excuse me, Ma'am, but I couldn't help hearing what you-all were saying. My name is Maroon, Ma'am—Clint Maroon. Texas."

Clio Dulaine looked up at him, she turned a bewildered face toward Bart Van Steed, then quickly to the men at the desk, "Well, really, gentlemen! This is too——"

"No offense, Ma'am," drawled Maroon.

Bart Van Steed now found himself not only aiding beauty in distress, but playing the defender of injured innocence: "Look here, Maroon, you can't address a lady you've never met."

"Listen at him! Introduce us, then, and make it legal. I'm aiming to help the little lady. She can have the rooms she wants right now. How's that, Ma'am!"

Grudgingly Van Steed went through the form of introduction. Again the Texan bowed with astonishing courtliness. Clio Dulaine held out her little gloved hand. He took it in his great clasp, he clung to it like an embarrassed boy.

"But I couldn't think of turning you out of your rooms, Mr. Maroon."

"Make nothing of it, Ma'am. It's thisaway. I'm just occupying two thirty-seven, thirty-eight and thirty-nine for the hell of it. Shucks, Ma'am, excuse me. I didn't go for to use language." He came closer. He still held her hand in his. She did not retreat. "No sense in my having it. I just like to spread out and be comfortable. I'll go get me my stuff and you can move in right now. I never really used those two extra rooms, anyway."

"How good of you, Mr.——"

"Maroon," he prompted her. "Clint Maroon."

"What a delightful name! So American."

"Texas, Ma'am."

"Texas! I should love to see Texas."

"Play your cards right and you will, Ma'am. No offense, Mrs.— uh——"

"De Chanfret."

"De—uh—yes. Well, I meant that was just an expression we use. I sure would like to be the one to show you Texas." He raised a hand toward the clerks behind the desk. "I'll mosey along and be out of there in two shakes. You-all can come on along right now, if you've got a mind to."

This surprising suggestion was seized upon by Mrs. De Chanfret with alacrity. "Kaka! Cupide!"

The room clerk, the manager, the assistant manager, the head usher, relaxed beaming. "Madame is wonderful," cooed Roscoe Bean, "to accommodate herself like this."

Clio graciously murmured something about being a woman of the world. Cupide, a gargoyle come alive, bestirred himself among the bags. Kaka moved to her mistress's side. The little procession formed again, now taking on the proportions of a safari. Bells were tapped smartly. Orders given. A squad of chambermaids and scrubwomen summoned. Clint Maroon did not precede the party. He waited. Clio turned to Batholomew Van Steed.

"How can I thank you! You have been so kind, so friendly. I feel, really, that we actually are friends."

Caution settled like a glaze over Van Steed's face. The quarry scented the pursuer. "I am happy to have been of service." He bowed rather stiffly. "I trust that you will be comfortable."

"And I hope," Clio said, all sweetness and light, "that your dear mother's telegram will soon be followed by her coming. But I can't help being selfish enough to realize that her failure to arrive was my gain. Good-by, Mr. Van Steed." She half turned away.

Caution fled. He took a step toward her. "I shall see you soon, I—that is—we shall meet again soon, I trust—guests under the same roof, naturally——"

She bowed, she smiled, she moved off with her entourage; she had given him a swimming glance intended to convey fatigue, gratitude, aloofness. Incredibly enough, she actually managed all three. But even as she turned away she paused a moment. "Who is this gentleman,"—she indicated the tall figure of the Texan strolling toward the elevator—your friend in the white hat? He is the real figure of an American. Who is he?" Her words were quite clear to the attendants at the desk.

Van Steed eyed him obliquely. "Maroon? Why—uh—Texas cattle man, I'm told. Some such matter. He's no friend of mine."

"A pity. In Paris he would be the rage." Bart Van Steed's pale golden eyes widened in surprise. How annoying those white eyelashes are, Clio thought, even as she smiled sweetly in farewell. Then the slender gray-clad figure moved off with a soft susurrus of silks, followed by the discreeter rustle of the majestic black woman's skirts. He was still looking after her as the elevator with its grillwork, its groaning ropes and clanking cables, lumbered heavily upward and bore her from his sight.

A little pink-and-white figure, pretty as a Dresden china shepherdess, approached the desk, paused a moment in passing and gave an extremely bad imitation of surprise at the encounter. "Your mother didn't come, Mr. Van Steed? What a disappointment for you!"

"Oh, howdy-do, Mrs. Porcelain! No—uh—that is—no."

"I do hope nothing's wrong," she cooed. "Saratoga isn't Saratoga without her."

A momentary gleam lighted his eye, then faded. "Nothing's wrong," he replied, as though thinking aloud. "The telegraph company must have made the mistake. Mother never does. I'm sending her a telegram now. The funny part of it is that I thought she was up in Newport at my sister's house. Mrs. Schermerhorn. She's expecting a—uh—she isn't well, that's why Mother—but her telegram was sent from New York."

Mrs. Porcelain wagged a coy forefinger at him. "Now, now! You're not playing a little joke on us, are you, Mr. Van Steed? You didn't drive down to the depot to meet a Certain Somebody Else? I just happened to be on the piazza taking a little constitutional when you drove up."

For years Madam Van Steed, that iron matriarch, had checked relentlessly on his every coming and going. His solicitude when she was present only testified to his guilty inner hatred—a hatred which occasionally brimmed over into a fury of resentment. So now he was seized with the seemingly unreasonable rage of the hag-ridden male.

"My dear Mrs. Porcelain, am I to understand that I am obliged to cloak my actions or explain my behavior to a lot of harpies on a hotel piazza!"

"Harpies!" The round blue eyes, the round pink mouth showed her shocked surprise, but the social training of years triumphed. "You're quite right, Mr. Van Steed. We do become like small-town gossips here in dear little old Saratoga, don't we?" She managed an arch smile. "She is really lovely."

"But I tell you I don't know the lady!" he almost shouted.

But Mrs. Porcelain was not to be diverted from her purpose by mere insult.

"You must introduce me some time soon. I should so love to meet her."

IX

✫

Clio Dulaine stood in the middle of the sitting room, surveying the suite with its grim and rigid furnishings. Black walnut chairs, mustard walls, a vast cuspidor. Through the open door of the bedroom she glimpsed the carved black walnut bed, the livery marble-topped table, the boxed-in washstand. Beyond that was the dim cavern of the bathroom with its zinc-lined tub. Bellboys were raising windows, lowering shades, muttering about ice water. Clint Maroon was standing discreetly in the outer hall doorway under the chaperonage of Roscoe Bean's eye.

"Looks like we're neighbors, Ma'am," he said, genially. "Seeing how I'm right next door." He waved his hand toward the closed double door.

"So kind of you to give up your rooms to me, Mr.—uh—Maroon. I really feel quite guilty."

"No call to. I never used 'em. Well, I'll be moseying along. Good day, Mrs. De Chanfret, Ma'am."

With considerable ostentation Roscoe Bean glided to the large double door between the sitting room and the bedroom just now designated by Maroon. "I'll lock the door on this side, Your Lady— that is, Mrs. De Chanfret—if you'll kindly turn the lock on your side, Mr. Maroon. It's a double lock, you see, both sides. Mmmm." His murmur conveyed a nice sense of the proprieties. He proceeded to turn the lock with precision and snap.

"Good day, Ma'am," Clint Maroon vanished from the doorway. Clio Dulaine waited. Roscoe Bean waited. Kakaracou waited. Cupide, grinning, cocked his impish head. A bolt shot into place, a key grated. "Ah!" sighed Roscoe Bean. Then, briskly, "The chambermaid and the scrub-woman and the housekeeper will be up at once. Have you had your dinner? Is there anything? Would you——"

Already Kaka was going about her duties with the utmost efficiency. She had immediately vanished into the bedroom to poke the mattress with an investigating forefinger. Now she was opening boxes, hanging clothes in the wardrobe, laying out toilet things, shooing the loitering bellboys. "*Allez, allez!* Go! *Carencro! Congo! Dépêche toi!*"

With a protesting palm and a voice of quiet authority Clio interrupted the usher's chatter. "Nothing more. Thank you. No maids. My maid will do all that is necessary for the present. Cupide, go with this gentleman. See that my trunks are brought up at once from the station. The hotel maids later, later. I must rest now."

She closed the outer hall door after them sharply, she turned the key, she stood a moment, listening, her head resting against the door. She turned, her body leaning against the door now, and surveyed the ugly room with a little secret smile of satisfaction and triumph. Her physical weariness was forgotten in a surge of elation. She listened again, her head thrown back. From the depths of her being she sighed with exquisite relief. The flurry of arrival was over, the fatigue of the trip was forgotten. From the bedroom came the reassuring sounds of Kaka's expert ministrations. Through the open windows facing the street she saw the green lace of giant elms, heard the clatter of horses' hoofs, snatches of talk, laughter, the cry of a vendor. Exultingly she thought, well, Clio Dulaine, here you are in Saratoga! You have left New Orleans and its sorrows behind you. You have already met the most eligible man in the East. You have money enough to last you the summer. You are a wonderful woman, Clio. But marvelous!

Swiftly she went to the forbidding slab of the somber double door, drew back the bolt, turned the massive key. But even as she did this she heard, in perfect unison, the bolt shot back, the key turned on the other door. Her hand never touched the knob, for as she instinctively stepped back the door was thrown open from the other side. As on their first real meeting the two burst into laughter spontaneous and a little hysterical before he gathered her up into his arms, caught her up and held her to him so that she lay in her gray and mauve like a scarf flung across his breast. There was no sound but the discreet rustling that betokened Kaka's hands busy in the adjoining room with tissue paper and silks. When, finally, he tipped her gently to her feet, one great arm spanned her shoulders, one hand tilted her face up toward his and silently, leisurely, he bent over her and his lips touched her hair, her brow, were pressed against her closed eyelids, her lips, her throat, her breast as he held her yielding as a reed.

"Send her away. Shut the door."

"Tonight, chéri. That endless journey. Tired."

He sighed, he released her, he passed a hand across his eyes with the old gesture of one dispelling a mist. "How are you, Ma'am?" Then they both giggled as though he had said something exquisitely witty.

"If you had called me Ma'am once more down there I'd have screamed."

"I sure would have admired to hear you, Ma'am. Only I'd hated to have you scared Bart thataway. Say, how in Sam Hill did you get him eating out of your hand? When I saw you come in with him easing along beside you I thought for a minute, well, hell's bells, how in tarnation can I stand here pretending I don't know her when that little mama's boy is bowing and scraping and running the whole she-bang!"

"Jealous already!"

"You're damn whistlin' I am!"

"There is much more to come. You must remember what we're here for."

"Look, honey. I've been thinking. I can make out for both of us. There's money to burn around here at the Club House and over at the track. I'm used to stud and red dog but I've been making out pretty good at roulette and faro. And I've been sitting in on poker games upstairs at the Club House in the private rooms. Say! Look!" He brought forth a wallet, his dexterous hands ruffled a sheaf of yellow-backed bills. "We can clean up pretty and then light out for somewhere else."

Anger, cold and hard, stiffened her whole body. Her eyes narrowed, her jaw set so that the muscles suddenly showed rigid. Maroon had tossed the fat wallet onto the marble-topped center table. Now her hand seized on it, she drew in her breath with a little hiss, then she hurled the leather-enclosed packet across the room where it lay in a corner of the floor, its golden leaves fluttering a moment before it subsided. He stared at her, uncertainly. He had never before seen her in such anger.

"Poker games!" Her tone was venomous. "Poker games, when there are fools here worth millions and millions! Do you think I came here to pick up dollar bills like those girls you told me of in your cheap dance halls in the West! Do you! Do you!" Then quietly, venomously, "Get out! Get out of my room."

Kaka appeared in the bedroom doorway, a silken garment in her hand. The bewildered Texan stared at her. Kaka tossed the garment onto a chair and glided swiftly to the distraught woman. Clio thrust her away, but the Negress heeded this no more than if she had been dealing with a tired child. She began to unfasten the snug bodice of Clio's dress, swiftly and deftly she peeled it from her as she stood, and the heavy silken garment slid to the floor with a soft slithering sound and lay in a crumpled circle at the girl's feet while she still glared at the Texan and he stared dazedly at her. "My poor little tired baby!" Kakaracou murmured to the figure standing there in the embroidered and beribboned corset-cover and petticoats. Then, over her shoulder to Maroon, "Come, lift her out, lak lil *bébé*, I put her in bed."

"Too hot," murmured Clio, her eyes half closed, her anger fled as suddenly as it had come. "I'll lie on that funny couch there in the bedroom. And you'll sit and talk to me, Clint, and Kaka will go on unpacking. I love it like that, cozy, and everyone near me, and things stirring."

As though she had been a doll he picked her up in his arms while Kaka scooped up the dress, and together they deposited her on the couch with its unyielding expanse of brocatel, its lumpy head-rest, in the room littered with the silks and ribbons and bottles and jars and gowns and bonnets only now unpacked by Kakaracou.

"Hep shoes," ordered Kaka. Maroon knelt with the Negress while each removed one of the little gray kid boots. She slipped a sheer white wrapper over Clio's head, thrust the girl's limp arms into the long beribboned sleeves, briskly buttoned it at the throat and tucked a tiny French hand-wrought pillow under the weary head.

"Ah-h-h-h!" breathed Clio, luxuriously. Suddenly she was wide awake; alert. "*Chéri,* I am so sorry. No, don't go away. Presently I will sleep. Not now. Come, sit here, talk to me. I didn't sleep, not one hour on that dreadful train, all the way from New Orleans I have not slept. Kaka can sleep standing upright like a cow. Really. And Cupide curled anywhere in a corner, like a monkey. Now, let us talk. This is wonderful. So cozy and gay but peaceful, too. I am happy! I am happy!"

"Hold on, look here," Maroon remonstrated, though only half-heartedly, for she looked so young and small there on the sofa amongst the cushions. "Now you say you're happy. But I've got a temper too, strong as horseradish. You ever let go at me like that again, why, I'm sure liable to punish you, pronto. Screeching at me like a crazy mare. You try that again, girl, you'll be here alone."

She pretended to cower in fright among the pillows, it was impossible to maintain a role of offended dignity in the face of her outrageous simperings. But he refused to smile, he took on a gruffly paternal tone. "Likely you're lightheaded on account of having no sleep and no decent food, probably."

He strolled into the sitting room, retrieved the scorned wallet, came back, still talking, and stuffed the billfold into his breast pocket. "Easy come, easy go, that's my motto, but just the same I've got more respect for money than to take and throw it thataway. Better let Kaka fetch you some dinner, maybe that'll settle you."

"No. When the train stopped at that town—Poughkeepsie— what a name! When the train stopped there everyone got out and there were women with baskets covered over with clean white napkins, and underneath the most delicious chicken and biscuits and cake. We bought everything. Even Kaka had to say it was not bad. Didn't you, Kaka?" Kaka made an unladylike sound. "Well, at least we could eat it."

The Texan was not yet quite mollified. "I never did see a woman grown treated like a baby before. Getting undressed and put to sleep in the middle of the day. Ma, she stayed on her feet and not a yip out of her when she was just about dying."

"I know. She must have been wonderful, like the pioneer American women in the books. I am not at all like that." She dismissed the whole matter with the air of one who finds it unimportant. "When I am ill I complain and when I am angry I shout and when I am happy I laugh. It is simpler." She stirred luxuriously among the pillows, she smiled engagingly up at him. "Stop scowling like a cross little boy! Let's talk, all cozy and comfortable. Kaka, move that chair nearer. Now. Tell me. Tell me everything. From the beginning." She clasped her hands like a child waiting to be told a fairy tale.

Rather sulkily he lounged in the armchair by the sofa, his long booted legs stretched out. "Nothing much to tell, comes to that."

"Clint, chéri, don't be like that. Here we are in Saratoga where we shall make our fortunes. Now then, those rich old men, those wicked old men who sit and rock on that huge fantastic piazza, tell me about them. Have you talked with them? Do they think you are big and important and Western, as we planned?"

In spite of himself he began to kindle to his story. "Well, it ain't as easy as all that, sugar. They're a special breed of varmints. I thought I knew something about what was behind men's faces from watching poker players. I've sat in twenty-four-hour games where I got to know that a muscle that kind of twitched in a player's jaw meant four aces, and once I spotted a royal flush from just happening to notice that Steve Fargo's face was dead pan but the pupils of his eyes had widened till you couldn't rightly see the real color of his eyes. But these fellas, they ain't human . . . Don't raise your left eyebrow when I say ain't. I know better but I'm talking Texas every day now, like you said, practicing . . . Well, there's a kind of coldblooded quiet about them you can't get at. It ain't money they're after. It's each other's skins. They've already got so much money they can't keep track of it, no way. I got it straight. Look at Willie Vanderbilt, his pa, the old Commodore—and say, he was no more a Commodore than I'm a Colonel—did I tell you they took to calling me Colonel around here, down at the track and over to the Club House—Colonel Maroon—well, as I was saying, the old Commodore left Willie ninety-four million dollars and damned if he hasn't run it up to two hundred million. Two hundred million, honey! We don't sit in that game, Clio."

"Why not! Why not, I'd like to know! Are you afraid?"

"No. I just ain't interested enough in money to go out and knife these sharks for it. It ain't money with them. It ain't even power. It's like they were playing a game, and the cards are people and the stakes are railroads or mines or water power. They ain't human. They don't care for human beings or for their own country or honesty or any decent living thing. These men, they're not like anybody you ever met up with. They don't run with the herd, they don't hunt in packs. They go it alone, dog eat dog. And yet you wouldn't rightly call what they've got by a name like—say—courage or independence. They put me in mind of jackals more than anything—they ain't dogs and they ain't wolves—they've just got the worst habits and make-up of both. You want me to be like them, Clio?"

"You don't have to be like them. You only have to be cleverer than they are."

"Yep. That's all. I could scheme to grab ahead of 'em. But you see, my folks, they were the giving kind, not the taking. They liked to build up, not tear down. When you think how people came over here from the old country and worked like slaves and went through hardships would kill us today. Pa clearing the land and planting it up and Grandpaw at the Alamo—why, say, my fingers they just itch to take out my gun when I see that pack of varmints sitting there, rocking, so soft-spoken and mild-looking. They're so poison mean their lives are threatened all the time. And that's why you never see them without two or three big kind of dumb-looking fellows standing around near by, faces like big biscuits with a couple of raisins for eyes. They're bodyguards. I bet I could pick one or two off right here from this window."

"Don't talk like a foolish boy, Clint. They must be quite simple, really, these American millionaires. Simple and cruel, like children. Taking each other's toys away by force and running off with them. This Van Steed—he seemed rather silly, I thought. Actually frightened of his mother. And a weak digestion. Pink cheeks and white eyelashes and stammers a little. Wouldn't you think he would have suspected my clumsy little trick! But he swallowed it. Well, now—really!"

He got up and began to pace the floor; then he perched on the footboard of the bed, slouching a little as though he were sitting on the top rail of a Texas corral fence. "Funny thing, they're all like that, one way or another. Sick men. It's like they knew death was on 'em, and they had to work fast. Vanderbilt looks like he'd burst a blood vessel any minute, his face is red but it isn't a red you get from health. Now Gould, he's got a bad heart and they say consumption. It's common talk he hardly ever sleeps, and times he spits up blood. Nights when everybody's asleep, two, three o'clock in the morning, he's sitting there on the piazza, rocking, and all day sending telegrams to New York or talking to the men he sends for, so quiet you couldn't catch a word if you were passing by slow. Asks the band to play his favorite tune, 'Lead, Kindly Light.' . . . You think you can come here and lasso a critter like this Bart Van Steed! He's one-third bronco, one-third mule and one-third Mama's boy."

"I thought he seemed quite charming."

"Quite charming," he mimicked in a maddening falsetto.

But she only smiled at him as at a rather naughty but engaging child. "Oh, I wish I weren't so sleepy. There is so much I want to know. Just to hear your voice. But this cool delicious air after all that heat. It is as if I were drugged."

He forsook his perch on the footboard to stand over Kaka busy with her bags and boxes. "Kaka, pull down the shades, she'll go to sleep, and we'll have a drive at five o'clock, or maybe a horseback ride if you feel like it, Clio."

Kaka glanced over her shoulder at her mistress, feverish and heavy-eyed. She spoke as if Clio were not in the room, her English very precise. "When she looks like that she will do things her own way. She has been like that for a month now, until she is ready to drop with fatigue, and me I ache in every bone and Cupide's legs are an inch shorter from running."

"Well, do something, can't you! She'll make herself sick."

"She was like that in Paris before we came to America. She was like that before she met you in the Market." She dropped her voice, she became suddenly the black woman, superstitious, witchlike. "She under a *wanga*."

"A what? What's that?"

"*Wanga*. A spell. I give her witch powder but"—her voice dropped so that her mobile lips mouthed the words almost sound-lessly—"no good because Miss Clio she a witch woman herself."

He laughed a little uncomfortably. "Listen at you!"

"What are you two whispering about? Kaka, don't unpack every-thing. We may not stay in these rooms."

He strode over to her then and stood over her menacingly. "What do you mean—not stay here! You're plumb crazy. You've been talking crazy ever since you got here. Where're you aiming to go!"

"He said the cottages—that man downstairs. Is it more chic, there in the cottages?"

"God, I don't know! Nothing you've said since you drove in

here makes a mite of sense. I've a mind to get out of here myself, and leave you."

"No, you won't, Clint *chéri*."

"Why won't I!" In a miserable imitation of truculence.

"You won't," she repeated, equably. Then, persisting, "The cottages. Tell me."

"Hell's bells! I don't know, I tell you! I don't even know why they call them cottages. It's crazy. They're the rooms at the back where the hotel's kind of U-shaped and verandas running all around. I don't want to talk about hotels!"

"He said a garden."

"Well, there's a garden back there, right pretty, with big trees and flower-beds. Mornings and evenings the hotel band plays there, and when there's a hotel hop, why, they string up colored lanterns. Some folks they like to sit there in the garden. Oh, God, I don't know! This is the looniest talk I ever heard! Look, you're what they call punch-drunk, you need sleep, you'd better let Kaka put you——"

She got up then, trailing her long white draperies over the oddments and elegancies with which the floor was strewn. "I tell you I must know a thousand things before I can sleep. Then I shall sleep and sleep and sleep, hours and hours, a thousand miles deep, and when I wake up everything will be clear and right in my mind. Isn't it so, Kaka! Tell him."

A certain affirmation was in Kaka's eyes, but she cackled derisively. "Hch-heh, yes, she think she a *mamulvi*, she go off in a spell and when she wake up everything come right like she want it."

"That's just dumb talk. All this milling around. What's eatin' on you, anyway! You don't rightly know what you're saying."

"But I do. Or I will. This little fellow—this little Van Steed—do you imagine he is cleverer than you and I?"

"Clever! It's money. They've got millions."

"They didn't always have millions."

"Listen, honey, you just don't understand. Why, the women around here, they'll tear you to pieces if you step in their way. You pretending to be here alone—that's bad medicine. A woman without a man here in Saratoga—they'll make cold hash out of you in a week."

"But I have a man. You. And in a week there will be two men—you and little Bartholomew."

"He's going to be too busy to bother about you, honey. I heard yesterday they're out to get him."

She whirled at this. "Who? How? Why?"

Restlessly he began to pace the littered room, stepping over piles of neatly stacked lingerie, trampling stray bits of tissue paper.

"I don't rightly know yet. I pieced it together from what I picked up. Van Steed owns a hundred miles of road between Albany and Binghamton. Right up near Saratoga here. It's what they call a trunk line. Only a hundred miles or thereabouts. Years ago his mama gave it to him to play with, his first little railroad. Now it's turned up worth millions."

"But why? Why? . . . Kaka, stop that rattling of paper! . . . Why is this—this Saratoga trunk worth millions? These—these are the things I want to know. How can I sleep when there are things like these I must know! Tell me—why millions?"

"Seems it's the link between the new Pennsylvania hard-coal lands and New England. That little stretch of one hundred miles is what they want to get their claws into. It's the coal has made all the difference. It's a coal haul, direct, for all of New England. Sure thing it's worth millions."

"Does he know this—Van Steed?"

"Why wouldn't he know it! He isn't as dumb as he looks. Van Steed, he's president of the Albany & Tuscarora, and this trunk line was just a kind of link—it didn't mean anything until these new coal fields were opened up. They've been fighting it out for months now. Gould's crowd have been buying up town councilors all along the line. The way they work it's so simple it sounds kind of crazy—or I'd think it was crazy if I hadn't heard the same kind of story all my life from the way Pa was treated. Honey, you wouldn't believe it. I can't even explain it to you. I won't try. It's everybody for himself and catch as catch can. Now Van Steed, he's got a smart fella on his side, a friend named Morgan, a banker lives in New York—J. P. Morgan his name is. He's a scrapper; they say he's smarter than Gould or Fisk was or any of them. But he hasn't started to fight the way the other crowd does, where anything goes. He's being legal, everything open and aboveboard. And Van Steed, he's the kind has got to have everything down on paper. Meantime, the Gould crowd, they're hitting below the belt. Gouge and bite and kick—that's their way. Talk about the East being civilized, why, say, it makes the West look like a church meeting. I have to laugh when I see these people here, dressed up in their silks and their swallow-tails, driving up and down, smirking and bowing."

"But these men with their railroads, what are they doing, then? What are they doing? Tell me."

"What they're doing they'd be strung up for as outlaws, West. You wouldn't believe. The Gould crowd, they hire gangs to go out and tear up tracks and chop down trestles. Folks won't ride the railroad any more. It ain't safe. That's just what the old crowd is figuring on. Run it down to nothing."

"But the government. Where is the government to stop these *apaches*?"

"Sa-a-ay, they took care of that right early. They've got the government bought up, hair and hide, horns and tallow."

Weary though she was, her mind persisted in its clear reasoning. "We will make ourselves valuable to this little Van Steed. He must be told that you are clever with railroads. I will tell him."

"Look here, Clio, honey, we don't aim to be any part of that crowd."

She ignored this. "If it's only a hundred miles—this road into the coal fields—why don't they—the Gould crowd—build their own hundred miles of railroad?"

"Because they can't get the land. Twenty years ago—even ten, maybe—they could have bought the land or stolen it from the government by going down to Washington and buying up Congress and so on. It's not so easy now. These railroad men——"

Suddenly she yawned prodigiously. "Railroads, railroads! Railroads bore me. I have no mind for railroads."

"But you said——"

"I know, I know. But you and I must do things very simply and directly, with our little minds. We have only a month, really."

"Do? Do what? What things?"

"Oh—I don't know, *chéri*. I think I shall marry this little Van Steed. Maybe——"

"Ha! Likely. I sure would like to know how you're fixing to do that."

"Oh, he is a simple fellow, really——"

"Don't fool yourself."

"Well——" She stretched luxuriously, then stopped abruptly, listening, in the midst of another yawn. "Cupide with my trunks. Kaka, quick, have them put in the hall and left there. My great new Saratoga trunk would hardly squeeze through the door, anyway. Quick, Kaka!"

Here Kaka rebelled. "How you going dress for dinner effen I don't take out and press!"

"Because I'm not going down, stupid! Do as I say."

"Not going down!" repeated Maroon. "Tonight!"

"Of course not. And probably not tomorrow. Where's your dramatic sense, Clint? I made a superb entrance. You will admit that was a great stroke of luck—of course I'd planned it, but who would have thought it would work so magically!"

But he was by now thoroughly exasperated. "Look here, you stop this play-acting or I'll light out. Hell's bells, you can't do this——"

"Wouldn't it be won-der-ful to have some champagne now—immediately—very very cold—so cold that a little mist stands outside the glass. Clint dearest, call Kaka—no, don't let them see you, of course—Kaka! Kaka! Tell Cupide to order me a bottle of champagne in ice—they will bring it up. Sit down, Clint, sit down." She picked up the pamphlet on the table by the sofa and flicked its leaves. "The waters, of course. Tell me, which one do you take?"

"Me! I wouldn't touch the stuff, I can't stomach it. Tastes worse than desert alky water."

"But doesn't everybody? Drink it, I mean. When I used to go to Aix with Mama and Aunt Belle everyone took the waters—there was a *régime* for the day—you took the waters, you walked, there were baths, you went to the Casino. Mama and Aunt Belle loved it— especially Aunt Belle. It made her thinner for a little while."

"That's the way they pass the time of day here. Out before break- fast, some of them over to the Springs. But mostly they don't take it the way you say—not to say seriously."

She was reading from the booklet, her pretty nose wrinkling a little with distaste. "M-m-m, let me see—uh—Empire waters. Rheu- matism, gout, irritated condition of the stomach, pimples, blotches, ulcers"—hastily she turned the page—"Columbia water. Possesses valuable di-diur—what is the meaning of that word, Clint? Well, anyway, I shall not drink Columbia water. Liver complaints— dyspepsia—erysipelas—gravel and vitiated condition of the— mmmmmmmm—— A pint mornings. Ugh! Excelsior Springs—kidney, bladder, gravel—— Congress Spring—*Mon Dieu!*"

"Congress is the one you want, honey. It's the stylish one. That's the place to go, mornings, before breakfast or after. Band plays. Every- body bowing and prancing."

"I can't imagine you——" She laughed deliciously at the picture of the Texan, booted, mincing, glass in hand, at Congress Spring.

"Me! No Ma'am! Mostly I'm over at the track, mornings, having my breakfast at the stables."

"Oh, Clint, I'd love that! Could I——" She stopped abruptly. From the street below came the call of a fruit vendor.

"Peaches! Fresh ripe peaches! Raspberries! Red raspberries!"

She was off the couch and across the floor, her head at the win- dow. "Heh! You! Peaches! Peaches here!"

He leaped to the window just ahead of the vigilant Kakaracou. "God A'mighty, Clio! You can't do that."

Unwillingly she turned away. "Well, send down, then. Cupide. Or you go. Fresh peaches bobbing in a glass of champagne. That is the way Mama used to eat them in Paris, and Aunt Belle. Delicious, and cool, cool. I am so hot and tired, *chéri*."

"*Stupide!*" Kaka scolded, thrusting her back from the window. "A fine lady you are, screaming into the street. You think this is New Orleans!"

"Well, where's Cupide? Kaka, see if he's outside the door. I told him to stay there. Send him down before the peach man is gone. Tell him big ripe yellow ones, with pink cheeks, and the pits like great pigeon-blood rubies in a nest of yellow velvet."

Cupide, stationed outside the door, was having a fine time. Already he had discovered that the exhilarating and speedy way to reach the ground floor was to slide down the banisters which curved from floor to floor around the stairwell. In Paris and in New Orleans he had had no fine slippery banisters. Now, cautioned by Kaka to make all haste in order to catch the fruit vendor, he nevertheless followed his usual procedure, which was to run up the stairs to the floor above in order to enjoy to the full his new and thrilling form of travel. Starting from these heights it was possible to attain sufficient momentum to swing round the polished curves and slide the entire distance down to the lobby itself, which was the end of the line. As he skimmed down from the third to the second floor a colored chambermaid, ascending the stairs with broom and pail, put out a horrified arm to stop him.

"You, little boy! Don't you know you ain't allowed to slide down no banisters you kill youseff! I going tell you mammy on you you do that again." His powerful arm jerked her hand that attempted to hold him, he leaped off the banister, the impish face confronted the girl, he scurried around and nipped her smartly behind and, amidst her shriek of surprise, leaped again to the rail, his gargoyle face grinning impishly up at her until he vanished round the curve.

Half an hour later Clio Dulaine was sipping from a tall dewy glass in whose bubbling contents a fat peach bobbed, fragrant and tempting.

"But won't you just try it, Clint? A sip. It's heavenly!"

"That's no drink for a man," Clint Maroon had said. "Champagne and peaches in the middle of the day. No Ma'am!" Then, as Clio sipped and purred contentedly, "Look, sugar. You put on one of your prettiest dresses and come down for supper tonight, won't you? There's a hop tonight. We were introduced downstairs, weren't we, all regular and proper, by Bart Van Steed. I can talk to you, same as anybody else. No secret in that."

"Oh, no. I must have my dinner up here."

"You feel sick, Clio!"

"No, no! I feel so well and happy—happier than I've ever been."

"Then why in tarnation do you want to mope up here?"

"Because they expect me to come down. Because they all saw me arrive and stood there gaping like a lot of peasants. Because they'll be waiting for me to come down this evening and tomorrow morning and tomorrow noon and tomorrow night. And I shan't. I shan't come down until day after tomorrow, in the morning, on my way to the spring. And by that time they will be dying with eagerness to see me. Especially little Van Steed."

"It sure sounds silly to me."

She looked at him over the rim of her glass, round-eyed. "Sometimes, Clint, I wonder if it was a good thing or a bad thing, for both of us—that day we met in the French Market."

"One thing's sure. If we hadn't, you wouldn't be here in Saratoga, drinking champagne out of a big water tumbler with a peach floating around in it."

She tapped the glass's rim thoughtfully against her teeth. "You are right." Suddenly she sat bolt upright, her eyes strained, her lips quivering. "What am I doing here!" she cried, wildly. "Mama is dead! Aunt Belle is dead! What am I doing here! Who are you! How do I know who you are! Kaka! Cupide!"

Swiftly, as before, the Negress ran to her, she took the hysterical girl in her arms. "Hush! Hush your mouth!" She turned to speak to Maroon over her shoulder, as she rocked the girl back and forth. "Champagne make her sad. My lil Rita was the same way, her mama."

Even as Clint Maroon stared at this new manifestation of his unpredictable lady, the sitting-room door opened to admit a Cupide almost completely hidden by an ambush of very pink roses. The years with Rita Dulaine and Belle Piquery and Kakaracou had accustomed him to more dramatic bedroom scenes than this, with its welter of gowns, shoes, hats, hysteria; and a discomfited male standing by in the background. He now advanced behind the thicket of roses. Unceremoniously he dumped them in the lap of the distraught Clio, who stopped in the midst of a disconsolate wail, her mouth open.

"I could hear you way out in the hall," Cupide announced, scrutinizing a thorn-pricked thumb and nursing it with his tongue. "There's quite a crowd out there—chambermaids, waiting, and a woman to scrub and a boy with ice water, and a woman who says she's the housekeeper. I told 'em if anybody tried to come in they'd probably be killed. The roses are from that man who drove us from the station."

"Dutch pink roses!" Clio exclaimed. "I loathe the color. No taste, that little man." And threw them to the floor. "Kaka, tell them to go away, those people outside. I shall be changing anyway, tomorrow, to the cottage side. Maybe even this afternoon if I'm not too tired——"

Maroon flung his arms out in a gesture that encircled the littered room. "Look at this place! It's enough to make anybody tired. You don't even know what you're saying. That champagne wine's gone to your head, middle of the day. There you've been, cooped up in trains this long trip. No real air. A drive would do you good. A little later, maybe, cool of the day."

Drowsily she shook her head. "No. I don't want to be wide awake. I don't want to drive. I want to be still, still. Talk to me. Tell me more. Little things that are important to know, and then I will dream about them and when I wake they will be settled in my mind. Who is the important woman, *par exemple?* Who is it among them that they all follow? This Mrs. Porcelain? Or the Forosini? Who?"

"Nope!" piped up Cupide in his clear boyish voice. "There's a fat old woman, I heard her talking to that man—the one who stays in the corner under the stairs. They call him the head usher. I heard her say De Chanfret, so I listened way back under the stairs. She said, 'I knew the De Chanfrets. Never heard of this one.' He said something about look it up in somebody's peerage; she said, 'That's no good, it's English.' " The midget's manner was somewhat absent-minded, for his attention was fixed on his thorn-pricked thumb.

"Get out!" scolded Kakaracou. "What do you know, imp!"

"No, stay. Kaka, make yourself neat, go downstairs, say I do not find it quiet here, I shall move into the cottage wing tomorrow. Go, look at the rooms. Don't take the first apartment they offer. It must have a servant's room for you. . . . Cupide, who is this fat woman?"

"Bellop," blurted Cupide.

"Don't make ugly noises."

"That's her name. I asked the bellboys. They call her Bellhop behind her back, but they say everybody in Saratoga is afraid of her. She looks like a washwoman. Big!" He stuck out his chest, he puffed his cheeks, he waddled, his voice suddenly became a booming bass. "Like that. And talks like a man. She called me to her when I was coming up the stairs just now and tried to question me. Where did you come from and how long had we been in this country and what was your name before you married. She gave me a silver dollar. I took it and pretended I spoke only French. I spoke very fast in French and I called her a fat old *truie* and what do you think! She speaks French like anything!" He went off into peals of laughter. "So I ran away."

"Oh, dear. I wish I weren't so terribly sleepy. You sound, all of you, as if you were speaking to me far away. Clint, who is this woman with the ridiculous name?"

Maroon, striding the room impatiently, tousled the dwarf's head not unkindly, and sent him into the next room with a little push.

"That's what I've been telling you. That's the kind of thing you get yourself into here. The town is full of bunko steerers. This crowd here in the hotel, millionaires and sharpers, they're onto each other, no matter which. Our best bet is to be ourselves, get what money we can, have some fun, and light out. I hate 'em like I hate rattlesnakes, but we'll never be able to sit in on the big game, honey."

"This woman," she persisted. "Who is this woman?"

"Well, far as I know, I'd say she looks about the way Cupide says, Mrs. Coventry Bellop. That's her name. Lives in New York but they say she hails from out West somewhere, years back. Got a tongue like an adder. Some say she gets her income from blackmail in a kind of quiet way. They say she lives here at the hotel free of charge, gets up parties, keeps 'em going, says who is who. Just a fat woman, about fifty-five, in black, plain-featured. I don't understand it. Maybe you do, Clio, but smart as you are I bet you'll make nothing out of her."

"I like the sound of her," Clio murmured, sleepily. "When a fat and frumpy old woman with no money can rule a place like this Saratoga then she is something uncommon—something original. I think we should know each other."

In a fury of masculine exasperation and bewilderment he stamped away from her. "Oh, to hell with all your planning and contriving, it's like something out of a storybook you've read somewhere." He came back to the couch. "Now look here, we're going to drive out to the lake at six, say, when it's cool, and have a fish dinner at Moon's, you can catch 'em yourself right out of the lake. I'm bossing this outfit."

She had fished the dripping peach out of the glass and had taken a bite out of its luscious wine-drenched cheek. Now, as he looked at her, the plump fruit fell with a thud from her inert hand and rolled a little way, tipsily. Clio didn't reply, she did not hear him. He saw that suddenly, like a child, she was asleep, the long lashes very black against the tear-stained white cheeks.

At the sudden silence Kakaracou looked up.

"Looks like she's clean beat out," Maroon whispered. "A nap'll do her good."

Quietly Kaka began to make ready the bed. "She will sleep," she said, and her tone was like that of a watcher who has at last seen a fever break. "She will sleep perhaps until tomorrow, perhaps until next day. Carry her there to the bed. That is well."

A sudden suspicion smote him. He strode over to Kaka, he took her bony arms in his great grasp. "Look here, if you've given her anything—if this is some of your monkey-shines I'll break every——"

The black woman looked into his face calmly. "It is bad to be long without sleep." She went about pulling down the shades. "I will rest here on this couch. Cupide will keep watch there in the next room. But here, until she wakes, it must be quiet. Quiet." She stood there, in silence, waiting. He paused, irresolutely. The room and the two women in it seemed suddenly of another world, eerie, apart. He turned and walked toward his own door. He felt a stranger to them. He heard the door close after him, the key was turned, the bolt shot. Then he heard the closing of the bedroom door. He stood in the center of his own room, an outsider. To himself he said, "Now's your chance, Clint. Vamoose. Drag it outa here and drag it quick. You stay in these parts you're going to get into a heap of trouble. If you're smart you'll git—pronto."

But he knew he would never go.

X

In the fortnight following Clio's arrival old Madam Van Steed was made to realize that her male offspring in Saratoga was even more in need of her maternal protection than was her ailing daughter in Newport. News of Bartholomew's preoccupation with a mysterious and dazzling widow traveled to her on the lightning wings of hotel gossip. Bag and baggage, the beldame arrived, took one look at what she termed the shenanigans of the dramatic Mrs. De Chanfret, and boomed in her deepest chest tones, "De Trenaunay de Chanfret de Fiddlesticks! The woman's an adventuress! It's written all over her!"

But before her antagonist's arrival Clio Dulaine had had a fortnight's advantage. And in less than two days after Madam Van Steed's announcement the Widow De Chanfret had managed to bring about a cleavage in the none too solid structure of that bizarre edifice called Saratoga society.

On one side were ranged the embattled dowagers holding the piazza front lines, their substantial backs to the wall at the Friday night hops. Behind their General, Madam Van Steed, rallied the conservatives, the bootlickers, the socially insecure and ambitious, mothers with marriageable daughters, daughters for whom Bartholomew Van Steed was a target. Defying these pranced Clio Dulaine and her motley crew made up of such variegated members as Clint Maroon, a frightened but quaveringly defiant Bart Van Steed, Kakaracou and

Cupidon, all the Negro waiters, bellboys and chambermaids, a number of piazza rockers who for years had been regularly snubbed by Madam Van Steed, and, astonishingly enough, that walking arsenal of insult, bonhomie, and social ammunition large and small, Mrs. Coventry Bellop of the Western Hemisphere.

The battle had started with a bang the very morning on which Clio, refreshed to the point of feeling actually reborn, awoke from a thirty-six-hour sleep. The hotel management had been politely concerned, then mystified, then alarmed by the tomblike silence which pervaded 237 and 238. Messages went unanswered, chambermaids were shooed away, food was almost entirely ignored, a discreet knock at the door brought no response, a hammering, if persisted in, might cause the door to be opened a crack through which could be discerned the tousled head and goggle-eye of a haggard Cupidon or the heavy-lidded countenance of Kakaracou looking like nothing so much as a python aroused from a winter's hibernation.

"What you want? . . . Madame is resting. . . . We have all that is needed. Come back tomorrow. . . . Go away. Go away. Go away."

Once a tray was demanded. The Negro waiter saw that the bedroom door remained shut, and it was evident that it had been the Negress and the dwarf who had partaken of the food.

Then, suddenly on the morning of the second day following the arrival of Mrs. De Chanfret and her attendants all was changed. The chambermaid slouching along the hall in her easy slippers at seven in the morning heard a gay snatch of song whose tune was familiar but whose words differed from those she knew. A fresh young voice, a white voice, for all its fidelity to the dialect:

> *Buckwheat cakes and good strong butter*
> *Makes mah mouf go flit-ter flut-ter.*
> *Look a-way a-way a-way in Dix-ay.*

"Them funny folks is up an' stirrin'," she confided to her colleague down the hall. "I thought they was sure 'nuff daid."

Except for three brief intervals Clio Dulaine actually had slept through that first night, through the following day and the second night. Once Kaka had brought her a *tisane* of soothing herbs brewed over the spirit-lamp, once she had fed her half an orange, slipping the slim golden moonlets between the girl's parted lips as you would feed a child. Clio's eyes were half shut during those ministrations, she murmured drowsily, almost incoherently, ". . . sleepy . . . what time . . . Mama . . . no more . . . Cleent . . . *chéri* . . . Cleent . . ." And she had giggled at this last coquettishly and then had sighed and snuggled her face into the pillow and slept again. During the heat of the noon hour Cupide had stood in his shirt sleeves, a tireless little sentinel fanning her gently with a great palmleaf fan as she lay asleep. Time after time Clint Maroon had knocked at the inner door. Sometimes he was admitted, often not. He had tiptoed away mystified and resentful but satisfied that nothing was seriously wrong.

"When she wake up," Kaka droned each time, "zoomba! Look out!"

Clio had opened her eyes at six in the morning. It was fresh and cool this early. Wide awake at once, alert, renewed, she stood in the middle of the room in her bare feet and nightgown and surveyed the world about her. Kaka, fully dressed, lay on the sofa, her tignon askew so that you saw her grizzled skull, so rarely visible that now it gave the effect of nakedness. She, too, was at once awake at this first sign of fresh life in her mistress. She got to her feet, her tignon still tipped rakishly.

"My *gabrielle*," Clio commanded, crisply. "Go down to your own quarters. Make yourself fresh from head to foot, everything. Roll up those shades. Where is Cupide? In there?" She passed into the sitting room where Cupide lay curled like a little dog in one of the upholstered armchairs. Awake, he was either merry or pugnacious. Now, asleep, he looked defenseless and submissive as a child. "Poor little man," murmured Clio, looking down at him. She picked up a shawl from a near-by chair and placed it gently over him. But at that he, too, awoke, he cocked one ribald eye up at her, then he leaped to the floor in his tiny stockinged feet, shook himself like a puppy, and, running to a corner, slipped into his boots, shrugged himself into his coat.

"Why didn't you sleep downstairs in the room provided for you?" demanded Clio, not unkindly.

"I wanted to be near you and Kaka," he answered, simply.

"Get down there now, both of you. I want you to wash and make yourselves neat and smart. You, Cupide, look to your shoes and your buttons. Be quiet. And above all, polite to the hotel servants." She eyed Cupide severely. "No tricks. And you, Kaka. No voodoo, no witchwork. Your best black silk. I am going to bathe in that funny box. Like a coffin, isn't it! But to have one's own bath in a hotel—how wonderful! America is really marvelous. When you are fresh and clean come back. Then you will make me a cup of your coffee, Kaka, hot and strong. How good that will be! Then I'll dress and we'll go to the Congress Spring, early. It will be the fashion to walk to the Congress Spring, early. I'll make it so. You'll see. Get along now! Quick. *Vite!*"

When the door had closed behind them she stood at the window a moment looking down at Broadway, watching the little green-shaded town come to life.

The long trancelike sleep had left her mind clear and sharp as mountain air. She felt detached from her surroundings, as though she were seeing them from some godlike height. Curious and haphazard as her life was, there always had been about it some slight sense of security at least. In her babyhood there had been her mother, the luxurious little house in Rampart Street; later there had been the orderly routine of school in France and the rather frowsy comfort of the Paris flat with Rita Dulaine and Belle Piquery and Kakaracou and Cupidon to give it substance. Even on her return to New Orleans, brief as the interlude had been, the Rampart Street house had again given her the illusion of security that accompanies the accustomed, the familiar or the remembered. Now, she thought, as she stared down at the main street of the little spa, what have I? In the whole world. Well, an old woman and a dwarf. In the next room a man I have known a few weeks. A *blagueur*, for all I know. Trunks full of clothes. Some good jewelry. Money enough to last me a year if I am careful. No home, no name, no background, nothing. I want comfort, security, money, respectability. Love? Mama had that and it ruined her life.

"Food. That is what I need," she said, aloud. She looked around the disheveled room. Hot, hot coffee, very strong. It was then that she began to sing as she turned on the water for her bath. By the time Kaka and Cupide returned and she had her second cup of Kaka's coffee she was buoyant, decisive, gay.

"Cupide, go downstairs, tell the man in the office that I have decided to move into the cottages. Kaka, you yourself look at the rooms. Make a great *bruit*, but everything dignified and proper. Tell them I will not pay more than I pay here in this location. Here it is noisy and hot, and anyway, for my plan it is better to seem to be alone. This is not discreet, here. The rooms must be ready when I return from the Spring."

Kaka, rustling importantly in her best silk and her embroidered petticoats, stood sociably drinking her own cup of coffee.

"How you going drink spring water after all that coffee?"

"I'm not going to drink the water, silly. Vile stuff!"

"*Faire parade*, h'm?" She rather liked this faring forth to stare and be stared at. "It's time. Two days lost."

"Not lost at all, idiot! I could go for days now without rest or sleep. I've stored up sleep as a camel stores water. . . . Let me see. I think I shall wear the mauve flowered cretonne and the shoes with the little red heels."

"Red heels are not for widows," grumbled Kaka. She began deftly to dress Clio's hair in a Marquise Cadogan coiffure, bangs on the forehead, very smooth at the back and tied in a club with a black ribbon à la George Washington. It was a youthful, a girlish arrangement.

Clio grinned. "But my dear husband, the Count de Trenaunay de Chanfret died—oh—at least two years ago. So I'm out of mourning. Even second mourning. I only keep on wearing it because my heart is broken. . . . The large leghorn hat, Kaka, with the black velvet facing."

It was scarcely half-past eight when they appeared in the hotel lobby. Clio, followed by Kaka and Cupide, looked spaciously about her, seeing everything, enjoying everything—the vast brass spittoons, the ponderous brass gas-chandeliers, the glimpse of garden at the back, the dapper and alert Northern black boys in uniform, so different from the slow-moving, soft-spoken Southern Negro.

As she approached the great open doorway Roscoe Bean, looking more than ever like Uriah Heep, slithered out of his cubbyhole under the stairs. "Why Your Ladyship—why Mrs. De Chanfret! You are an early riser indeed! Is your carriage at the door? May I assist you?"

"I am walking to Congress Spring."

"Walking!" His surprise and horror could not have been greater if she had said crawling.

"Certainly. I am in Saratoga for my health. I shall do here as I and everyone else did in Aix-le-Bains, in Vichy, in Evian, in Wiesbaden. No one in Europe would dream of driving to the springs. It is part of the *régime* to walk."

Bean, murmuring at her side, was all deference. "Of course. Naturally. So sensible."

She stood a moment in the doorway, surveying the vast spaces of the piazza. A scattering of portly and rather puffy-eyed men smoking large cigars. A few very settled matrons in the iron embrace of practical morning costumes—sturdy sateens, bison serge, relentless brown canvas, snuffy cashmere, high-necked, long-sleeved. Clio thought, I'd as soon wear a hair shirt for my sins, and done with it.

Well back near the wall in a rocking chair that almost engulfed him sat a little man, thin-chested, meager, with brilliant feverish eyes. With sudden conviction, "That is Mr. Gould, isn't it?" Clio demanded.

"Yes." Bean managed magically to inject awe, admiration and wonder into the monosyllable.

Audaciously she moved toward him, Kaka and Cupide in her

wake, a reluctant Bean deferentially at her side. "I must speak to him. Though perhaps he may not remember me. Perhaps you'd better introduce us."

"Oh, Mrs. De Chanfret! I really——"

But it was too late. Deftly she covered his remonstrance by taking the office from him. "Oh, Mr. Gould, I was just saying to him— uh—to this—I used to hear my dear husband speak of you. I am Mrs. De Chanfret."

He rose, his eyes hostile, his face impassive. "I do not know the name."

Nasty little man, thought Clio. She smiled sweetly. "You will recall him as the Count de Trenaunay de Chanfret, no doubt. Please don't stand. After all, we're all here for our health, aren't we? So charming. So American!" Rather abruptly she moved away toward the street steps. No knowing what a man like that might do, she thought. But I've been seen in conversation with Mr. Jay Gould. All these frumps on the piazza saw it. That should soon be spread about. She dismissed Bean with a soulful smile and a honeyed good day and moved down the street, her attendants in her wake. She looked about her with the liveliest interest. A neat New England town with a veneer of temporary sophistication, like a spinster schoolteacher gone gay. Wall Street tickers in the brokerage branch occupying a little street-floor shop in the United States Hotel; millinery and fancy goods, stationery and groceries in the windows of the two-story brick buildings to catch the fancy of the summer visitor. A spruced-up little town with an air of striving to put its best foot forward, innocently ignorant of the fact that its white-painted houses, its scroll-work Victorian porches, the greenery of lawn and shrub and ancient trees furnished its real charm. Past the Club House, Morrissey's realized dream of splendor, its substantial red-brick front so demure amidst the greenery of Congress Spring Park.

Clio Dulaine was ecstatically aware of a lightness and gayety of spirit and body and mind such as she had never before experienced. She had eaten almost nothing in the past three days. The hot, strong coffee had been a powerful stimulant. Every nerve, artery, muscle and vein had been refreshed by her trancelike sleep. After the clammy and stifling heat of New Orleans the pine-pricked air of Saratoga seemed clear, dry and exhilarating as a bottle of Grand Montrachet. Added to these were youth, ambition and a deadly seriousness of purpose.

Here, in July, were gathered the worst and the best of America. Even if Maroon had not told her she would have sensed this. Here, for three months in the year, was a raffish, provincial and swaggering society; a snobbish, conservative, Victorian society; religious sects meeting in tents; gamblers and race-track habitués swarming in hotels and paddocks and game rooms. Millionaires glutted with grabbing, still reaching out for more; black-satin madams, peroxided and portly, driving the length of Broadway at four in the afternoon, their girls, befeathered and bedizened, clustered about them like overblown flowers. Invalids in search of health; girls in search of husbands. Politicians, speculators, jockeys; dowagers, sporting men, sporting women; middle-class merchants with their plump wives and hopeful daughters; trollops, railroad tycoons, croupiers, thugs: judges, actresses, Western ranchers and cattle men. Prim, bawdy, vulgar, sedate, flashy, substantial. Saratoga.

I knew America would be like this, Clio Dulaine thought, exultantly. Everything into the kettle, like a French *pot-au-feu*. Everything simmering together in a beautiful rich stew. I'm going to have a glorious time. How Aunt Belle Piquery would have loved it, poor darling. She'd have had one of these dried-up millionaires in no time. Well, so shall I, but not in her way. Though I'm more like Aunt Belle, I do believe, than like Mama.

She turned her head to catch Kaka's jaundiced eye and the strutting Cupide's merry look. "It is well," she said, speaking to them in French. "This is going to be very good. I can feel it."

Kaka shrugged, skeptically. "*Peut-être que oui*. Not so fast, my pigeon." But the volatile Cupide whistled between his teeth, slyly, and the tune was Kaka's old Gombo song of "Compair Bouki Et

Macaques"; Compair Bouki who thought to cook the monkeys in the boiling pot and was himself cooked instead.

Sam-bombel! Sam-bombel tam!
Sam-bombel! Sam-bombel dam!

Now there was the sound of music. The band was playing in Congress Spring Park. They turned up the neat walk with its bordering flower-beds of geraniums and petunias and sweet alyssum. There at the spring were the dipper boys, ragamuffins who poked into the spring with their tin cups at the end of a long stick and brought up a dripping dipperful. Kaka had brought her mistress's own fine silver monogrammed cup, holding it primly in front of her as she walked. The little crowd of early-morning walkers and drinkers gaped, nudged, tittered, depending on their station in life. Saratoga's residents, both permanent and transient, were all accustomed to all that was dramatic and bizarre in humanity. But this beautiful and extravagantly dressed young woman with her two fantastic attendants were more than even the sophisticated eye could assimilate. One tended to reject the whole pattern as an optical illusion.

Dipper boys stared, promenaders stared, the band trombone struck a sour note. Clio, enjoying herself, walked serenely on toward the little ornate pavilion with its scrolled woodwork and colored glass windows and its tables and chairs invitingly set forth. Kaka, very stiff and haughty, held out her cup to be filled. Then she turned and marched off to tender the brimming potion, while Cupide, in turn, flipped a penny at the spring boy and strutted on. Strolling thus while Clio seemed to sip and contemplate the scene about her, they circled the little green square three times, and three times the cup was filled. If Clio poured its contents deftly into the shrubbery, no one saw. And now fashion began to arrive. They came in carriages, in dogcarts, on horseback; a few nobodies came afoot, the women's flounced skirts flirting the dusty street.

The crowds began to arrive in swarms. Clio had been waiting for this. She would leave as they came, moving against the incoming tide of morning visitors to the Congress Spring. She did not know these people but she marked them with a shrewd eye. Later she was to learn that it had been the Jefferson Deckers who had dashed up in the magnificent Brewster coach, black, with the yellow running gear, drawn by four handsome bays. The black-haired, black-eyed beauty, partridge-plump, guiding two snow-white horses tandem with white reins, for all the world, Clio thought, like a rider in a circus, could be only Guilia Forosini. The handsome old fellow beside her, with a mane of white hair and the neat white goatee was her father, of course, Forosini, the California banker-millionaire. There came Van Steed. Now he had seen her. The doll-like blonde stopping him now must be the Mrs. Porcelain that Clint wrote about. Where is he? Where is he? Some left their carriages and walked into the park to the spring; others were served at the carriage steps, the grooms or spring boys scampering back and forth with brimming cups.

There he was at last! There was Clint Maroon in the glittering dear familiar clarence with the fleet bays. Now Clio made her leisurely way up the path, her head high, Cupide following, Kaka, stately and rather forbidding, walking, duennalike, almost beside her.

And now she was passing Van Steed. She did not pause, she nodded, her smile was remote, almost impersonal. She felt the light brown eye appraising her—figure, gown, hat, face. Van Steed was not accustomed to being passed thus by any woman. These past two days he had watched for her.

"Mrs. De Chanfret! I heard you were—have you been ill? You haven't been down. I hope——" Van Steed at his shyest.

"Not ill. Weary."

"I can understand that. But you look—uh—you seem quite recovered if appearances are any—uh—that is, Mrs. Porcelain would like to meet you. . . . Mrs. Porcelain . . . Mrs. De Chanfret."

Mrs. Porcelain's was a little soft chirrupy voice with a gurgle in it. "Oh—Mrs. De Chanfret, you must have driven down very early."

"I didn't drive. I walked."

"Walked!"

Van Steed waxed suddenly daring, emboldened as he was by temporary freedom from maternal restraint. "Then you must allow me to drive you back."

"No. No, I'm walking back. There is that fascinating Mr. Maroon. Isn't it? You presented him—remember? And he will ask to drive me back, too. You are all so kind. But I really never heard of driving to a spring when one is taking the waters. I intend to walk down and back every morning, early, as everyone does at the European cures. . . . I must say *au revoir*, now. *Au revoir*, Mrs. Porcelain." She was moving on, then seemed suddenly to recall something, came back a step, held up a chiding forefinger. "*Méchant homme!* It was naughty of you to pretend you didn't know that this Mr. Maroon is a great famous American railroad king, dear Mr. Van Steed. You were having your little joke with me because I have been so long in France. Was that it?"

"Who?"

"That Mr. Maroon. Do you know, that is why I have been so weary until now. All that first night I was unable to sleep. Talk, talk, talk in the next room. Railroads, railroads! I thought I should go mad. I am moving to a cottage apartment this morning. For quiet."

Bart Van Steed's pink cheeks grew pinker, and the amber eyes suddenly widened and then narrowed like a jungle thing scenting prey. Ah, there it is, thought Clio. Those eyes. He isn't such a booby after all.

"Oh, talking railroads, were they? Now what could they say about railroads to keep a charming woman awake?"

"Dear me, I don't know. Such things are too much for me. But they argued and shouted until really I thought I must send one of my servants to protest. Albany and Something or Other—a railroad they were shouting about—and trunk lines—tell me, what is a trunk line?—and—oh, yes, they were talking about you, too, Mr. Van Steed. I even heard Mr. Maroon's voice say that you were smarter than any of them. By that time they really were shouting. I couldn't help hearing it. But maddening it was. No repose. You have such vitality here in America."

"Who? Who was there?"

"Why, how should I know! I know no one in Saratoga. When I was talking with Mr. Gould early this morning on the piazza I thought his voice sounded like the one that was disputing Mr. Maroon. Of course, I don't know. Perhaps I shouldn't have mentioned it. I don't understand such things. I just thought I would twit you with it because you had said he wasn't a friend of yours, teasing me I suppose, and I couldn't help overhearing him say that he was with you, or something like that . . . *Mon Dieu*, have I said anything? You look so troubled. I am so strange here, perhaps I shouldn't have . . . Please don't repeat what I have said. It is so different here in America after . . . Good-by. *Au revoir*." She was thinking, even as she talked, it can't be as simple as this. Now really!

They saw her move on. The eyes over the cups of water followed her as she went, dipping and swooping so gracefully in the flowered cretonne and the great leghorn turned up saucily at one side to reveal the black velvet facing. They saw White Hat Maroon jump down and bow low with a sweep of the sombrero, they saw him motion toward the clarence in invitation; there was no mistaking the negative shake of her head, the appreciative though fleeting smile as she moved on down the street, the Texan staring after her.

"Dear me!" tittered the pink Mrs. Porcelain. "You don't think she's strong-minded, do you? Walking!"

"I admire strong-minded women," declared Bartholomew Van Steed somewhat to his own surprise. "Excuse me. I must speak to Maroon." But Maroon had turned the clarence on one wheel and was even now driving away from Congress Spring toward the United States Hotel. But the spirited bays had been slowed down to a walk. They stepped high and daintily so as not to overpace the woman walking. It was as though the equipage and its occupant were guarding her.

XI

✣

Though for two weeks they ran as fast as they could, feminine Saratoga could never quite catch up with Mrs. De Chanfret. Clio Dulaine's instinct as a showman was sound; and if it had not been for the arrival of old Madam Van Steed, Clio's success might actually have been assured at the end of a fortnight. Certain sly letters of warning must have been dispatched to the matriarch watching over her female progeny in Newport. Torn between fear and duty, she must have convinced herself that while nature, even lacking her supervision, must inevitably pursue its course with her daughter, the enceinte Mrs. Schermerhorn of Newport, it could be thwarted if it threatened her son Bartholomew, weakest of her offspring and the most cherished. "Your dear son," the letters had said, "seems to be really interested in a charming widow, a Mrs. De Chanfret. . . . Bart has at last . . . they say she is the Countess de Trenaunay de Chanfret . . . no one seems to know exactly . . ." Like a lioness scenting danger to her young, Madam Van Steed descended upon Saratoga, claws unsheathed, fangs bared.

But those two weeks before the arrival of the iron woman had been sufficiently dramatic to last Saratoga the season.

You never knew. You never knew what that Mrs. De Chanfret was going to do or wear or say next. By the time they had copied her Marquise Catogan coiffure, she had discarded it for a madonna arrangement, her black hair parted in the middle and drawn down to frame the white face with the great liquid dark eyes. She had attended the first Saturday night hop escorted by that rich Texan Clint Maroon and wearing a breath-taking black satin *merveilleux* trimmed with flounce after flounce of cobweb fine black Chantilly lace as a background for a fabulous *parure* of diamond necklace, bracelets, rings, brooch, earrings. The Mrs. Porcelains, the Guilia Forosinis, the Peabody sisters of Philadelphia, the feminine Lispenards and Rhinelanders and Keenes, the Denards, the Willoughbys appeared at the following Wednesday hop in such panoply of satins, passementerie, galloons and garnitures as to call for a hysterical outburst of verbiage from Miss Sophie Sparkle, the local society correspondent for the New York newspapers. Into this blaze of splendor there entered on the somewhat unsteady arm of Bartholomew Van Steed a slim figure in girlish white china silk, the front of the skirt veiled by two deep flounces of Valenciennes lace, the modest square-cut corsage edged with lace, the sleeves mere puffs like a baby's. A single strand of pearls. Every woman in the room felt overdressed and, somehow, brazen.

Everything she did seemed unconventional because it was unexpected. The women found it most exasperating. The men thought it piquant.

On that first morning at Congress Spring she had returned to the hotel at a serene and leisurely gait and had waved demurely once to the dashing Texan, Clint Maroon, as he kept pace with her in his turnout. Arrived at the hotel, she had again encountered the full battery of the piazza barrage and had crossed the vast lobby to the dining room.

"Oh, no!" she cried at the door of that stupendous cavern. "I couldn't! I could never breakfast here!"

The headwaiter, black, majestic, with the assurance of one who has been patronized by presidents and millionaires and visiting nobility, surveyed the vast acreage of his domain and bestowed a reassuring smile upon his new client.

"No call for you to feel scairt, Madam. Ah'll escort you person-ally to your table."

Startled, she recovered herself and bestowed upon him her most poignant smile. "I so love to breakfast out of doors. It is a European custom. I would so like to have my breakfast out there under the trees in the garden. Or perhaps on the gallery just outside."

"We are not in the habit of serving meals out of doors, Madam. Our dining room is——" But his eye had caught the verdant promise of a crisp bill as her fingers dipped into her purse. "It might be arranged, though, Madam. It might be arranged."

Clio turned her head ever so slightly. "Kaka." Kaka advanced to take charge, fixing the man with her terrible eye. "Kaka, an American breakfast, just this once. Enormous. Everything. *Je meurs de faim.*"

As she turned away she heard Kaka's most scathing tones. "*Canaille!* You know who that was you talking to! La Comtesse de Trenaunay de——"

I could almost believe it myself, Clio thought, strolling toward the garden, Cupide strutting in her wake. "Cupide, run, find Mr. Maroon, tell him I am breakfasting in the garden."

Cupide looked up into her face, all eagerness. "When we go to the stables he promised to teach me roping as they do it in the Wild West. The lariat. He can lasso anything that runs. Like this Z-z-zing!" He swung an imaginary rope round his head and let it fly.

"M-m-m," said Clio absently. Then, "In the garden, while I am having my breakfast. I should like to see that. Tell Colonel Maroon that I should love to see an exhibition of this Wild West roping with the lariat. In the garden."

So the guests of the United States Hotel, breakfasting sedately in the dining room or returning from the springs or emerging from their bedrooms, saw the beautiful Mrs. De Chanfret seated at breakfast on the garden piazza, polishing off what appeared to be a farm-hand meal of ham and eggs and waffles and marmalade and coffee, pausing now and then to applaud the performance evidently in progress for her benefit. On the neat lawn of the garden just below the piazza rail the dashing Texan, Colonel Clint Maroon, was throwing a lariat in the most intricate and expert way, now causing it to whirl round his booted feet, now around his sombreroed head, now unexpectedly snaking it out with a zing and a whining whistle so that it spun round the head of the entranced dwarf who was watching him and bound the little figure's arms to its sides.

"Bravo!" Mrs. De Chanfret would cry from time to time, between bites of hot biscuit topped with strawberry jam. Maroon had supplied the little man with a shorter and lighter rope of his own, and with this he was valiantly striving to follow the wrist twists of his teacher. The front piazza was deserted now. Out of the tail of her eye Clio saw Van Steed's astonished face; the nervous smile of Roscoe Bean as he peered over the shoulder of Hiram Tompkins, the hotel manager. Here was a situation outside the experience of the urbane Bean. He writhed with doubt. Was this good for the United States Hotel? Would the conservative guests object? Breakfast on the veranda! But now they'd all be demanding breakfast on the veranda. Black waiters, white-clad, skimming across the garden, were carrying breakfast trays to the cottage apartments, balancing them miraculously upon their heads in the famous Saratoga manner but threatening now at every step to send their burdens crashing as they gazed, pop-eyed, at the unprecedented goings on in the sedate and cloistral confines of the elm-shaded garden. Now the hotel band was assembling in the stand for the ten o'clock morning concert under the trees. Instinct told Clio that the moment was over. Abruptly she motioned Cupide to her, she rose and leaned a little over the veranda rail, smiling down upon the gallant Maroon who now stood, hat in hand, idly twirling his lariat as he received her praises. "Oh, Colonel Maroon. Brilliant! As good as a circus."

Very low, without moving her lips, she was saying, swiftly, *Moving into the cottages, chéri. I think it is better. I must talk to you. Van Steed.*

"Will you honor me by driving to the races with me, Ma'am, at eleven!"

"I shall be delighted." *Go quickly. Before he can talk to you. I'll tell you then.*

She turned to encounter a stout, plain woman in dowdy black standing directly in her path. Fiftyish. Formidable. "Mrs. De Chanfret!" she boomed. "I am Mrs. Coventry Bellop." Remarkably beautiful eyes in that plain dumpling of a face. Gray eyes, purposeful, lively, penetrating. *En garde!* Clio thought.

"Ah, yes?" With the raising inflection indicating just the proper degree of well-bred surprise at being thus accosted by a stranger.

"I want to welcome you to Saratoga."

"So kind." Coolly.

"And to tell you that I had the great pleasure of knowing your late departed husband. Dear, dear Bimbi!"

The polite smile stiffened a little on Clio's face, but she was equal to the occasion. "Is it possible!"

Clio was aghast to see Mrs. Coventry Bellop close one lively eye in a portentous wink. "Well, isn't it?"

"Hardly. He was almost a recluse. Perhaps you are thinking of his younger brother the—the black sheep, I'm afraid. I believe he was known as—uh—Bimbi among his friends."

To her relief Mrs. Coventry Bellop now patted her smartly on the shoulder. "I shouldn't wonder. If you say so. Well, let me know if I can be of any—assistance. I really run Saratoga, you know," she boomed. "Though old lady Van Steed thinks she does."

"Indeed!" Vaguely.

"You'll soon be in a position to judge, I should say." With which astonishing prediction Mrs. Coventry Bellop again patted her arm and waddled off with surprising lightness and agility for one of her proportions.

Escorted by the ubiquitous Bean to her new quarters in the cottage section, Clio graciously expressed herself as pleased as she looked about the cool veranda-shaded apartment. It boasted its own outer

entrance and hallway, its row of bells meant to summon chambermaid, waiter, valet (none of which functioned and none of which she
needed, luckily, what with Kakaracou and Cupidon), its own cryptlike
bathroom, a grim little sitting room, a black walnut bedroom. The
garden greenery could be glimpsed just beyond the veranda.

"Now then," Clio announced, briskly, as she looked about her
after Bean's departure. "This is more like it. Privacy. Here, Cupide!
Take this note to Mr. Maroon quickly. Kaka, I can't go to the races in
flowered cretonne. I think the almond-shell *poult-de-soie*. The straw
bonnet with the velvet ruche and the flower melange. My scarlet
embroidered parasol for color. Brown silk stockings, brown shoes."

"M'm. *Chic,* that," Kaka murmured in approval. "I am happy to
see the widow now vanishes."

"While I am at the races unpack the scarves and shawls and ornaments. The clock put there on the mantel. The photographs on the
table and the desk. The ornaments the *bibelots*—those I'll place
about when I return. There will be fresh flowers sent by Mr. Van Steed
and Mr. Maroon from the hotel florist. At least there should be. What
horrible furniture! But it won't be so bad and it won't be so long—I
hope. Though I like it, on the whole. Here I can receive—guests.
With no maids poking about in the halls."

Kaka sniffed maddeningly. "High-heeled Texas boots make a
great deal of noise on a wooden veranda floor."

"Oh, you old crow! Always croaking, croaking. A bundle of
dried sticks! I tell you I like it here in Saratoga. I feel gay and young
and light for the first time in my life."

Panic distorted Kaka's face. "Don't say it! The *Zumbi* will hear
and be displeased. Here, quick! Touch the *gris-gris.*" She groped in
her bosom and pulled out an amulet on a bit of string that hung
around her scrawny neck. She snatched up Clio's hand and forcibly
rubbed her fingers over the dingy charm, muttering as she did so.

Clio slapped the woman's hand smartly. "Stop it, you witch! I'll
send you back to New Orleans; you'll live there in a wretched hovel
the rest of your life."

"*Laissez-donc!* You know I speak the truth." She thrust the gris-gris back into her bosom and went equally on fastening her mistress's smart little brown shoes.

Cupide poked his head in at the door. "He's at the curb with the carriage. What do you think! It's a new one to surprise you!" His voice rose to a squeal. "It's a four-in-hand! Everyone's out to see it. Two bays and two blacks, and a regular coach to match, black with red wheels. And the harness trimmed with silver!" Unable to contain himself, he flung open the door that led to the veranda, and the next instant the two women saw the impish figure in its maroon livery turning an exultant series of handsprings past the veranda window.

Escorted by Cupidon, Clio was horrified to see, as she reached the street doorway, that the situation she had schemed to avoid had taken place. There at the curb was the splendid coach and four, like something out of a fairy tale. There in the driver's seat in a white driving coat, fawn vest, fawn trousers and the now-famous white sombrero, was Clint Maroon, his expert hands holding the ribbons over the backs of the four horses whose satin-smooth coats glistened in the sun. Looking up at him, deep in earnest conversation, one foot on the step, was Bart Van Steed.

"*Dieu!*" exclaimed Clio, aloud; skimmed across the piazza and down the steps at such speed that Cupide, having opened the scarlet parasol, was a frantic little figure pattering after her, his tiny arm stretched full length to hold the parasol high.

Her quick ear caught the Texan's words as she came toward them. From his vantage, perched on the driver's seat, he had seen her approach. Van Steed's back was toward her.

". . . Texas is a young state run by young men. You Easterners take no account of Texas. That's where you make a mistake."

"Oh, Mr. Maroon! I do hope I haven't kept you waiting!" Van Steed spun on his heel. His pink cheeks flushed pinker, "What a glorious coach! And four—— Oh, Mr. Van Steed. Oh, dear! You haven't repeated my indiscreet conversation!" She put her palm prettily to her cheek as though she, too, were blushing, which she wasn't.

His girlish skin now took on a definite rose tint as he handed her up to the seat beside Maroon and Cupide proffered her the crimson parasol. There was something anguished in the amber eyes of young Van Steed as from his position at the curb he looked up at these two resplendent figures, young, seemingly carefree, certainly beautiful. Clio's crimson sunshade cast a roseate glow over them both. It was as if these two dwelt aloft in a glowing world of their own.

She leaned a little toward him over the wheel, her lovely ardent eyes meeting his. "I didn't thank you for the roses. That Mrs. Crockery was with you . . . no, that's not right . . . Porcelain . . . Porcelain, that's it . . . so stupid of me . . . she's really charming . . . may I, an utter stranger, offer you my congratulations . . . I hear you are to be married . . . Mrs. Porcelain . . . really enchanting . . ."

"Married!" His voice was a shout. Then he remembered the piazza and repeated, "Married!" in a voice that rose to a squeak vibrant with outrage. "Mrs. De Chanfret, whoever told you that is a liar!"

Clint Maroon's drawl cast its cooling shadow upon the heated words. "Why, Mrs. De Chanfret, Ma'am, you-all certainly are putting your pretty little foot in it today. First you tell this gentleman here that I'm out to get his railroad off him——"

"Oh, then he did tell you that! How naughty of you, Mr. Van Steed. Especially as I said that Colonel Maroon admired——"

"Shucks, he didn't rightly say that, no. It was this way. I told this little runt of yours to go fetch you my message I was waiting. He says you've moved to the cottages. It's natural I'd be surprised, being as I'd given up my rooms—not that that matters, Ma'am, I'm glad to be of service—but when I remarked how come you went and did that, why, friend Van Steed here speaks up and says it's because I and my friends raised such a holler up there last night talking railroads. Seems he got the idea I was fixing to skin him out of his millions, or some such sorry trick."

Her lips quivered. There were tears in her eyes. She looked at

Maroon, she turned her stricken glance down upon Van Steed's upturned face.

"How dreadful! How really frightful. How could I be so clumsy. Dear Mr. Maroon! Dear Mr. Van Steed! After you've both been so kind, so helpful to a weary stranger. To have made trouble between you! How can I make amends!"

"Married!" Van Steed was still quivering. "I must ask you, Mrs. De Chanfret, to tell me who gave you that piece of complete misinformation." So that's stabbed him deepest, Clio thought. Poor little man.

"I don't know. Really! I've talked to so many people. I'm all confused and oh, so unhappy. It may have been Mr. Gould, it may have been the chambermaid—or Mrs. Coventry Bellop—or the hotel manager—or perhaps Cupide picked it up from the bellboys—yes, now that I recall it, I seem to remember it was you, wasn't it, Cupide?"

The dwarf poured out his protest in a flood of colloquial French that was, fortunately, completely unintelligible to all but Clio. Much of it was highly uncomplimentary to Mr. Van Steed, to Saratoga, and to the human race in general.

"En voilá assez!" She was all concern as she bent toward the injured Van Steed. "He swears it wasn't he. But I'm quite certain now. Please forgive me." She turned to Maroon. "And you, too. How could I be so tiresome!"

Maroon laughed an easy laugh, his warm gaze upon her. "Why, Ma'am, just to know you've had my name on your lips gives me pleasure. And I'm not denying I'm interested in railroads. And if I didn't feel the way I do about Mr. Van Steed here, and his road we were talking about, why I'd say leave him roar. But I'm for you, Mr. Van Steed. Not against you. There ain't any call for you to be wrathy. I happen to know something of the fix you're in. Down in Texas we'd know what to do, but maybe we're too rough for you Eastern folks. Leastways, for folks like you." He gathered up the reins. The horses were stamping restlessly, the silver harness jingled, the piazza by now resembled a group of statuary frozen into vain attitudes of strained attention. "But I know what I'd do in your place."

Bart Van Steed did not take his foot off the carriage step.

"Just what would you do, Colonel Maroon! I'd be interested to know."

"I'll bet you would. Well, sir, that's something to talk about sometime, friendly, over a cigar. It might be worth nothing to you; it might be worth a million." He leaned over so that his shoulder pressed against Clio, he lowered his voice confidentially. "I might as well tell you I'd go the whole hog to put my brand on a certain crowd—and a certain man in that crowd. If I ever aim to get tangled with that bunch, look out! I been studying railroads a good many years now——" He broke off suddenly. "Shucks! This here's no place to talk business. With this little lady looking like a thoroughbred rarin' for the races. Well, we'll be easin' along."

It was plain the conversation was ended. Curious that Van Steed had been the suppliant, there at the curb, and Clint Maroon a splendid figure with his lady beside him high up on the glittering coach. Van Steed's face, upturned, was almost wistful. Reluctantly he took his foot from the step. The reins became taut in Maroon's gloved hands.

"Ma'm'selle!" came Cupide's voice from the curb. "Ma'm'selle Clio! You're not going without me! Ma'm'selle!" His voice rose to a squeal of anguish. He held up his two little arms like a child.

"Let him come, Clint," she said, very low.

Maroon beckoned with a jerk of his head. Like a fly blown by the wind the dwarf soared up the side of the coach, perched on the edge of the rear seat.

"*Ne bougez pas de là,*" Clio commanded. But she could have saved her breath. His arms folded across his chest, his head held high, he was the footman in livery, a statue in little. Only the fine eyes danced as he watched the movements of the splendid horses and heard the music of their fleet hoofs accompanied by the clink of the silver-mounted harness. The coach and four dashed down Broadway on its way to the races.

Clio gave a little childish bounce of delight. "Clint, I am so happy. Forgive me for behaving so badly the day I came." He did not reply. She turned to look into his face. It was stern and unsmiling. "Clint! *Chéri!*"

Still he said nothing. They whirled among the sun-dappled streets. His eyes were on the horses. She put a hand on his arm. She shook it a little, pettishly. The off lead horse broke a trifle in his stride, regained it immediately.

"Take your hand off my arm," Maroon said between his teeth. "What d'you reckon I'm driving—cattle!"

"How can you talk to me like that? No one has ever talked to me like that!"

"Time they did, then. You've been high-tailing it about long enough."

"What is that?"

"Back in Texas the menfolks run things. You've been living with a bunch of women so long it's like a herd of mares think they can run a stallion right off the range. I've got every reverence for womenkind. There'll never be anybody like Ma. And there's others back home——"

"Like the finest little woman in the world," she put in, mischievously.

"That's so. My way of thinking, women should have minds of their own and plenty of spirit. But back in Texas it's the men who wear the pants. Looks like you listened to so much poison talk back there in Paris on account of your ma and your aunty, they figured they'd been done wrong by, why, you've taken on a kind of sneery feeling about menfolks. You got 'em all scaled down to about the size of that poor little fellow perched up back there. Well, you're dead wrong."

"What have I done! What have I said?"

"I'm aimin' to tell you. I'm crazy about you, honey, but I reckon you'd best know that if you try to run me I'll leave you, pronto. I don't mean your pretty little ways, and thinking of things that are smart as all get-out, and trying 'em to see if they work. That's all fair enough."

"But Clint, we said this was to be a partnership."

"That's right. But that don't say you can put words in my mouth I never said. I'm just naturally ornery enough not to want to be stampeded into doing something I didn't aim to do. I can be nagged by women and I can be fooled by women and I can be coaxed by women, but no woman's going to run me, by God! Now you pin back those pretty little ears of yours and take heed of what I'm saying. I'm boss of this outfit or I'll drag it out of here and drag it quick. You heard me."

If he had anticipated tears and protestations he was happily disappointed. Like all domineering women she wanted, more than anything in the world, to be dominated by someone stronger than she. Now, at her silence, he turned his gaze from the road ahead to steal a glance at her. She was regarding him with such shining adoration as to cause him to forget road, coach, four-in-hand. *"Chéri,"* she said in her most melting tones; and then, in English, as though the French word could not convey her emotion, "Darling! Darling! Darling!"

"Attention!" screamed Cupide from the back seat. *"Nom d'un——"*

Almost automatically Maroon swerved the animals to the right, missing by a fraction of an inch a smart dogcart whose occupants' faces were two white discs of fright as the coach swept by.

"Hell's bells!" yelled Maroon. But the danger seemed to restore his customary good humor. "See what you do to me, honey? Good thing you coaxed me to let Cupide come along. Don't look at me like that when I've got a parcel of horses on my hands or we're liable to end in the ditch."

"With you I'm never afraid."

"Uh-huh."

"Tell me, Clint, have you really a plan, as you said to Van Steed? I mean, really?"

"Well, not to say rightly a plan. Anyway, nothing he'd hear to. I don't want to get mixed in with that crowd. Look, Clio. I came up here to Saratoga to get myself a little honest money—cards, roulette, horses and so forth. I figured we'd have a high old time, clean up and get out. New York, maybe, September, though it's not my meat. But here you are, starting trouble, cutting up didoes, acting downright locoed."

"What have I done! I arrived only a day—two days——"

"And then what! Screeching out of hotel windows, champagne and peaches in the middle of the day, sleeping like drugged straight through for better than thirty hours, sashaying over to the cottages after all that hocus-pocus about the rooms, and now telling the doggonedest mess of lies—excuse me, honey, I didn't go for to sound mean-tempered, but you going to keep this up?"

"Oh, yes. I've thought of the most wonderful things. It's going to be better and better all the time."

He regarded with great concentration the glistening haunches of the four fine horses speeding so fleetly under his expert guidance. But it was plain that his horse-loving mind was not really on them. "Well—uh—now countesses, they don't carry on thataway, do they? I mean, for a girl that's up to the tricks you are, why, you sure are getting yourself noticed."

"That's my Paris background, I suppose. It's the Aunt Belle in me. We never went out in Paris that people didn't stare and even follow us. I'm used to it."

"It don't make good sense to me."

Out of her murky past she waxed sententious beyond her years. "The only people who can afford to go unnoticed and quiet are the very very rich and secure and the really wicked. No one would know I was here if I didn't make a great furore. *Faire le diable à quatre*. It was a success in New Orleans, wasn't it? My little technique?"

He laughed tolerantly at the memory of her recent triumph.

"Yes, those sure were cute didoes you cut down there. But this is different. I didn't mind—much. But you don't figure on catching a husband any such way, do you? Leastways, not Van Steed. He was brought up prim and proper."

Into her voice there came a hard determination. "He was brought up by a woman who was stronger and harder and more possessive than he. His mother. Well, I'll be stronger and harder and more possessive than she. And cleverer. You wait. You'll see."

"Uh-huh," he said again.

Pleased with herself she smoothed the shining folds of her silken gown, she looked down at the glittering coach, at the four superb horses, at the silver harness. She just touched his knee with one gloved forefinger. "This is rather wonderful. I feel like Cinderella. You haven't told me how you came by this splendid coach and four. How Aunt Belle and Mama would have adored it!"

"Right nice little poker game at the Club House night before last," he explained, laconically. "I was kind of put out when you went off into the Sleeping Beauty act of yours, so I figured I might as well get me a little extra change. Nothing better to do with my time. Ever since then I've been real worried about your friend Bart Van Steed."

"You have! Why?"

"You know that old saying. And he sure is unlucky at cards."

Now she looked at the coach and four with fresh appreciation and with a kind of proprietary approval, as though she had earned it. They were passing the stables now. With his whip he pointed to one. "Alamo's in there. We'll go down to the stables tomorrow morning and see him."

"And breakfast at the stables?"

"I don't know about that. Women don't do that. Men go down there and eat, early mornings, six seven o'clock. But no women."

"I'm going. I don't care what other women do. I'm different."

"You are. You sure are. That's what——" He stopped.

"What's what?" she asked mischievously. But he did not go on, and they swept dramatically into the race-track enclosure, the most spectacular coach among all the glittering vehicles gathered there. Down jumped Cupide and scurried round and stood at the near lead horse's head, his hand on the bridle rein; and at sight of this diminutive figure pitted against the huge equipage and the four fiery horses, the staring crowd burst into laughter; a voice shouted, "Hold 'em, Goliath!" Another yelled, "Look out they don't eat you for a fly." But Cupidon spat between his teeth, taking careful aim, and his deriders were seen to wipe their faces hastily.

"We can watch the races from up here," Maroon said. "Only I reckoned maybe you'd like to stroll around some. Cupide can't hold these critters, though."

"He's got the strength of an orang-utan in his arms. All his life he has been around horses."

Maroon looked dubious as he stepped down. "I don't know about that. Up on that box." He walked over to Cupide and stared down on him. "You sitting up there I'm afraid if they took a notion to pull a little, why, you'd be over the dashboard and landed on one of their ears."

The impish face peered up at him wickedly. "If I wanted to I could lift you off your feet where you stand, and carry you."

Maroon backed away, hastily. "God A'mighty, don't do that! All right, get up there on the seat. Anybody starts monkeying with the horses, scaring 'em, give him a cut with the whip. We'll be back, anyway, in two shakes."

There they all were—the Rhinelanders, the Forosinis, the Vanderbilts, the Lorillards, the Chisholms, Mrs. Porcelain. Mrs. Coventry Bellop, looking more than ever like a cook, was squired by three young dandies who seemed to find her conversation vastly edifying, judging by their bursts of laughter. No sign anywhere of that meager figure, those burning eyes.

"They're all here except Mr. Gould. Doesn't he care for races?"

"Gould, he doesn't care for anything that's fixed as easy as a horse race. He's been playing with millions and whole railroads and telegraph companies and hundreds of thousands of human beings and foreign empires so long he wouldn't get any feeling about whether a horse came in first or not. Do you know what he does for a pastime? Grows orchids out at his place in the country. Nope, you can't figure him out the way you can other people. Or get the best of him."

"There is a way," Clio persisted; "a very simple way. We will find it. No big thing. Something childish."

"I just like to hear you talk, honey. I don't care what you say."

"You will listen, though, won't you? And if we have a plan you will help? You promised."

"Why, sure thing. Fact is, I have got an idea, like I said to Van Steed. Don't know's it's any good, though. It came to me while I was talking to him. I was so riled at the way you'd gone and mixed me up with him that it came into my head, just like that."

"Listen, chéri, we won't stay here long at the races. There are other things to talk about much more exciting than this. Are you going to enter Alamo sometime soon?"

"He hasn't got much of a chance in this field. He's a little too young, anyway. And I haven't got a jockey I just like."

"Cupide will ride him."

"You're crazy."

"I say he can. He can ride anything. In France he used to be always around the stables; they called him their mascot at Longchamp and Auteuil; they let him exercise the horses at the tracks. He used to run off and be gone for days. Mama was always threatening to send him back to America. It would be chic to enter your horse; it would look successful and solid. Cupide knows a hundred ways, if Alamo is good and has a chance. Cupide would get something from Kaka; he would give the other horse something; no one would suspect it."

"Holy snakes!" Maroon glanced quickly around in horror. "If anybody hears you say a thing like that! We'd be run out of town on a rail."

"Pooh! These piazza millionaires they cheat and rob and kill people, even. You've said so yourself."

"That's different. If you steal five millions and a railroad, that's high finance. But if you cheat on a horse race, that's worse than murder."

"I just thought you'd like to win. And you said Alamo wasn't very good yet. Why did you have him sent up here then?"

"Because. A hundred reasons. God A'mighty, women are the most immoral people there is. Don't seem to know right from wrong."

"Such a fuss about a horse race."

"Look, Clio, be like you were in New Orleans that first month, will you?"

"But how is that possible, Clint? I am at least ten years older since then."

"Let's be young again, just for now. Let's quit figuring and contriving. Here it is, midday, middle of the summer. Look at that pretty little race track! Even if you had you your million right now what could you get with it you haven't got this minute?"

Half-past eleven in the morning. Saratoga managed somehow to assemble its sporting blood at this matutinal hour. Even rakish New Yorkers whose lives were adjusted to a schedule in which night ended at noon were certain to appear at the Saratoga track by eleven, haggard perhaps, and not quite free of last night's fumes, but bravely armed with field-glasses, pencil, and strong black cigars. Even those imported flowers of the frailer species arrived in wilted clusters, buttressed by their stout black-satin madams and looking slightly ocherous in spite of the layers of rouge and rice powder.

Against the background of elms and pungent pines, richly green, the little track lay like a prim nosegay with its pinks and blues and heliotropes and scarlet of parasols and millinery.

Descended from their gaudy coach, Clint and Clio prepared to take their places, but not before a stroll in the paddock so that Clint could inspect the horses and the feminine world could inspect Clio's Paris *poult-de-soie* glowing under the rosy shade of the scarlet embroidered parasol.

Smiling, exquisite, seeming to glance neither to right nor left,

Clio saw everything, everyone. "Who's that?" she said again and again, low-voiced, and she pinched Clint's arm a sharp little tweak to take his attention from the horses. "Who's that? Who's that? Why are they standing around that stout, homely little peasant? There, with the red face."

"Because that's Willie Vanderbilt, that's why."

"That! *Dieu!* That clod is a millionaire!"

"Only about a hundred and fifty million, that's all."

"But he looks wretched!"

"Sure does. They call him Public-Be-Damned Vanderbilt on account of what he said. They hate him. He's scared of his life. I bet he wishes he could have stayed there on Staten Island, farming, and hauling scows full of manure across the bay from the old Commodore's stables. He and Gould, they're dead enemies. In Texas they'd be shooting it out. Here they just try to steal each other's railroads."

"I'm almost sorry that I must marry a millionaire. They are so unattractive."

"You can't have everything, honey. Little Van Steed isn't so bad looking," he observed, with irritating tolerance. "Get him to grow a beard, now, hide that place where his chin ought to be, why——"

She pinched his arm now, in sheer spitefulness. Leisurely, they strolled toward the grandstand. Suddenly there was a tug at Clio's skirt. She turned quickly, but she knew even before she turned that she would see the goggle-eyed Cupide looking up at her. His voice was a whisper.

"Ma'm'selle, bet on Mavourneen in the third. Everything. Fixed. *Mais soyez sur de là.* Tell to Monsieur Clint."

"Heh! What the hell you doing away from those horses! Who——"

But the little man had darted off, was lost in the crowd.

"It's all right," Clio assured him placidly. "He would not neglect them. He has someone watching them, be sure of that. He has found valuable information, little Cupide. How much money have you?

Here is my purse. In the third—Mavourneen—everything. He has ways of knowing, that *diablotin*. He has just now found out."

Together they walked to their places, a thousand eyes followed them. Curiously enough, aside from Clio the most distinguished feminine figure to be peered at by the crowd was not that of the beflowered Mrs. Porcelain or the overdramatic Guilia Forosini but the stout black-clad Mrs. Coventry Bellop, whose rollicking laugh boomed out as she chatted and joked with her three attendant swains.

"She is good company, that one," Clio observed to Clint, very low. She was shutting her rosy parasol and adjusting her draperies as she looked about her languidly. "I've seen her sort in France, she is like one of those fat, mustached old women who sell fruit in the Paris market—tough and gay and impudent and full of good bread and soup. I like her, that one."

The first race was about to start. Suddenly, above the buzz of voices in the grandstand there could be heard the booming chest tones of Mrs. Bellop calling, "Countess! Countess!"

"She means you, Clio," said Clint out of the corner of his mouth. "The old trollop!"

"Countess!"

Clio turned her head ever so slightly. Sophie Bellop's ugly, broad face was grinning cheerily down at her. "Are you betting, Countess? You look to me like somebody who'd be lucky at picking winners."

"I am," said Clio, very quietly, just forming the words with her lips. Smiled her slow, sad smile for the benefit of the crowd and turned back to Maroon. "I think she means me well, that cow. I feel her friendly."

"I wouldn't give you a plugged nickel for any of 'em," Clint observed, morosely.

"Oh, come now, *chéri*. How could she harm me, that one?"

"She runs this place, I tell you."

"All the more reason, then. She took care to call me Countess though she surely knows——"

"She's after something. When an old coyote comes prowling around the chicken roost it ain't because she's friendly to the hens."

"Clint, Clint! You are suspicious of everyone. You probably are suspicious of me, even."

"No, sugar, I'm not suspicious of you. I'm dead sure of you. I know you're crooked, so I don't have to worry none."

Her lovely leisurely laugh rang out.

It was just after the second race that she said, "Your pencil," as Clint was leaving to place his bet and hers. "I want to write a note."

"Don't be foolish," he said.

"Wait a moment. I will go with you. Look, there is Van Steed arriving. How hot and cross he looks. There, the little Porcelain is happy; see how she grows all pink, like a milkmaid; and the one you tell me is the Forosini she shows all her teeth with happy hunger. Let us place our bet and go."

"Now!"

"After this race. Let us watch it from the carriage, standing. This grows a little tiresome, don't you think? After all, I know that one horse can run faster than another."

She scrawled one word in her childish hand on a scrap of paper, she folded it tight and cocked one corner. As they rose to leave she tossed it swiftly and accurately into Sophie Bellop's capacious lap. As that surprised face looked up at her, Clio put a finger to her lips, the ageless gesture of caution and secrecy. They had scarcely regained the carriage when they saw the stout black-clad figure rushing toward the window.

"Did you tell her Mavourneen?"

"Yes."

"Kind of foolish, weren't you? It's all right us throwing away a few hundred dollars on a chance. But what does that little imp know!"

"He doesn't always know. Only sometimes. But when he says he knows, like today, then you can be sure. He has ways, that little one."

"What kind of ways?"

"Never mind. You will see Mavourneen come in. And we shall

leave here, and the Bellop will tell everyone she has won. There will be great *réclame*. And we will have—how much will we have in our pockets?"

"Thousand, maybe. I don't know's I like it, myself. I—there they are. Wait a minute. Here, take the glasses. That one. Seven. Green and white."

"M'm. Seven is lucky for me. And I adore green. But I think I must be like this Mr. Gould and even that little stubborn Van Steed. I would find it more exciting to gamble with railroads and millions and people and the law than with horses running. You see, I am by nature mercenary. How lucky for you that we are not serious, you and I."

"Yeh," said Maroon. "I'd just as soon take up steady with a rattlesnake." But his tone was hollow.

XII

✶

By the end of that first week the women had their knives out. A prick here, a prick there, the ladies of Saratoga's summer society were intent on drawing blood from their thrusts at the spectacular, the unpredictable Mrs. De Chanfret. But as yet they had been no match for her. She parried every thrust, she disarmed them by her sheer audacity. She was having a superb time, she was squired by the two most dashing bachelors in Saratoga. If she went to the races with Clint Maroon in the morning, then she drove to the lake with Van Steed in the afternoon. Occasionally she vanished for twenty-four hours. Resting. Madame is resting, Kakaracou said, barring the cottage suite doorway with her neat black silk, her stony white-fichued bosom, her basilisk eye. Bart Van Steed stood at the door; he actually found himself arguing with the woman.

"But Mrs. De Chanfret was going to have dinner with me at Moon's Lake House. I've ordered the dinner, exactly as she wanted it. Lobster shipped down specially from Maine." As though the mention of this dish could somehow bring her out of her retirement.

"Madame is very sorry." Kaka was being very grand. "Madame Le Com—Madame De Chanfret is fatigued. She asked me to tell you she is *désolée* she cannot go. Madame De Chanfret is resting today."

No one had ever before done a thing like this to the most eligible bachelor in New York—in the Western Hemisphere. He was piqued, bewildered, angered, bewitched.

When later he reproached her she said, "You are angry. *Vous avez raison.* You will never again ask me to dine with you."

"You know that isn't true."

"After all, why should you bother about a poor weary widow about whom you know nothing? I may be an adventuress for all you know. And there are such lovely creatures just longing for a word with you—that pretty little Porcelain, and that big handsome Forosini with the rolling dark eyes, and those really sweet little McAllister sisters. And Mr. Maroon tells me that there has come to town a new little beauty, Nellie Leonard. He says she is escorted by a person called Diamond Jim Brady. What a freshness of language you have here in America! But surely a man like that would have no chance if you happened to fancy this pretty little Leonard."

"Thank you." He was stammering with rage. The amber eyes were like a cat's, the pink cheeks were curiously white. "I am quite capable of selecting my own company. You needn't dictate to me the company I may or may not keep. It's bad enough that my mother——" He stopped, horrified at what he had almost said.

Instinct told her the right thing to do. As though to hide her hurt, she lowered her eyelids a moment in silence; the long lashes were dewy when she raised them.

"Why will you misunderstand me! You are so strong and powerful. I have known such unhappiness in my marriage—I mean, you have been from the first so kind when you rescued me at the station—I only want you to be happy. Forgive me if I seemed presumptuous and managing. Women are like that, you know, with men they—they admire and respect. Especially women who have known misfortune, perhaps, in—in love."

Mollified, bewildered, but still sulky, he floundered deeper in confusion. "But suppose I don't like the kind of women you keep throwing at my head! You and my mother."

"Do you think of me as of your mother, dear Mr. Van Steed!

Oh, that is sweet of you. But though I have seen so much of the world I am, after all, young and sympathetic and at least I hope——" She faltered, stopped.

In desperation he almost shouted, "I always seem to say the wrong thing to you."

"But no, no. It is I who am clumsy—*sans savoir faire*. You must help me to do and say the right thing. Will you?"

He sent flowers, remorsefully. Mounds of them.

Kaka, divesting these chaste offerings of their tissue-paper wrappings, surveyed them with a jaundiced eye. "Flowers! Posies!" Her tone should have withered them on their stems. "That's a Northerner for you! Your mama, gentlemen just see her riding out in her carriage would send her jewelry. You say he got money—this little pink man?"

"Millions. Millions and millions and millions!"

"Why'n't he send you jewelry gifts, then? Diamonds and big stone necklace and ruby rings like your mama got."

"Because I'm a respectable widow, that's why. To take jewelry from a man who isn't your husband, that is not *convenable*."

"Your aunt Belle was a widow. She never had a husband no more than you. But she got jewelry. She never had to put up with no flowers."

Clio regaled Clint with this bit of conversation; she gave a superb imitation of the black woman's disdain for mere roses; she enjoyed her performance as much as he. The two conspirators, at ease with one another, went into gales of laughter.

He said, ruefully, "You haven't had any jewelry off of me, either. I sure would like to load you with it, honey. You can have my diamond stud, and welcome, if you'll take it."

"Clint! I'm ashamed of you. Where is your loyalty! You know that diamond is for the ring when you marry the little blonde Texas beauty—the finest little woman in the world."

Morosely he retorted, "Some day you'll be play-acting yourself right out of Saratoga if you don't watch out."

"No," she said, "I was quite wonderful with Van Steed. Real

tears. I must make him think he is strong and masterful. He must feel he is deciding everything. You know, it's a great strain, this pretending. Mama never had to pretend. She was actually like that. Languid and lovely and sort of looking up at one with those eyes. I try to be like that—when I think of it."

"You're really a strong-minded female, honey. No use your soft-soaping and fluttering around. You wouldn't fool any man."

She flared at that. "I never bothered to try to fool you."

"Yessir, Countess," he drawled, "that's right. I reckon I just wasn't worth fretting about, that day in the French Market."

"*Touché,*" she laughed, good-naturedly.

Sometimes even she found it difficult to tell when she was herself and when she was the mysterious Mrs. De Chanfret. Perhaps no one enjoyed her performance more than she. Frequently she actually convinced herself of her own assumed role. In a way she enjoyed everything—even the things she disliked.

She regarded the vast dining room with a mingling of amusement and horror; rarely entered it. The crowd, the clatter, the rush, the heavy smells of too-profuse food repelled her. When she did choose to dine there it always was late, when the hordes were almost finished. She kept her table, she selected special dishes ordered ahead by Kakaracou, she tipped well but not so lavishly as to cause the waiters to disrespect her judgment. She refused to countenance the heavy midday dinner.

"Barbaric! All that rich food in the middle of the day. I dine at night."

Her cottage apartment was situated on the other side of the U-shaped wing. She frequently dined or lunched in her own sitting room. You saw the black waiters in stiffly starched white skimming across the garden, mounting the wooden steps, racing along the veranda toward her apartment, their laden trays miraculously balanced atop their heads. The dining-room meals were stupendous; the United States Hotel guests stuffed themselves with a dozen courses to the meal, for everything was included in the American plan. Clio fancied the specially prepared delicacies for which the outlying inns and restaurants were famous. There she grew ecstatic over savory American dishes, new to a palate trained to the French cuisine.

"I never saw a woman enjoy her vittles more than you do," Clint Maroon said admiringly, as she started on her third ear of hot corn on the cob, cooked in the husk and now dripping with butter.

"Mama said always that the only decent food in America was to be found in New Orleans. Of course the food at the hotel is—you know—no imagination. And cooked in such quantities, as for an army. How can food be properly cooked that way! Naturally not. But here it's delicious—all these American dishes, what a pity they don't know of them in France. In France, they think Americans live on buffalo meat and flapjacks."

Woodcock, reed birds, brook trout, black bass, red raspberries at Riley's. Steak, corn on the cob, at Crum's.

Maroon said, "I get to where I can't look at all that fancy fodder at the hotel. I just want to wrassle with a good thick T-bone steak." The two enjoyed food and understood it. They would taste a dish in silence, let the flavor send its message to the palate, then they would solemnly look at one another across the table and nod.

"Ma, coming from Virginia, she fancied her food. I reckon that's how I came to be a kind of finicky feeder. Ma, she used to say she didn't trust people who said they didn't care about what they ate. Said there was something wrong with them. Texas, though, it isn't a good-feeding state. Everything into the frying skillet."

It was at Moon's that Clio first tasted the famous Saratoga chips, said to have originated there, and it was she who first scandalized spa society by strolling along Broadway and about the paddock at the race track crunching the crisp circlets out of a paper sack as though they were candy or peanuts. She made it the fashion, and soon you saw all Saratoga dipping into cornucopias filled with golden-brown paper-thin potatoes; a gathered crowd was likely to create a sound like a scuffling through dried autumn leaves.

Concluding a dinner with Maroon, she was conscious of her

Not present

tight stays. In contrast, dining with the dyspeptic Van Steed was definitely lacking in gusto. The De Chanfret veneer frequently cracked here and there so that Belle Piquery, Rita Dulaine and the hotblooded Nicolas showed through to the most casual observer. But in Saratoga it was, for the most part, put down to the forgivable idiosyncrasies of the titled and the foreign.

The first time she lighted a cigarette in public the piazza shook to the topmost capital of its columns. A woman who smoked! But even fast women didn't smoke in public. She had lighted a tiny white cylinder one evening strolling in the hotel garden under the rosy light of the gay Japanese lanterns. It was just before the nine o'clock hop. She was accompanied by the timorous Van Steed and she was looking her most bewitching in a short Spanish jacket over a tight basque, a full skirt of flowered silk with a sash draped to the side and caught with a tremendous bow.

Van Steed had watched her with dazed unbelief that grew to consternation as she extracted the cigarette from a tiny diamond-studded case which she took from her flowered silk bag, tapped it daintily and expertly, placed it between her lips and motioned him wordlessly for a light. He struck a match, his hand trembling so that the flame flickered and died. He struck another; she smiled at him across the little pool of light that illumined their two intent faces.

"You smoke cigarettes, Mrs. De Chanfret!" This obviously was a rhetorical question, since she was now blowing a smoke spiral through her pursed lips into the evening dusk. "I—I've never seen a lady smoke cigarettes before." His shocked tone had in it a hint of almost husbandly proprietorship. Even the stout professional madams who marshaled their bevy of girls in the afternoon Broadway carriage parade knew better than to allow them to smoke in public.

Clio shrugged carelessly. "It's a continental custom, I suppose. I've smoked since I was thirteen. There's nothing so delicious as that single cigarette after dinner."

Nervously he glanced about, sensing a hundred peering eyes in the dusk. "People will—people will misunderstand. In a hotel, people talk."

"Oh, how sweet—how kind of you to protect me like that! Perhaps you are right. I am not used to American ways. But a cigarette"—she held it away from her delicately, she looked at it, she laughed a little poignant laugh—"a cigarette is sometimes cozy when one is lonely. Don't you find this so, dear Mr. Van Steed?"

"Cigar smoker myself," he said gruffly.

She murmured her admiration. "But of course. So masculine."

He cleared his throat. "I shouldn't think you'd be lonely, Mrs. De Chanfret. You never—that is, you're so popular—a woman of the world." She was silent. The silence lengthened, became unbearable. In a kind of panic he looked at her. Her face was almost hidden from him; she had turned her head aside, the lashes lay on the white cheeks. "Mrs. De Chanfret! Have I said something! I didn't mean——"

Still she was silent. They walked beneath the rosy glow of the Japanese lanterns. Inside the hotel the orchestra struck up the popular strains of "Champagne Charlie." Now she turned to him, she just touched her lashes with her lace handkerchief. "A woman of the world," she repeated, very low. Her tone was not reproachful; merely sad. "Imagine for yourself that your dear sister should suddenly find herself a widow, and her dear mother dead, too, suddenly—forgive me that I even speak of such a thing—but *par exemple* only—and she finds herself alone in—shall we say—France. Alone, with only a servant or two, and knowing no one. No one. She follows the ways to which she is accustomed in her own loved America. Is that a woman of the world!" She pressed the handkerchief to her lips.

"Mrs. De Chanfret! Clio!"

Her face was suddenly radiant; she just touched his arm with the tips of her fingers, and pressed it gently and gave the effect of gazing up at him, starry-eyed, by leaning just a little. "You called me Clio. How dear, how good, how friendly! Bart!"

"Shall we go in? The—uh—the music has started."

"She's smoking a cigarette!" It was as though the scarlet tip of the little white cylinder had lighted a conflagration in the United States Hotel. "He lighted it for her right there in the garden as bold as you please, and now she's smoking it, walking up and down with a lace thing over her head, and a short velvet jacket like a gypsy. . . . She's thrown away the cigarette. . . . She's taking his arm!"

These were the oddments which were dispatched by letter to old Madam Van Steed maintaining her grudging vigil over her expectant daughter in Newport. With the breath of the harpies hot on her neck, Clio Dulaine went her unconventional way.

It became known that she frequently rose at six and ate breakfast with the stable-boys and jockeys and grooms and trainers and horsemen at the race-track stables. Later, this became the last word in chic. Now the very idea was considered brazen beyond belief. The early-morning air was exquisitely cool and pungent with pine; the mist across the meadows pearled every tree and roof and fence and paddock. Clio made friends with everything and everyone from waterboys to track favorites. She was fascinated by the tough, engaging faces of the stable hangers-on. Theirs was a kind of terse astringent wit. Their faces were, for the most part, curiously hard-bitten and twisted as to features; a wry mouth like a crooked slit in a box; a nose that swerved oddly; an eye that seemed higher than its mate, or that dropped in one corner, with sinister effect. Their hands were slim, flexible, almost fragile looking; their feet, too, slim and high-arched. They wore jerseys, shapeless pants or baggy riding breeches that hugged their incredibly meager knees. There was about them an indefinable style.

"*Chic, ça,*" Clio would say. "*Un véritable type.*"

"What's a teep?" Maroon asked.

"Uh—I must think——" She was being very French for the benefit of Van Steed. The three were breakfasting together.

Van Steed now said, yes, indeed, you're right, he is, and nodded to show that he too was familiar with the French language. This did little to soothe Maroon's irritation.

"Spell it," demanded Maroon.

"Why, t-y-p-e. *Type*." She gave it again the French pronunciation.

"T-y—well, hell's bells! Teep! Type, you mean. Well, it's too bad you can't speak American. Are you fixing to stay over in this country long, Mrs. De Chanfret? You ought to learn the language."

"That depends, dear Colonel Maroon, on so many, many things."

"What, for instance?" Van Steed asked with pronounced eagerness.

"Oh, things you would consider quite sordid, I'm afraid, Mr. Van Steed. Everything is so expensive over here. It takes so many francs to make one American dollar."

He spoke with a rush, as though the words had tumbled out before he could check them. "You should never have to worry about money. You're so—so—you ought to have everything that's beautiful—and uh—beautiful." He stammered, floundered, blushed furiously.

"Perhaps," wistfully, "if—ah—Edouard had lived."

"Edouard?"

"My husband."

"Oh. Oh, I thought you said—that is—I understood his name was Etienne."

"It was. I—I always called him Edouard. A little pet name, you understand."

Phew, Maroon thought. That'll learn her not to be so cute.

Unruffled, she went placidly on eating the hearty stable breakfast of scalding coffee and ham and eggs and steak and fried potatoes and hot biscuits. Everything seemed to her serene and friendly at this hour of the morning. Even the race horses, so fiery and untouchable as they pranced out to the track a few hours later, haughtily spurning the ground with their delicate hoofs, seeming scarcely to touch it, like the toes of a ballet dancer, now put their friendly heads outside their stalls looking almost benign as they lipped a bit of sugar.

Cupide usually accompanied her on these excursions to the stable. It was his heaven. The stables were quick to recognize his magic with horses. They permitted him to exercise their horses, grudgingly at first but freely after they had seen what he did with the fiery Alamo, who was as yet not entirely broken to the race track.

Darting in and out of the stables and paddocks, under horses' hoofs, into back rooms, he picked up the most astonishing and valuable bits of information, which he imparted to Clint and Clio.

"That Nellie Leonard is an actress, they say she is going to be famous because that James Buchanan Brady has lots of money to put into plays for her. She is taking singing lessons every day. . . . Bet on Champagne Charlie in the third race, don't let them talk you out of it. I know what I know. . . . That girl in the cottages with Sam Lamar isn't his daughter at all, she's his mistress. . . . President of the United States Arthur is coming to the United States Hotel next week. . . . They are going to have a great ball. . . . The Forosini has a new riding horse, pure white. He is trained to bow his head and swing toward her when she mounts the block. . . . Gould is going to buy the Manhattan Elevated Company. He is trying to ruin them so he can get it cheap. I listened at the keyhole when he was talking. . . . Kaka is teaching Creole cooking to Mrs. Lewis at the Club House, and Kaka is playing the roulette wheel from the kitchen. The waiters place her money for her. She won seventy-five dollars last night. They're afraid to keep any out for themselves because they know she is a witch. . . . The old lady who is the mother of that Van Steed is coming to Saratoga. She doesn't like you. . . . Tonight Mrs. Porcelain is going to wear a pink dress, tulle, with rosebuds. . . ."

He knew everything. His sources of news were devious but infallible. Bellboys, chambermaids, waiters, grooms, bartenders, faro dealers, stable hands, jockeys, trainers, prostitutes all brought him tidbits and spices with which to flavor the *pot-au-feu* which was forever stewing in his great domed skull. When he slipped into the hotel front lobby (where he was not permitted), the Negro boys swarmed around him, their faces gashed with anticipatory grins. He postured for them, he danced, he told droll dirty stories, he fabricated tremendous gar-

gantuan lies. For the chambermaids he seemed to have a kind of fascination that was at once unwholesome and maternal. At the track the
stablemen and even the jockeys admitted that his knowledge of horse-
flesh was uncanny.

Now he began his campaign. He wanted Maroon to enter
Alamo. He begged to be allowed to ride him. Dawn daily found him
at the track. He cajoled, begged, bribed, pleaded until Maroon,
trainer, stable-boys, all were worn down. He took the horse into his
charge, bit by bit. Soon he was riding him daily in the early-morning
track work. Crouched over the neck of the beautiful two-year-old he
looked like a tiny bedizened monkey.

"Let me ride him, Mr. Clint. Let me race him; I promise you he
will win. I swear it. Perhaps not first, but we will not shame you,
Alamo and I. Think how chic it will be, your own horse to race at
Saratoga . . . Miss Clio, speak for me. Speak for me!"

He was like a thwarted lover pleading that they intercede with a
mistress. It was difficult to tell whether he was motivated by his slavish
admiration for Maroon, his doglike devotion to Clio, or his worship
of the spirited animal.

In the beginning Maroon had laughed indulgently at the dwarf's
pleadings as one treats a child who cries for the moon.

"Listen at him! You'd be a sorry figure and so would Alamo,
trailing along at the end of the field like a yearling strayed from the
herd."

Cupide turned to Clio. "Mad'moiselle, tell him how in France I
rode in all the most famous races. Tell him——"

"What a lie!" Clio retorted.

Maroon roared good-naturedly. "Get going, Cupide, before I
take a boot to you. Why, Alamo's a big critter; he'd likely turn his
head if you were up there on his back, racing, and eat you for a fly."

"I've mounted him every day. You know this!" The little man
was near to tears. His barrel-like chest was heaving. "I have the
strength of a giant." He clenched his fists, he made the muscles bulge
in the tight sleeves of his uniform.

"Git, Scat! Drag it out of here!"

Suddenly the little man began to shake all over as with a chill. His popeyes searched the room wildly. With a bound he stood before the dreary little fireplace, he seized the iron poker, took it in his two tiny hands and bent it into a circle as though it were a willow twig. As suddenly, then, he threw it, rattling, to the floor, burst into tears and ran from the room.

Maroon, staring after him, shook his handsome head in bewilderment. "How come I ever got mixed up with a hystericky outfit like you folks I'm damned if I know! Why, say, that midget's downright dangerous. If he was mine I'd sure enough tan him good. Did you see what he just did there! Why—say!"

Unreasonably, then, Clio turned about-face and sided with Cupide. "He's wonderful with horses. You yourself have seen that. He can ride anything. You are jealous because Alamo loves him more than you."

"God A'mighty!" shouted Maroon. "Let the sorry scoundrel ride him then. Serve him right if he gets throwed and killed. Only don't blame me." He stamped from the room as irate as a humdrum husband.

Cupide was not yet finished. He knew power when he saw it; he had not listened at keyholes in vain. Straight as his little bandy legs would take him he ran to the room where power resided. It was napping time for the feminine guests of the United States Hotel—that hour which stretched, a desert waste, when the heavy midday meal was in the process of digestion and the three o'clock Broadway carriage parade had not yet begun.

Smartly, peremptorily, he rapped at the door of a third-floor suite. There was no answer. He rapped again.

"Go away!" bellowed the voice of Mrs. Coventry Bellop. "I'm sleeping."

Rat-a-tat-tat, went the knuckles. Then again. Silence within the room. Rat-a-tat-tat. To a mind keyed to plots and petty conspiracies the peremptory knocking spelled exigency. A key turned, the door was opened, Mrs. Bellop, a huge shapeless mass in a rumpled muslin wrapper, peered out into the hall, saw nothing, then, feeling a tweak at her skirts, looked down in amazement over the shelf of her own tremendous bust to see the tiny figure hovering in the neighborhood of her be-ruffled knees.

"Good God!" she boomed. "You gave me a start. What are you doing down there?"

"I must talk to you." He laid one finger alongside his nose like a midget in a pantomime. Perhaps he had, in fact, seen this gesture of secrecy in some puppet show and with his gift of mimicry was unconsciously using it now.

She stood a moment, staring down at him. Then, without a word, she stood aside to let him enter. Accustomed to the fastidious neatness of Clio Dulaine's apartment, he looked about Mrs. Bellop's chamber with considerable distaste. A cluttered place in which chairs, tables, shelf were littered with a burden of odds and ends of every description. The froglike eyes of the little man saw everything, made a mental note of all they saw. Garments, letters, papers, half-smoked stubs of very small black cigars; food, gloves, wilted flowers, a hairbrush full of combings; stockings, a cockatoo in a cage, a fat wheezing pug dog whose resemblance to Cupide was striking.

"What do you want?" demanded the forthright Mrs. Bellop. "Who sent you?"

He put his hat in his hand, the polite and well-trained groom, but his tone was that of a plotter who knows an accomplice when he sees one.

"No one sent me. I came."

"What for? Nothing good, I'll be bound."

He looked pained at this. "Would you like to make a thousand dollars?"

"Get out of here!" said Mrs. Bellop.

He put up his little hand, palm out, almost peremptorily. "You need only say one word to Mad'moiselle—to Mrs. De Chanfret, I mean. And spend fifty dollars. You have fifty dollars?"

"Get out of here!" Mrs. Bellop said again. But halfheartedly. It was plain that her interest was at least piqued.

"Madam Bellop," he began, earnestly, "I am a great and famous jockey."

"Likely story."

"It is true. Look at me. Imagine my featherweight on a good horse, with my hands of iron. Listen. I am serious. I want to ride Alamo. You know—Monsieur Clint's horse. If I ride him I shall win."

"Ride him then. What d'you mean, rousing me out of my sleep! What's behind all this twaddle? Quick, or I'll have you thrown out of the hotel!"

Yet storm as she would, the sad eyes, the sardonic mouth, the stunted body commanded her interest, held her attention. He spoke simply, briefly, like one who is himself so convinced that he feels he will have no trouble convincing another.

"I will ride Alamo. I will win. That I can assure you."

"Bosh! How?"

"I will win. Will you tell Mad'moiselle that it would be a good thing for Monsieur Clint and for her? To have a winning horse is very *chic*. All my life I have wanted to ride a winning horse. But all my life. It is my dream."

"Look here," interrupted Mrs. Bellop, testily. "Sometimes you talk like a nigger bootblack and sometimes you talk like a character in a book. I can't make it out. For that matter, I don't know why I'm wasting time on you. Get along, now, before I call the front office." But her tone lacked conviction.

The midget could not be serious long. He shook himself like a little dog, he grinned engagingly, the big front teeth, spaced wide apart, were friendly as a white picket fence. Suddenly he was all Negro. "Please tell her like I say, Miz Bellop. She do what you say. Looky, effen you ain't got fifty, why, I put it in for you, you win a thousand dollars. Only"—his face now was a mask of cunning—"only you mustn't speak a breathin' word to any folks about it. Just you and Mr. Clint and Miss Clio."

"Dirty work if I ever saw it," said the forthright Mrs. Bellop. "She send you?"

"No *ma'am!*"

"He send you?"

"No *ma'am!*"

It was impossible to doubt his sincerity. Mrs. Bellop possessed the spirit of adventure; and she was not a lady to forego a chance at gain. Still she hesitated, pondering. Her fine eyes, shrewd, intelligent, searched the froglike face upturned to her. Honor among thieves. Desperate, he played his last card. "No call to feel backward about the fifty, Miz Bellop. No call at all. I can spare it and you can pay me back when you win. I stole it."

At this engaging example of candor she burst into rollicking laughter, her bosom heaved, her sides shook. "Run along, you imp! I've a mind to do it, just out of curiosity. If you're lying——"

Always dramatic, he finished the sentence for her. "You can kill me."

"I know worse ways than that to punish you. Get, now! Shoo!"

But he must have final assurance. "You the boss of this here whole Saratoga. You going to do it, Miz Bellop? I I'm?"

"I might." But he saw that he had won.

It was almost too simple. Sophie Bellop, bidding her usual train of attendants to remain where they were, waddled into the paddock at next day's race, alone. Her sharp eye had caught sight of Clint and Clio, but even if she had not seen them she need only have followed the turning of heads, like the waving of grain in the wind, as they passed through any crowd. Accustomed though Saratoga was to the dramatic, there always was a stir when these two handsome and compelling creatures appeared together.

Mrs. Coventry Bellop wasted no time on finesse. Hers was an almost brutal directness of method, always. "Good morning, Countess! How are you, Colonel Maroon!" She scarcely paused to hear their courteous return of greeting. "What's become of that horse of yours, Colonel?"

"He's here, Ma'am. In the stables. Eating his pretty head off."

"Race him, why don't you? Isn't that what a race horse is for?"

A light leaped in Clio's eyes. So! she thought. Cupide. She said, aloud, "I've been urging Colonel Maroon to enter him, Mrs. Bellop."

"Certainly," said the blunt Sophie, brisk and businesslike as any bookie. "Get that little dwarf imp of yours to ride him, he's just made for a jockey. I've watched him with horses; he's born to ride. Saratoga needs a new sensation. Come on. Surprise them."

The man's mind sensed intrigue; he looked from the girl's sparkling face to the purposeful countenance of the powerful woman. "What're you two girls cooking up!" His caressing laugh was sheer flattery, as always, but his eyes were unsmiling. He had a feeling of helplessness, of being propelled into something by wills stronger than his. This very morning Kaka had fixed him with her hypnotic eye and had murmured, "I had a dream last night, Mr. Clint. I saw a horse and it seemed like the horse belonged to you and yet it didn't. And the jockey, he was Cupide and yet it wasn't, riding him. And it was like a race, and at the same time it wasn't exactly a race, neither."

"M'm," Clint cut in, laconically. "You'd better change your voodoo powers, Kaka."

Gently, persistently, they wore down his resistance.

"It would give you great *réclame,*" Clio said. "The New York papers."

An unknown horse. An unknown jockey. They ordered—rather, Clio ordered—for the diminutive figure a suit of silks in the historic colors of the stormy Texas flag. Kakaracou, when the shining suit arrived, embroidered the Lone Star on his sleeve.

"All right, all right," Maroon had said. "You'll make a laughing stock of me, but maybe it'll teach you a lesson."

But he knew Cupide; he had watched Kaka's secret impassive face. He had taken his own precautions the night before the race.

In the sitting room of Clio's apartment the big Texan had called Cupide to him. The little man had trotted over to him and the Texan, lolling in an armchair, had locked the midget firmly between his steel-muscled horseman's knees.

"Now listen at what I'm fixing to say, Cupide. I'm not just passin' the time of day. You're riding Alamo tomorrow. You haven't a Chinaman's chance to win, but you might bring him in fourth or even third, if you're smart. But if I hear you've been too smart, you might as well light out somewheres right from the stables and never come back. I reckon you know what I mean. Don't you touch another horse, hear me! Don't you even show your ugly little face in another stall, only Alamo's. If I hear of any monkeyshines I'll tie you to the bedpost here and I'll pay Kaka to do such voodoo over you that——"

"No!" Cupide screamed. "I promise. I promise."

"All right. Now fork over, pronto, before I shake it out of you. Everything you got on you, because I'm going to search you, later, down to your toenails. Don't figure to throw off on me, because I'm watching you."

For a moment the midget was still, still. His lips drew back from his teeth like those of an animal about to sink his fangs into an enemy. Then he looked up pitifully into Maroon's stern face. "You going to make me?"

"Surest thing you know."

"You'll be sorry."

Maroon made a threatening gesture.

"Here!" squealed Cupide. From the inside hidden pocket of his tight little jacket he took a tiny folded packet like a powder paper; from the lining of his hat he took another; he took a stubby pencil from some inner recess of his clothing, unscrewed its top and brought forth a vial hardly thicker than a darning needle. "Here. Take them. This is only a powder, it makes a horse sneeze and his eyes water, it does no harm—after the race. This makes him chill. And cough. This, under the hoof, you can't even find it once it's in, but——"

Maroon turned him inside out. He threatened to scratch Alamo in next day's race. He himself put Cupide to bed, took away his clothes.

"I'm driving you to the track myself," he said, next morning, "and staying with you till you're mounted."

"Mais certainement," Cupide said, amiably, "why not? Have I not been good, Monsieur Clint! I have not smoked a single cigar now for two weeks, so well I have trained."

"You're up to something," Clint mused, regarding the midget thoughtfully. "When you get to putting on French like that it means mischief."

"I must say good-by to Kaka, she will make magic to help me win."

"M'm. I'll go with you."

But though Kaka did a good deal of eye-rolling with facial contortions and mumbling and passing of hands over the little man's head and down the length of his body, her hands were flat, her fingers spread. In spite of himself Maroon watched her fascinated. He drove Cupide to the track, stayed with him until he actually was mounted, a grotesque little bundle of satin in the brilliant colors of the state of Texas.

"Phew!" he exploded, mopping his face as he joined Clio just before the start of the race. "Why in tarnation I ever said I'd leave him ride Alamo! He shouldn't ought to be allowed to enter any kind of sporting event except maybe to see who can spit the farthest. He's got no moral sense, no more than a goat."

"Such a fuss, *chéri!*" Clio laughed. "You've upset him, poor little man! Taking his silly powders away and watching him as if he were a criminal. What harm to give another horse a bit of something, not to hurt him?"

"God A'mighty, the both of you'll end in jail yet, doggone if I don't think so!"

Maroon sat moodily as the race began, staring as Alamo cantered to the head of the stretch. But when the field broke away suddenly he stood up, wildly waving his white sombrero, shouting, "Eeeeee-yipeeee! Stay with him Cupide! EEEEE-YOW!" Something very odd seemed to be happening. Alamo had started at a curiously mincing gait, more like the spirited step of a high-bred horse showing his paces in the Broadway carriage parade than the swift steady pace of a racer. The field swept past him, left him behind with two straggling nags. The tiny mounted figure crouched almost astride the animal's neck, and now Cupide's stumpy arm, whip in hand, came up, came down, came up, down. "Leave him be!" howled Maroon. The grandstand and paddock roared. Who had ever heard of whipping a horse at the beginning of a two-mile race! And the whip came down on Alamo's neck, not his rump. Alamo lurched, recovered, abandoned his high-school gait for a curious bunching of the four feet followed by flinging them wide. It gave him a ridiculous plunging gait like that of a nursery rocking-horse. "Oh, my God!" groaned Maroon; and covered his eyes. But Clio remained smiling, smiling. Mrs. Coventry Bellop was staring at them. Clio smiled. Bart Van Steed, very pink-cheeked, shook a sympathetic head. Clio's smile grew sweeter. "I'd give a million dollars to be out of here," groaned Maroon. "Twenty to one shot. Well, anyway, nobody bet on him, that's sure. Only our couple of hundred between us."

"He seems to be running quite well," Clio now observed, mildly. There was something unnatural in her serene composure. Women take things different from men, Maroon thought, somewhat to his own surprise. She's a wonder and no mistake. His hand rested on her knee, he looked again at the track.

"Take your hand away. They're watching us," Clio said, between her teeth. But she need not have bothered. He had leaped again to his feet, the white sombrero was describing circles in the air. Alamo's gait still was grotesque but it was covering magnificent distances in the beginning of the second mile. He was running, not like a horse, but as a greyhound runs, or a jack rabbit. All four feet bunched under him, then all four spread to unbelievable length. He seemed to go through the air in a series of leaps. From a roar of amusement the crowd now grew hysterical.

"Kangaroo!" they were yelling. "Go it, Kangaroo! Tom Thumb! Let him out, Tom Thumb! He wants to fly!"

The tiny arm had ceased to rise and fall. Cupide, against the dark sweating neck, was like a bluebottle that will not be shaken off.

"He—why he's—he's—Clio, it looks like he's got a chance to win!"

"He will win," Clio said, calmly.

The curious bounding gait passed the last half-mile, passed the last five in the field of seven, passed the favorite Oh Susanna, reached the post and kept steadily on, bunch and spread, bunch and spread until a score of trackhands and stable-boys swarmed out to stop him. He stopped, too, in a bunch. "Four feet on a dime," Maroon said later, ruefully. With difficulty they brought him to a standstill, his eyes were rolling, he jerked, pranced, reared.

It was Maroon who lifted Cupide off the horse, hugged him, lighted for him the huge black cigar that he had denied himself like any jockey in training. And Maroon, smiling now, smiling a curious smile with Clio at his side, said, over and over, "Yes, it sure surprised me as much as anybody. I just entered him to please the little fellow, but he like to sawed Alamo's head off; it was a wonder the poor critter didn't roll him off his back. . . . Well, thanks . . . Well, that's mighty kind of you. . . . Why, no, I just had a few dollars up, not anything to speak of . . . I'd no i-dea he'd come in, his first race like that."

But once Clio's sitting room sheltered them, Maroon confronted her. He was white with rage.

"What did he give him? I'm going to wring his neck, and Kaka's too. But first tell me—what did he give him?"

"Give him? But who? What is this you are talking?"

"Don't start that Frenchified stuff with me. You and that witch bitch in there. Disgracing me for life! Kaka!" He strode toward the inner door. "Kaka! Come on out of there or I'll drag——"

As though on signal there came a knocking at the outer door even as Kaka flung open the bedroom door. She was an imposing figure in her best black silk, stiff and rich, a filmy fichu crossed on her flat breast, her gold earrings dangling, her brooch flashing, her turbaned head held high. In her hand was a silver tray holding small amber-filled glasses.

"Come in! Come in!" Clio called gaily in answer to the knocking at the outer door.

"Coquetier?" said Kaka, gently, proffering her tray to Maroon. *"Coquetier?"*

A Negro bellboy stood in the hall doorway. "Gepmum from the newspapers like to speak to Colonel Maroon. New York papers and everywhere."

"I won't see 'em. Tell them to go to hell!"

"Oh, I'd see them if I were you, dear Colonel Maroon," cooed Clio. "They'll think it so very queer, if you don't. Isn't that true?"

Sulkily he followed the boy across the balcony, down the stairs.

"How much you win?" Kaka asked her, smoothly.

"Ten thousand."

"M'm-m'm! The Colonel's wrathy. But he wouldn't let Cupide give the other horses the stop powders, like he wanted to, so he had to give Mr. Clint's horse the go-ahead medicine."

"True. In some ways—a few only—Colonel Maroon *il n'a point de raison.*"

"Mais un homme comme il faut, toutefois," Kaka tittered. "Only we must keep away from him for a few days that other one—that monkey—that *homme des bois.*"

"Quick, stop that giggling, put down that glass, run after that bellboy, tell him to tell the newspaper reporters that the beautiful Mrs. De Chantret won ten thousand dollars. Make it fifteen. And let it be known that Mrs. Coventry Bellop, too, was a winner. The well-known society leader . . . That stuff Cupide stuck into him with the butt of his whip—it won't hurt Alamo, will it? After?"

"No." Kaka scurried toward the door with a swish of her silks. "Only hurry-up powders. Wouldn't hurt a fly."

XIII

✦

"It is an interesting thing," Clio *reflected, her eyes narrowed in her* thoughtful expression. "He's as shy as a bird, Van Steed, but he likes to be seen with women who are *dramatique*—spectacular—is that the word?"

"No spika de Angleesh," retorted Maroon, sulkily. He had not yet quite come round, though three days had elapsed since the race—the Kangaroo race it was called in Saratoga. There had been some ugly talk, but this had quickly died down when it became known beyond a shadow of a doubt that Maroon himself had had a mere hundred dollars on his own horse.

"Clint, I don't understand you now. You are so different."

"So are you."

"No. I am exactly what I said I would be when we planned it all in New Orleans. I did not pretend. I did not try to make you believe that I was one of those good women like your dear mama, and that other you so admire. Everything *convenable*. I am here to make somehow a great deal of money—by marriage, if possible. But safely. You know that."

"You make me sick," he said, brutally.

But her tone was equable. "Yes, it makes me a little sick, too. But Mama—and Aunt Belle—and all that in New Orleans—that I saw for years, and there if you like was something to make one really sick. I won't be like them. I won't be. I won't be!" The tears streaming from her wide-open eyes, her lips quivering.

"You sure cry pretty." But he came over to her and ran his hand almost roughly over her sleek black hair, and then the hand gripped her shoulder, her arms were about him, they clung together, he drank the tears from her eyes.

"You will help me, won't you, *chéri?* Darling. Darling." Always she accented the last syllable—dar-*ling*. Dar-*ling*. It seemed to make the word a thousand times more caressing.

"Now what?"

She sat up, flushed but composed again and almost businesslike. "That Forosini. He rides with her sometimes in the afternoon."

"I reckon he's still got the right."

"But it's because she behaves like a circus rider. I want to do something that will make her seem dull."

"Well, get yourself pink tights and spangles and ride down Broadway bareback." But even as she pouted he said, thoughtfully, "S-a-a-ay! Maybe we can teach Blue Blazes to do her licking trick with you. She likes you."

Like a child she hugged him. "Clint, you are a good, good man!"

"Oh, my God!" he groaned in protest.

She ran into the next room. "Quick, Kaka! My riding habit."

Guilia Forosini in her trim black habit was the center of an admiring crowd when she mounted her white horse every afternoon at five. It was quite a ceremony. Her father, white-haired, military of bearing, known to all by his shock of curly white hair, his iron-gray imperial and mustache, led her by the hand down the piazza steps. Always, as she approached her horse, the animal bowed his beautiful head and swung toward her as though inviting her to mount. Usually two grooms accompanied the dark-eyed beauty, often one of the young bloods among the summer visitors; occasionally even Bart Van Steed had been seen to canter with her through the pine-scented paths.

After that first afternoon at five when Mrs. De Chanfret had

descended the piazza steps to mount Colonel Maroon's horse, Blue
Blazes, the fickle crowd had deserted the Forosini en masse. The reason was simple enough. Mrs. De Chanfret gave them a better show.

Blue Blazes was blue black. His coat was the color of Clio's hair.
Her gloves were white, her stock was white, she sported a fresh white
flower in her buttonhole, her boots shone like Blue Blazes' back.
There was about her the indefinable neatness of the Parisienne. She
made the Forosini in contrast seem somehow blowzy. But it was not
this alone the crowd had come to see; it was not for this that they had
deserted the Forosini just in the act of mounting there at the other
horse block. For as she reached Blue Blazes' side, Clio lifted her veil
and Blue Blazes turned his magnificent head and kissed her cheek.
The crowd was rapturous.

"Just a little sugar water on your cheek, honey," Maroon had
said when he taught her the trick down at the stables. "Blue Blazes
he'll do anything for a lick of sugar water. I taught him that little
knack when he was just a foal."

Mrs. De Chanfret. That Countess de Traysomething de Chanfret. She uses mascara on her eyelashes you can't tell me they can be
as long and black as that and kind of thick looking. (She used mascara
quite artlessly, having seen Aunt Belle Piquery do it for years.) They
say she walked right into the gambling room at the Club House where
ladies simply aren't allowed and when they told her that it was against
the rules she just smiled and stayed on as brazen as you please. Al
Spencer, the manager, came up and spoke to her. She was with that
Colonel Maroon. And she stayed, mind you. She says it's the fashion
in Europe, well, all I can say is she'd better go back there—bringing
ideas like that into the minds of American womanhood! Even Mrs.
Coventry Bellop never went that far, and she certainly does as she
likes.

Though Clio Dulaine was busily throwing dust in the eyes of
Saratoga so that her real business could be accomplished, she now and
then found herself the center of a sensation out of sheer innocence or
worldliness; it was difficult to say which.

Though she enjoyed the al fresco dining at the outlying inns and restaurants, there was something very gala about dining at the ornate Club House with its mirrors and gilt, its frescoes and chandeliers. The full-length portrait of John Morrissey, its founder, hung in the hallway, black mustache, gold watch-chain, the famous $5,000 diamond stud, the diamond sleeve links, Prince Albert coat and all. Though death had ended his reign, the lavish standard of the Morrissey ménage persisted.

As for the blatant bronzes and flowered carpets and the writhing figures carved in every defenseless inch of wood, Clio, after one look, said, "Isn't it frightful! I adore it! And that portrait! His coat of arms should be over the door. A cuspidor couchant, with two cigars and a plug of tobacco rampant."

This got about and caused mingled resentment and hilarity.

But even Clio's fastidious palate, accustomed to the most artful French and Creole cookery, could not deny the flavor and variety of the gaudy Club House restaurant. On cool evenings it was pleasant to dine where wines actually were known by name and age and where caviar and *crêpes suzette* were recognized as the alpha and omega of a good meal. It was pleasant, too, to be squired by the flamboyant Colonel Maroon or the shy but equally sensational Bart Van Steed.

She had been accompanied by Maroon on that first night when she entered the gaming rooms in defiance of the house rules. There were women in the parlors, in the lounge, but certainly they were not the cream of Saratoga summer society. They were adventurous nobodies who derived a vicarious sense of sin from being so near its portals; all the more titillating because it was forbidden them.

Clio had by now had quite enough of the hotel parlors with their shrill feminine chatter; she had had enough and to spare of the restaurants, of the drives, of the gargantuan hotel dining room. At the Club House she had eaten her dinner with enormous gusto, had mopped up the last drop of fragrant cointreau and orange sauce with a little pillow of pancake.

"That was heavenly! Now I am going to play a little roulette. I'm always lucky at roulette."

"Womenfolks not allowed in the gaming room. You know that, honey."

"*Ridicule!* Provincial nonsense. Tell me about the owner of this Club House. Who is he?"

"There's two of them. They bought it after Morrissey died. Charley Reed, he killed a man back in New Orleans in 1862 and they sentenced him to death but there was a lot of hocus-pocus and they got him pardoned. The Federal troops were in there by that time and the head of the gambling outfit was a fellow named Butler, brother of Major General Benjamin Butler. So Reed he got off and went right on with his gambling place. Well, say, now he's all for society here in Saratoga; built himself a fifty-thousand-dollar house on Union Avenue, goes to the Episcopal church every Sunday. At the races every day, but you don't see him around the Club House much."

"And the other?"

"Al Spencer, he's the quietest spoken fellow you'd ever meet, stingy as all get-out. He's got a hobby of collecting paintings but it isn't just for fun. He buys 'em cheap and sells at a profit."

"What a country! A convicted murderer and an art dealer conduct a gambling house in the most famous watering-place in America."

"That's so. But look at us!"

"Look at all of them," Clio interrupted. "I only marvel more and more that any country could be so rich and so vital as to survive the plundering of these past years. We are all thieves together, the lot of us."

She actually entered the gaming room, a thing unheard of in the history of Saratoga. Followed by the protesting and rather sheepish Maroon, she had swept past the doorman before he could recover from his surprise and was strolling past the faro and roulette tables with a professionally interested eye.

"Madam," an attendant protested. "Ladies are not allowed in the gaming rooms."

"Nonsense. Send for Mr. Reed. Send for Mr. Spencer." The pious ex-murderer was not to be found, but Spencer, resembling a shabby clerk in a lawyer's office rather than the owner of the most notorious and gaudy gambling house in America, glided in and surveyed Mrs. De Chanfret with a fishy eye before he turned his reproachful gaze on Clint Maroon.

"Now, Colonel Maroon, after all the money you've taken out of this place——"

"It isn't his fault, Mr. Spencer," Clio interrupted quickly. "I am Mrs. De Chanfret. I have begged Mr. Van Steed and Mr. Maroon to escort me into your beautiful gaming rooms but they said it was forbidden. I couldn't believe it. I have been everywhere in Europe— Monte Carlo, Aix, Nice, Cannes—and never have I heard of such a thing."

"Hear of it now," replied the laconic Spencer.

"Think of all the money you're losing. Women are bad gamblers they say."

"Yes, ma'am. That's just it. Hystericky. Get to screechin'."

Every eye in the room was on them. She was wearing her dress of crème Beaupré veiling in the shade of Kioto porcelain and a blue surah vest bordered with red velvet. It was a costume in which she would have attracted attention under the most conventional circumstances. Now, in the midst of the men's dark coats and snuffy midsummer seersuckers, she stood out like a flag in a breeze. Only the fish-eyed Spencer surveyed her unmoved.

"Thanks, Al," Maroon said, uncomfortably. "Come on, Cl— uh—Mrs. De Chanfret. We'd better mosey along now."

But as always, opposition made her the more determined. "Mr. Spencer, I'll make a confession to you. Colonel Maroon wagered me five hundred dollars that you wouldn't let me play. I bet five hundred you would. If you'll let me play just once I'll put the five hundred on Number Five and, win or lose, I'll go. Will you? Just this once?"

The chance to recoup something, if only five hundred dollars, from the lucky Texan proved too much for the avaricious Spencer.

"Win or lose. Promise?"

"Win or lose. Promise."

Without a word Maroon peeled five one-hundred-dollar bills from the sheaf in his wallet and handed them to Spencer. Spencer in turn gave them to Clio. Wordlessly, without waiting to buy chips, she flung them down on the five.

Five won. She pointed to the winnings. "Thank you so much, dear Mr. Spencer. The original five please give to Mr. Maroon. The rest you will please give to your favorite charity in Saratoga"—in a definitely clear tone. The cream-and-blue Beaupré veiling floated out of the room followed by a fuming Maroon and leaving in its wake a buzz of talk that sounded like a badly directed mob scene in a pageant.

"Now what in tarnation did you do that for, Clio!"

"You're not angry, are you Clint *chéri?* I had to play, once. It's very bad for me to be forbidden things I want to do. Harmless things, I mean."

"Suppose you'd lost the five?"

"I'd have paid you back. You know that."

"God help any man who takes up with you for life. I wouldn't be in his shoes, not for a million."

"Oh, I'm hoping he'll have more than a mere million."

"Pretty sure of yourself, aren't you?"

"No. No, I'm not. Not sure of myself or of you or anything or of anyone——" Her voice trailed off into wistful nothingness.

"There you go! Hard as nails to begin with, and then you get to feeling sorry for yourself and next thing you've got me and Kaka and Cupide and everybody else babying you like you were two years old. Well, that's about what you act like—two years old."

They were walking toward the hotel in the soft midsummer darkness. "Do I? Yes, I suppose I do." There was something disarming about her unexpected acquiescence. "But what chance had we here in a place like this unless we made a great fuss? My little plan with Van

Steed—it has thrown you two together, hasn't it? Everyone here knows you and me, they think we are rich and important. They suspect nothing."

He put his hand over hers that lay on his arm as they walked. "Honey, this kind of game, you've got to work quick and get out before they find the pea under the walnut shell."

"Then what have you done with Van Steed? I have done what I could. I've told him that he is wonderful. I've told him that you are wonderful. If I can have ten more days I think he would have the courage to be serious. You say you have a plan. Why don't you tell me! I can see no chance for big money unless this plan of yours is one that he——What is it, this plan, anyway? I've no head for railroads. Railroads bore me. But tell me simply."

"Same old plan we used to use when the sheep men tried to crowd the cattle men off the range. The quickest draw and the hardest fist and the smartest one to outguess the other, he won."

"Yes, but tell me. Tell me what is being done with this railroad. I'll try to understand."

"Anybody could understand. That's the trouble. Did you ever hear of a fellow named Morgan—J. P. Morgan?"

"You once spoke of him."

Strolling along in the soft darkness, his hand on hers, he told his story of ruthlessness, and his gentle drawling voice that she so loved to hear made it seem stirring and almost romantic.

"Well sir, he's a scrapper for you. New fellow. Banker. Smart as Gould and just as hard, but he ain't rough. Not poor white trash with no bringing up, like Rockefeller and Huntington and Gould and Jim Hill, Carnegie and Vanderbilt and Astor. Morgan, his pa was a banker before him. I don't mean he's any sissy, even if his name is Pierpont. But he sits quiet; he's as close-mouthed as an Indian. Matter of that, they're all in the same kettle. Yellow-livered, wouldn't fight in the Civil War, Pa said. Paid substitutes to fight for 'em; they were too busy robbing the country, themselves. But this Morgan, he's been to Europe, worked in a bank there; he's had a college education."

"Is he rich?"

"Rich! Hell, yes!"

"Married?"

His laugh rang out. "No, honey, no. I mean, no for you. Seems he married young, and she died. But no, sugar."

"*Eh bien!* One never knows. Do go on, *chéri*. I am fascinated."

"Folks have a lot of respect for him. Scared of him, too, I reckon; because he keeps his mouth shut they don't know what he's thinking. I told him what I wanted to do——"

"When? Where?"

"Oh, last week, you were busy as a bird-dog hatching one of your plots with Kaka and Cupide, I guess, and off making little Bart think butter wouldn't melt in your mouth. I went to New York."

"New York! Without me!"

"Honey, you can't go traveling around with Colonel Maroon—a respectable widow like you. You got your work cut out, according to your own pattern."

She jerked his arm, irritably for her. "Go on, then. Go on! Never mind about my plan. Yours."

"You couldn't call it a plan. It's so dumb and simple nobody's willing to believe it'll work. That's Easterners for you! Course, it is rough, maybe, a mite. But not any rougher than they were with Pa. Now, that hundred miles of road between Albany and Binghamton, it keeps on breaking down all the time. The other crowd sees to that. The trains go off the tracks. The trestles break down. There's fights in the trains and people get hurt. It's got so nobody'll use the road for freight or passengers. Scairt to. It's all done by Gould and his gang. They're trying to make the trunk line worthless so little Bart will sell it to them cheap and good riddance. He's tried law and order by calling on the citizens of the towns the road runs through. Well, the Gould gang gets them beaten up, and now he's got agents going through the towns with bundles of cash buying up stock that's held by the townships. They even tried to take over the books and the headquarters by force. That's always been the system of men like Fisk and Gould and Drew—you don't know about 'em, but I've heard of 'em all my life. Their scheme is, run it into the ground, make it worthless and you'll get it for nothing. The Delaware, Lackawanna & Western crowd would help little Bart Van Steed—that's a coal company—and back of it all that J. P. Morgan—if Van Steed would only fight. I mean, fight. I'd be willing to lead a gang down there. I'd get together a certain crowd I know. I'd put men in every office and railroad yard and station, and on every train and in every engine. I'd battle 'em bloody. I'd run 'em off the range."

They had reached the hotel. She took her hand from his arm, she stopped dead in the light that streamed from the open windows facing the piazza. "But this is a civilized day. These are like stories of Indian fighters. It is savage. I can't believe that business in America is conducted like this! You are laughing at me!"

"Nope. That's the straight of it."

She shook her head, she looked up at him. "Poor little Bartholomew Van Steed!"

"Honey, come on away from here with me."

But now she shook her head again, and this time it was for him. "When I leave Saratoga I intend to be settled for life—settled and safe and sure. But sure."

"I can always make enough for the two of us."

"But you just said God help any man who takes up with me for life."

"Who's talking about a lifetime!"

"I am."

Up the broad piazza steps and into the lobby. The cream-and-blue veiling, the white sombrero immediately were aware of an overtone of shrillness, an added quiver of excitement in the babble that issued from the hotel parlor.

Roscoe Bean skimmed by, his coat-tails vibrant. "What's up?" drawled Maroon. "The cats seem to be miaouing louder than ordinary tonight."

"Sh-sh!" Bean's unctuous smile had in it a touch of apprehension. "Oh, Colonel Maroon, you kill me the way you put things." He dropped his voice as though speaking of the sacred. "It's Madam Van Steed. Madam Van Steed has arrived."

XIV

Madam Van Steed sat on the piazza next morning, and her subjects paid her court. Frelinghuysens and Belmonts, Burnsides and Stewarts were reduced to their proper stations in the presence of royalty. Even Miss P. Vanderbilt, aunt of the fabulous William, whose first name no one seemed to know and wouldn't have dared use if they had, paid her respects to the monolithic figure whose iron-gray hair and iron-gray eyes and iron-gray gown seemed hewn from the very material of which she was made. Miss P. Vanderbilt ruled her own Vanderbilt clan with a terrible and devastating sweetness, a wistful blue eye, a tremulous smile, a tiny childlike voice. She wore little white *lisse* caps beneath which her faded curls bobbed jauntily. In the hotel dining room the Vanderbilt table was fourth from the door but the Van Steed table was second from the door and on the garden side. Madam Van Steed conducted herself like a comedy duchess in a bad American play about a duchess. Yet, once explained, her foibles were legitimate enough. Her companion, Miss Diggs, was there to drape shawls, read aloud, fetch and carry, pat pillows, write letters. Her crook-handled walking stick was a necessary adjunct to one who was ridden by rheumatism. The temper was induced by pain, for the arthritic right hand was curled into a claw. Her possessiveness toward her son was the frustrated love which had been rejected by the philandering Van Steed *père*. Her arrogance, her spitefulness and her domineering habit were probably glandular, but added up to pure meanness, and could have existed only in one to whom the grace of humor had been completely denied.

This bulky and aged Borgia now sat enthroned in her corner of the United States Hotel piazza. Each subject received his meed of poison as he approached the presence. The strident, overbearing voice carried up and down half the length of the enormous promenade.

"Oh, it's Miss Vanderbilt! Still wearing your little caps, I see." Then, in a piercing aside to Miss Diggs: "Bald as a billiard ball. Those curls are stitched to the cap."

Bart Van Steed hung over her chair, captive. "Well, I'll just drive down to Congress Spring, Mother. Shall I bring you a fresh bottle of water?"

"Diggs fetched it early this morning. Stay here with me, Bartholomew. After all, I arrived only last night, I haven't had a chance to talk to you. . . . Who's this? Oh, Mrs. Porcelain. You are still Mrs. Porcelain, I suppose? What's the matter with the men these days! They want nothing but young chits of sixteen. The sillies! As soon as a woman gets along toward her thirties and has some sense they count her as shopworn. . . . Is there a circus in town? But then who's that driving tandem with the white reins? Oh, the Forosini! No wonder. The old man himself looks like a ringmaster and now all the daughter needs is spangles and a hoop to make it perfect."

Only Mrs. Coventry Bellop gave her dart for dart. For well over a decade these two had been coming to Saratoga to partake of the waters and to enjoy their ancient feud. Madam Van Steed had the money, Mrs. Coventry Bellop the blood. She regarded Madam Van Steed as a parvenu and the Goulds, the Vanderbilts, the Astors, the Belmonts as upstarts. She loathed stupidity and dullness, played poker with the men; it was said she had been seen to smoke a pipe. Madam Van Steed, the conventional, regarded her with horror mingled with a wholesome fear. Bellop made no secret of her poverty. She knew the characters and the scandals of the Club House since the day of Morrissey; every hotel register was an open book to her. She knew how much the faro dealers were paid; which actually were secretaries and which were not in the cottages of the lonely millionaires whose wives were in Europe; had the most terrific inside political information about the doings, past, present and future of the late Boss Tweed, and of Samuel Tilden, James G. Blaine, Sanford Church. The lives of the Lorillards, the Kips, the Lelands were not only an open book to her but one from whose pages she gave free and delightful readings. She boasted that she was helping General Ulysses S. Grant with his memoirs; she gossiped with Mark Twain when he came to near-by Mount McGregor to visit General Grant. She was the confidante of chambermaids, racetrack touts, millionaires, cooks, dowagers, bookies, debutantes, brokers, jockeys and, amazingly enough, she rarely betrayed a genuine confidence. Hers was the expansive, sympathetic and outgoing nature which attracts emotional confession. She was at once generous and grasping. She never had a penny long.

Clio had been conscious that this woman marked her comings and goings; suspected her plans; coolly appraised her jewelry and her exhibitionistic outbursts. The plump good-natured face, like the Cheshire Cat, seemed to materialize out of thin air. The humorous intelligent eyes seemed to be weighing her, evaluating her.

This morning, as Clio ascended the steps of the United States Hotel with Clint Maroon at her side, her quick eye noted the staring group in the center of the piazza, her dramatic instinct sensed a tense moment impending. A bevy of sycophantic mamas and daughters clustered round the chair of an imperious old woman; the captive Bart leaned over her, offering filial attentions.

Clio had walked to Congress Spring, she had taken a glass of the water, she was conscious of a feeling of unusual alertness and excitement. Maroon, having breakfasted at the stables, had driven swiftly to Congress Park and had picked her up and driven her to the hotel in spite of her halfhearted protests. Kaka and Cupide, who had accompanied her as always, had been tucked into the back seat of the high cart. It was this picturesque company upon which Madam Van Steed's eye now fell—fell, flickered and widened in astonishment. Cupide leaped down to hold the horses, Maroon in white hat, white full-skirted coat, Texas boots and fawn trousers, handed down a Clio all cream and black in cool India silk and a lush leghorn hat trimmed with lace and yellow roses. Cream lace and leghorn enhanced the black of her smooth hair, her creamy skin, accented the dark eyes, the cream-colored India silk was set off by black velvet bows. A lace-ruffled parasol made perfect the whole.

Up the piazza steps, Maroon's eyes warm upon her. The statuesque Kakaracou walked behind. Cupide scrambled up to the driver's seat to await Maroon's return.

"Bless my soul!" came the trumpet tones of Madam Van Steed. "What's this? We've not only a circus but a sideshow!"

There was a murmur of remonstrance from the wretched Bart and a snicker of amusement from the piazza collection.

Clio heard a murmur of French from Kaka in the rear. "The old devil has arrived, then, to protect her imp."

Clio nodded coolly in the direction of Van Steed, Maroon swept off the white sombrero in salute, the little group entered the hotel, but not before they heard the beldame's next words shrilled from her nook and evidently addressed to her son. "Who? De Chanfret? What's the world coming to! Well, run along, run after them, fetch her over to me, and the cowboy too. I want to see them."

Another murmur of remonstrance from the wretched Bart; another titter from the group. Hurried footsteps behind them; Bartholomew Van Steed caught up with them. He stood before them, his cheeks were very pink, his amber eyes held a look of pleading.

"Mrs. De Chanfret, my mother arrived unexpectedly last evening—she wants so much to meet you—uh—you, too, Maroon—if you'd—do you mind—she's out on the piazza—not very well, you know—heard so much about you——"

"But I'd be enchanted to meet your dear mother," Clio said; and tossing her parasol to Kaka she gaily tucked one hand in Bart's limp and unresponsive arm, the other in Maroon's, and so through the screened doorway and down the piazza's length, a radiant smiling figure squired by two devoted swains. Now Clio saw that the stout black-clad Bellop was among the group and yet apart from it. She was leaning against one of the piazza pillars, her hands on her broad hips, her mocking eyes regarding the scene before her with anticipatory relish.

She called out to Clio in her deep hearty voice, "Good morning, Countess! *Comment ça va!*" A look of friendly warning in her eye, a something in her tone.

Clio grinned. *"C'est ce que nous verrons."* That remains to be seen.

Stumblingly Van Steed began the introduction. "Mother, this is Mrs. De Chanfret—Colonel Maroon—my——"

"Howdy do! I hear you call yourself a countess."

"I call myself Mrs. De Chanfret."

"Touché!" boomed Mrs. Coventry Bellop.

"Colonel Maroon, eh?" the rasping voice went on. "What war was that? You look a bit young to have been a colonel in the Civil War, young man."

The Texan looked down at her, the sunburned face crinkled in laughter, the drawling voice had in it a note of amused admiration.

"Shucks, Ma'am, I'm no Colonel, any more than old Vanderbilt was a Commodore. You know how it is, Ma'am. Vanderbilt, he ran a Staten Island ferry and some scows loaded with cow manure, and that's all the Commodore he ever was."

In the little ripple of laughter that followed this the cold gray eyes shifted to Clio's lovely face. "That ninny, Bean, the head usher, couldn't find your husband's signature in the old hotel register. Isn't that odd!"

This is going to be bad, after all, Clio thought. Aloud she said, "Signature?"

"I've been coming to the United States Hotel for years. Before it was burned down and after it was rebuilt. I've met every well-known person that ever stopped here—in my day, that is. They saved the old registers from the big fire, you know. You'd be interested to see the signatures. There's the Marquis de Lafayette and General Burnside and General Grant and Washington Irving and even Joseph Bonaparte, the late King of Spain. But no Count de Trenaunay de Chanfret. You say he stayed here?"

"Incognito." Serenely. "When a French diplomat is in America on affairs of state connected with his country, it is sometimes wise to discard titles."

"Mother doesn't mean——" stammered Bart Van Steed, miserably.

Mrs. Coventry Bellop's hearty voice cut in. "She doesn't mean a thing—do you, Clarissa? It doesn't pay to inquire too closely into the background of us Saratoga summer folks. Now you, Clarissa, you call yourself a lady. But that doesn't necessarily mean you are one, does it! Come on, Mrs. De Chanfret. Let's take a turn in the garden along with this handsome Texan. It's too hot out here in the sun for a woman of my girth."

"Good day to you, Ma'am," said Maroon to Madam Van Steed; and bowed, the white sombrero held over his heart.

Clio looked into Sophie Bellop's steady eyes, and her own were warm with gratitude for this new ally. "The garden? That will be charming, dear Mrs. Bellop. . . . Enchanted to have met you, Madam Van Steed. You are all that your dear son had led me to expect."

Into the grateful coolness of the hotel lobby. "Phew!" exclaimed Mrs. Coventry Bellop inelegantly and wiped her flushed face. "The old hell-cat!" Then, as Clint Maroon stared at her with new eyes, she proceeded to take charge. "Look, Colonel, I want to talk to this young lady. You're probably off, anyway, to the track. By the way, that little jockey of yours—where did he ever race before?"

"Why—uh——" floundered Clint.

"He rode Sans Nom at Longchamp two years ago," Clio snapped, for she was by now cross, tired, hot. "What a curious custom you Americans have of asking questions!"

Mrs. Bellop's round white cheeks crinkled in a grin. "You're a

wonderful girl," she boomed. "Run along, Colonel. Mrs. De Chanfret and I, we're going to have a little chat, just us girls."

He looked at Clio. "Would you care to go to the races at
eleven?"

"I am weary of the races."

"We'll drive at three."

"I am bored with the parade. of carriages, like a funeral procession, up and down this Broadway."

"What do you say to dinner out at the Lake?"

"I am sick to death of black bass—corn on the cob—red raspberries—ugh!"

"Why—honey——!"

Sophie Bellop's comfortable laugh cut the little silence. "That's
Saratoga sickness. Everybody feels that way after two weeks. If you
can stand it after two weeks of it you can stand it for two months, and
like it." She waved him away with a flirt of her strangely small, lean
hand. "She'll be all right by this evening. You run along, Colonel
Maroon."

He looked at Clio. She nodded. He was off, his Texas boots tap-
ping smartly on the flagstones, the broad shoulders straightening in
relief at being out of this feminine pother.

Clio thought, I must be rid of this woman. There is a reason for
this sudden friendliness. She held out her hand. "I hope you weren't
too sharp, after all, with that very provincial old lady. But thank you.
Good-by."

"Nonsense. I want to talk to you. It's important. Don't be silly,
child."

"The garden?"

"No. Your room. We can talk there."

With a shrug Clio turned toward the cottages. Kakaracou was
accustomed to surprises. Her face, as she opened the door, remained
impassive. Only the eyes narrowed a little in suspicion.

"Make me some coffee, Kaka. Will you have some, Mrs. Bellop?
I've had no breakfast. But these huge trays of heavy food—I can't face

them any more. How I should love a crisp *croissant* with sweet butter! Ah, well." She took off the broad-brimmed leghorn with its heavy trimming of blond lace and roses and ribbons, she flung it on the table among a litter of books and trinkets and *bibelots*. The grim little hotel sitting room had, with her occupancy, taken on a luxurious and feminine air. Sophie Bellop's eyes, intelligent, materialistic, encompassed the room and its contents, stared openly, without obliqueness, into the bedroom beyond with its lacy pink pillows, its scent bottles, its flowers and yellow-backed French books and its froth of furbelows.

"If you'd ask me," boomed Sophie Bellop, "who I'd rather be than anyone in the world this minute, I'd say—you."

Clio had gone straight to the bedroom and, Southern fashion, she was unconcernedly getting out of her elaborate street clothes and into an airy ruffled wrapper. Thus she had seen Rita Dulaine and Belle Piquery do, thus she always would do. Kaka, on her knees, was unlacing her. Now, as Clio, in petticoats and corset cover, moved toward the door the better to gaze upon the astonishing Mrs. Bellop, Kaka too moved forward, still on her knees.

"Me!" Bare-armed, her hands on her hips, Clio stared in unbelief. "But why?"

Mrs. Bellop had discovered a dish of large meaty black cherries on the sitting-room table and was munching them and blowing the pits into her palm. "No reason. No reason, my girl, except that you're young and beautiful and smart and brassy and have two dashing young men in love with you—at least, poor Bart would be dashing if that old harridan didn't catch on to his coat-tails every time he tries to dash—and are going to be rich if you use some sense. That's all." She popped another cherry into her mouth.

Clio said nothing. She moved back into her bedroom. Her corsets came off; you heard a little sigh of relief as lungs and muscles expanded. The cool flimsy gabrielle enveloped her. "The coffee, Kaka. Quickly. In there. A napkin and bowl for Mrs. Bellop's hands."

She crossed the little sitting room then with her easy indolent stride and sank back against the lumpy couch whose bleakness was enlivened by the Spanish silk shawl of lemon yellow thrown over its back.

Mrs. Bellop, relieved of the cherry pits, relaxed in her chair, belched a little and began to drum dreamily on the marble table top with her slim sensitive fingers. A silence fell between the two women—a silence of deliberate waiting, weighing, measuring.

At last Clio spoke, deliberately. "Just what is it you want of me?"

"Money."

"I have no money."

"You will have."

"How?"

"By listening to me."

"You have no money. Why have you not listened to yourself?"

"Because I'm not you. I explained that to you a minute ago. And I've been a fool most of my life."

Kaka brought the coffee, fragrant, steaming. Clio sugared it generously, drank it, creamless, in great grateful gulps. "Ah! That's wonderful! Another cup, Kaka." Kaka, in the bedroom, busied herself with the India silk, the froth of garments lately discarded.

"Tell your woman to shut that door."

"It doesn't matter. Kaka knows everything. She never talks. If you mean me harm she would be likely to kill you. She would make a little figure like you, out of soap or dough, and she would stick pins in it through the place where the heart and the brain and the bowels would be if it were alive. And you'd sicken and die."

"Not I," retorted Mrs. Coventry Bellop, briskly. "I've had pins stuck in me all my life, and knives, too. Clarissa Van Steed alone would have been the death of me if I hadn't the hide of a rhinoceros."

Clio, sipping her second cup of coffee, set the cup down on the saucer now with a little decisive clack. "All my life, Mrs. Bellop, I have been very direct. If I wanted to do a thing, and it was possible to do it, I did it. I say what I want to say. That old woman on the piazza, she is a terrible old woman, she dislikes me, she makes no pretense. I rather admire her for it. I shall be grateful if you will be as honest."

She placed the cup and saucer on the tabouret at her side; she leaned back and regarded the woman before her with a level look.

"You're a babe," Mrs. Bellop began, briskly, "if you think that old adder is honest. She isn't. But that's neither here nor there. You're right, she hates you and she wants to run you out of Saratoga and she'll do it unless——"

"Unless?"

Sophie Bellop spread her feet wide apart, leaned forward, rested her hands on her plump knees and looked Clio straight in the eye. "Look, my girl. I know you're no more the Comtesse de Trumpery and Choo-Choo than I am Queen Victoria. But if I say you are, if I take you in hand, if I stand up for you against this old buzzard and her crew, the world will believe you are. I've watched you now for two weeks. And I'll say this: you've been wonderful. Bold and dramatic and believable. But from now on you'll need a strong arm behind you, and that handsome Texan's arm won't be enough. It's got to be a woman who's smarter than old lady Van Steed and who they're scared of."

As the woman talked, Clio was thinking, well, here it is. I wonder if she knows everything. I suppose I was foolish to think that America was so simple. It's no good being grand and denying things and telling her to go.

"What is it you want?"

"I'm coming to that. Let me just rattle on a little, will you? I'm gabby, but what I've got to say to you is important to both of us. And I like you more than ever for not trying to pretend you don't know what I'm talking about. Now listen. I know my way around this world. I've known what it was to be very rich. I know what it is to be very poor; I've lived on nothing for years. In luxury."

"Blackmail?" inquired Clio, pleasantly, as one would say, for example—farming?

"Give me credit for being smarter than that. Listen, my child. You've been shrewd, but you can't beat this combination without inside help any more than you can beat the roulette and faro games at the Club House simply because you happen to win once or twice. You lose in the end unless you know how the wheel is fixed or can fix it yourself. Same with Saratoga; same way with everything. I know everybody. I've been everywhere. I know Europe. I know America. If I give a party that somebody else pays for, everybody comes because I'm giving it. Don't ask me why. I don't know. I'm nearly sixty. I dress and look like a washwoman, so the women are never envious of me and the men never fall in love with me and I have a fine time. I'm afraid of nobody. If you know anything about America, which you probably don't, you know that Coventry Bellop was one of the wealthiest of the really rich men of the 1860's. He was in on Erie—maybe you don't know what that meant and I won't go into it now—but the New York Central crowd took it away from him, and then Astor and Drew and Van Steed and Fisk and Gould came in on Erie—well, when Covey died of a stroke in '69, I was left as bare as the day I was born and people began to call me not Sophie Bellop or Mrs. Coventry Bellop, but Poorsophiebellop, just like that, all in one word. Poorsophiebellop. The wives of the very men who'd ruined him. Not that I blame them. Covey'd have done the same to them if he'd been smart enough to beat them. Well, they thought Poorsophiebellop would take their old clothes and live in that fourth-floor back bedroom in a rich relation's house and be glad to be asked in for tea. Right then I made it my motto to insult them before they could insult me. I was earning my living—and fairly honestly, too—in a day when it wasn't just downright common and vulgar for a woman to work for her living the way it is now—it was considered criminal. Not that I really worked. I schemed. I planned. I tricked and contrived. I made certain hotels fashionable by touting for them. I put Saratoga on the map. I made Newport, though I must say I can't bear the place. Remember, I've known the cream of two continents in my days—Daniel Webster, Washington Irving, Henry Clay, William Makepeace Thackeray, Henry James, for brains—not to speak of rich riffraff like the Astors, Drew, Jim Hill, the Vanderbilts, the Goulds, and plenty of dressed-up circus mountebanks like Jim Fish and his brawling crew.

As for the gloating friends like Clarissa Van Steed and the rich rela-
tions—I threw their cast-off clothes back in their faces and I snapped
my fingers at the hall bedrooms. If I'd been a beauty, like you, I could
have had the world. I don't know, though. There's always been a soft
streak in me that crops out when I least want it. Now Bellop. I knew
he was weak when I married him. But his eyes were so blue and he
cried when I refused him. I thought I could make him strong and self-
reliant. But you can't make iron out of lead. . . . So then, there I was,
a widow and a pauper; I had two black dresses, one for daytime, one
for evening, and that's been my uniform ever since. I don't bother
about clothes and it's wonderful. Nobody cares how I look, anyway.
I'm the life of the party. Most people don't know how to have a good
time, any more than spoiled children. I show them. I spend their
money for them, and they're grateful for it. I've got nothing to lose
because I live by my wits. They can't take that away from me. So I say
and I do as I please. It's a grand feeling."

Clio laughed suddenly, spontaneously, in sheer delight. "You're
like Aunt Belle. It's wonderful!"

"Who's she?"

"Mama's sister. My Aunt Belle Piquery. Only she was more—
well—*légère*. But she used a word—a Northern word. Spunky. She
used to say she liked people with spunk."

"M'm. I know about your mama. I made it my business to find
out. I've got connections in New Orleans."

"Then it is blackmail, after all?"

"No, child. I tell you I like you. And I hate Clarissa Van Steed
and everything she stands for. She and women like her have kept
America back fifty years. Hard and rigid and provincial. And mean.
She's got the ugliest house in New York; the curtains at her front
windows amount to a drawbridge moat and bastion. What's a bastion,
anyway?"

Clio laughed again. "You came here just to talk. But I think you
are really wonderful. The one amusing person I have met in America."

"That's right. Keep up that French accent. Your natural theater sense is one of your most valuable assets—though sometimes you overdo it. . . . So you're set on marrying little Bart Van Steed, eh?"

"I do not think that concerns you."

"You can't do it without me. He hasn't asked you yet, and he never will, now that the old devil's here, unless he's properly managed."

Suddenly, "I do not think I care to go on with this conversation."

But Sophie Bellop blithely waved aside this blunt statement which Clio had followed by rising as though to end the visit. Brightly, chattily, she went on, her attitude more relaxed now, her big body leaning comfortably against the chair back.

"Sit down, child, and stop fussing. Now then. Bart's really rich. I don't mean just rich—he's got seventy, eighty millions if he's got a cent and even if the Gould crowd trick him out of the trunk line——"

Clio sat down then. "You know about that, too?"

"Of course. I'm coming to that later. Maroon. Let's see—what was I saying? Oh, yes. Well, I've watched you like a hawk, you're a smart girl, you've got the jaw of success, and if you manage that big handsome brute right, even if he isn't as smart as you are—oh, I forgot, you're set on marrying Van Steed instead. Well, perhaps you're right, but I suppose if I had it to do I'd be a fool and marry the Texan though he hasn't a penny. I never could resist a magnificent specimen like that. Those shoulders, and small through the hips, and the way he looks at you. Ah, me! Well, lucky I haven't turned silly in my old age. I play the piano like an angel, I never forget a face, I'm healthy, I don't nip away at a bottle the way some women do, my age, poor things."

She had not yet put her cards on the table. Her handsome shrewd eyes were on Clio; she was talking now in order to give the girl time in which to digest what she had heard. "They'll be after you now; they've only been waiting for a leader; they'll tear you to pieces if you try to go it alone from now on. But they're afraid of me. It was I who fixed on the number Four Hundred for the Centennial Ball in

'76. You probably don't know about that. Most of the world thinks that Ward McAllister and Mrs. William Astor picked the Four Hundred. But the inner circle knows I did it. More heads fell that winter than at the time of the Bastille. Those daughters and granddaughters of peddlers and butchers and fur dealers and land grabbers are afraid of me because I'm not scared of them. And I give them a good time, poor dears, and show them how to have fun with their money."

Now that Clio Dulaine understood thoroughly, she put her question bluntly. "How much do you want?"

"Understand," parried Mrs. Coventry Bellop, "you don't need anyone to manage you; you've been clever as can be from the very first. That spectacular entrance and then disappearing for two days. They nearly died. I see you've got a crest on almost everything. Can't make it out, though."

"Kaka embroiders so beautifully. My name is Clio. She combined that with the crest of the Duc de Chaulnes and part of the coat-of arms of the Dulaines. Sometimes I use just the plain letter C, with a vine or a wreath."

Sophie Bellop burst into laughter. "That's what I mean. You're a natural success. You have the right instinct. Nothing can stop you—with me behind you."

"How much do you want?"

"Of course," Mrs. Bellop rattled on, "you've got the right to help yourself to a couple of crests and titles. Look at the people who've come over this land like vultures. Not only Americans. Lord Dunmore's got a hundred thousand acres of good American land if he's got a grain. Dunraven's got sixty thousand up in Colorado. We're fools. We're fools. We think it can go on forever. Too much of everything. I'll bet in another hundred years or even less we'll find out. We'll be a ruined country unless they stop this grabbing. We'll be so soft that anybody can come and take us like picking a ripe plum. It's something to scare you, this country, I always say. There's never been anything like it. Floods, grasshoppers, snowstorms—never anything in moderation. Too hot or too cold or too high or too big. The whole

West from North Dakota on buried in snow last winter. You can't begin to——"

"How much do you want?"

"I think you can get him if you want him. Mrs. Porcelain's too Dolly Vardenish and pink for him. And the Forosini's too common. I'm nearly sixty. I won't live more than another ten or twelve years. I'll take twenty-five thousand down on the day of your settlement and ten thousand a year for ten years. I don't want to be grasping."

"How do you know—how do I know—that I can't do this alone?"

"Very well. Try it."

"Or suppose, together, we don't succeed. Then what?"

"Nothing. You'll have learned from me and I from you. You can give me a present—something negotiable, I hope. Now then, I like everything in writing, black on white. It saves a lot of rumpus in the end."

The sound of swift, light footsteps on the cottage veranda, the hall door opened and shut, a tap at the door of the little sitting room. Clio stood up, an unaccustomed scarlet suddenly showing beneath the cream-white skin.

"Come in!"

Maroon's height and breadth seemed to fill the little room. He brought with him the smell of the stables and of barber's ointment and cigars and leather.

The lusty Sophie sniffed the air. "You smell nice and masculine. It's grand."

His blue plainsman's eyes looked from Clio to Sophie and back again. "You two plotting something? You look guilty as all hell."

Clio trailed her laces over to him, she picked up his great hand, she looked at it intently as though examining it for the first time. An intimate gesture, childlike. "Mrs. Bellop is going to be my—my chaperon."

He grinned. "Little late, I'd say."

Mrs. Bellop stood up and shook herself like an amiable poodle. "Not too late. We hope."

He eyed Clio straight. "Not too late for—what?"

Clio dropped his hand then and walked to the window that looked out on the sun-dappled garden. She shrugged her shoulders evasively.

Mrs. Bellop furnished a brisk answer. "For social success and a brilliant marriage—with someone who is really mad about her. You know who." She came over to Maroon, the plump poodle looked saucily up at the mastiff. "Though I'll say this: how any girl can look at any other man when you're around is more than I can see. If I was twenty years younger—well—twenty-five, say—I'd snatch you off if I had to drug you to do it. Speaking of drugs, that horse of yours—well, we won't go into that. Thanks for the tip, though. Comes in handy when a girl's got her own way to make. . . . What was I saying—oh, yes. If she wants to marry money, why, that's her business. I did. And now look at me. But don't think I'm going to neglect you, dear boy. I've got a scheme I want you to present to Bart Van Steed—you can say you thought of it—and I'll swear it will save that trunk line of the Albany and Tuscarora from falling into the clutches of——"

"Hold on there! Hold on! Just because Clio there has got me saddle broke don't get the idea that you can gentle me. If Clio is hankering for social success and a brilliant marriage, and you're the one to rope and tie the bridegroom, why here's wishing you luck. But you got me wrong, sister. When it comes to riding my own range, why, I'm the one that wears the pants. That matter, Clio, I'd say— only I don't want to get mixed up in any woman business—I'd say you've gone this far alone, I'd go the rest of the way and play the game out."

Slowly, as though emerging from a spell, Clio turned from the window. "You would?" she said, uncertainly. "You would?"

"Sure would. You're smarter than any woman in this town. Go it alone. . . . Sa-a-ay, that coffee sure smells good. Kaka! How about rustling me a cup!"

Clio Dulaine walked over to Mrs. Bellop. She held out her hand. "Thank you so much, Mrs. Bellop. You have been so kind. Don't think me ungrateful. I like you. But he is right."

Mrs. Bellop looked from one to the other, she laughed a little discomfited laugh. "Well, you can't say I didn't warn you."

"You are wonderful. So honest. And really good. Here. Please take this." To her own surprise Clio took a ring from her finger, pressed it into Mrs. Bellop's hand. "You are the only woman who has shown me kindness."

"Women," murmured Mrs. Bellop as she turned the ring this way and that to catch the light, "are a hundred years behind the times. They don't know their own strength. Some day they'll catch up with themselves and then this will be a different world. Look here, Clio, I'm going to stay behind you anyway, not being bossy but just in case. And just to prove to you I like you I'm going to keep your ring. Giving it to me is the first foolish thing you've done. Hang onto your jewelry, I always say. It's a woman's best friend."

XV

★

Suddenly Clio Dulaine felt herself curiously alone in Saratoga; not alone merely, but neglected. She had arrived in an impasse. She knew she must break through this or devise another way. Her flouncings, her paradings, her dramatic entrances, her outrageous flouting of the conventions had begun to pall on her audience. Her sure dramatic sense warned her of this. At this crucial moment her two swains had grown distrait and even neglectful.

"Business," Clint would say, when she reproached him. "I'd like to go along with you, honey, but I've got a little matter of business to tend to. Now, Bart, he'd come a running if he knew you wanted to drive out. Why'n't you send Cupide over with a note?"

"How dare you!" she would say, melodramatically.

Innocently, almost absently, he would stare at her. "What's up? Have I said something? I didn't go to."

"How dare you say to me that you're busy! And suggest that I go about begging other men to take me here and there! Perhaps the kind of women you have——"

"Hold on! I didn't say anything about other men. I said Bart. He's the man you're fixing to marry."

"Oh, so that's it. You're jealous."

"Oh. Yes. Uh-huh. Leastways, I would be if I had time. But I am busier than a sheep dog. Look, I'm seeing Van Steed right soon. Shall I tell him?"

"Get out! Get out of my sight!"

There was about him nothing of the chagrined suitor. On the contrary, he seemed elated and thoroughly the male pleased with himself. This in itself was sufficiently annoying to the high-handed Clio. But now, to her bewilderment, the timorous Van Steed was sometimes guilty of similar conduct. Even in her company he actually seemed unconscious of her presence. It wasn't a lessening of his devotion, she felt, nor of Clint's. It was an intangible barrier that had come up between her and them. Her small personal plans seemed insignificant. From first place she sensed herself relegated to second position. Awaiting a reply to a question, she could find Van Steed's face blank. A silence. Then, "Oh, I beg your pardon! What was that you said? I was thinking——" he would stammer.

Baffled, Clio turned waspishly on Kakaracou and Cupidon. But in Cupide she encountered the same maddening preoccupation with something beyond her ken. Do this, do that, she would snap at him. But his goggle gaze would be fixed dreamily on some inner vision. "Do you hear me, you *suppôt!*"

"Did you say something, Ma'm'selle?"

Kaka, brushing the girl's hair and seeing the wrathful face in the mirror, attempted to offer her soothing solution.

"They cooking up something. Don't you fuss your head. They doing business."

"I don't care what they're doing. I'm bored with it here, anyway. Silly place, third-rate, provincial. Mama would have loathed it. I think I shall leave next week."

At this Cupide set up a howl of protest. "No! I won't go! I won't go!"

Clio surveyed the dwarf through narrowed lids. "Oh, you won't go, is that what I hear!" Then, in a surprising shout that topped his own, "Why not? Why not, *petit drôle?* Quick! Answer me!"

"Business," said Cupide. "I have business."

With practiced ease he dodged as she reached swiftly for the hair-brush and let fly at him.

The truth of it was that he had. Van Steed had business. Maroon had business. Cupidon, blessed by nature with keyhole height, had made their business his.

Even when they had no engagement, Clint had always rushed to her side at sight of her, whether in the garden, at the springs, in the lobby, or the piazza. Van Steed's method had been less forthright, yet he too had seemed always somehow to be standing near, even if his mother's hand clutched his arm as she leaned on him not only for support but to stay him. Yet now she could pass the two men as they stood in the lobby talking together earnestly, seriously, and her bewilderment mounted to fury as they bowed and held their hats aloft with the kind of exaggeration which comes of absentminded courtesy. They were thinking of something other than herself; they were so deeply interested in what they were saying that she, Clio Dulaine, was actually only another woman passing. She listened sharply as she undulated by. The Texan's drawling voice:

"The government ought to get back of the railroads. Now, take Texas. It's a young state run by young men. Neither I nor my father before me cared a hoot for public office but railroads——"

"In arriving at the cost of production less depreciation, why, the local conditions such as service required and maintenance——"

Then for three days he was gone. He had announced his going, casually, the night before his departure. A shade too casually.

"Almost forgot to tell you, honey, I'm taking a little trip on business." This was the new Clint Maroon, in the saddle, and, as he phrased it, rarin' to go.

"Where? Where are you going?"

"Oh, Albany. Albany and New York."

"What for? You used to tell me everything. What are you keeping from me?"

"I'm showing your little friend Van Steed that he can't go on trying to make agreements with these pirates. Next thing he knows they're going to get more than that little trunk-line railroad away from him. Maybe his pa left him millions, but hanging on to 'em is something different."

"Oh, really! If you know so much about making millions why don't you tell him this?"

"I did. I said, look, Van Steed, the way you're going I reckon you'll lose your piece of railroad and what goes with it. What's it mean to you, losing that hundred miles of coal haul? In figures, I mean. You know how he is, him and his kind. Afraid to give you a straight answer to a straight question. Well, what do I know about railroads and so on? Nothing! I said, will you give me a share in the road if I save it for you? Save it how? he said. Fighting it out, I told him, the way we used to fight the sheep men to save the cattle range."

Clio stared, aghast. "But Clint, you can't do that! This isn't the Wild West."

"Worse. It's the wild East. They've got the shareholdings deadlocked down there now. The board of directors are divided, half the Erie crowd, half the Morgan-Van Steed crowd. They actually wrestle for the stock books. I mean wrestle. Van Steed, he's about ready to give up; he's not much of a scrapper. But this J. P. Morgan, he's the boy for my money. I never thought I'd be in a railroad fight, but say, honey, this last week I've had more fun than any time since I came up North from Texas. And they're paying me for it. A fistful of shares if we——"

She grasped his arm, she shook him as though to bring him to his senses. "This is a dangerous business. What do they care for you! What are you doing down there! What is it you have been doing this week away from me? Tell me!"

"Well, I got a gang together from here and around. Went away to New York for some of 'em—there's quite a bunch of Texas boys around, you'd be surprised. Hard times. Hard times. Look at the wealth in the country, and hundreds and thousands begging in the streets. Look at Frick, a millionaire at thirty! Look at Carnegie down at the Thompson Steel Works, getting a hundred and thirty percent for his money. Pirates. You can't deal with 'em. You have to fight 'em, barehanded. That's how I put it to Morgan, and I'll say this for him, he was with me. There's been scraps in every railroad station along the line, but last week—time I was away there—we got wind of the plan they had to take over the office headquarters at Albany by force. Sent up a bunch of brass-knuckle boys and mavericks, said they were deputies, with fake badges pinned on 'em. Well, say, honey, force is what they got. I had the boys rounded up, so when Jim Briscoe and his gang of thugs stepped through the door expecting to find nobody but old Gid Fish with his eyeshade on and sleeve-protectors, why, Briscoe he yelled, 'Rush in, boys, and take possession! Throw him out! Grab the books!' That's where we came in, yelling like Comanches and threw the whole crowd, Briscoe first of all, right down the stairs of the Tuscarora office. You never saw such a boiling or arms and legs there at the foot of the stairs. Nobody hurt serious—couple arms and legs and so on—but we were laughing so, seeing their faces, we like to fell down the stairs ourselves, on top of 'em."

Clio clasped her hands to her head, as nearly distraught as he had ever seen her. "I won't listen. I won't listen!"

"Why, Clio, honey, you asked me what I'd been up to, didn't you?"

"But it's savage! It's disgusting!"

"Y-e-e-es," he drawled. "Perfectly disgusting." His tone, so quiet, so even, was venomous. "Almost as disgusting as what they did to my folks. A real delicate little flower like you, brought up in Paris and so on, you wouldn't understand. No! Van Steed, he's more your kind. Ladylike, he wouldn't hurt a fly. Pay somebody, though, to swat the fly for him."

"Chéri, we didn't come here to this Saratoga to fight railroads."

"Oh, yes we did."

"To fight them with tricks, yes, and to get some of their millions if we could. But not to fight with fists and boots, like savages. I am frightened. I am frightened—for you."

But the surly mood was still on him. There had been a time when he would have melted at this evidence of her solicitude, but now he said sneeringly, "Say, that's fine! I've got you to look after me, and little Bart, he's got his mama, why, no boogy man can get us that-away."

Clio had battles of her own in plenty by now, but these brutal tales of Clint Maroon's adventures in railroading filled her with apprehension. Bewildered, she brought up the subject as casually as possible when next she saw Van Steed. It was interesting to see his struggles, buffeted as he now was between the filial habit of years and the powerful new emotion which this beautiful and unconventional woman had aroused in him. Inexperienced in love and wary of its unexplored dangers, he tried rather clumsily to be in her company when the maternal eye was not upon him.

"Uh—Mrs. De Chanfret—I—I hear you have a charming apartment in the cottages with your own beautiful—uh—bric-a-brac and ornaments and—uh—so forth. I never have had the privilege of seeing you surrounded by your—uh—own personal—that is——"

"Who told you this?"

"Why, Mrs. Bellop, I believe. That is, Mrs. Bellop."

"What an amazing woman! What energy! She has been most friendly to me."

"Would you—could I come to call some—some afternoon, perhaps, and have—that is—tea? You never have invited me, you know." He felt very audacious.

"Tea! I never could understand tea—except as medicine, of course. At night, when I am weary, Kaka brews me a tisane to soothe me. But tea as tea!"

"Oh, well, I just meant—you know—tea as a—a—symbol—I mean——"

"Dear Mr. Van Steed, that is almost as if you meant to sound improper!"

"Oh, no, Mrs. De Chanfret. I assure you!" It was too easy to bring the deeper pink into the already roseate cheeks.

"I was only teasing. Do come—tomorrow afternoon? And perhaps your mama would like to come, too." With innocent cordiality.

"I'm afraid not. She rarely goes anywhere; she isn't well, you know. Rheumatism—her age—difficult."

"So I have heard. It is difficult to believe. She is so very—alert." Then the direct attack. "Your mama does not like me."

"Oh, I wouldn't say that, Mrs. De Chanfret."

"Oh, it's quite natural. There are reasons, natural and unnatural. She wants to keep you by her—wait! I don't mean to offend you. She herself probably would be the first to deny it. She fears—and hates—any young and attractive woman who may snatch you from her. Particularly one like myself who is not of her little world—who is not *chacalata*."

"Not what? What's that mean?"

"Oh, that's a word, a foreign sort of word, it means conventional—*comme il faut*. It's a word out of my childhood. Well, she has nothing to fear from me, dear Mr. Van Steed. My heart lies buried in my beloved France." She saw the stubborn look come into his face. I've almost got him, she thought, exultantly. And even as his conviction came to her she perversely put it away from her. How silly he looks simpering at me like that! "Tomorrow afternoon, then. And do bring your dear mama if she cares to come."

He came alone, as she had known he would. She had set her stage. The heritage of Great-Grand'mère Bonnevie, the actress, always welled strong in her at times such as this. She wore simple white with the little girlish strand of pearls as ornament; she looked young, cool, virginal. Bart Van Steed, staring at her in the dim seclusion of the sitting room, blurted his thoughts as always.

"You look—different."

"Different?" She put one hand to her breast, posed fingers up like that portrait of the Empress Louise.

"Younger. That is, younger."

"Oh dear Mr. Van Steed! Have I seemed so old!"

It was too easy to make him blush, stammer, fidget. "No! No!

Only about the hotel and in the evening and at the races you always seemed so much more—that is—your clothes usually so sophisticated and now you look"— fatuously—"you are like a little girl."

"Oh, Mr. Van Steed! How sweet! How sweet of you! After all, I was widowed at nineteen——"

Kaka and two black waiters crackling in stiffly starched linens now appeared with the tea-things. "Tea!" Van Steed cried in considerable dismay.

"You said tea," Clio reminded him, gently.

They sipped, stirred, munched. Years of this, Clio thought, grimly. Millions and security—but years of this.

Kaka in her best silk and best manner served them, shooing away the hotel waiters who had brought the tray.

"Wouldn't you rather have something cold to drink, perhaps?" Clio suggested, for he had placed the cup, almost untouched, on the table beside his chair. "Lemonade, or one of Kaka's delicious rum——"

"No. No, really, my digestion. Uh——"

"I have asked dear Mrs. Bellop to drop in, since your mama couldn't chaperon us. Not that we need a chaperon. A poor old widow like myself."

His pink face clouded with displeasure. "Mrs. Bellop!" Then hastily, "I wanted to ask you—could I fetch you for the ball tonight? I'd be delighted to call for you."

"I should have loved it. But I've promised to go with Colonel Maroon."

"Maroon's away." Bluntly.

"Yes. Yes, I know. But he'll be back. He assured me he would be back." She leaned forward. Something in his face alarmed her. "He went only to Albany, he said. Tell me, isn't this Albany very near Saratoga?"

"Why, yes. You passed it on your way traveling here in the train. Must have."

"Colonel Maroon has told me it is the capital of the state of New York."

"Yes. That's right."

"But Mr. Van Steed! I am bewildered. I cannot understand! What manner of country is this! There is Albany, the capital of the state, I hear that hordes of—of roughs they fight like savages for a railroad. Where are the laws! Where are the police! The military!"

The tale of banditry had seemed fantastic enough coming from the lips of the big Texan; but now to hear it retold and augmented by the shy and pink-cheeked Van Steed had the effect of wild absurdity.

"Oh. Well. You see, they've bought up the town councilors and so on." Very matter-of-factly. "We've met trick with trick and bribe with bribe. It's a matter of—uh—force now, you know." He patted her hand timidly. "You shouldn't worry your pretty head about such matters, dear Mrs. De Chanfret. In fact, Colonel Maroon shouldn't have told you. It's—uh—man's business."

She looked at him scornfully. "Really! What are you doing about it? You yourself, I mean."

He smiled tolerantly. "I'm afraid you wouldn't understand. But I may tell you—in confidence—that we now have possession of the Albany end of the road. Briscoe and his crowd have retreated to the Binghamton end." He looked about him, cautiously. He lowered his voice. "Traffic has stopped entirely. The people living along the line are terrified. We are planning to send down fully five hundred men by train and take the stations along the Binghamton route by force."

"Whose plan is this?"

"Well, Colonel Maroon proposed it, really——"

Suddenly, like a madness, little darts of rage and hate shot through her body; she wanted to hurt this shy and nervous little man, she hated him, she hated Saratoga, she hated the hotel, Madam Van Steed, Congress Spring, the race track, the lake, the food, the piazza, the world. She felt her fingers tingling with the desire to strike him—to slap him across his delicate pink face.

In a fury of cruelty she said, "You are afraid. You are afraid to fight for your own railroad, you are afraid of your mother, you are afraid of me, you are afraid of life, you are afraid of everything! Go away! Go away! I want to be alone."

She saw the look in his amber eyes; she saw the color drain out of his face. Abruptly she left him, flew to her room, fell to berating Kaka, and ended in a burst of tears, a thing in itself so rare in her that even Kakaracou was alarmed. The man in the front room stood a moment, his palms pressed to his eyes. Then he went, closing the front door gently.

In Kaka's arms, her head against the bony breast, she sniffled, "I detest this place! I wish I had never come. I wish we had stayed in Paris. I wish we had stayed in New Orleans. At least we belonged there. After a fashion. Even he doesn't care any more; he leaves me alone. Alone!"

Kaka rocked her to and fro. *"Pauvre bébé!* My pretty one, like my beautiful Rita! Alone."

But at that Clio Dulaine sat up, dried her eyes. *"Idiote!* I am not Rita! I am Clio! And I shall make my life as I said. No whining and weeping for me. There! I'm strong again. I'll show them, those devils who sit all day on the piazza brewing their witches' brew! And what do you think, he goes to fight like a common *Apache* in railroads!"

Kaka sniffed her disdain. "That *vacher!* That *gascon* with his swagger!"

Hearing him attacked by another, Clio now sprang to his defense. "He is no *gascon.* He doesn't swagger. He is too brave, that's the trouble. He fights the battles of little men who are too weak and cowardly to fight their own."

"You know what I think?" Kakaracou went on, maddeningly. "I think we have seen the last of him, that one. I hear he is to have a big lump of money for this work he is doing like a roustabout on the docks in New Orleans."

Fortunately it was a powder puff that Clio was holding in her right hand. If it had been a paperweight, a knife, a lump of iron, it would have been the same. She threw it into Kaka's face, she began to scream in French, English and Gombo, somewhat to her own surprise, epithets she had not known she knew. *"Cochonne!* Black devil! *Carencro!* Congo! Witch from hell! How dare you say he will not come back! He'll be back for the ball tonight. He promised me. He is going in real cowboy costume—chaps and spurs and lariat—and Cupide is——"

"Cupide is—where?" Kaka interrupted, her voice ominous.

"Cupide? Why—I haven't seen him today. I suppose he's over at the stables again; he fancies himself since he stole that race. I'll have a talk with him, that *suppôt!"*

"Cupide is with him."

"He can't be! How do you know?"

"For days now he has been pleading to go with him."

"Yes, but he refused to take him. I heard him."

"They have some big dangerous plan. I know that. Cupide knew it too. He listened. He must have hidden himself somewhere when the Maroon went off, and now he is with him. I know. I am sure."

"I'll whip him myself. I'll take my riding crop and I'll—— What's that plan? What dangerous plan? Tell me!"

"Something crazy. He is driving to this Albany, then a train, the lot of them, toward a town——"

"Binghamton?"

"Yes, that's it. There are a lot of them, they are going to take each station along the way, Cupide said, as if they were fighting in a war—it is crazy I tell you—bizarre, like this place—this Saratoga—I tell you if anything happens to Cupide because of him, I'll kill him, I'll——"

Now it was Clio who was comforting the black woman, her arms about Kaka's meager shoulders, her lovely cheek pressed against the withered one.

"What stupid talk, Kaka. Nothing will happen to them. We are simply not used to the way things are done here. We've been gone so long. It is like that in America. It is quite the thing. If you want a thing—land—a railroad—you simply take it. *Drôle, ça."*

The Negress shook her head. "I tell you it's not good, I don't like it. Railroads. And fights with engines. What has Cupide to do with railroads! I tell you——" Her high thin voice rose in a wail.

Brisk knuckles rapped at the door. A hearty voice boomed, "What's going on here!"

Kaka jerked herself erect. "That great cow!" Miraculously she assumed her usual dignity like a garment as she opened the door. Sophie Bellop bounced in, a bombazine ball.

"What a to-do! I could hear you across the garden, screeching like a couple of fishwives. And Bart Van Steed looking up at your window as if he had seen a ghost. You can't afford to do this, Clio."

"I can afford to do what I please. What do I care for these old gossips? I spit on them. . . . Kaka, mix me a *coquetier*. I have been very upset. Will you have a *coquetier*, Mrs. Bellop?"

"What's that?"

"That is a little drink to hearten and steady one. A *coquetier* it is called. Aunt Belle used to take one when she felt upset. She used to let me taste hers, and Mama would scold her, but I loved it."

"Oh, no! Not for me. It's a drink, is it? I take nothing. You know that."

"No, no, it's a medicine, really. Aunt Belle said it was brought to New Orleans from Santo Domingo by Peychaud, the apothecary. Bitters, and a dash of cognac, and a twist of lemon peel. He mixed it in an egg-shaped cup. That's why it's called a *coquetier*. Lovely. Do just sip it, to try."

"Well, I'll just taste it, that's all, to please you."

Kaka glimpsed a black waiter, white-coated, crossing the garden. "Ice!" she bawled, thrusting her head out of the window. "Ice! For *coquetier!*"

Sophie Bellop shook her head reproachfully. "You folks have outlandish manners. It's all very well to be original, I think that's very clever, but with everyone against you as they are now——"

"Pooh! What do I care!" Clio curled herself up on the hard little sofa, she kicked off her slippers, she rolled up the voluminous sleeves of her gown. "Phew! It is hot here in this miserable Saratoga. I shall be glad to go. I think I shall go to the mountains. Where are there mountains here? Like the Alps."

Sophie Bellop's usually placid face was serious. "In this country we'd consider the Alps as foothills. Anyway, you're not going. Now look here. You've done wonderfully until now. All of a sudden you're behaving like a ninny. What's come over you?"

"*Ennui.* I am bored with Saratoga. With these railroad *parvenus.* I thought it would be wonderful to be very rich and secure and respectable for the rest of my life. Well, look at them. They're afraid of one another, they're afraid of me! Bart Van Steed is a *lâche.* The old one is a shrew and a devil. That Forosini and the Porcelain have the taste of vulgar provincials."

"Yes, well, let's stop all this fancy talk and be sensible."

"Sensible! Sensible! Sensible about what?"

"About the way you're behaving. It's really kind of crazy."

"Oh, *zut!* You have found out. You learn everything. Very well. I have done something wrong. I told little Van Steed he is a coward. What do I care! I managed before I came to this Saratoga. I can manage again."

"But it's turned out right—or it may. Listen to me, child——"

But an imp of contrariness dominated the girl. "Ah, Kaka! There you are! Drink that, Mrs. Bellop, and then we shall be as sensible as sensible can be." She took the little glass from Kaka, she sniffed, she tasted, she nodded in approval, she quaffed it down. Potent, slightly bitter, the *coquetier* seemed to leap like a tiny tongue of liquid flame from her throat down to her vitals. Mrs. Bellop sipped, said, "Ugh! Bitter as gall," made a wry face, drank it down. "What's that you called it?"

"*Coquetier.*"

"Oh, now I get it. *Coquetier.* Cocktail! Of course. What's that in it? Brandy? Well, if that's medicine, everybody in Saratoga is going to have the complaint it's good for. I'll tell the barman at the Club about it. No, I won't have another, and neither will you. Give me the recipe, there's a good girl. I'll make old Spencer pay me for it."

Clio's lip curled a little, contemptuously. "Kaka, Mrs. Bellop would like the recipe for the *coquetier*. Tell Cupide to write it out——" Suddenly she remembered, she sat up, she pushed her hair away from her brow with a fevered frantic gesture. "Cupide went with him. He ran away and went with him to that mad—that insane—place where they battle like savages for a piece of railroad track! I don't understand this country! I don't understand. And now Clint is gone and Cupide is gone and you"—she turned blazing eyes on Kakaracou—"you will go next, I suppose. Why don't you go! Why don't you——"

Calmly and majestically, Kaka gathered up the little glasses and the great tumbler in which she had mixed the drink. A portion of the red-brown concoction still remained. "Is too hot for *coquetier*," she observed, and nonchalantly emptied the contents of the tumbler into the hotel cuspidor. "Why'n't you catch yourself a little nap, Miss Clio?" She shot a malignant glance at Sophie Bellop, patted a couch pillow invitingly, then pressed her strong withered hand on the girl's shoulder. "Kaka is not going leave her Clio *bébé*."

"Everybody can leave me! I don't need anyone! I'm not like Mama and Aunt Belle. I'm strong, I'm clever, I'm free!" The tears were rolling down her cheeks.

"Well, good God!" exclaimed Mrs. Bellop. "What was in that cocktail thing, Kaka?"

Kaka shook her head. She was all deep-south Negress, the veneer of Paris, of Northern travel was gone. "He like this when he tired."

"He! He who? Oh, my God, I never heard such talk. What's wrong with you two! You've reverted right back to—to whatever it was you came from. Now you listen to me, Clio."

"Go away," Clio said, sleepily. "Go away."

"I'll do nothing of the kind. You're right on the doorstep—or threshold or whatever they call it—of success, and I'm not going to let you stop now. So quit rolling your eyes and listen to me. You can make the match of the year. I know a man head over heels in love when I see one. And he is, even if you did screech at him like a fish-wife. He's used to being screeched at by a woman. He'd never marry anyone who wasn't stronger than his ma. And you're that. Besides, I need the money—and I like you. Are you listening?"

"You have said nothing."

"All right then. You're going to hear something. Bart and his ma have had a terrible quarrel. Oh, I thought that would make you open those eyes. The old devil is wild. Bart told her that he wasn't afraid of her any more—that he hated her—that he was in love with you. The chambermaid on their floor is paid to—that is, she does some laundry work for me, you understand. She said it was awful; she thought the old lady would have a stroke. Miss Diggs was dousing her with eau de cologne and spirits of ammonia and she slapped Diggs' face—not that that matters, but I just thought you'd like—well, she said she was going to run you out of town—out of the country—out of——"

"There is no other place," Clio murmured, her lids half closed, "except out of the world, and I don't think the poor old lady will have the courage to murder me. Do you?" She cocked an amused eye at Sophie Bellop. One eye. The other was closed.

"Stop that! This is no laughing matter, I tell you."

"Oh, but let us laugh, anyway. The world—life—is no laughing matter. But one must laugh."

"If I hadn't seen with my own eyes that you'd had only one of those cocktail things, I'd say you were just plain drunk. Even though you're not, I ought to march right out of here and leave you. But I'm not going to be beaten by that old buzzard, Van Steed. It's a matter of pride."

"Pride," echoed Clio in a maddening murmur. "That is what the Dulaines have. I am a Dulaine, but not *chacalata*. I have very little pride, really."

"You're talking nonsense. Listen. Do you know what the old woman said to her son? And what she's saying to everyone in the hotel? That you're not a countess at all; that you're not even Mrs. De

Chanfret; that you're an adventuress; that you've got a touch of the tarbrush!"

Clio now settled herself rather cozily as for a nap. "There is much in what she says. She is no fool, that old *mégère*."

The patience of the good-natured Bellop snapped. She bounced out of her chair, she shook Clio's shoulder, she stood over her in elephantine anger. "No, but you are. If I weren't sure that creepy woman of yours would put a knife into me, I'd slap you here and now. I'm only talking to you out of kindness of my heart."

"And out of your hatred for Mama Van Steed."

"You're an ungrateful brat!"

Clio sprang up, she took Sophie Bellop's hand, she looked beseechingly into her face. "I am! I am! But I am so troubled. I don't know what is the matter with me. Suddenly I don't care. I don't care about the very thing for which I've worked and planned and schemed."

"Maybe that's because you've almost got it."

"You think so?"

"Of course. Where's your spirit! He's never looked at a woman before, except just by way of politeness. When he came here today it was on the tip of his tongue to ask you to marry him. I'm sure of it. That's why I stayed away until I saw him come out, wobbling like a man who'd been hit. I don't say you'd make a suitable wife for him— but then, you wouldn't make a suitable wife for anyone—unless it was a Bengal tiger. You like him, don't you? Of course you're not in love with him. He doesn't expect it. Look here, are you listening to what I'm saying?"

"What? Who?"

"Good God! She says who! A fortune of millions in her very hand, and she says who!"

"Oh. Yes. You mean little Van Steed. Do you know, Mrs. Bellop, the women in America are very powerful. The men seem to spend their whole time and their energies on business matters while the women manage their lives for them. Here in the North, especially. I myself seem to be like that now. In France I remember it was quite different, it——"

"We haven't time to talk about France now, or whether American women are strong-minded. You know perfectly well that I got up this fancy-dress ball just for you. It won't be like the regular hops. We're having a supper at eleven—not just fruit-punch and cakes. Every millionaire in Saratoga will be there. The New York newspapers will call it the Millionaires' Ball. And that old harpy, Van Steed, is arranging to have everybody cut you."

"How nice!" cooed Clio at her most French.

"But I'll be there. It's my ball—at least, I got the hotel to give it. The Grand Union is wild with jealousy. I've found out that Guilia Forosini is coming as a Spanish gypsy—orange satin skirt, red velvet jacket, gold braid, epaulets, gold-ball fringe. Mrs. Porcelain's wearing a rose trellis costume. Ankle length skirt of ciel blue tulle and satin, garlands of roses on her shoulders, and a headdress made to represent a gilt trellis covered with roses. Now you—what's the matter!"

Clio was laughing. She was laughing as she hadn't laughed since she came to Saratoga; she was staggering with laughter; the tears of laughter were filling her eyes.

Kakaracou, grimly disapproving, was in the bedroom doorway. "I told you leave Miss Clio alone when she like this."

"It's all right," Clio gasped. "Go away, Kaka. Dear Mrs. Bellop, forgive me. But the Spanish gypsy—and the gilt trellis on the head—it is so—so——" She was off again into the peals of hysterical laughter.

But even the good nature of the ebullient Sophie Bellop was cooled by now. "I'm going. You're right, Kaka. For that matter, I'm beginning to think that old viper Clarissa Van Steed is right, too, for the first time in her life. I came here to tell you that I think you ought to outdo them by coming as a French marquise—satin hoops, powdered wig, all your jewelry. I would help you, and your woman here is a seamstress, I'm sure."

Clio was suddenly very sober, deeply interested. "Pink satin, do you think? Over great hoops. With flounces of fine black Spanish lace? It was my mother's. I have it here in my unopened trunks."

"That's it! Wonderful!"

"Satin slippers with great diamond buckles?"

"Really! Can you manage?"

"It is nothing. And powdered hair and a little black patch here— and here—and all my jewels. All, you think?"

"Certainly. All. You'll look dazzling. Simply dazzling."

"How nize! How nize!" Clio's eyes were very narrow. There was something in her face and in the face of the Negress that made Sophie Bellop vaguely uncomfortable.

"You'll have to send him a note telling him you were ill or hysterical or something. He'll understand—I hope. Look, I'll tell him myself. You've got to make an entrance with him—not too early."

"I am coming to the dance with—with him. With Clint."

"But you can't. It'll spoil everything. Besides, he isn't here."

"He will be." Her face set in iron stubbornness. "No matter afterward. But I am going with him."

XVI

✣

Thirty miles to Albany. Clint Maroon was tooling along in the cool of the August day. Day, in fact, had not yet come. At two in the morning the road between Saratoga and Albany was still a dark mystery ahead, but the twin bays, fresh, glossy, restive after forty-eight hours of idleness, swung along as sure-footed as though the bright sun shone for them. For this trip Maroon had abandoned the clarence for a light, springy cart. Its four wheels seemed simultaneously off the ground, the cart and driver suspended in mid-air, so little did the bays make of the weight they were pulling along the road to Albany.

Clint Maroon was happy. He was happier than he had been in months. The reins in his hands, the cool moist air against his face, no sound except the hoofbeats and the skim of the wheels over the hard-baked road. No sun, no moon, no stars, no women, no fuss, no crowds; and the exhilarating prospect of a tough fight ahead. As blackness melted to a ghostly gray the good burghers sleeping lightly in the gray dawn stirred restlessly between rumpled sheets and started up in nightmarish fright, recalling the legend of the Headless Horseman of Sleepy Hollow, or old Indian stories of the region in earlier days—tales of sudden massacres and Iroquois uprisings. But it was only Clint Maroon, though they did not know, whirling along behind the light-stepping bays, high, wide and handsome, and singing the cowboy songs of old Texas as he went his nostalgic way.

> *I jumped in my saddle*
> *An' I give a li'l yell*
> *An' the swing cattle broke*
> *An' the leaders went to hell.*
> *Tum-a-ti-yi, yippi, yippi, yea, yea, yea.*
> *Tum-a-ti-yi, yippi, yippi, yea, yea, yea.*

Aside from Van Steed he had taken no one into his confidence. To Clio he had said, "I'm fixing to go away, Clio, on business. Couple of days."

"Business. What business?"

He evaded this. "Cupide'll look after you. And Bart." He grinned.

Her hand on his arm, her tone wistfully reproachful. "But I thought we were here as partners, Clint. When we talked in New Orleans of this Saratoga we made the adventure together."

"Shucks, honey, you don't need me any more. You set out to catch you a millionaire and you've got him, roped and tied. All you've got to do now is cinch the saddle on him. He's already been gentled by his ma."

They glared at each other, the two partners. "Yes, I know I have been successful," she said, evenly. "I shan't forget you. When the time comes."

"Poor little Bart! If I didn't hate him and all his kind like poison I'd have a mind to warn him he was making a misjudgment. In his place I sure would feel cheap to think I was being married for my money."

"You need never fear. When you win five hundred at cards you feel yourself rich. The sweet little woman in Texas has just such ambitions, I am sure—she who makes the ravishing white satin neckties with the blue forget-me-nots."

"Yep, sure is comical the way a woman likes to put her mark on a man with a needle. You couldn't sit nor sleep till you had me crawling with those fancy initials all over my handkerchiefs and shirts. I looked to wake up any morning and find a big C, with a pretty vine, branded on my rump."

With the most disarming candor she said, "He hasn't asked me to marry him."

"Bart, he isn't the asking kind. You have to tell him."

They fell silent there in the dim coolness of her cottage sitting room. It was a warm pulsating silence such as they often had known in the dusk of the fragrant little garden in Rampart Street. As though sensing this he said, "It was different in New Orleans. Why can't it be like that here? You were mighty sweet, those days. Ornery—but mighty sweet."

In sudden fright, "Clint! Chéri! You're not leaving me!" She flung herself against him, she clung to him.

"Times I wish I could."

"Where are you going? Don't go! Don't go! Stay, stay!" Her arms about him, her scented laces smothering him.

He took her head in his two hands and looked down into her face. "Do you want to come away from here now, honey? Say the word."

But at that she hesitated a moment. In that moment he put her gently from him. "I have to go get some sleep," he said, soberly. "Up before daybreak tomorrow." He strode toward the door.

"But you will be back for the hop—no, it is a ball that the Bellop is giving. A ball, no less, for these canailles. If you like you may escort me."

"I reckoned you were fixing to go with Bart."

"I was, but——"

"Better go with him. Adios, honey. Pleasant dreams." Suddenly he strode over to her, caught her up and kissed her roughly, punishingly, set her down so that she swayed dizzily. The next instant she heard the tap of his high-heeled boots on the veranda stairs.

Now, as Clint Maroon drove along toward Albany in the dawn,

he thought, why don't you light out of here, cowboy? High-tail it out of there, and stay out. What call have you got to get yourself mixed up with railroads and foreign women and voodoo witches and dwarfs? You're Clint Maroon, of the Texas Maroons. Why don't you just keep on traveling away from here? They'll ship Alamo after you. That's about all you got to leave.

Clint! *Chéri!* You're not leaving me!

He knew he could not do it. Not yet.

The sun was higher now. The world was beginning drowsily to awake. From roadside farmhouses, as the turnout whirled by, there came the scent of coffee and of frizzling ham.

I'd like mighty well, Clint thought, to stop by and sit down to a good farm breakfast of biscuits and fried potatoes and ham like I used to back home. None of this la-de-da New Orleans and Saratoga stuff. Another month of that, I'm likely to be a sissy worse than Van Steed. Van Steed. No real harm in him. Not to say, harm. Not pure cussedness like the others. I wonder what the Gould crowd will do if they're licked. What was that Pappy said old Neely Vanderbilt said—it never pays to kick a skunk. Well, stink or not, I'm enjoying this. I don't recollect when I've felt more like tackling a job. Getting soft as mud sitting around eating quail, drinking wine, parading good horse-flesh up and down that sinkhole Broadway in Saratoga like a damned Easterner.

He had not pressed the bays, for he knew he was in ample time. Nevertheless they had, in five hours, easily covered the distance between Saratoga and Albany. He made straight for the Albany station. He knew he could get breakfast there. And there his drive would end and the business of the day begin. Few people were astir in the early-morning streets of Albany, yet those few stared, smiled, and a few even waved and broke into laughter as the handsome bays and their dashing driver and the dusty light cart flashed past. What the tarnation is eating on folks in this town! Clint thought, puzzled. You'd think they'd never seen a horse before, or a man driving. He whirled up to the Albany station, drew up at a hitching post and saw the faces of the loungers and Negro porters break into broad grins. Instinctively now he turned to glance over his shoulder. There behind him, snug as a jack-in-the-box and markedly resembling one, sat Cupide. Grinning, goggle-eyed, he was wedged neatly into the back of the cart. His glossy hat sat at a debonair angle, his maroon uniform was neatly buttoned, his arms were folded across his chest, his smile was an ivory gash, but his gaze was apprehensive as it met Maroon's stupefied stare.

In what seemed like a single fluid motion Clint Maroon had leaped to the ground, had thrown the reins to a waiting boy and advanced on Cupide, whip in hand.

"Get down out of there, you varmint! Get down or I'll haul you down."

Cupide stood up while the onlookers guffawed as for the first time they realized the stature of this strangely attired passenger. Nimbly he leaped to the ground, his tiny feet in their glittering top boots landing neatly as a cat's. As Maroon reached for him, the sad eyes looked up at him, the clear boyish voice broke a little with a note of pathos beneath its engaging humor.

"It was like riding on a donkey's tail, Monsieur Clint. Bumpitty-bump, bumpitty-bump. I'm hollow as a drum."

Maroon laid a heavy hand on the dwarf's shoulder. "What do you want here?"

"Breakfast. I am hungry for my breakfast."

Maroon's voice dropped. "Did she send you?"

"No. I ran away. I hid in the back of the cart. It was fine—but bumpy."

"You get out of here."

"No, Monsieur Clint. No! I want to fight, too, with you and the rest. I'm strong. You know how I am strong."

"Doggone if I haven't got a mind to tan you good, here and now, you little rat. Skin you and pin your hide to a fence, that's what I ought to do. How'd you know where I was going?"

The old face on the childlike body was turned up to him, its look all candor and simplicity. "I listened at the keyhole. I heard everything. It's going to be a fine fight." He rubbed his tiny hands together. "I can't wait until I begin butting them in the stomach, the *canailles*."

Maroon's reply was a venomous mutter, out of which son-of-a-bitch emerged as the least offensive term. "You're going to get the hell out of here. . . . Hi, boy! What's the next train to Saratoga? . . . D'you want to earn five dollars? You go rustle some breakfast—coffee and so on—for this little runt. You've got a good half an hour before train time. You buy a ticket and set him on that train headed for Saratoga, and don't you let him out of your sight till the train's started. Go on, get going, act like you're alive!"

"Monsieur Clint! You're not going to send me back!"

"You're damn whistlin' I am!" An aggrieved note crept into his voice. "Tagging me around. I bet she put you up to it."

"No, no! No one. Not Mad'moiselle, not Kaka. No one knows. Please let me stay. I will help, I will work, I will fight——"

"Shut up!" He dropped his voice, his very quietness was venomous. "And if you let out a word of what you know, here or in Saratoga, I'll kill you when I get back, sure as shooting." He turned to the fellow who now had emerged from the depot, railway ticket in hand. "Now, you. Hang on to that ticket till he's on the train. Give him his breakfast. If he gets balky leave him go without. One thing. Look out he don't butt you."

A bewildered look came into the face of the newly appointed guardian. "Don't what?"

"Butt you. He's got a head like a cannon ball. . . . I'll learn you to tag around after me. And remember! One word out of you about you know what and——" He snapped his fingers and flung the sound away, dead. Suddenly, to his horror, the little man dropped to his knees, he clasped his arms about Maroon's legs.

"Don't do this to me! Don't! Don't! I am strong. You know how strong. I am stronger than three regular men, I will fight——"

With terrible ruthlessness Maroon plucked the dwarf from him as you would fling off an insect. "Get away from me, you varmint you! I'll learn you to flap those big ears of yours at keyholes!"

The childlike figure was on its feet at once, like a thing made of steel springs. Even as the onlookers guffawed Clint Maroon felt his first pang of contrition, felt his face redden with shame at what he had done.

Cupidon brushed himself off, methodically. Quietly he looked at Maroon. His eyes gazed straight into those of his idol. "Monsieur, I am a man," he said. For that instant he was somehow tall.

A moment the two stared at one another. Then Maroon turned and walked quickly away.

He knew where he must go. He was late, and cursed his lateness and the cause of it, but his heart was not in it. You'll be hitting children next, he said to himself, and women too, likely. What's come over you! He strode along in his high-heeled boots, his great white sombrero, his fine cloth suit with its full-skirted coat, but he felt a diminished man.

The light cart and the bays would be cared for. That had been carefully arranged days ago. Everything had been arranged. All that money could insure had been carefully planned and carried out by men of millions. Only physical courage and devil-may-care love of adventure had been lacking. And these he, Clint Maroon, had provided.

Into the hot, dusty office of the stationmaster. Sparse, taciturn, Gid Fish looked up under his green eyeshade at the dashing figure in the doorway. His voice was as dry, his gaze as detached as though sombreroed figures in high-heeled Texas boots were daily visitors in the Albany depot office. The physical contrast between the two men was ludicrous—the one so full-blooded, so virile, so dramatic, the other so dry, dusty and sallow. Yet the two seemed to like and respect one another; their speech had the terseness of mutual understanding.

"Howdy, Gid!"

"Howdy, Clint!"

"Came in my rig like I said."

"Seen you."

"Boys in?"

"Yep."

"Steam up?"

"Yep."

"Road clear?"

"Yep."

"Well, *adios!*"

Maroon turned to go, his coat-tails flirting about his legs with the vigor of his movements. Gid Fish's rasping voice suddenly stopped him, held him with its note of urgency. "Somebody must of blabbed."

Maroon whirled. "Who says so?"

"Just come over the wire. They got wind."

Maroon's right hand went to his hip. "Who blabbed?"

"Gould's a smart fella."

Even as he said this there came the clack-clack-clack of the telegraph instrument on Gid Fish's desk. A moment of silence broken only by the clacking sound. "Says there's hell to pay in Binghamton," said Fish, laconically. "Git."

Clint Maroon's high heels clattered on the bare boards as he dashed from the room. Across the tracks, down the yards to where an engine waited, steam up.

The head that now thrust itself out of the engine-cab window was surmounted by the customary long-visored striped linen cap, the body was garbed in engineer's overalls, but the face that looked down at the hurrying figure of Clint Maroon was not an engineer's face as one usually sees it—the keen-eyed, quizzical and curiously benevolent countenance of the born mechanic. It was a hard-bitten ruthless face, but the eyes redeemed it. Devil-may-care, they were merry now with amusement and anticipation.

"You're going to get them nice clothes mussed up, Clint."

Maroon ignored this. His eye traveled the engine, end to end. "Sure enough big."

Pride irradiated the face framed in the engine cab. "She's the heaviest engine in the East."

"Better had be. Gid Fish says they got wind of us down in Binghamton. No telling what they'll do. Of course they don't know about the boys. Can't. They all back in there?" He nodded in the direction of the two coaches attached to the puffing engine.

"Yep. Rarin'."

"Get going, Les. I'll go talk to the boys. After the first stop I'll come up there in the engine with you. I want to see what's ahead. Where at's Tracy?"

Like a figure in a Punch and Judy show a smoke-grimed face bobbed up in the window beside that of Les, the engineer. His teeth gleamed white against their sooty background. "Feeding the critter," he said. "She eats like a hungry maverick." Les, the engineer; Tracy, the fireman; Clint Maroon, the leader. All three had the Western flavor in their speech—laconic, gentle, almost drawling. Les surveyed Clint with a kind of amused admiration.

"You come up here you're liable to ruin them pretty pants, Clint."

Maroon grinned back at him good-naturedly. "Got any coffee up there, left over?"

"Sure have. Wait a minute."

"Can't stop for it now. When I climb up in there I'll take it, and welcome. Get her going. We got to lick the whey out of the Binghamton outfit before noon and clean up all along the line to boot."

The two heads stuck out of the cab window turned to gaze after him a moment; they saw him leap into the doorway of the first car with a flirting whisk of his coat-tails.

"Son-of-a-gun!" said Tracy, affectionately. In another moment the big engine moved.

Passing swiftly from car to car, Clint Maroon faced three hundred men; he stood swaying at the head of each car, he repeated his brief speech, they made laconic answer.

"Howdy, boys!"

"Howdy, Clint!"

They strangely resembled one another, these silent men. Lean, tall, wiry; their faces weather-beaten, their eyes had the look of those accustomed to far horizons. Yet they were ruined faces, the faces of men who, though fearless, had known defeat and succumbed to it. Hard times had searched them out with her bony fingers and sent them wandering, drink-scarred and jobless, into the inhospitable East. Danger meant nothing to them. Risk was their daily ration. Violence flavored their food. Life they held lightly. Guns were merely part of their wardrobe.

"Like I said, no guns—only maybe the butts in a pinch. You got your clubs and spades and axes and your fists, and you'll likely need 'em. No shooting. Every station between here and Binghamton we're out quick before they can telegraph word ahead. We throw 'em out, take the books, and leave a bunch behind to hold the fort. Where we're in we stay in, and we've got to be in every station between here and there before nightfall, sure. Whenever you hear three screeches from the engine ahead—no matter where we're at or what you're doing—that means out, pronto. We're going. Hold on to your hats."

It was child's play to these men. They treated it as though it were a roundup; they felt that they lacked only the horses under them to make their day perfect. Town followed town, station followed station. The procedure never varied; it even took on a sort of monotony after the first hour. The train would come to a grinding, jolting halt that shook the marrow of even these hard-boned Westerners. Three shrill screeches from the engine. Out the men swarmed armed with bludgeons, spades, shovels; their guns handy in their holsters in spite of Clint's warning. Quick as they were, Maroon was quicker. The crew was, for the most part, sombreroed as he, but it was the figure in the great white sombrero and the flying coat-tails that led the charge into the station. A rush into the ticket office, bursting into the stationmaster's room; a scuffle, oaths, yells.

"Come on, you son-a-kabitchee!"

"Stay with him, cowboy!"

"Heel that booger, Red. Heel him!"

"Hot iron! Hot iron!"

The old language of the range and the branding pen and the corral returned joyously to their lips. The West they had known was vanishing—had vanished, indeed, for them. Resentful, fearless, they were blurred copies of Clint Maroon. The thing they had been hired to do was absurd—was almost touching in its childlike simplicity and crudeness. But then, so, too, were they.

In each town they left behind them the bewildered buzz and chatter of the townspeople. Long-suffering as these were, and accustomed to the violence and destruction with which the now-notorious railroad fight had been carried on in the past year, the lightning sortie of these Westerners was a new and melodramatic experience. There was, in the first place, a kind of grim enjoyment in their faces, a sardonic humor in their speech, as they poured out of their modern Trojan horse. Booted, sombreroed like the dashing figure that led them, they seemed, in the eyes of the staid York State burghers, to be creatures from another world. Binghamton was their goal, Binghamton was to be the final test, for there the enemy was fortified in numbers probably equal to theirs, if not greater. Meanwhile their zest was tremendous, their purpose grim, their spirits rollicking. Strange wild yells, bred of the plains, the range, the Indian country, issued from their leather throats. Yip-ee! Eee-yow! And always, bringing up the rear, though the white-hatted leader never knew it, was a grotesque little figure rolling on stumpy legs. In wine-colored livery and top hat and glittering diminutive boots he was, the staring onlookers assumed, a creature strayed from a circus. The whole effect was, in fact, that of a circus minus its tent and tigers and elephants. This little figure followed an erratic pattern of its own, dodging, hiding, mingling whenever possible where the melee was thickest, darting back to the refuge of the train coaches before the white-hatted leader strode back to his eyrie in the engine cab. Evidently there was some sort of understanding between him and the tall rangey fellows who made up the company. Almost absentmindedly they seemed to protect him;

they shielded him in little clusters when it appeared that Maroon's eye might fall upon him. Here was a mascot. Here was a good-luck piece. Look at the little runt, they said. Says he's Maroon's bodyguard. Reckon he's lying.

In the engine cab Clint Maroon, incredibly neat in spite of the heat, the dust, the soot that belched from the smokestack, leaned far out of the window to peer up the track. Each time he withdrew his head from this watchtower he heaved a sigh of relief.

"No sign of them, hide nor hair," he remarked to Les, the engineer. "D'you reckon Gid Fish was just throwin' off on me, saying he'd heard somebody'd blabbed up in Binghamton!"

"Nope," said Les, cheerfully, above the roar and jolt of the massive engine.

"We've only got a matter of fifteen miles to go," Clint argued.

Tracy, the fireman, his red-rimmed eyes rolling grotesquely in his sooty face, turned his head away from the fire to throw a terse reminder over his shoulder.

"Long tunnel between here and Binghamton. Keep your head stuck out going through there. You're liable to get kind of specked, but you sure might see something at the end of it."

Maroon's hand went to his hip. "You keeping back something you know!"

A grin gashed the black face. "My, my, ain't you touchy, Clint, since you come East and got to going with New York millionaires!"

With an oath Maroon lunged forward, but the drawling voice of Les with a sharp overtone in it now served to stop him short.

"Something down the line," he yelled. "I can feel it. On our track. God A'mighty, they wouldn't mix it in the tunnel!"

For an instant the three men stared, each seeing in the other's eyes confirmation of his own worst dread. "Open her up!" yelled Clint. "Wide! We've got to get out of here." For they had slowed down going through the tunnel. From his window Clint could now see the blue sky through the tunnel mouth a hundred yards ahead.

"They can't jump if I speed her up."

"They've jumped off wild bucking horses, they can clear a greasy train, you got to get us the hell out of here. We'll be caught like rats in a——" His head was far out of the window, he was peering through the curtain of smoke and soot and cinders that belched from the smokestack. The heat in the tunnel was insufferable, the blazing temperature in the engine cab was indescribable, Maroon's face was ludicrously streaked now with sweat and grime, his white hat was polkadotted with black, his diamond scarfpin sparkled bravely in the sullied nest of the satin necktie. He leaned perilously out, he turned his head now to peer back at the laden cars and he could dimly discern the heads and shoulders of the men thrust far out of the train windows and hanging from the car steps. Theirs had been perilous paths; instinctively they sensed danger; they were ready to jump. Now by straddling the car window Clint could see ahead. There it was, down the track, down their own track and headed straight for them. He could see the locomotive, it was sending out a column of smoke like a fiery monster breathing defiance.

"Give 'em the whistle!" yelled Maroon. "They're on the track!"

Three shrill blasts seemed to rend the roof of the tunnel. Three more. The figures in the cars behind now leaped, tumbled from the train, shouting, cursing, running.

"Jump!" howled Les above the turmoil. "Jump, you crazy sons-of-bitches, I'm letting her out."

Poised for the leap, with Tracy behind him, Maroon clung by one hand. "Come on! God damn it, come on, Les."

They had cleared the tunnel. "Coming. Jump! I'm letting her out. They didn't get us in the tunnel, the stinkin' yellow-bellies."

Neatly and without fluster, as though he were sliding out of a saddle onto the ground, Clint Maroon stepped to the ground, swung round like a dancer, caught his balance magically and started to run as Tracy landed just behind him. He had had, as he leaped, a last glimpse of Les's face as he bent forward to give the powerful engine its last notch of speed before he, too, leaped for his life.

Bells were ringing, whistles tooting, sparks pouring from the two engines, men were leaping from doors and windows, they ran wide of the track, they yelled like Comanches as the two engines, like something out of a crazy dream, met in the terrible impact of a head-on collision. The heavy engine crumpled the lighter, pushed it aside like a toy. Above the crash and the splintering of wood and the smashing of glass sounded the wild shouts of the men in the blood-curdling yells of the Western plains. Yip-eeee! Eeeeeee-yow! Clubs in their hands, axes, guns, shovels. Swarming along the tracks they came toward each other, the two bands of men. It was plain that Maroon's crew outnumbered the Binghamton crowd, but on these you saw the flash of deputies' badges glinting in the sun. But the faces above these were the flabby drink-sodden faces of such Bowery toughs and slum riffraff as the opposition had been hastily able to press into service when news of the Albany foray reached their ears.

"Heel them! Catch them! Brand them! Go get 'em! Go get 'em! Hot iron! Hot iron!"

At the head of the throng ran Clint Maroon. He was smiling, happily. His men were at his heels, and in another moment the two sides had met with an impact of blows, oaths, shouts. It was a glorious free-for-all, a primitive battle of fists and clubs and feet. The thud of knuckles on flesh; grunts; the scuffle of leather on cinders; the screams of men in pain; howls of rage.

"No guns!" Clint shouted. "Ear 'em down, slug 'em, kick them in the guts! Hammer 'em! No guns."

Here was a strange new rule of the game to these men accustomed to fair gun play in a fight, but they cheerfully made the best of it. Fists, boots, axes, clubs. The early training of their cowboy days stood them in good stead now. Five hundred men writhed and pushed, stamped and cursed, punched and hammered and wrestled in a gargantuan bloody welter.

Suddenly, out of a corner of his eye, Clint Maroon glimpsed a familiar figure, diminutive, implike, in a wine-red coat and a shiny top hat, a grin of dreadful joy on his face. Busily, methodically, he was running between men's legs, he was butting them behind, tipping them over neatly and jumping on them, a look of immense happiness and satisfaction irradiating him as he did so.

Beset though he was, Clint stopped to stare, open-mouthed, then he burst into laughter, and even as he roared with mirth he waved the dwarf back and shouted at him above the din. "Get out of here, you son-of-a-gun! . . . Get out of here, run away from here! Drag it, or I'll bust every——"

The little man came running toward him, dodging this way and that. He was making frantic motions, he pointed with one tiny hand at something behind Maroon and mouthed as he ran. Instinctively Maroon whirled to look behind him. There stood a stubble-bearded ruffian, arms upraised to bring down a shovel on his head. He had only time to duck, an instinctive gesture, and to raise one arm to shield his head. The flat of the shovel crashed down on his elbow and came to a rest against his ribs. Maroon stumbled, sank to one knee, and saw with horror that the fellow again held the shovel high, poised for a finishing blow. Into Clint's mind flashed the thought, here's a Maroon being killed with a shovel and disgracing the family. Then Cupide leaped, not like a human being but like a monkey; he used his head as a projectile and landed squarely in the man's stomach as he stood arms upraised. There was a grunt, the shovel flew from his hands, and, falling, nicked Maroon smartly just above the eye. Then shovel-wielder, Cupide, Maroon, and the shovel itself mingled in a welter of legs, arms, curses, pain. But Maroon's shattered arm was doubled under his shattered rib and both felt the weight of his own body and that of the fantastic combatants. He was conscious of a wave of unbearable nausea before the kindly curtain of unconsciousness blacked out the daylight.

XVII

✦

*In a society which dined in the middle of the day and had supper at half-*past six, the hour set for the grand ball of the United States Hotel season did not seem at all unsophisticated. But then, Saratoga, which considered itself very worldly and delightfully wicked, still had a Cinderella attitude toward the midnight hour. Eight-thirty to midnight the announcement had said.

Supper had been rushed through in the dining room or ignored completely by the belles of the evening. From behind bedroom doors and up and down the hotel corridors could be heard the sounds of gala preparation—excited squeals, the splashing of water, the tinkle of supper trays, the ringing of bells, the hurried steps of waiters and bellboys and chambermaids, the tuning of fiddle and horn. Every gas jet in the great brass chandeliers was flaring; even the crystal chandelier in the parlor, which was lighted only on special occasions. In the garden the daytime geraniums and petunias and alyssum and pansies had vanished in the dusk. In their place bloomed the gaudy orange and scarlet and rose color of the paper lanterns glowing between the trees.

Grudgingly, yet with a certain elation, the United States Hotel had permitted a very few choice guests of their rival, the Grand Union Hotel, to attend this crowning event of the hotel's summer season: the Jefferson De Forests, the Deckers of Rittenhouse Square, Mrs.

Blood of Boston, the Rhinelanders, the Willoughby Kilps, General Roscoe E. Flower.

At the head of the ballroom, directly opposite the musicians' platform, enthroned among the dowagers, sat Madam Van Steed. About her clustered her ladies-in-waiting—the insecure, the jealous, the malicious, the grudging, the envious. They made elegant conversation and they watched the door; they commented on the success or the dismal failure of the costumes which had been devised under the generous rules of fancy dress; and they watched the door.

"How sweet!" they had cooed at sight of the rose-trellised Mrs. Porcelain. "How dashing and romantic!" on the entrance of the Spanish gypsy. They made stilted talk, generously larded with hints concerning their own lofty place in society.

"I had a letter today from my cousin, Mrs. Fortesque, of London. She says the Queen is suffering from low spirits. She will take no exercise. Letitia—that's Mrs. Fortesque—says the dear Queen will go to Italy in the autumn."

"I see that Mrs. De Chanfret isn't here yet. Do you think she's not coming! Dear me, I hope . . ."

"Letitia says that the Prince of Wales—they call him Jumbo, isn't that shocking!—no longer wears a buttonhole flower. . . ."

"A draft, Clarissa! Dear me, it's really very warm in here. I don't believe they'll want to shut the garden doors, so early . . ."

"They say it is a diet for corpulency devised by a Mr. Banting. I don't think it can be good for one's health, starving oneself. The Banting Regimen For Corpulency it is called. My dear, for breakfast you're allowed white-fish and bacon, or cold beef or broiled kidney, toast, and tea with milk and no cream, the way the English take it. For dinner some fish and a bit of poultry or game, a green vegetable, fruit. For supper only meat or fish, a vegetable . . . for tea . . ."

"My maid who has a friend who is a friend of a maid who knows Sophie Bellop's maid happened to mention to me—I didn't ask her—she just spoke of it the way they do—she happened to mention that she had heard that the De Chanfret woman, or whatever she calls herself, is coming as a French marquise in a powdered wig. Well, really! Couldn't you die! After all we know . . ."

"I always thought Creoles were colored people. . . ."

". . . New Orleans aristocracy—French and Spanish blood . . ."

"But where is she? Your son seems worried, Clarissa dear. . . ."

"I see your son isn't dancing, dear Mrs. Van Steed."

"He is worried. It's about business. I almost had to use force to keep him from going to Binghamton tonight. Something about a railroad. Some railroad trouble. Nothing to speak of. Bart is so clever. He'll make it come right."

Eight-thirty. Nine. Half-past nine. Ten. At half-past nine Mrs. Bellop had sent a bellboy with a message to Clio's rooms. He had returned with the news that the cottage apartment was in darkness, the door locked, the windows closed. No sound from within.

"But I felt," he said, solemnly, "like eyes was watching me."

Decidedly the ball was not going well. There was about it a thin quality, as though a prime ingredient were lacking. People danced, but listlessly. Mrs. Porcelain, the ciel tulle somewhat wilted, the rose trellis headdress askew, smiled and cooed unconvincingly, her eyes on the doorway. The rolling-eyed Forosini found that a velvet gypsy jacket for dancing in August was a mistake. The dowagers grouped against the wall were tigresses robbed of their prey.

"It doesn't seem to be going, Mrs. Bellop," complained Tompkins, the hotel manager. "It's too early for supper. They've just stuffed themselves with dinner. What's wrong?"

"It's that Mrs. De Chanfret."

"Why, what's the matter with her? I don't see her. Has she done something?"

"No. That's the trouble. She isn't here. And they've got so used to seeing her and expecting her to do something dramatic that when she isn't around everything goes stale, like flat champagne."

"Well, fetch her then. Fetch her."

"I can't find her."

"Nonsense! She must be somewhere. I can't have the Grand Union saying this ball was a failure. If they do, it's your fault, Mrs. Bellop."

"Oh, run along, Tompkins. Who do you think you're talking to! A chambermaid! I could make the United States Hotel look like a haunted house in two weeks if I chose. So mind your manners. Where's Van Steed? Now he's disappeared, too. Drat the man!"

She left the listless ballroom, her eyes searching the corridors, the lobby; she sent bellboys scurrying into the garden, the men's wash-room, up to Van Steed's apartment, out to the piazza; she even tried Clio's apartment again, in vain. "The bar. He wouldn't be there. He doesn't drink anything. Can't. Well, try it, anyway." She herself followed the boy; she poked her head in at the swinging door to survey the territory forbidden to females. There sat Van Steed at a far corner table. "Fetch him! Fetch him at once. Tell him it's important."

As the boy bent over him he raised his head, his eyes followed the boy's pointing finger to where Mrs. Bellop stood in the doorway. Knowing her, perhaps he feared that she was not above coming in and buttonholing him in the bar itself. He rose and came toward her, and she saw that his cheeks had lost their wonted pink and were a curious clay-gray. He had had a drink too potent for the hot night, for little beads of moisture stood out on his forehead, yet his hand, when she grasped it, was cold. A grin that was a grimace sat awry on his lips. My, he's taking it hard, she thought.

"What's wrong? Are you sick? Has something happened to her?"

He opened his clenched left hand. In it was a moist wad of yellow paper. Mrs. Bellop had met enough bad news in her day to recognize it at sight. Yet the staring grin baffled her.

"Not bad news I hope, Bart. No, of course—you're smiling—that is—not bad news I hope."

He looked up from the slip of paper. He stared at her. He wet his lips with his tongue.

"Where is she?" he said, without preliminaries.

"I don't know. I sent over. The place is dark."

"Maybe she's heard."

"Heard what?"

"It's stifling in here. Come out on the piazza a minute, will you? I'm——"

She followed him. The piazza was almost deserted. A few solid couples sat there taking the evening air before their bedtime. A little low-voiced knot of sporting men talking of the day's races and tomorrow's possibilities. Van Steed glanced around quickly, seeking a secluded spot. Far off, in a dim corner at the end of the long piazza, there glowed the red eye of a cigar. They could not discern the lonely, meager, hollow-chested figure behind it, but they knew. And the grin came again, fleetingly, into Van Steed's drawn face.

"Well, we've licked him, anyway."

"So that's it!"

"He knows it. He's been sitting there like that; they've been sending him messages ever since this afternoon. I guess that will show him there are some people smarter than the Gould gang." Then, "Oh, my God!" The exclamation was wrung from him like a groan.

"For heaven's sake, what is it! Tell me quickly. I've got to go back in there. There's a musical concert at ten-thirty. Not that I care a damn about those ninnies. Stop staring like that and tell me!"

But shrewd and quick as her mind was in its workings, she could make little of his whispered babble. "They took every station between Albany and Binghamton——"

"Who? Who did?"

He ignored her question. "I didn't think he could do it—I thought he was all blow and bluster. Pierpont Morgan knew better; he took to him right away . . . Maroon had almost five hundred men . . . Gould's gang had more . . . but that Texas crowd six feet all of them and made of iron like him . . . engine too . . . the Binghamton locomotive rolled right off the track but they backed their own way down to . . . jumped first . . . if he's alive but he's disappeared and the dwarf . . . Morgan sent the telegram a thousand words . . . Morgan says he's a wonder Morgan thinks he's the biggest . . . of course maybe it's not so bad . . . but they can't find the little chap . . . only his hat that top hat of his mashed in . . . she'll never forgive me . . ."

Mrs. Bellop actually shook him. "For God's sake stop standing there mumbling! I can't make out what you're saying; it sounds crazy."

Here she jumped and uttered a little scream as an oily voice sounded close to her ear. "Oop, sorry!" It was Bean, the head usher, unctuous, deferential. "They're waiting for you in the ballroom, Mrs. Bellop. Mr. Thompkins. The concert, you know."

Mrs. Bellop clapped a frantic hand to her head. "No need to scare me to death with your pussycat ways. Look here, Bean, have you seen Mrs. De Chanfret? D'you know where she is? You make it your business to know everything."

Bean's fatuous smile gleamed in the light from the parlor win dows. He giggled a little. "I regret to say that I have not set eyes on that fairest of her sex since an early hour this m——"

"Oh, shut up!" barked Sophie Bellop. "Bart, pull yourself together."

"——orning," the usher went on, urbanely. "And Mr. Van Steed, sir, your lady mother asked me to request you to come to her side, she seemed much perturbed, if I may venture to say so."

"Go away, Bean. Run along! Scat!" She eyed the man sharply. "I suppose you were listening to everything we said. Read telegrams, too, before they're delivered. I'm sure of that. Oh, well."

Sophie Bellop took Van Steed's arm; briskly she began to propel him toward the door. "Now pull yourself together, Bart. You're the color of dough."

"He can't be hurt badly, can he?"

"My land, I don't know. I suppose he's made of flesh and blood like the——"

"Blood!" echoed Van Steed, and went a pale green.

"Come, come, he's probably all right, celebrating somewhere with his Texas friends. And the dwarf too."

"But where is she? Do you think she's heard and has gone off to find him? Perhaps he sent for her. Perhaps——"

Mrs. Bellop looked serious. "I never thought of that. It's like her to do that. But this very evening she was planning to come in pink satin. I had planned it as a kind of triumph for her against all those harpies like that precious mother of yours."

A changed man, he made no protest at this. He had transferred his every emotion to another strong woman. And of her, as had been true before, he stood in fear. "Do you think she'll blame me? It wasn't my plan, you know. It was his idea. I didn't approve, really. I thought it was crazy. I said so to Morgan. He'll have to admit that himself."

Sophie glared at him with considerable distaste. "He grabbed your railroad for you, didn't he? Took it with his bare hands, like—like a hero—or a bandit—I'm not sure which. Anyway, you've got it."

"I know," miserably. "I know."

"If she comes down—maybe she's just overdoing her entrance—if she comes down don't say anything to her about Maroon being hurt or—well, hurt. Or the dwarf. Not tonight. Tonight is your chance. Now come along. Perk up! Be a man!"

Even this he did not resent.

As they entered the ballroom doorway, five hundred reproachful faces turned toward them like balloons pulled by a single string. The United States Hotel grand ball had bogged down in a morass of apathy. Leaderless, it flopped feebly, lifting first one foot then another, but without progress.

"Really, Mrs. Bellop!" hissed Tompkins, the manager, reproachfully. "Really, Mrs. Bellop! I haven't deserved this at your hands."

"Oh, hush your fuss!" snapped Sophie. Nimbly she clambered to the musicians' platform, she motioned the drum to beat a ruffle for silence. "Ladies and gentlemen! Before partaking of the magnificent collation which our genial host, Manager Tompkins, has ordered prepared for us, there has been planned a surprise concert in which the most talented of Saratoga's visiting guests will favor us. The first number is a bass solo entitled 'Rocked in the Cradle of the Deep,' rendered by Mr. Archibald McElroy of Cincinnati. Following this, Miss Charlotte Chisholm will lend her lovely soprano to the musical number entitled 'Her Bright Smile Haunts Me Still.' . . . Comedy number rendered by Mr. Len Porter, entitled 'I've Only Been Down to the Club.' . . . Duet by the justly popular Pettingill twins: 'Wait Till the Clouds Roll By, Jennie.' . . . Seats will be placed by the ushers, following which supper will be . . . and a prize will be given by the management for the most original fancy dress costume in this evening's . . ."

There followed a spatter of appreciative applause, the buzz of conversation; a fiddle squeaked, a flute emitted a tentative giggle. But their hearts were not in it. "A circus without the elephant," said Mrs. Bellop to Van Steed. "They're so disappointed they could cry. Your lady mother looks as if she'd have a stroke."

"Praw-leens! Praw-leens!" A clear powerful voice sounded from the outer corridor. In the doorway appeared a black mammy in voluminous calico and a vast white apron, a kerchief crossed on her bosom, her head swathed in a brilliant orange tignon. Gold and diamond hoop earrings dangled from beneath the turban's folds (Aunt Belle Piquery's jewelry). The teeth gleamed white in the blackened face, the dark eyes flashed, on her arm was a great woven basket neatly covered with a white napkin. The slim figure was stuffed fore and aft into ponderous curves. "Praw-leens! Praw-leens!"

The basket actually was laden with the toothsome New Orleans confections; she was handing out pralines here and there as she made her way through the crowd; they were gathering round her laughing; the adventurous were biting into the sugary nut-laden circlets.

Sophie Bellop stood up, shaking. "They'll never forgive her for this," she muttered aloud to no one in particular, "they'll never——" With amazing agility for a woman of her weight, Sophie scurried through the crowd; she reached Mrs. De Chanfret's side just as the buxom calicoed figure stood before the anguished Bart Van Steed, just as his voice pleaded in an agonized whisper, "Mrs. De Chanfret. Go home. Please. Please. Don't!"

She tossed her head so that the earrings bobbed and glittered.

"Go 'long, honey chile, you quality folks, you don't want no truck with a no-count black wench like me! You jes' shut you mouth with one o' these prawleens, Mammy made um herself, yassuh!" She laughed a great throaty Negro guffaw; she actually thrust a praline into his wretched hand and went on; she traveled the leisurely circle toward Madam Van Steed; her rolling eye encompassed the group; her grin was a scarlet and white gash in the blackened face. Recovering from their first surprise, the orchestra now entered into the spirit of the thing. They struck up the strains of "Whoa, Emma!" Clio Dulaine hoisted the basket a trifle higher on her arm, she raised the voluminous calico skirts a little, the feet in the white cotton stockings and the strapped flat slippers broke into the shuffle of a Negro dance as in her childhood she had been taught it by Cupide and Kaka in the kitchen of the Paris flat. Madam Van Steed's face, the faces of the satellite dowagers were masks of horror as they beheld the shuffling slapping feet, the heaving rump, the rolling eye, the insolent grin.

"Whoa, Emma!" boomed the band.

"Whoa, Emma!" yelled the crowd, delighted. The party had come alive at last.

Clio's hand, in its white cotton glove, plunged into her basket; she began to throw handfuls of pralines, like giant confetti, into the gray satin lap of Madam Van Steed, into the brocade and satin laps of the ladies grouped about her. "Praw-leen for sweeten dem sour faces! Praw-leens!" She rolled her eyes, she raised her hands high, palms out, she threw back her head, she was imitating every wandering New Orleans minstrel and cavorting street band she had ever seen, every caroling berry vendor from the bayous; she was Belle Piquery, she was Kakaracou and Cupide in the old carefree Southern days of her early childhood; she was defiance against every convention she so hated. And so shuffling, shouting, clapping her hands, the empty basket now hooked round her neck by its handle and hanging at her back, Clio Dulaine made her fantastic way to the veranda door that led onto the garden and disappeared from the sight of a somewhat hysterical company made up of the flower of Saratoga.

The length of the curved veranda, down the steps to the floor below, running along the veranda tier and into her own apartment, the heavy basket bobbing at her back. A wild figure, her eyes rolling in the blackened face, she stood in the center of the little sitting room, laughing, crying, while Kaka divested her of the ridiculous garments—the full-skirted calico, the padding that had stuffed bosom and hips, the brilliant tignon, the dangling hoop earrings.

"Their faces, Kaka! Their silly faces with their mouths open and their eyes staring, and those stiff old women in their satin dresses. And Mrs. Porcelain with her trellis! Kaka! Kaka!" Tears streaked the blackened cheeks.

With cream and a soft cloth Kaka was cleansing the girl's face and throat, and as she worked she kept up a grumbling and a mumbling, as though to herself.

"Somepin fret me . . . maybe now we come away from here but where at is Cupide where at is Cupide I got a feeling deep down somepin fret me . . . I know you turn out like your mama . . . no luck with menfolks . . . plan and contrive but no luck with menfolks . . . you fixing to marry a millionaire but all the time you crazy in your head for that *vacher* he leave you . . . just like Mister Nicolas he leave . . ."

With the flat of her hand Clio slapped the woman full in the face. But Kakaracou caught her hand and kissed it and said, "Now! That is better. Now will you put on the pink satin and your mama's diamonds and Kaka fix your hair *à la marquise!*"

"Yes," said Clio, laughing. "Yes. Why not! Quick! Quick! I could marry him yet, if I wanted to."

The black woman's fingers were lightning. Powder on the piled black hair; the pink satin and black lace springing stiff and glistening from her slender waist, the necklaces, bracelets, the pendants, the parure, the flashing earrings; the rings with which Nicolas Dulaine had loaded his mistress. "There! Now, Kaka, you'll come with me, my attendant, all very proper, since I have no man now. I really do look beautiful, don't I! Am I as beautiful as my mother was? I am! I am!"

But Kakaracou shook her head. The two fantastic figures, the girl in her powdered hair and her pink satin hoops and her blazing jewels, the stately black woman in her turban and stiff silk, swept down the cottage balcony stairs and were halfway across the garden when a distracted figure stumbled toward them. His face was in shadow, but the light from the ballroom windows was full on the two women.

"Clio! Clio!"

"Oh, Mr. Van Steed, how you frightened me! I was just coming to have a little peek at the ball. The music sounded so enticing."

"Clio!"

She slipped her hand in his arm, she pulled him round with quite a hearty jerk. "Will you be my escort, since Colonel Maroon could not return in time?"

"Clio, I must talk to you. How could you——"

"Not now. Later. Who is that, singing? How sweet! How very sweet!"

They stood together in the ballroom doorway. On the platform Miss Charlotte Chisholm's soprano warbling wavered, faltered, went bravely on. Clio did not enter; she did not take advantage of a chair indicated by a dazzled usher; she stood there with the wretched Van Steed; she shook her lovely powdered head; she put a finger to her lips for quiet and glanced toward the platform; and if Miss Chisholm had been turning cartwheels, uttering the notes of a Patti meanwhile, no one in that crowded room would have seen her or heard.

The singer finished, lamely. Clio applauded delicately and said, "Charming, charming!" She smiled across the room at the glaring Madam Van Steed, she waved to Sophie Bellop, who was waddling toward her, making her way through the crowd with astonishing swiftness.

"Clio, will you come into the garden for a stroll? I must talk to you. Now."

"Wouldn't it look strange?"

"No. No."

But Mrs. Bellop was upon them. "Well, young lady, you must have taken leave of your senses!"

"Why, dear Mrs. Bellop!"

"A pretty how-d'you-do! It's sure to be in the New York papers. They'll never forgive you, those——"

Clio laid a hand affectionately on the arm of Saratoga's social arbiter. "Dear, dear Mrs. Bellop, don't scold me! And you, too, Bart. The party seemed so dull and stuffy I thought I would liven it up a little. It was in fun. I am so sorry. Tell me, have you heard news of Colonel Maroon? He was to have been my escort, the naughty man." A lightning look leaped between Sophie Bellop and Bart Van Steed. But swift as it was, Clio caught it. The day's vague unrest, the fear that had held her all evening, now became a terrible certainty. "What is it? You two. What's happened?"

"Nothing. Run along into the garden. You've made trouble enough for one evening."

Clio's face hardened into a dreadful mask of resolved fury. "Tell me. Tell me what you know or I shall do something dreadful. But really frightful. I shall tear off my clothes and scream. I shall beat you with my fists. I care for nothing. Tell me! Tell me!"

"Sh-sh-sh! All right. All right. Later."

"Now! Now!" Her voice was rising.

Mrs. Bellop spoke soothingly while Bart's mouth opened and closed like that of a gasping fish. "The railroad—they—Bart got word that everything was—was—successful—isn't that lovely!"

Clio spat the word through her teeth. "Successful! Successful! Clint! Where is he?" She actually shook Van Steed's arm as one would try to shake an answer out of a stubborn little boy.

He had not the gift of dissembling. Her fingers were biting into his arm. Ruthless in business, he was water-weak against the brow-beating of a determined woman. "It's nothing. We heard that little—uh—the dwarf was hurt somewhat. Somewhat. Quite a fight," he went on, with a rickety attempt at jocularity. "Quite a little fracas the boys had. But you'll be glad to know that they won."

"Do you want me to strike you here before all these people! Maroon! Tell me what has happened to him! Maroon!"

"Well, I understand he was hurt a little—nothing serious—no direct word from him, but you know how he is—he can take care of himself——"

Her face was livid, her eyes narrowed to black slits, her lips drew back from her teeth. It was a face venomous, murderous, terrible.

"He's dead. He's dead. I can see it in your face. Your cowardly face. He fought for you and your miserable crawling railroad that brings you your dirty coal. I tell you I despise you. I would sooner marry a snake that crawls on its belly. I would——"

But they were not looking at her, they were looking at something beyond her, down the long hallway. She turned, then, to see Clint Maroon almost in the doorway. A stained and soiled bandage wrapped his head, his right arm rested in a sling, he leaned a little sideways as though to ease some inward strain. And behind him strutted a grotesque little figure on whose head rose a bump the size of an egg—a figure in a stained and ragged uniform of wine red and muddied boots whose left member lacked a heel, so that he limped and hopped as he came.

"Howdy, folks," drawled Maroon. "My, my, Mrs. De Chanfret, you look right pretty. I reckon I'm a sight——"

She seemed not to run to him merely but to spring like an arrow shot from the bow. "Clint! Clint *chéri!*"

But at the impact of her body flung against his Clint Maroon said, "Ouch!" like a little boy. And then his long body crumpled to the floor, dragging Clio to her knees as he went.

XVIII

✦

Propped up among the pillows of his bed, Clint Maroon looked out almost sheepishly from beneath his head bandage at the faces turned so solicitously toward him. The bandage was a proper one now; the arm in its splint rested comfortably against his side; the room smelled of drugs and eau de cologne and coffee. He looked very clean and boyish. The doctor had come and gone.

"Shucks! I feel fine. That's the first time a Maroon ever did a sissy thing like that. I sure hope you-all will excuse me being so womanish. Fainting away. I'm plumb ashamed."

"Don't talk now, *chéri*. Rest. Here. Another sip of this."

"Why, say, many a time back in Texas I've been hurt worse than this throwed by a bucking horse. Never made such a to-do about it. Nothing to eat all day—that was it, only a swallow of whisky one of the boys—say, that cup of Kaka's good coffee, the way she makes it, is better than any medicine. Where's Cupide?"

Two hands grasped the bed's footboard, the dwarf's powerful arms pulled him up so that the great head, decorated now with a plaster where the lump had risen, rose like a nightmarish sun over the horizon.

"You would have been killed—but smashed dead—if it had not been for me, Monsieur Clint."

"I know, I know. I reckon it might have been better, at that, than having you around my neck the rest of my life."

"Then why you take him along?" Kaka demanded.

"Take him!" Maroon yelled. "I tried the worst way to get shut of him." He glared wrathfully at the gnomelike figure perched now on the footboard. "How come you got on that train, anyway, after I turned you off at the Albany station?"

"Oh, that was easy," Cupide explained. His tiny hands made an airy nothing of it. "I butted him in the stomach, he grunted like a stuck pig, then I took the five dollars you had given him and I ran just as the train was moving—it was dangerous, I can tell you it was—and I hid in the water closet or under the seats when you came near. The boys were very nice to me—*mais gentil*—very."

"*Insecte!*" said Kaka, fondly. "*Fou furieux!*"

Clio pushed the hair back from her forehead with a frantic gesture. "I tell you, I don't understand, I don't understand such people. You are hurt and broken and this monkey here might be dead—you, too—and all that a fool who has already millions may have another million. What nonsense is this!"

"You didn't think he was such a fool a week ago."

"I did. I did. But when I heard you were hurt I hated him, I called him every name, I said terrible things."

"Sorry?"

"Only if I have hurt the little man. Clint, let us go away from here. Take me with you. I have decided I do not care so much to marry a man with millions."

"Looks like you'll have to now, care or not."

She stared, uncomprehending, startled. "What is this! Clint! What are you saying!"

"Well, sugar, it's like this——"

But she knelt at the side of his bed, she put her head on the pillow beside him, she cradled his head in her arms. "I won't leave you. I tell you I will follow you, I will make such a *bruit* that you will be ashamed."

"Now, now, wait a minute. Hold your horses. I got a taste of this railroad and money thing, and say, it's easier than riding fence. Even a dumb cowboy like me can get the hang of it. These fellows, they don't only skin the country and the people—they're out to skin each other. I've got a piece of that little Saratoga trunk railroad; Mr. Morgan gave it to me if I licked the Gould crowd, and I did. So now I'm figuring to get the whole of that railroad away from little Bart, and I will, too. I'm going to be hog rich. Just for the hell of it. And it's all your doings, Clio. Only now things have got to be different between us."

"Different?" she repeated with stiff lips.

"Sure thing. There's no way out, honey. I aim to be worth millions and millions. That's the way you wanted it. But our fun's over. Folks as rich as we're going to be, why, we just naturally have got to get married. Yes ma'am. Married and respectable, that's us."

XIX

There was a light knock—light but firm—on the sitting-room door of the Maroon suite, and Mrs. Maroon entered, cool, smiling, lovely. The newspapermen scrambled to their feet.

"I'm sorry, but the time is up. I said fifteen minutes, and it has been nearly half an hour." She looked up at him, anxiety in her eyes. "Tired, *chéri?*" Her hand on his arm.

"No. You'd think I was ten years old—instead of nearly ten times ten."

She still smiled, her eyes were questioning them—what had he said, how much did they know? "You know, Mr. Maroon was hurt some years ago in a—in an accident. And sometimes now, when he overexerts himself, he feels it."

"What accident was that?" the *Post* reporter asked.

"Uh—railroad accident, you might say," Colonel Maroon replied.

"Recent?"

"Well, no, you couldn't exactly call it recent. Matter of, say, sixty years ago."

The reporters relaxed. "Now you're kidding us again, Mrs. Maroon. Honestly, how a woman who looks the way you do can have a stony heart like that!"

She glanced up at her handsome ruddy husband; her eyes were

searching to know more than the question implied. "Did you tell the young people what they wanted to know?"

There were lines of weariness in his face; he was polite, but it was plain that he longed now to be rid of them.

"Yes, honey. They wouldn't listen to what I wanted to tell 'em. So I told them what they wanted to know. It's their job to get what they were sent for." He raised a hand in farewell. "Good day to you, boys and girls. I wish some time before the last roundup you'd listen to the story I want to tell you. I could show you this country's gone a long ways in the last fifty years. I don't mean machinery and education and that. I mean folks' rights. They've clamped down on fellows like me who damn near ruined this country."

"Oh, now, Colonel! You've been reading books. You're one of America's famous citizens. No kidding."

"Famous for what! Another quarter of century of grabbers like us and there wouldn't have been a decent stretch of forest or soil or waterway that hadn't been divided among us. Museums and paintings and libraries—that was our way of trying to make peace with our conscience. I'm the last of the crowd that had all four feet in the trough and nothing to stop 'em. We're getting along toward a real democracy now and don't let anybody tell you different. These will be known as the good new days and those were the bad old days. The time's coming when there'll be no such thing as a multi-millionaire in America, and no such thing as a pauper. You'll live to see it but I won't. That'll be a real democracy."

"Sure, Colonel. That'll make a great story."

"That'll be swell. Don't forget to tell us all about it next time."

"Thanks, Mrs. Maroon. Thanks, Colonel. Look, we've got to beat it."

Standing there, handsome and straight, his wife's delicate hand resting on his arm, he waved to them a Western salute with his free hand as though he were whirling a sombrero round his fine head. They were gone.

"They didn't want to hear it, Clint?"

"No." Gruff with disappointment.

"Ah, well, it doesn't matter now."

"But honey, I sure would have liked to have them hear it. We were a couple of bad characters, I suppose, the way you'd look at it now."

She looked down at the simple flowing folds of her white gown. She smiled her lovely smile. "Streamlined. Saratoga trunks are streamlined now, and so are railroads and houses and people. Everything except this hotel. It's kind of wonderful to come back and find it the same."

He wiped his forehead with his fine linen handkerchief. "The storybooks made the old days seem right pretty. But it's better this way. I'll be glad to get rid of the money. . . . Want to go to the races, honey? Like we did in the old days!"

"But do you think you could stand it, *chéri*? The noise, the heat, the cameras, the crowds staring."

"Shucks, I've stood it for sixty years. I guess I can stand it a while longer. Anyway, if it's going to kill me I don't know anywhere I'd rather die than sitting out there at the Saratoga track watching the horses coming round the curve. Remember the time that little devil Cupide——?"

EDNA FERBER

"I didn't want to be a writer," Edna Ferber admitted in her 1939 autobiography *A Peculiar Treasure*. "I never had wanted to be a writer. I couldn't even use a typewriter, never having tried. The stage was my one love. . . . I go to the theater because I love it; I write plays for the theater because I love it. I am still wrapped in my childish dream [of being an actress, but]. . . . At seventeen my writing career accidentally began."

That accidental career, of course, was an astounding success. Beginning as a "Girl Reporter" for the Appleton, Wisconsin, *Crescent* at age seventeen, Ferber parlayed a short stint as a journalist into a long career as a writer of short stories, novels and plays—a career that lasted more than sixty years and brought her great fame and wealth.

Ferber was born on August 15, 1885, in Kalamazoo, Michigan, to Jacob and Julia Ferber, a Hungarian-born Jewish merchant and his American-born wife. Throughout Edna's childhood, the family moved several times throughout the Midwest before settling in Appleton, where the Ferbers ran a general store. When Jacob began losing his sight to a degenerative eye disease, Julia took control of the family fortunes, running the store with indefatigable shrewdness. A formidable woman, Julia would later appear, fictionalized, in many of her daughter's novels.

For financial reasons, Ferber set aside her plans to study for a career on the stage and took a job right after high school on the *Crescent*. After a year and a half covering every imaginable type of story, she was fired by a new editor who disdained her "feminine" writing style, but she was hired immediately by the *Milwaukee Journal*. Young and enthusiastic, she took her job seriously, neglecting her personal well-being. When she collapsed from exhaustion, she returned to Appleton for what was supposed to be a temporary leave. Except for some freelance assignments during political conventions, however, Ferber never returned to newspaper work. While she was recuperating she wrote her first short story, "The Homely Heroine." It was published in *Everybody's Magazine* and Edna Ferber's career as a writer of fiction took off.

More stories followed, and a novel, *Dawn O'Hara*, was published in 1911. In a short story called "Representing T.A. Buck," Ferber introduced the unusual character of Mrs. Emma McChesney, a divorced traveling saleswoman with a young son, who worked for the T.A. Buck Featherloom Petticoat Company. *American Magazine* published the story and asked for a second installment. Without having planned it, Ferber embarked on a string of Emma McChesney stories that appeared in *American Magazine* and *Cosmopolitan*, were collected into three volumes, and had a huge following (Theodore Roosevelt was a fan). When a reviewer of the third volume, *Emma McChesney & Co.* (1915) accused Ferber of beating a dead horse, Ferber realized "I had been sliding to oblivion on a path greased by Emma McChesney." She immediately stopped writing the stories, despite an offer from *Cosmopolitan* to name her own price. Nonetheless, Ferber did dramatize the stories for the stage, working in collaboration with George V. Hobart. The play, *Our Mrs. McChesney*, was produced in 1915 and starred Ethel Barrymore.

Ferber's second novel, *Fanny Herself*, was published in 1917, her third, *The Girls*, in 1921. It was Ferber's next novel, *So Big* (1924), that established her as a major writer. It won the Pulitzer Prize and became the first of many best sellers she would produce.

While she worked on novels, Ferber continued to publish short stories in magazines and books. One story, "Old Man Minick," caught the attention of playwright George S. Kaufman, who asked her to collaborate with him on adapting it for the stage. The play, *Minick*, was the first in an impressive list of collaborations between the two writers. After *Minick*, Ferber topped the success of *So Big* with the novel *Show Boat* (1926), which served as the basis for the now classic 1927 Broadway musical and three film versions. In what surely must be considered a coup for any writer, *Show Boat* opened on Broadway December 27, 1927, and another Ferber hit, *The Royal Family*, written with Kaufman, opened the next day.

By this time, Ferber was living full time in New York and hanging around with the legendary wits of the Algonquin Round Table, including Kaufman, Alexander Woollcott, Marc Connelly, Robert Sherwood, Heywood Broun, and Dorothy Parker. But her rigorous work schedule precluded social lunches, and she admitted that she managed to grace these legendary gatherings only three or four times a year.

After *Show Boat*, many of Ferber's novels were large-scale social histories that dealt with regional America. *Cimarron* (1930) recreates the Oklahoma land rush of 1889, *American Beauty* (1931) is based on a wave of immigration of industrious Polish farmers to New England in the late Nineteenth Century, *Come and Get It* (1935) deals with the rape of Wisconsin and Michigan forests by the Robber Barons. Other novels include *Saratoga Trunk* (1941) and *Great Son* (1945); her other plays with Kaufman include *Dinner at Eight* (1932), and *Stage Door* (1936).

Ferber's 1952 novel *Giant*, a sprawling contemporary satire of the newly wealthy in Texas, caused quite an uproar in the Lone Star State, but was a huge commercial success. The 1956 film version of the book, famous for being the last film of screen legend James Dean, was nominated for seven Academy Awards, winning the Oscar for its director, George Stevens. *Ice Palace* (1958), her last novel, was set in Alaska. She published two volumes of her memoirs, *A Peculiar Treasure* (1939) and *A Kind of Magic* (1963). Ferber, who never married, died of cancer on April 16, 1968.

Hugely successful in her day, Ferber's novels have fallen out of favor, perhaps because commercial success often breeds contempt among the intelligentsia. Ferber was a quintessentially American writer, choosing American settings—often huge panoramas—and themes for her work. "Each one of them had been written with a definite underlying theme in mind, and this had, for some baffling reason, been almost entirely overlooked by the average reader," Ferber once complained. "I found myself regarded as a go-getting best seller and a deft writer of romantic and colorful American novels."

In her obituary, the *New York Times* said, "Her books were not profound, but they were vivid and had a sound sociological basis. She was among the best-read novelists in the nation, and critics of the 1920s and '30s did not hesitate to call her the greatest American woman novelist of her day."

Ferber herself once wrote, "Those critics or well-wishers who think that I could have written better than I have are flattering me. Always I have written at the top of my bent at that particular time. It may be that this or that, written five years later or one year earlier, or under different circumstances, might have been the better for it. But one writes as the opportunity and the material and the inclination shape themselves. This is certain: I never have written a line except to please myself. I never have written with an eye to what is called the public or the market or the trend or the editor or the reviewer. Good or bad, popular or unpopular, lasting or ephemeral, the words I have put down on paper were the best words I could summon at the time to express the thing I wanted more than anything else to say."

Saratoga Trunk

✴

1941

Edna Ferber first intended to write Saratoga Trunk *as a play, and she* went so far as to involve the great acting couple Alfred Lunt and Lynn Fontanne in its development. But, when she brought the idea to George S. Kaufman, with whom she generally collaborated on plays, he proved lukewarm to the idea. A disastrous scouting trip to Saratoga in December—where the glamorous resort hotels that played host to the wealthy in the summer were not heated for the winter— completely soured Kaufman. Ferber temporarily shelved the idea, later resurrecting the material for a novel, which was published by Double- day in 1941.

Given its theatrical origins, it is not surprising to learn that the few negative reviews Ferber received for the book faulted its staginess. By far the worst was Edward Weeks's assessment in the *Atlantic*. "The novel wears too much make-up," he wrote. "Clio is play-acting too often, Clint is too stagey a Texan, and the millionaires at Saratoga are comedians—not people of power. Despite Mrs. Bellop's breezy can- dor, despite the delectable food and the charming clothes, despite Clio's Parisian turn of phrase, there is throughout an unmistakable trace of musical comedy in this prose." And *Time* complained that

"Miss Ferber's noisy, flashing manner never really gives you a period, but always makes you enjoy the fraud. *Saratoga Trunk* is so neatly made that the scenarists need only bracket the non-dialogue as stage direction, and call it a half-day's work."

But other critics applauded Ferber for these same qualities. Fairfax Downey, in the *Saturday Review of Literature*, wrote, "Unpacking it is absorbing entertainment. There's everything in it but the kitchen stove—no, that's in it too. . . . Successful playwright that she is, she knows good theater. *Saratoga Trunk*, of course, is just that. Good theater." The *Christian Science Monitor* felt that "in Miss Ferber's skillful hands, the story, for all it worldliness, acquires so much vigor and color that it has indubitable entertainment value. It may be garish, theatrical, and no more subtle than a circus, yet the sparkle is genuine. Nothing of Miss Ferber's could ever be tawdry."

Indeed, the majority of critics embraced the book, noting that Ferber's achievement lay in her masterful, atmospheric recreation of time and place. Reviewing it for *Library Journal*, S. E. Sherman called *Saratoga Trunk* "an utterly delicious concoction. This expertly written, absorbingly entertaining satire likewise adroitly contrasts the ideals of a plutocratic America gradually emerging into a true democracy." "One closes *Saratoga Trunk* with the feeling of having lived in a rich and exciting world, peopled by fascination and exciting characters no less real because they are eccentric and romantic," wrote Rose Feld in *Books*. "The secret of Miss Ferber's achievement is rooted in many things—her vitality and belief in the people she creates; her meticulous care with all the details of background and characterization; her unfailing sense of drama. Possibly this adds up to genius."

In the *New Yorker*, Clifton Fadiman said, "The author draws a sound, truly patriotic moral from her story, but it won't disturb anyone excessively. As flashing and agreeable a yarn as Miss Ferber has fashioned for some time, it should be a walkaway for La Dietrich and Mr. Gary Cooper." Indeed, when the movie version of *Saratoga Trunk* appeared in 1943, Gary Cooper had been cast as Clint Maroon, but it was Ingrid Bergman who played Clio Dulaine. Coming full circle, the book also was adapted as a Broadway musical in 1959, with Howard Keel and Carol Lawrence in the leads. It closed after 10 weeks. Ferber herself played no active part in either of these incarnations of the story.

By the time she published *Saratoga Trunk*, Edna Ferber was already one of the country's most successful writers. She had won the Pulitzer Prize for *So Big*, and *Show Boat* had taken on a life of its own as a novel and as the now classic Jerome Kern-Oscar Hammerstein II musical. In collaboration with Kaufman, Ferber had written such hit plays as *The Royal Family, Dinner at Eight,* and *Stage Door.* So it was not unexpected that her latest novel would become another best seller.

In the November 2, 1941 *New York Times*, Margaret Wallace emphatically stated that "the most cautious reviewer can predict skyrocket success for *Saratoga Trunk*—and not feel that he is getting out on a limb, either. Few of Edna Ferber's vastly popular novels of the past decade have arrived on the book counters with more fanfare. In abridged form it has been serialized by a national magazine, and it will be seen on stage and screen as soon as the ponderous machinery for producing an A spectacle can begin grinding it out. *Saratoga Trunk* is what is known in a field of human endeavor only slightly less hazardous than the publishing business as a natural."

PERENNIAL ■ CLASSICS

Books by Edna Ferber:

SO BIG

ISBN 0-06-095669-0 (paperback)

The Pulitzer Prize–winning novel about the life of a gambler's daughter and of her son, Dirk. A critically acclaimed masterpiece that deals with such contemporary issues as poverty, sexism, and success.

"A thoughtful book, clean and strong, dramatic at times, interesting always, clear-sighted, sympathetic, a novel to read and to remember."
—*The New York Times*

GIANT

ISBN 0-06-095670-4 (paperback)

A tale of power, love, cattle barons and oil tycoons in a place racked by noise and heat, big men and bourbon, and the high shrill voices of Texas women.
Giant was the basis for the epic 1956 motion picture starring Elizabeth Taylor, Rock Hudson, and James Dean.

"A powerful story . . . truly as big as its subject." —*Los Angeles Times*

SARATOGA TRUNK

ISBN 0-06-095671-2 (paperback)

A classic novel about a New Orleans vixen and a handsome Texan who are so obsessed with acquiring everything they have ever wanted, they fail to realize they already have all they will ever need . . . each other.
Saratoga Trunk was the basis for the classic film starring Ingrid Bergman and Gary Cooper.

"The greatest American woman novelist of her day." —*The New York Times*

Available wherever books are sold, or call 1-800-331-3761 to order.